MINISTRY OF ANGELS

A Novel of Hope and Restoration

In World War Two

JOAN LA BLANC

Northampton House Press

This is a work of fiction. All of the characters, organizations, and events portrayed in this novel are either products of the author's imagination or are used fictitiously.

Cover design and NHP logo by Naia Poyer.

Northampton House Press edition, 2014. ISBN 978-1-937997-45-8.

10 9 8 7 6 5 4 3 2

MINISTRY OF ANGELS

CHAPTER ONE
October, 1943

As she left the ladies' toilet and swayed through the crowded day coach, Anna Donovan began to suspect the gargoyle-faced geezer in the seat next to hers was dead, not just asleep. As if he'd given up the ghost since he'd gulped half her chicken sandwich, belched and begun to snore. She hadn't noticed when the snoring stopped, but now his head lolled against the smeared window, mouth sagging and breathing too shallow to be discernible. If he even was still breathing.

The train was slowing for her stop, so Anna wrestled her Pullman case from the overhead rack. Even when it slammed to the floor, the man didn't stir. Sighing, she sat gingerly beside him again and wondered if she should check his pulse. Easy enough with hands dangling in his lap, bony wrists within reach. But if he had expired, she'd have to tell the conductor, who'd have to notify some authority, who'd have to remove the body. Leaving her to make a statement to the police or coroner. A cumbersome, tedious process that would cause her to miss the bus to Rockhampton, where Dr. Millett was expecting her at 4:15. A hell of a way to start a new job, even for a humanitarian reason.

Yet the idea of leaving a hapless corpse alone and unnoticed in a train full of strangers repulsed her even more than the potential consequences of reporting his death. As a nurse and a Christian, her duty was clear. And inarguable. So, after the conductor announced Brunswick, she reached over and lifted the ancient fellow's limp wrist. It felt like part of a chicken, ready for frying—tissue-paper skin noticeably cool, prominent veins, fragile bones. Please, Lord, she prayed; let him be alive even if he'd rather not be. Even if the son he'd talked about didn't want him living in his home. Please, let him just be in a nice deep sleep so she could get on with her new life.

When she felt nothing after thirty seconds, she probed closer to the heel of the thumb. More nothing. Edging toward panic, she pressed against a tendon. And found a small, tenuous throb, barely palpable. By the second hand of her watch, she calculated the rate at about thirty per minute. So slow that if he were her patient, she'd be worried. But he wasn't. Thanks be to God, he wasn't in her care.

Sense of duty assuaged, she replaced the fragile claw on the old man's thigh. He stirred slightly, snorted and turned his face to the window as the train screeched into the station. She exhaled with relief, then, clutching purse and overnight bag, pushed the larger suitcase into the vestibule. When they'd jolted to a stop, the conductor hoisted it to the platform. She grabbed it and headed toward a line of busses. Even focused on locating the one she needed, she couldn't help glancing up at the fifth window of the dusty coach. Inside, the old man sat blinking and drooling. She smiled, but he gave no sign he remembered he'd shared his life story. Or half her lunch.

Scanning the buses angled in along the platform, she

dragged her bags toward the one for Camden. The driver tossed them in the luggage compartment and squinted at her ticket. Behind her, a male voice said, "Headed for Bath, ma'am?"

The Chief Petty Officer in Navy Air greens had been on the train when she'd boarded at Dover, had helped her father lift the monster suitcase to the rack. She made her voice friendly. But crisp. He was, after all, an enlisted man. "Bath? Uh…what makes you think that?"

"The pin on your jacket. And the wedding ring. Just wondered if your husband's at the shipyard."

She touched the insignia on her lapel, a miniature of those on naval officer's caps. "I didn't know that was a base."

"It isn't. But BuShips has a unit there. Keeping an eye on the tin cans they're building."

A familiar twinge tightened her chest. "Oh, I wish he was there. But he's on a sub. In the Pacific." She had to bite back the rest of the story; one didn't share personal troubles with total strangers, even friendly Navy men who might understand. And sympathize.

He let her precede him toward the line waiting to board. "Sorry. Just thought…" He cleared his throat. "Myself, I'm at the air station outside town here. With an ASW squadron. You know. Anti-submarine warfare?"

Nervous, she glanced about in case his frank talk might be considered the loose lips that were said to sink ships. Probably not; everyone else in the nearby crowd seemed occupied with tickets, luggage, timetables. The temptation to tell him about Dan grew stronger. Still, she let herself say only, "I hope they don't have bases like that on the coast of Japan."

He drew a sharp, startled breath and his eyes went wide. "Oh no, ma'am, reckon not. Don't let that worry you one little bit."

She hadn't noticed the Southern accent before. It was so comfortingly avuncular, she wouldn't have minded sharing a bus seat with the man. And perhaps also the fact that Dan's boat was missing in action. By the time they boarded, however, all the doubles were taken, so she slid into one beside a woman whose face was half-buried in *Silver Screen.* A black bandana—probably some sailor's neckerchief—was tied turban-style over pin curls, and she was holding a glowing cigarette, crimson lip prints vivid on the tip. Besides a pall of smoke, the vehicle reeked of hot oil, gasoline fumes, and the other woman's perfume. Cheap and cloying, but an improvement over the urine odor that had hung like a yellow cloud around the old man on the train.

Every seat in the bus was taken by the time a southbound train pulled in, disgorging a gaggle of workmen who ran over and packed the aisle. One lodged beside her, where he exhaled whiskey fumes and talked loudly to his buddies about his date the night before. A soldier's wife, he bragged, lonely and starved for love. Obviously every letch's dream.

Disgusted, Anna fixed her gaze over the other woman's shoulder at movie stars' pictures: Lana Turner working at the Hollywood Canteen, Jimmy Cagney selling war bonds at a rally, Betty Grable helping Mrs. Roosevelt christen a new cruiser. But when the workman said his date was "One of them blondies that gotta have it every night," she felt her face flaming. Her hair was only dishwater blonde, but she knew she was the butt of his remark. Indeed; before long she felt his erection against her arm. Without debating whether she should, she used a move Dan had taught her — jerking her elbow into the guy's crotch hard enough to cause pain, if not permanent injury.

He staggered backward. "Jesus, girlie. What'd you do that for? I ain't talking about you."

She compressed her lips into a tight line and fixed her

gaze out the window on an inlet they were crossing. The tide was out; a trickle of water reflecting the sky was a bright blue thread through black mud studded with mossy boulders.

"Don't pay him no mind, honey," said her seat-mate. "Feeble-minded Four-F creep."

Breathing deeply, Anna was only dimly aware when the chief from the train pushed forward and seized the loudmouth by the collar. "Listen, buddy, you better shut that big yap of yours, or you and me are gonna get off and have a little talk."

The wise guy muttered a string of obscenities, but retreated to the rear. To her relief, the chief stood nearby till he left the bus a few miles later. He didn't talk to her again, but his presence reassured her that decency still ruled some men's hearts. By then they were passing the air station he'd mentioned. Mile after mile of hurricane fence enclosed acres of Quonset huts, control tower, checkered water tower, and rows of two-engine planes. She recognized their distinctive silhouettes from her Official Airplane Spotter's Guide: Amphibious patrol bombers, with high tails and top-mounted wings. PBYs, also known as Catalinas.

When the bus stopped at a sentry post, he stepped off, grinning back at her and making the V-for-Victory sign with his fingers. She gave him a thumbs-up as they surged forward again. Kind of him to assure her the Japs had no bases like this, but she recognized this as pure wishful thinking. Like a popular belief soon after Pearl Harbor that it wouldn't take long—a year at most—to run the Japs out of the Pacific. Now, almost two years into the war, no one was making any rose-colored predictions. Even she, with all her faith that the Lord was on the Allies' side, was having trouble with optimism. Especially about Dan's safety.

After the chief got off, she sat stiffly upright in case the offensive workman returned. But he stayed in the back till the next town where he and his buddies shuffled off toward an arched sign: “Bath Iron Works.” Even if the chief hadn’t told her, she’d have guessed they were building warships—patriotic posters on the fence, armed guards at the gate, stork-like cranes in the distance and a Navy E pennant on the flagstaff. And evidently these hard-drinking toughs were working on them. Good Lord, were all the decent men in the service?

Revolted at the notion, she paged rapidly through the magazine her seatmate had left behind. When she was unable to distract herself with this silly movie trivia, she moved over and rested her forehead on the cold window glass. And remembered Dan’s complaints about engineering malfunctions the Portsmouth yard hadn’t fixed before his boat had left for New London. And the problem plagued O-boat her crew had considered jinxed long before she disappeared on a test dive. Or was *jinxed* a euphemism for crippled by sloppy workmanship, not random Fate? Another possibility she preferred not to consider: If these men were typical of shipyard workers all over the country—including the Hunters Point Navy Yard in San Francisco--no wonder *Wolf Fish* hadn’t returned from her last patrol.

Anger flooded into her like seawater into the tanks of a crash-diving sub. And made her clench fists and jaw alike. Anger was an emotion her mother always warned was unbecoming in a clergyman’s daughter. Yet sometimes it felt powerful, even comforting. As it had when she’d used the elbow-to-the crotch maneuver on the shipyard worker.

For the rest of the trip, its residue inspired a dozen scathing comments. She filed them away for future use, for such a time as a sharp blow to some other lecherous creep’s gonads didn’t make her point

Chapter Two

Flaring behind the bus, the sun was a low red fireball when they pulled into Rockhampton. At first glance, a typical New England town clustered around a central square dominated by a high-steepled white church, autumn-bright trees, a brick hotel, a three-story department store, the Roxy movie theater and a string of small shops. Anna was ready to be the first off after the bus turned south, crossed the green, then headed north again. It finally sighed to a stop in front of the Rexall Drug Store, where a small crowd waited to board.

Filling her lungs with brisk, salt-tinged air, she dragged both bags toward the awning to wait for whoever would meet her there. Dr. Millett had assured her if he couldn't, he'd send someone else. But after the bus left for Camden and no one had shown up, she was about to hail a green and white checkered taxi when an angular chap in denims came hurrying up the street, his anxious gaze fixed on her.

"Nurse Donovan?" He yanked off a battered slouch hat. Wispy gray hair blew in the wind, and faded blue eyes squinted from a face as tanned and leathery as old cowhide.

She'd expected someone in suit and tie, but extended her hand. "Dr. Millett?"

"No, miss. Cap'n Fletcher Hood at your service." He

shook it loosely, like someone unaccustomed to greeting this way. "Doc ain't finished house calls yet, so he asked me to fetch you down to his place. These here your bags?"

She nodded. He grasped them as if they were weightless, then led her down the street to a Model-A pickup with the top half of the headlights painted black. He helped her into the battered passenger seat and loaded the luggage in the back. After he slid in behind the wheel, he gave her a lopsided grin. "Doc said you come up from Portsmouth just now. That right?" She said it was. "Got the blackout down there too?" She said they had. When the engine was sputtering, he offered a Chesterfield. She declined. He struck a match to one for himself before he pulled onto the street. Dan's brand. As evocative as a strain of half-remembered music, the fresh smoke filled her with sudden longing. And a passing jolt of familiar sorrow. With a deep breath, she switched focus to the view unwinding in the windshield. Nothing memorable—ordinary little houses, gas stations, stores, tiny churches with old cemeteries, a few down-at-the-heel cinder block industrial buildings. A lot like Kittery, but without Navy vehicles and Navy men. Without those constant reminders of Dan.

Driving even slower than her father, Mr. Hood picked his way through the town's ragged outskirts. Dusk was purpling around them, but as they crossed a long bridge over an inlet, the sky was still so bright she could see long dark cloud stripes in the west. He said they foretold rain; a fisherman knew the signs.

"Oh, you're a fisherman?" She should have known; he wasn't a retired naval officer at all, but a man whose title derived from owning and piloting his own boat.

"Ay-yuh. Trouble is, I can get all the gas I need, but with so many grounds off-limits, these days takes twice as long to catch half as much." He chuckled. "Market's real good, though. Hardly any boats out of East Point nowadays, so many boys gone to war. Tried to join up myself, but they said I was too old. So now I haul mail and freight out to the island, and keep Doc's car running. He's busier'n a one-armed paperhanger since they started drafting docs. Make matters worse, near a year since he had a nurse out to the island. Don't have none to the house either. Last one left around the time his wife did. Right before Pearl Harbor, it was." He paused for breath as the truck chugged up a slight hill, even balkier than her father's Packard.

"Oh, he lives alone?"

"Ay-yuh. Don't know why the wife took off. Doc, he never talks about things like that. Personal, I mean. 'Course, could've been she got bored. Not much to do around here except go to the picture show." He glanced over in the dimness. "Ain't going to be a problem with you, I hope. Being you're from a big town like Portsmouth."

"I grew up in a minister's home. I never went in for night life."

"Well, good. Hate to see Doc disappointed again."

So the man who'd offered the job on the phone had suffered some sort of disappointment, she presumed in love. Curious but aware her employer's personal life was none of her business, she said only, "I don't intend to be a disappointment to anyone," in her most resolute tone.

He didn't answer but lit another cigarette. Between puffs, he fell to whistling a medley of *Coming in on a Wing and a Prayer* and *Praise the Lord and Pass the Ammunition.* The cheerful piping lifted her spirits for the rest of the ten-mile drive.

With the town blacked out, she could see few details of the doctor's house when they pulled into the driveway, only that it was a big square Victorian. Fletcher Hood handed her a flashlight, then hefted her luggage to a ginger bread-trimmed porch. Inside was a vestibule and a hallway dimly lit by a wrought iron floor lamp at the foot of the stairs.

"I'll just set your bags here till Doc gets back," Mr. Hood said. "Now, you come wait in the parlor." Entering a room off the hall, he switched on a table lamp with a stained glass shade so she could see a mishmash of dark, carved tables, mohair sofas, sagging easy chairs, faded hooked rugs. Benign neglect hung in the stale air as perceptibly as the ghosts of old varnish, dust, cigarette smoke. And faintly, the clean sharpness of antiseptic.

Embarrassed, she asked, "Uh… is there a bathroom I can use first?"

He gestured across the hall. "Just through Doc's office there. At the back. But it ain't much. So don't plan on taking a bath."

She laughed and groped through a dim examining room to the closet-sized lavatory. In the washstand mirror, her hair looked dull and greasy, as if she hadn't just washed it that morning. Combing did little to improve it but a touch of lipstick brightened her face. She washed the travel smell from her hands, then took the torch back to Cap'n Hood. "Thank you for picking me up. And carrying my bags in."

To her surprise, he looked embarrassed, and tipped his hat again. "Don't mention it, nurse. Guess I'll be getting home, then. See you in the morning, I expect."

"The morning?"

"Ay-yuh. When we go over to the island. Don't want to miss that, do you?"

"No. I can't wait." A lie; she was too weary to think beyond the rest of the day. Weary in her bones, more deeply weary than she'd ever been before. Like a woman of fifty, not twenty-five. Like a refugee she'd seen in a newsreel, pushing her few possessions across Europe in a baby carriage without a baby. God only knew what had become of that baby.

As soon as the door had closed behind Cap'n Hood, she

dropped onto a sagging davenport. For a moment the hush of the elderly house pressed on her like a dark presence, until a nearby clock went into full Westminster chimes then bonged five times. When it finished, she realized the place was full of clocks, all ticking busily. In the distance, another struck the hour. Who kept them wound? she wondered, as if it somehow mattered. If Dr. Millett had no nurse or wife, perhaps a housekeeper handled that chore. And in what appeared to be the patients' waiting room, also kept the stand ashtrays emptied and piles of *The Saturday Evening Post, Life* and *Liberty* neatly stacked on end tables.

She shuddered, relieved that she wasn't going to work here as his office nurse. However primitive the island clinic, it would surely be less confining than this stuffy, antiquated house. Especially since she'd be in charge, except for the one day each week the doctor spent there.

When she'd talked to him on the phone; he'd sounded kindly and sincere. Modest, middle-aged and weary. But even if he was a martinet to work for, she knew how to get along with doctors. In three years of nursing at the Portsmouth Naval Hospital, she'd been associated with an infinite variety of them, including the one who'd put her in touch with this one. If he was anything like his friend Jeff Fielding, Jim Millett would be reasonable, competent and easy to work for. Which was actually beside the point: she wasn't looking for ease and comfort, rather a job that would keep her so busy she'd have neither the time nor the energy to wonder endlessly whether Dan was still alive.

Jim Millett parked the Buick in the entrance to the drive, then felt his way through the familiar twilight up the steps and across the porch to the front door. The sky was a dusky violet, and the air held the dank scent of tidal water as it did whenever the wind died. As he came into the tiled vestibule, he noticed the suitcases. His spirits rose at this confirmation that the new nurse had arrived as scheduled.

"Hello?" he called. "Anyone here?"

A young woman he hadn't seen before stepped through the archway from the waiting room. Her smile was tentative. "Doctor Millett?"

He nodded, aware that her gaze dropped--everyone's did at first--to his built-up shoe, the cane, the halting walk. "Mrs. Donovan, I presume."

She walked closer, hand extended. He wasn't used to women who made this gesture, but probably a minister's daughter would be trained to greet people this way. Their fingers touched briefly. She was tall, gray eyes level with his, and the blue tweed suit hung loosely on her frame, as if she'd lost weight since she'd bought it. Her overall appearance too—limp hair, pale face, dark-circled eyes--suggested some malaise she hadn't hinted at when they'd spoken on the phone. But she'd told him her husband's submarine was missing in action, so perhaps what he was seeing were the physical traces of prolonged anxiety.

"Hope I haven't kept you waiting. Come on in the office so we can talk." He went in first and switched on the green-shaded lamp on the desk; both had been his grandfather's. Like the wooden armchair beside the desk, worn slick by sixty years of patients' butts.

When she sat, it was heavily, almost like a collapse, with head lowered and one hand pressed to her mouth.

Alarmed, he asked, "You all right, Mrs. Donovan?"

She took a deep, unsteady breath. "Sorry. Just A little vertigo. Probably low blood sugar."

He eased into his swivel chair, wheeling it closer so he could wrap his fingers around her wrist. Pulse racing but strong. "Eaten anything today?"

When she looked up and nodded, he reached over and

gently pulled down one lower eyelid. Pale mucosa, he noted, then studied the beds of her fingernails long enough to see further confirmation of anemia.

"On the train," she said. "Half a chicken sandwich my mother packed. And a deviled egg. And some cake. I gave the rest to an old man in the next seat. He seemed starved."

So she was a compassionate soul, he observed; a good quality in a nurse. "I see. Now, what about your periods. Heavier than usual lately?"

She averted her gaze, compressed her lips. "No. But two months ago I had…uh, an emergency C-section. See, I started hemorrhaging while I was working in the OB clinic, so they took me right to surgery." She shrugged. "Too late to save the baby, though."

He murmured, "Sorry," and stared at her with the sense of watching a monster wave suck someone out to sea while he stood by, helpless to intervene. Nothing new; this same impuissance seized him whenever he was confronted with someone else's unspeakable, irreversible loss. "Full term?"

"Twenty-seven weeks." The color had begun seeping back into her cheeks, but her voice was faint.

"Boy or girl?"

"Boy."

"Sorry." He swallowed hard. "My friend at Portsmouth told me you lost your husband, but didn't mention a stillbirth. What was it, a *placenta praevia*?"

She shook her head. "An abruption."

He winced, imagining the bloody process. "Transfusions afterward?"

"No. The blood bank was low, and my case wasn't life or death. So they gave me iron pills. And they told me to eat lots of liver."

"So…are you?"

The corners of her mouth lifted slightly. "No. I hate liver."

"Me too." A faint, conspiratorial smile connected them a moment. Then the hall clock chimed five-thirty and brought him back. "Well now. Ready for supper? Mrs. Goulding's keeping it hot for us."

"Won't be liver, will it?"

He chuckled and got to his feet, grabbing the cane for support. "If it is, we'll go to the coffee shop in Rockhampton."

It was a short four blocks to the boardinghouse, but he toured the village first so she could see the sheen of the harbor, the dark shapes of boats and rocks, the stark silhouettes of hillside houses against the sky. Heading up the slope again, he asked, "How long since you lost your husband?"

"Actually, he's just missing in action. His sub's overdue from a patrol. I only got word in June, so it could still show up. I really don't consider him lost."

"Of course. One must never lose hope."

She didn't answer. Huddled across the front seat, she stared into the twin paths cast by the dimmed headlights. But when he switched off the engine in front of the boardinghouse, she said, "I hope it doesn't matter about the stillbirth, Dr. Millett. Because I've had the postpartum checkup and everything's fine. Except the low red count. The other…the grief, I mean… I'm over that now. After all, it's been two months. It's not going to interfere with my job."

He said, "I'm not worried," but wanted to tell her she hadn't even begun to get over such a major double loss. Recovering from any sudden deprivation was relative, a matter of comparing how you felt from one day to the next. So if today was better than yesterday, you thought you were over it. He'd never been widowed, never had kids, but he supposed losing a spouse or a child was like losing anything else, including the use of one leg. His had been warped and atrophied by polio when he was twelve. And though he was used to living with its limitations, he could never pretend he was over it. Because it was always there in plain sight, to prove he wasn't. This woman, on the other hand, carried no visible evidence of bereavement, only a scarred soul. And though he'd known her for less than an hour, he sensed she wouldn't let it keep her from honoring her commitment to this job.

Mrs. Goulding's boardinghouse was a no-nonsense place, shake-sided and narrow, not a chink of light showing under the blackout curtains. Inside the hallway, the smell was the same that met him whenever he took supper here—of stale cooking and cigarettes, kerosene and incontinent elderly women. In the dining room, two places were set at one end of a long bare table, the other occupied by the widows Mrs. Goulding took in as wards of the state. Some were knitting, others just staring at big Philco floor radio. In high volume, an announcer with a stilted, pseudo-English accent was telling of Allied daylight air raids over Germany. He called them "daring" and mentioned "heavy losses," but cheerfully, the way even the grimmest news seemed to be reported.

When Jim introduced Anna, the women nodded or grunted, but said nothing by way of welcome. He held her chair, then sat beside her while Mrs. Goulding's son brought out chipped china bowls of red flannel hash, cabbage boiled to a mush, sweet pickles, store-bought white bread with uncolored margarine, and the remains of an apple pie. Seth was a squatty wall-eyed fellow, neither boy nor man, with bowl-cut orange hair, short, blunt fingers and an unlit cigarette dangling from his lips. His gaze remained downcast the whole time he served them.

As they regarded this feast, Mrs. Goulding, the gaunt, raw-boned widow of a drowned lobsterman, told them, "Take all you want, but mind you, eat what you take. Waste not, want not, I always say."

Jim began dishing food onto Anna's plate. "Not too much, please," she whispered.

"Why? Not hungry?"

"No, not very. And I don't want to leave anything."

He had to smile, noticing she ate silently, determinedly picking up even the crumbs. Someone's dutiful daughter, he thought. Some Navy man's dutiful wife. Well, good. Exactly what he needed—a nurse whose dutifulness would outlast the island's long winter. And Jean Cropper's hot and cold moods. A sturdy woman with New England starch in her veins, one who wouldn't quit after a week or a month to look for romance in the night clubs of Portland or Boston. Her only disadvantage, to his reckoning, might be that wounded soul.

While she worked through one paltry serving, he plowed through two platefuls, then cut them wedges of the pie. The bacon grease in the crust didn't shock him, but after the first bite, Anna set down her fork and asked Mrs. Goulding for a cup of tea. "If it's no trouble, please," she added dutifully.

Mrs. G. yelled for Seth. Five minutes later, he slammed down a chipped brown tea pot, two stained ironstone cups without saucers and a can of condensed milk.

Anna poured, then drank half of hers before she resumed eating the pie. Finishing, she murmured, "I must say, I've never had anything like this before. Maybe if it was warmed up, with some good cheese…."

He grinned. "And if wishes were horses…." Another fleeting, shared smile.

When they stood to leave, Mrs. Goulding directed Anna to a room at the top of the stairs, warned there'd be no hot water till morning, and, "Mind you, breakfast at six-thirty sharp. Don't be late if you want to eat."

Jim led her toward the front hall where the stairs rose, uncarpeted and steep between walls papered in faded pink peonies. "Best you do eat something. At least toast. Long trip to the island. Sound can be rough even in fair weather. Less chance of motion sickness on a full stomach."

"Thanks. I'll do my best." At the front door, she picked up her overnight case and offered her hand again. "What time in the morning?"

"Eight." Her fingers were cold, even after hot tea. He reached into the breast pocket of his jacket and withdrew an envelope. "Meanwhile, here's the contract for your job on the island. Look it over, and if you decide to stay, you can sign it. But you'll want to see the clinic first, of course."

She took it, nodded. "From everything you've told me, I'm sure it'll be fine."

"That's good news. Well, then, good night. I hope you sleep well."

"I expect to. Been a long day. And tomorrow will probably be another."

"Afraid so." To his surprise, he felt apologetic. Nonsense; long days were the stuff of any medical practice. A nurse would understand that. "See you in the morning then."

When she turned to climb the steps. He watched a moment, noticing her strong legs, the straight seams in her hose, the sensible shoes. Then, uncommonly and inexplicably wistful, he opened the door and stepped out on his cane. After the overheated house, the chill outside seemed more intense than before. Now the night smelled of rain, wind rising, a cold front predicted. He shivered and got into his car. And wondered, as he drove across the village, how Anna Donovan perceived him. Probably as old and desiccated, vital juices turning to dust. He wasn't yet forty, but suspected his patients already called him "Old Doc Millett" as they had his grandfather. Even sixteen years after his death, some locals claimed Jim was his spit and image.

Home again, he phoned two patients he'd seen that afternoon, then hobbled up the long front stairs to his bedroom. Stairs were the hardest part of his routines, so he tried to limit himself to one trip a day at home, though the hospital entrance had wide marble steps, and often homebound patients were in a second-floor bedroom. So it was a rare night that his crippled leg didn't ache. Now, as he unstrapped the clumsy brace that gave it rigidity, his gaze fell on the studio portrait of his former wife on the bureau. Two years now since she'd packed up, returned to Boston and asked him to divorce her on grounds of desertion.

Wanting to be shed of the charade that marriage had become, he'd agreed without reservations. Since then she'd married some Back Bay lawyer and now seemed deep into happily-ever-after.

Odd, he thought; he usually avoided recollections of her as assiduously as he avoided old seafood. Tonight, however, he felt powerless to resist her memory. And why? Because a new nurse had entered his professional life? Or to remind himself not to imagine her in any other context?

Leaning on the crutch, he walked across the room to study the photograph--dark eyes, well-groomed brows, slightly parted lips. For so long he'd been convinced his libido had turned to ashes, yet now he felt a pulse of warmth, as if a coal still glowed. Still smoldered, ready to flame. And burn the hell out of him again.

Masochist, he rebuked himself, slamming the picture frame-down beside the lamp. And a fool to acknowledge this faint residual yearning for the heat he'd known with Ellen. Other men, he was quite sure, took heat for granted. He never had, so after it had run its course, the other side of passion had deadened his soul the way polio had his leg. Or so he'd previously been convinced.

Before he got into bed, he raised the window sash just enough to hear the trickle of rain on the porch roof. The scent of it always evoked faint nostalgia for something he sensed he'd missed, but could never pinpoint. Tonight it also stirred curiosity about what Anna Donovan would be feeling in her shabby boarding house room. Women's emotions were a mystery to him, but logic suggested she'd be anxious about the new job, and worried about her husband, and sad about her baby; with those feelings compounded by being alone and isolated from everyone she loved. Yeah, that'd be it. Alone and isolated. Well, they had that in common then. Yet how very unlikely they'd ever talk about it. How very unlikely they'd ever share much of anything beside medical matters. Of course, wasn't that better than nothing?

Indeed. For a man like him, it was far better than nothing. Especially with a fine young woman like Anna Donovan.

Chapter Three

Standing behind Captain Hood in the pilothouse, Anna watched the East Point wharf recede as he maneuvered the big steel trawler *Molly B* toward the channel. In the slanting golden light of a clear autumn morning, the village reminded her of an impressionist painting-- rocky harbor, weathered pilings and shanties, clapboard and shingled houses rising steeply behind them, lobster boats and pots stacked for the winter, gulls screeching and diving. And in the inky water below, their mirrored images, rippled by the wake. Like a Monet scene, except he'd never come to New England.

Half-nauseated by diesel exhaust, Cap'n Hood's latest cigarette and the stink of old fish, Anna gulped fresh air as they churned past a channel marker and turned north into cold wind. Fletcher pointed toward the open water he'd called The Sound. "Now, nurse. Make out Hope Island yonder?"

She squinted at a cluster of hazy blobs on the horizon. "Which one?"

"Big one on the far left. That's Little Hope to the right. Nothing there nowadays but falling-down summer places. Next to that's Little No Hope." He chuckled, sucked on his cigarette, then tossed it overboard through the open window.

"Only scrub pines and rocks. Might be a few deer left if hunters ain't picked them all off since meat got so scarce." He handed her a pair of heavy binoculars. "Here, have a look-see." With a minimal glance at the compass, he adjusted the wheel on a course parallel to the shoreline. "Use to be, we could come out of East Point and head straight to the island. Nowadays, though, gotta know what you're doing, 'cause they got the old channel mined."

"Mined! What for?"

His eyes narrowed to indigo slits. "Never know what them Huns'll do next with them U-boats. Heard they tried landing spies down to Long Island, but the Coast Guard got them afore they ever set foot on American soil. Might try that here too. Likely won't bother with Portland, 'cause there's artillery all over them islands." He sniffed. "But up here? Hell, no. Damned government don't think this part of Maine's worth wasting men they need in combat."

Dr. Millett slid the window closed and seated himself in one of the chairs bolted to the steel deck. In a fresh shirt and a navy blue tie, he looked younger than he had the evening before and no longer a study in beige -- hair and eyes, necktie and jacket, even the rims of his glasses. "Don't worry, Mrs. Donovan. We're perfectly safe."

"I'm not worried. But yesterday, the bus went by a Navy air base outside Brunswick, and I understand they're building warships at the Bath Iron Works. Saboteurs could do a lot of damage in this area."

When he and Fletcher exchanged amused glances, she realized she sounded naïve, even melodramatic. Embarrassed, she focused the glasses on the large whale-shaped island, but blowing spume blurred the view. Except for one large building that stood out against the sky. "What's the big place on the hill?"

Fletcher said. "Old hotel. Not near as famous as the Wentworth down your way, but maybe you heard of it.

Hope Island House?"

She shook her head.

"Thought you could stay there," Jim said. "At least for a while. Jean--I told you about her; she runs the clinic. Anyway, she lives there. Hotel's been closed since the war started, but she has a room you can use. If you want to."

"That'll be fine." They were passing a wooded point where waves pounded rocks at base of a stumpy lighthouse. Beyond it was a curving sand beach, and a spit of land studded with the charred skeleton of a house. The sight sent a sudden dark horror shuddering through her. Almost like the emotions that had predicted Dan's loss. What would this one be—confirmation? No, she rebuked herself; there was no sense leaving Portsmouth if she was going to let those old fears pollute her new life here.

With a last drag on his smoke, Fletcher put the wheel over in a sharp arc toward the sea, then slid open the window just enough to toss out the butt. Heading into the waves, the trawler's bow rose so steeply Anna lost her balance and toppled into the other chair in the pilothouse.

"Made this trip almost every week the past four years," the doctor called above the stepped-up rumble of the engine, "but each time, it's different. Even rougher in a storm, though."

"Is it ever so bad you can't get out there?"

Fletcher glanced back, one hand on the wheel, the other massaging his stubbled jaw. "Now and then in a big blow. Shallow water always riles up more'n deep, don't you know?"

Her mind quickly converted this information into a new what-if. "Dr. Millett, you told me OB cases go to the mainland before their due date. But suppose there was some other emergency during a storm. Say, a case of acute appendicitis?"

His glance was curious. "That actually happened a few

years back. But Fletcher got me over so I could remove the appendix before it ruptured. Damned rough ride, though."

She was tempted to ask what would have happened if he hadn't managed to reach the island in time, but shouting over engine noise was no way to have a serious medical discussion. So she tried to relax in the stiff chair, and closed her eyes against the dizzying rise and fall of the horizon. After a few minutes, however, she realized the pitching of the boat and the smells in the pilothouse were about to make her lose her breakfast. Not much of a meal-- thin oatmeal and a cup of Postum with condensed milk- - but not one she wanted to part with in these conditions.

When bile rose in her throat, she bolted from the chair, wrenched open the heavy door and stepped onto the afterdeck. Clutching the rail, she breathed deeply of the cold, salty air and focused on the horizon. And sensations other than nausea: sunlight warm on her skin; wind shrieking in the rigging; gulls coasting above the wake. Behind them, the lighthouse had receded to a white slash against evergreened hills, while ahead, Hope Island assumed shape and definition. Soon she made out that the hotel had a red mansard roof, and that a white spire rose from a lesser hill behind the village.

Her stomach settled as the waves diminished. She was about to return to the pilothouse when Dr. Millett came out, leaning heavily on his cane. "Everything all right, Mrs. Donovan?"

"Oh Yes. Thanks. Just a touch of mal-de-mer. I haven't been on a boat in a while."

"Bothered me at first too. Fortunately, I got over it."

Without meaning to notice the affliction he hadn't gotten over, she glanced down at his cane, then quickly gestured at the island. "How soon till we get there?"

"Oh, half hour, more or less. Why? Still seasick?"

"No, I'm fine now. Just excited to start a new job."

He took off his hat and raked his fingers through his hair. Wind erased the tracks before he covered his head again. "Well, I hope you go on feeling that way. Because there's not much excitement on the island."

"That's okay. I've never been bored in my life. And I won't be now."

Squinting, he studied her through his glasses. In the sunlight his eyes seemed more gold than beige. "Well, good. One less thing for me to worry about then."

Exactly what Dan had said when she'd agreed to go home to have the baby instead of staying in San Francisco after his boat left. Coincidence, she told herself. This colorless middle-aged man would have almost nothing in common with her handsome naval officer husband. Except intelligence and diligence, of course, but not the submariner's daring, the craving for adventure. Or the same passionate nature. Definitely not the passionate nature. Even as she thought it, she felt a blush rising.

"In the meantime," he added, "if you ever want to talk, I'm a good listener. Or so my patients tell me."

She cleared her throat to dispel the errant thought. "Thanks for offering. I'll keep it in mind. Now. Tell me more about what we're going to do today."

While she listened, she had a sense she was finally slipping the bonds of dependency on parents and husband. Becoming a woman on her own, about to step into a new life on an island that so far seemed rather picturesque. Of course, there'd be more to it than superficial charm. No job, no situation was free of challenges; as a priest's daughter she knew even churches had their share of the malicious, the hard-hearted and the self-righteously judgmental. Plus a few other varieties of Good People, including the pious martyrs from whom her father often prayed privately for deliverance.

Fortunately, she told herself, she had no illusions left to

be shattered. Therefore, by the time *Molly B* passed a stone breakwater, exhilaration tingled in her, leaving her more animated than she'd been since San Francisco, and conscious of teetering on the brink of adventure in a strange place. Not so strange, actually; the harbor looked like every other small New England harbor she'd ever seen, with a sliver of sand beach and ramshackle sheds perched on skinny legs. Behind it was a village with a general store and Texaco gas pumps, a barber shop with a striped pole, a red-painted firehouse, a luncheonette with a Coca-Cola sign and a smattering of small shops. Even a Civil War Monument. The spire she'd seen earlier rose from a white church on a hillside punctuated with gravestones.

Evidently following her gaze, the doctor said, "Church closed up around the time the hotel did. Except every now and then the Congregational minister from town comes over for a special service. Hope not having regular services won't be a problem for you."

She shook her head. "Not at all. Don't think I mentioned it before, but my father's an Episcopal priest. So I know every service forward and backward. And every prayer in the book by heart."

A smile abruptly softened his face, momentarily turned him boyish, then faded as fast as it had come.

Fletcher cut the engine and they glided toward a pier where a lineup of horse-drawn wagons and vintage pickup trucks waited. The doctor pointed: "Blue wagon's Cleve Cropper's, come to fetch coal for the hotel. And your bags, of course. Jean's probably already at the clinic. Started working there right out of high school, mostly keeping records. Now she handles a lot of the nurse's duties too. Lucky she does; hard to get one to stay more'n a month or two." He grinned. "Guess I shouldn't tell you that, should I?"

She smiled minimally. "Why do they leave? Not that it

matters. I intend to stay the year of my contract."

He shrugged. "Likely not enough social life. Or eligible men."

"Those things don't matter to me."

"Well, good. Anyway, Jean's not trained as a nurse, but she's picked up so much I tell her she ought to make it official. Go to school, get her license."

Anna squinted into sunlight dazzling off slick water between boat and pier. "Will she stay on after I get there?"

"Well, she'll keep doing records. And handling the books. The rest'll be up to you."

Suddenly she had to ask, "If she's doing such a good job, why do you need me?"

His scowled at his hands on the rail, at the immaculate nails, at a small signet ring on the right little finger. "Well, by law, any island with more than a hundred residents is supposed to have a full-time RN. Jean's competent, but in emergencies, we need someone with a medical background. Plus, we're supposed to give a civilian first aid course, and only an RN can teach it." He cleared his throat as the mate tossed the bowline to a bewhiskered man on the pier. "Since the war, the state's been looking the other way. But if they ever got serious, we could lose funding."

"Oh, I see." She hoped she didn't sound disappointed. Yet she was. And why? After all, he'd offered her the job, and she was qualified. Never mind his reasons. If she wanted to make a success of it, she couldn't react with hurt feelings. That was childish. And she was anything but a child.

Once they'd tied up, she followed him down the gangway, squared her purse and slowed her steps to match his hobbling gait as they crossed the pier toward the waiting vehicles. The blue wagon he'd pointed out was drawn by a black mare that stomped and snorted above steaming clumps of manure. There, the doctor introduced her to Cleve

Cropper, Jean's uncle---a rangy man in overalls, flannel shirt and battered fedora.

Ignoring her extended hand, he tipped his hat, said he'd put her bags in her room at the hotel, if that was all right? She thanked him, said it was fine. She and Dr. Millett walked on, met two other middle-aged men, both equally taciturn. And Cleve's wife, Lorraine, en route to the boat for mail sacks. Dark of hair and eyes, she struck Anna as exotic, with a smile framed in fuschia lipstick and a skin-tight rose sweater accentuating pointed breasts. She took a pack of Lucky Strikes from her skirt pocket and extended it. "Pleased to meet you, honey. Care for a smoke?"

Anna smiled. "Thanks, but I don't smoke."

"Well, be seeing you around then. Any questions about this place, just ask me. I'm the postmistress; I know everybody's secrets." The smile flashed again; she put a cigarette to her lips and walked on, high heels clicking on cobblestones.

The town square was nothing more than a circle of dead grass surrounding a tall granite obelisk commemorating the victory of Joshua Chamberlain's Maine Regulars at Gettysburg. On the next corner, the sturdy-looking brick town hall housed a library, auditorium and the clinic. Inside, the doctor led her to a door with a frosted glass panel marked with a red cross, then let her precede him into an institutional waiting room - green walls, gray-painted floor, steel chairs with leather seats, stand ashtrays and low tables on which issues of *Colliers, Popular Mechanics* and *New England Farmer* were haphazardly stacked. Sagging Venetian blinds covered the windows. The air was stale with old smoke, yet faintly medicinal. The only decorative touches were Red Cross posters promoting blood donation and the first aid course.

"Darn, forgot the magazines from the house," said the doctor, "Wanted to bring that Life everybody's talking about. One with the full-page picture of dead GIs. You seen it?"

She winced, recalling uniformed corpses on a New Guinea beach. "Pretty awful. But then, war is, isn't it?"

"Never been in one, but General Sherman said it was hell. Cruelty that can't be refined. Maybe I'm lucky to have this game leg after all. Now then, let me find Jean."

Suddenly uneasy for no sensible reason, she pressed her fingernails into her palms and watched him limp down a hall behind the check-in counter. He passed two open doors, stopped at a third, face brightening. "Ah, here you are, Jean. Come meet our new nurse."

For fully five minutes after he returned to the desk, Jean Cropper busied herself in the clinic's back room, a haphazard office/kitchen jammed with a fridge, hot plate, table and chairs, typewriter, filing cabinets and a score of printed regulations thumb-tacked to the walls. The nurses Jim hired had often tried to organize this clutter, at least for a week or so before frustration convinced them to leave it alone. This pleased her. The clinic had been her domain for ten years; she knew where everything was, could put her hands on it in the dark if she had to. Same with the two exam rooms and the front desk. Only area she didn't intrude on was Jim's office, though she often ran a feather duster over the desk when he wasn't around.

A compact woman of twenty-nine, she'd never been married, though for a while she'd been engaged to a merchant seaman who'd died when his tanker was torpedoed in November, 1942. She'd lived her entire life in the hotel on Hope Island, except for the high school years when she'd stayed in East Point with Jim's parents and his younger sister, her best friend, her only friend. And might still be if she hadn't been thrown from a horse during her second semester at Mount Holyoke. Died, and left a hole in Jean's life, and her family's.

She wasn't sure what her death had done to Jim; he'd been in Boston for eight or nine years by then, training for his medical career. His parents, however, had moved to Florida afterward and never come back, even to visit. Jean couldn't understand their wanting to live elsewhere; tragedy went with you, even to exotic places like Florida. She herself had never been tempted to leave the island. Except once, when she'd taken a series of trains down to Bayonne, New Jersey to visit Ken Renaldi before he sailed on what proved his last voyage. A week in a boarding house there snuffed out any remaining interest in travel. So when she got word of his death, she consoled herself that it probably wouldn't have worked out anyway: his post-war dream was to work in the family winery. Being in the same state as Bayonne, Hammonton was the last place she wanted to live.

From the front, Jim's voice reminded her she was supposed to meet the latest of his clinic nurses. She stubbed out a cigarette in an ashtray decorated with the Trylon and Perisphere from the New York World's Fair, buttoned her lab coat and ambled toward the check-in desk. The woman beside him was a head taller than she, skinny and plain, and though she wore red lipstick, not nearly as pretty as the other nurses he'd hired. That was good. Only thing not in her favor was, she was a lot younger than Jean expected.

He stopped talking, face brightening as he introduced them. Anna Donovan held out her hand. "Nice to meet you."

Jean ignored the proffered shake. Instead she said, "Doctor, I thought you were looking for somebody older."

His eyes narrowed. "No, just someone with a wide range of experience. Which Mrs. Donovan's had in the years she's been in nursing."

Anna's smile touched off dimples, revealed white, even

teeth. Like an Ipana ad. "Dr. Millett's told me so much about you, Jean, I know you'll help me learn everything I need to know."

"Please, nurse. Miss Cropper, if you don't mind," she corrected. "We try to be professional here. If you stay at the hotel, then we can use first names. But you'll probably want to know more about the job before you take it, won't you?"

"No. I've already made up my mind."

Yeah, for today, she thought. Just wait till winter. Wait till you have to go out at night in a snowstorm and the damn car won't start. "Well, good for you. I'll get you a lab coat so nobody bleeds all over that swell suit. Then I'll show you the ropes."

Jim excused himself to phone housebound patients; Jean reached into the closet for a fresh coat. Handing it over, she added, "Hope you've brought a uniform so patients know you're the nurse."

"Three. They're in my luggage. Your uncle's taking it up to the hotel."

"Oh, so you're staying there, are you?"

Her eyes widened. "Dr. Millett suggested it. But if it's not convenient with you, I'll find a boarding house." She took off her suit jacket, eased into the starched white coat. "Now then. I'm ready for all those ropes you're going to show me."

We'll see how ready you are, Jean thought as she launched into the same rigorous routine she'd used with the other nurses, six of them in the four years since Jim had taken over the clinic. Important stuff, of course, like contents of filing cabinets, drawers, closets, locked medicine chests and refrigerator. Plus procedures for patient check-in, completing forms, transcribing notes. Most of the women only half-listened, as if they already knew everything. Or had no intentions of staying a moment longer than they had to.

This one paid attention, however. Or seemed to, even asked a few sensible questions. Well, maybe being a widow had made her appreciate a good job like this.

While Jean was showing Anna around, Doris Godwin came through the waiting room and shuffled to the desk in worn-down felt slippers. Probably her bunions, judging by the bulging toe joints. Though with her it was rarely the same complaint twice. "Nurse, get Mrs. Godwin's chart from the files," Jean ordered.

Doris Godwin scrutinized her across the counter. "You the new nurse Doc's been promising?"

Anna turned, smiled, nodded. "Yes, ma'am. Anna Donovan."

She sniffed. "Hope you stay longer than the last one. Or the one before. No sooner get here than off they go to greener pastures. Meaning, some place there's more single men."

"That won't happen to me, ma'am. Because I'm a married woman. My husband's in the Navy. In the Pacific." She paused, color draining from her face. For a moment, she grasped the counter for support. Then, excusing herself, fled down the hall toward the rest room.

Mrs. Godwin watched her retreat. "Well now, Jean. What was that all about?"

"Husband's missing in action," Jean murmured. "Must be sensitive about it."

"Hmmph. Can't be sensitive if you work here."

With a faint smirk, Jean recorded Doris's latest medical complaint, told her to have a seat in Exam Room One, then glanced into Jim's office. "Don't know about that new nurse of yours. Thought she was going to pass out just now. Hope she's strong enough for this job."

"Give her time, Jean," he said without raising his gaze from the chart on his desk.

But she didn't need time. Right from the start, she'd

taken the measure of the nurses he'd hired, had met enough now to trust her first impression. The really pretty ones were the worst, constantly preening, flirting with every man that came near, even plain-as-dirt Uncle Cleve. "Well, if this one doesn't work out either, you can always count on me."

"Of course. Now, what ails Doris Godwin today?" He pushed his chair back and thumped toward the door on the cane.

"Sore throat. Said she could hardly talk, then talked my ear off." She was ready to remind him she knew the patients better than any off-islander ever could, but he was halfway down the hall.

By then Anna had returned to the front desk and was trying to log in Chester Philbrick, an islander famous for a natural body odor enhanced by the emanations of his hog farm. Now he seemed reluctant to give his full name, said only, "Philbrick. Jeannie can tell you the rest. She's knowed me all her life."

"Go on, Nurse," Jean prompted.

Anna nodded. "All right. I'll leave that blank for now." She spelled out P-H-I-L-B-R-I-C-K. "And what's the nature of your complaint?"

The scowl deepened; he shifted from foot to foot. "Being you're new and all, I'll just tell you what I always tell her. Only Doc needs to know."

"Okay, we'll leave that blank too."

"Now pull his chart," Jean said. "Then take him back to the examining room and leave it in the holder on the door."

"Shall I take his vital signs?"

"Doctor likes to check them himself."

"Whatever you say." Anna riffled through files for the record, led him down the hall. It was a while before she returned. "When I told Mr. Philbrick to sit on the edge of the table, she said he'd rather stand. So I figured he must have hemorrhoids."

Jean glared. "Why do you need to know anyway?"

Anna blinked a couple of times. "Just trying to learn as much as I can about the patients as fast as I can."

Sounded commendable, Jean thought. But she'd see how long that lasted. She glanced up at the regulator clock on the wall. "Well, if you really want to be useful, go down the street and get our lunches. Doctor and I always have hamburgers and Coca-Cola. Order yourself whatever you want." The nurse nodded, and reached for her purse. "Tell them put it on the clinic's bill. Now don't forget, two hamburgers and two sodas."

Anna's complaisant smile faded as her lips tightened. "Think I can remember that. The Lunch Box. Down the street. Anything else I should know?"

"Not right now. But this afternoon you'll have plenty to learn."

"This afternoon?"

"When we make house calls. Didn't the doctor tell you?"

The younger woman's face crumpled, as if she might cry. Jean hoped she did; that'd tell her everything she needed to know about the latest hireling. But this one only shrugged, said, "I'll try not to be long," and hurried out through the waiting room. Jean watched her go with a the sense that she had more backbone than any of the others. Or was more serious about working here than they'd been. As if she was looking for something other than an easy job, with short hours, and lots of fun during her time off. Well, if that's how it was, then she'd certainly come to the right place.

The harbor was spangled by mid-day sunlight, but the wind had a crisp, salty edge as Anna left the building. The scene with Jean had tempted her to blurt out, "I may be young but I'm not feeble-minded." Except that the first day on an unfamiliar island a hundred miles from home seemed neither the time nor place for a smart mouth. Especially if she had to live with Jean at the hotel.

Still bristling, she came down the hill toward the center of the village. As she passed the general store, a woman's voice called, "You headed for lunch too, nurse?" Coming down the steps, Lorraine Cropper gave her a brilliant smile.

She paused to let the older woman catch up. "Yes I am, Mrs. Cropper. I think Jean sent me as part of my training."

"She treating you okay?"

"She's very helpful," Anna said cautiously.

Lorraine's plucked-thin brows rose. "You know, since her fiancé died, that job's her life. Wouldn't be surprised if she's peeved Doc brought in another mainlander. Especially a looker like yourself."

Having never considered herself a "looker", Anna ignored the comment and swung open the Lunch Box door. Inside, the place was arranged like a diner, booths along the windows and an interior counter with barstools. It also smelled like every such eatery she'd ever known-- of hot fat, frying onions, steam, overheated coffee, cigarettes. The same noises too: clatter of plates and cutlery, din of conversation, and from a neon-flashing Wurlitzer jukebox, the Andrews Sisters blasting out *Boogie-Woogie Bugle Boy.*

Lorraine wedged herself between two men on stools, pushed close to the counter and beckoned a waitress with frizzy yellow hair. "Mabel, this here's the new nurse up to the clinic. She's come for lunch. And mind you, she don't have all day."

Anna ordered for the others, plus a ham on rye and Nehi for herself. Lorraine invited her to sit till the food was ready, so she slid into a booth and watched the older woman stir canned milk into her coffee. "Stuff's half chicory these days, but it beats nothing."

Not sure she should ask what she intended to, Anna

clasped her hands atop a wooden surface scarred with a welter of carved initials. “Uh, Mrs. Cropper, I was wondering. Is there any place to stay here besides the hotel?”

“Call me Lorraine, why don’t you?”

“Okay. Anyway, I thought you might know.”

The mascaraed eyelids narrowed. “How come? Ain’t the hotel to your liking?”

“I haven’t seen it yet.”

“Oh. Then you mean, in case you and Jean don’t get on?”

“No, no,” Anna said hastily. “I just thought maybe there’s some place closer to the clinic.”

Lorraine blew across her cup. “Well, there’s the boarding-house down the next corner, but it ain’t somewhere a lady’d stay.” She sipped, added more milk. “Tell you what, though. If Jean gives you any guff, you just move in with me and Cleve. Got all sorts of room in that old house. And it’s just up the road.”

“Thanks. That’s kind of you. I’ll keep it in mind.”

“Don’t mention it, honey. Fifteen years ago, I was a stranger here myself. And let me tell you, not one woman made it easy for me. Except Jean’s mother, God rest her soul. The men, though, they were a different story.”

Sensing Lorraine was about to launch into a faintly-sordid tale, Anna was relieved when the waitress brought the grease-spotted paper bag. Taking it, she got to her feet. “Nice talking to you, Mrs. . . uh, Lorraine. I’ll be in for stamps one day soon.”

“Bet you write that hubby of yours every night, don’t you?”

She managed to keep smiling. “Usually. But I don’t mail the letters anymore. Since his sub went missing, the Navy sends them back.”

Lorraine rose-tipped fingers flew to cover her mouth.

"Oh, honey, I'm sorry. Nobody told me nothing about it. But don't you give up hope, you hear?"

"No, I never will." Aware people were watching—and no doubt whispering, "Doc's latest nurse" to one another--she hurried toward the door. As she opened it, the jukebox went into the familiar introduction to *All the Things You Are.* The first song she and Dan had ever danced to. Their song. A few years old now, no longer on the Hit Parade. So maybe hearing it today was a good omen for the new job. She decided to take it as one anyway, especially coming right after Lorraine's counsel not to give up hope.

Chapter Four

Jim was still scribbling on the Hooper girl's chart when Jean sidled into the office, lunch bag in hand. Without waiting for an invitation, she pulled up a chair and began removing the sandwiches. He capped the pen, closed the chart. "Wait a minute, Jean. Thought I'd eat with Anna today. Find out how she's doing. Ask her to come in, please."

Jean's green-olive eyes went wide. With surprise? Or shock? Maybe even dismay. "But why? You never did that with any other nurses."

"Yeah. And I should have. Might've stayed longer if I'd taken an interest in their progress."

"Now that's nonsense. You shouldn't have to mollycoddle grown women."

"Just ask Anna to bring her lunch up here."

She sniffed, stepped into the hall, called. "Anna? Doctor wants you to eat with us."

"Not us, Jean. At least not today, if you don't mind."

She drew a quick breath and hunched her shoulders. Scowling, she removed one hamburger and a Coke bottle from the bag, then marched out, brushing past Anna in the doorway without a word.

"Come on in," he said. "And close the door behind you."

She nodded; he pointed to the chair Jean had dragged up to his desk. Shoving the chart aside, he unwrapped his burger; condiments dribbled from the bun like molten confetti. "Sorry to intrude on your lunch hour, but I wanted to see what you think of the job so far."

She sat cautiously, the way well-bred girls were trained to in case they had to rise unexpectedly. "It's about what I expected. Of course, there's a lot to get used to, but I will eventually." With exaggerated care, she unwrapped a sandwich oozing yellow mustard and pink ham slices, then set it on her lap.

"Good." He bit into the paper-thin burger, swigged from the green bottle. "That mean you've decided to stay?"

She nodded. "Actually I read the contract and signed it last night. And so far, nothing I've seen today has changed my mind. So…it's in my purse in the closet out front. I'll get it when I finish lunch. I mean, if you think I'm what you need here."

He stifled the exuberant smile that tempted him as he recalled Jeff Fielding's high praise of her work at Portsmouth. As well as her fine character and stoic commitment to duty even in the face of personal sorrows. "I'm quite sure you are. But take your time."

"Very well." Nodding, she neatened the wrappings on her lap.

"And how're you and Jean getting on?"

He sensed the slightest hesitance when she said, "We're…uh, we're becoming acquainted." She nibbled at one end of the diagonally-cut sandwich. "Oh my goodness. Haven't seen this much ham since rationing started."

He laughed. "It's bootleg. Hog farmers here sell us all we want before they send it to market."

She chewed slowly, sipped from the soda bottle. "Doubt I can eat more than half. Would you care for the rest?"

"That's a tempting offer." He attacked the burger again, a

huge mouthful he barely chewed before he gulped it down. "That reminds me. I've asked Jean to serve wine before supper every night. To help your appetite. And another at bedtime, if you have trouble sleeping."

She stared, chewing more slowly.

"See, her cellar's full of the stuff. Fiancé brought a couple cases every time he came to visit. He was Italian; they drink it instead of water." Unable to read her expression, he added, "Or do you object for religious reasons?"

"Oh my, no. Episcopalians aren't Puritans."

He chuckled. "So I've heard. Anyway, remind her this evening." He finished his sandwich. "Now, if you're sure you can't eat the other half…"

She leaned over to hand it to him. "But getting back to routines. What exactly do we do days you're not here?"

Holding the tempting new sandwich, he described visiting homebound patients, taking vitals, keeping up their meds. "And make sure they're following orders." He grinned. "If you can." Then, savoring the smoky flavor, he allowed himself a restrained bite before he mentioned the first aid course she and Jean were to teach.

Anna scanned the diplomas on the wall behind him. "Something else I'm curious about. Wouldn't it save time if I took patients' vitals instead of you? Usually, they're the nurses' job. Drawing blood is, too."

He had to smile. "Yeah, I know. And whenever I've had an RN, she's done them. Because Jean's not comfortable taking anything but temps. So feel free to add them to your other duties." The smile widened to a grin. "Might wish you hadn't once things get busy here."

"No, I won't, Dr. Millett. It's my job to make your job easier."

He studied her with faint curiosity. "Learn that at Mass General?"

She blushed, which surprised him. "Among other things."

He wanted to smile at her penchant for sententiousness, but instead concentrated on the remains of his sandwich. Gulping down the last bite, he said, "That's another thing, Anna. It's okay to call me Jim."

"Oh. Very well, thanks." She crumpled the wax paper, drained the soda and seemed about to spring from her chair. "But when we're with patients, I'll call you doctor. That's the professional thing to do. As Jean reminded me earlier."

"Well, it's fine to be professional, of course, but you'll find we're a lot less formal here than they are in Navy medical facilities. Don't have time to stand on ceremony like they do."

She nodded. "Will that be all then?"

"Unless you can think of something else."

"No. Not at the moment." She got to her feet. "Now. When do we start house calls?"

"Soon's we finish office patients and lunch. Any minute now. Maybe you can help Jean pull the charts beforehand."

She nodded, got to her feet and left, closing the door behind her. Damn; she hadn't told him much at all, had seemed evasive about Jean. Another thing well-bred girls were trained to do—if they couldn't say something nice, they said nothing at all. Not that he needed chapter and verse. He'd observed Jean with nurses he'd hired before; she didn't sabotage them outright but offered no help, no advice, not so much as a voluntary smile. Maybe it'd been a mistake to arrange for Anna to stay at the hotel, as the others had. Then again, maybe the wine would relax the tension. Another innovation, like the impromptu mid-day interview.

By the time they'd made the last house call, dusk was

thickening over the island, and he was bone weary, bad leg throbbing with the day's exertions. In and out of the station wagon nine times, often with steps to climb or a rocky path to walk. All his patients had been chattier than usual, thrilled to have a new nurse to listen to their symptoms. Most were chronic, routine cases—congestive heart failure, diabetes, hypertension, effects of stroke, crippling arthritis and just plain old age. Except for Beth Carter, a bright and pretty 16-year- old with rheumatic fever. Anna had only stood by, observing while he palpated the girl's swollen knees and listened to her heart, but had asked nothing until they were heading back to the village. She was in the rear seat with her lap full of charts, Jean driving, Jim beside her in front. As they bounced over the rutted gravel track from the island's north end, Anna asked if he expected the girl to make a full recovery.

He half-turned toward her. "Well, so far her heart sounds are good, no sign of damage. And the mother's enforcing the bed rest and aspirin regimen, so I'm hopeful she'll come out of it without residual effects."

"Must be hard for someone that age to be so isolated."

"Don't worry about Beth," Jean put in tartly. "She's an island girl. They know how to follow orders. Why, she's even keeping up with her homework so she doesn't fall behind. And after she graduates, she's going to nursing school so she can come back and work here." She smiled at Jim. "Sooner or later, we'll have someone we can count on."

He wanted to say, "I believe we have one now," but decided not to set Jean off with a contrary opinion. Especially when there was no valid reason to argue the point.

When he got out at the pier, his bad leg was barely able to support his weight, even with the brace. Exiting behind him, Anna offered to carry his bag. He was tempted, but said, "I can manage, thanks. See if Ruthie could use a hand instead."

She jumped to take the small cardboard suitcase from the patient, a woman with such severe fibroid tumors she was going to the Rockhampton hospital for a hysterectomy. When they were halfway across the pier, Fletcher Hood started the trawler's engine in anticipation of a quick getaway. He liked to brag he knew the Sound better than his wife's moods, but he still seemed uneasy at night without navigation lights. Jim always tried to finish house calls quickly, but today all the extra talk had used almost an hour. Nearly five now, he observed as he dragged himself up the gangway. An hour to cross the sound, then another thirty minutes to drive Ruthie to the hospital, an hour to make rounds, and eat supper somewhere. If he was lucky, he'd get home by eight, finish calling patients by nine. After that the night was his own. Barring emergencies, of course.

Ahead of him, Anna led Ruthie into the pilothouse, then waited for him on deck. "Good night, Jim. Thanks for helping me today."

"Glad to. See you next week then. Remember, call if you have any questions. Anything at all." He stepped onto the deck as she went back down the gangway. Immediately, the mate swung it alongside and cast them off. The engines roared, foam spewed behind them as they came about. The smell of diesel exhaust mingled with the faint fishiness of harbor water and smoke from Fletch's most recent cigarette.

Aching to get off his leg, Jim nonetheless stood at the rail as they headed toward the breakwater. Anna was still on the pier by the station wagon, watching them recede. He raised his hand in a brief wave. When she returned the gesture, he was surprised. And pleased, taking it as a good sign. Then he went into the pilothouse and crashed gratefully into the empty deck chair across from Ruthie Bowen.

Chapter Five

Impatience tempted Jean to lean on the horn when Anna stood gazing after the receding trawler for what felt like ten minutes. Not that Jean had anything to do back at the hotel: this was the free-floating annoyance that took her over whenever she had to wait for anything. It abated only slightly when the nurse finally slid into the front seat. "Sorry to make you wait. But I wanted to watch the boat leave."

Jean started the engine. "Wish you were on it, don't you?"

"What? Why do you say that?"

"Listen, I know the signs. Any idea how many nurses Jim's hired the past four years?"

Anna shook her head and turned to look behind them as they backed into the street. Still following the trawler with her eyes, Jean surmised. Silly woman.

"You're number seven. One left the third week because we were having a nor'easter. Another lasted four months. That was the longest."

"Did they all stay at your hotel?"

"Yep."

"Then maybe I'd better find a room somewhere else."

Jean snorted. "Go ahead. Just try and find one half as

nice. With meals thrown in. And now Jim's paid me for a case of wine so you can have a drink before supper. Let me tell you, he never did that with the others. Must think you need special handling.

Anna seemed to stiffen. "If he does, it's only because I'm anemic. And he may think I'm not eating right."

"Anemic? Is that all? Well, you're certainly getting the red carpet treatment. Guess he'll try anything to keep a nurse here."

Anna sighed, frowned. "He doesn't have to worry me. We have a contract. And I need the job. I had a good one at the naval hospital down home, but …" She shook her head, lowered her voice. "I couldn't go on living with my parents?"

Jean glanced across the seat. "Oh yeah? What's the matter with them?"

"Nothing. They're wonderful people. They'd do anything for me. Except…"

Spoiled rich kid, Jean thought. "Then why did you leave?"

Anna sighed. "Hard to explain. Except…well, they've been treating me like a child. It was bad enough when I got word my husband's missing in action. But after I lost a baby, they started watching me as if they expected me to break. Acting so damned sorry for me I couldn't stand all that sympathy."

Jean took a deep breath. "A baby! Jim told me about your husband, but he never mentioned a baby. Well, that's too bad. But lots of women have miscarriages. It's not the end of the world."

"I was almost seven months. It wasn't a miscarriage. The baby might've had a chance if he hadn't been stillborn. There's a difference."

Jean nodded. "Yeah, I know the difference. But these things happen. You can't stop living."

"Of course they do. You just don't expect them to happen to you. I'd think you'd understand that after losing your fiancé."

"That was totally different. See, he's not just missing. Hell, he was in the engine room when they took the torpedo. A tanker full of aviation gas. Went up like a damned torch, they said. On the other hand, your husband could still come back. You can still have other kids. Nothing to feel sorry for yourself about. Plenty of women worse off than you, don't you know?"

Anna didn't answer, face turned to the side window, profile silhouetted against the last pink light. The gears whined as Jean coaxed the car up the long hill. "Oh, and something else. You shouldn't have offered to carry Jim's bag just now. He may be a cripple, but he hates to be treated like one."

Anna turned suddenly. "Oh, for the love of God. Do you have to lecture me about absolutely everything? I was only being kind."

"Huh. Looked like pity to me."

The other woman was silent for a moment. Finally she said, "Tell me something, Miss Cropper. Or Jean, since we're alone. Is this how you treated those other nurses? I mean, did you go out of your way to give them a hard time about absolutely everything?"

Jean snorted. "If I did, it was only because it's a damned hard job and you might as well find out right away."

"Then why aren't you glad you don't have to do it yourself anymore? Why do you act…oh, like I'm stealing it? Or are you scared Jim's going to fall for somebody but you?"

"What?" Without meaning to, she eased up on the gas pedal. "Now that's just crazy. Jim Millett? Like I said, he's a cripple. And old. Almost forty. He's like a brother, but he's the last man on earth I'd ever fall for."

"Well, you seem so jealous and possessive, I had to wonder."

"Take my word for it. I've known him all my life. Used to be best friends with his sister. Once when he was home from medical school, the three of us went to the movies. I was embarrassed in case anybody thought he was my boyfriend. See, even then, I couldn't stand to think of him that way. Don't know how he ever got that woman to marry him; she was a real dish. And rich, everybody said. Didn't take her long to wise up, though, only a couple years."

"That's a shame. He's such a nice person."

"Sure he is. But could you stand him touching you? You know. Down there?"

Anna inhaled sharply and swung her gaze back to the window again. Probably shocked her, Jean thought, hoping she had. High time somebody shocked her into adulthood.

Disgusted by Jean's question, Anna was relieved when she said nothing more as she drove them through a dim landscape of somber, boxy houses, cedars and pines, bayberry bushes and boulders. Then they rounded a curve and there was the hotel, silhouetted against the lavender sky. Three stories, a porch wrapped around the first. Beyond, silver ocean reflected the last daylight.

Jean parked in a shed, then led her along a sand path to the porch steps. In the stillness, she made out the sibilance of breakers somewhere below, and now and then, the distant, lonely hum of the trawler's engine on the Sound. The air was icy but when they came into the foyer, she was enfolded by heat heavy with the smell of old varnish, and something fragrant baking. They followed it back to the kitchen where Jean opened the oven of a black coal range, lifted the lid of a blue-enameled roaster then peered into pans atop the stove.

"Well, we're in luck tonight. Mrs. Leech's roasted a chicken. In your honor, I guess. Jim probably put her up to it." Next, she looked into a big refrigerator with a top-mounted condenser. "Yep. Even made cranberry sauce. The works."

Well, Jean might not be happy with her there, Anna thought, but at least Jim wanted her to feel welcome.

"Now. About that wine. Got two kinds. Chianti and Sauterne. Sauterne's sweeter. Jim said give you whatever you want."

"I guess the Sauterne. Will you have some too?"

Jean shrugged. "Might as well. Kenny used to say I was more fun after a little wine."

Maybe they'd get on better then, Anna thought. Or maybe not. She'd known other girls like this, angry from the core out for no reason anyone could tell. Maybe in Jean's case, bitterness was the fruit of loss, first of Jim's sister, then her fiancé. And before that, according to Jim, of both parents. So maybe there was lingering heartbreak from their deaths too. And heartbreak made people behave in ways that were often unrecognizable as grief.

Lord God, she thought suddenly; could that even be true of her?

The hotel's dining room was closed for the duration, so they ate in the parlor from a drop-leaf table by a heavily-draped window. Jean poured wine into small, cut-glass goblets and they sat across from each other, tentatively, stiffly, like combatants in an enforced and reluctant truce. Still, Jean lifted her glass. "Here's to you, Anna. Hope you last here as long as you want to."

Surprised, Anna sipped the sweet liquid. "I will," she said firmly, omitting the next thought, No matter how hard you make my life. Then it came to her to lighten the moment. "But if you short-sheet my bed, I swear I'll move somewhere else."

For a moment she saw traces of a smile flicker across Jean's face, but she only snickered.

By the time they'd carried their plates to the kitchen, it was after seven. More relaxed than she'd been in weeks, Anna asked for a second glass of wine. "I'll take it to bed in case I can't sleep."

"Take the whole damned bottle, if you like. Now. I'll get the flashlight and lead the way."

Then, following the light from the torch, she led her up the wide front steps into a hallway heavy with the pervasive, omnipresent reminders of old varnish and mildew. Beyond a string of closed doors they came to a bathroom with a claw-foot tub and an overhead toilet tank. "We have to share this. But there's no hot water till Mrs. Leech lights the bucket-a-day stove in the morning."

In the front room, Anna's suitcases were set atop a walnut sleigh bed flanked by a marble-topped washstand and a tufted red-velvet chair. A converted glass oil lamp reflected in the gilt mirror of a carved bureau.

"Comforter on the bed," Jean said, "blankets in the armoire. Window faces the ocean, so sunrise'll likely wake you if you leave the curtains open. Towels're in the bathroom, and a new bar of Camay. My room's just across the hall in case you need anything else." She backed into the hallway. "By the way, Anna. Chester Philbrick's problem's a boil on the buttocks. He gets a lot of them."

"I know. I read his chart later. Maybe we ought to give him a cake of Lifebuoy. Might not help the boils, but it'll get rid of the BO."

Jean actually smiled. Finally. "Hog farmers need more than soap."

When she'd closed the door, Anna hung the contents of her larger bag in the dark Victorian armoire. Last, she took Dan's picture from the overnight case and set it by the lamp.

As she got into flannel pajamas, she wondered if she'd ever love him in the warmth of a big bed again. Sure she would, she told herself. If the boat had been captured, it might be another six months before the Navy got word. And if he ended up in a Jap prison camp, even longer till he got mail. So far he had no idea she'd even lost the baby. The news was in a letter the Fleet Post Office had sent back.

Suddenly, that they'd returned it made no sense: if the Navy expected the sub to return, why didn't they hold the mail till it did?

Oh God; every time she thought about Dan, her mind flipped to a new likelihood. Impossible anymore to remain steadfast in the faith that he'd come home safe. Several times, she'd considered asking her father if he'd ever doubted, ever yielded to hopelessness. But even more so since she'd lost the baby, she didn't want him to know her faith was wavering. His example had always been so strong, such apostasy would have more potential for breaking his heart than her leaving home did.

Ready for bed, she switched off the light and opened the drapes. The darkness outside was total, except for a faint orange rim on the northern horizon. Half a day too early for sunrise. What then, another ship burning?

She yanked the curtains closed, groped back to bed, and asked the Lord for some indication Dan was either alive or dead. Not just a song on a jukebox, but a sign as unmistakable as a slap on the face. High time she found out if she was still his wife. Or his widow.

Chapter Six

Cleve Cropper was sinking into the sweet depths of sleep when a strong-fisted pounding on the front door brought him reluctantly back to the surface. He'd already been in bed for hours, working on what Lorraine called A Night of Love. Once he'd had the stamina to pursue carnal pleasure for hours; now, at sixty, he was content to get it over with as fast as possible, then turn to what beds were mainly created for--sleep. But not Lorraine. Even after the main event, she wanted to cuddle and talk about romantic matters till nearly midnight. Tonight it was an old theme: how remarkable it was that of all the letters responding to his newspaper ad for a bride, he'd chosen hers. Her theory was that Fate had ordained them to be together. He'd never let on that he'd left it up to his brother's wife, who'd believed marriage to a good woman would reform him of the drink. He didn't care, either about marriage or being reformed, but at forty-five he was too old to work the New Bedford long-liners. So he'd come back to the island to help Eve run the hotel after Malcolm died, which was when she'd noticed his fondness for the booze. So, he thought, what the hell? And let her choose his mail-order bride, this big-tittied, black-haired half-Cajun woman from Louisiana who liked screwing even better than he did.

It had worked out well. Fortunately, these days she didn't expect such evenings more than once a fortnight, which gave him a chance to rest up between performances.

That night, as he tried to wake up, he hoped he'd only dreamed the knocking. Not so; it went on and on, Jean's muffled voice behind it. "Uncle, uncle. Get up. Something's happened."

"Good God, Cleve," Lorraine mumbled from her pillow. "Go see what she wants before she breaks the door down."

Feeling every minute of his hard-lived years, he slid his stocking-clad feet to the cold floor, grabbed the moth-eaten robe she kept trying to throw away, and plodded down the steps by the light of an electric torch. "Hold your horses, Jeannie. I'm a-coming."

When he swung the door open, his niece and the new nurse were silhouetted against the silver luminescence of a just-past-full moon. "What the hell, girl? Why you banging on a man's door in the middle of the night?"

He barely had time to step aside as she charged into the front room. Like her mother, she was short and squat, physical qualities enhanced by a thick fisherman's sweater, slacks, scarf and knit cap over dark auburn waves, also like her mother's. Behind her, Anna Donovan was similarly bundled but still thin as a rail. The hotel station wagon was parked at the gate. "Sorry, uncle," Jean gasped out. "But we just saw a German sub blow up. And we don't know what to do."

"What? A German sub?" Scowling, he slammed the door and switched on the floor lamp beside the coal stove. "Slow down now, girlie. And tell me what happened, real slow so I don't miss nothing."

Her voice was high with excitement. "It was a sub, uncle. A sub, sure as we're standing here! Came through the Cut in the old channel, and then a couple hundred yards into the Sound, it must've hit a mine."

"Actually, two mines," said Anna. "At least, there were two explosions. Then we couldn't tell if it sank, or submerged and kept going."

He squinted at them as the unfolding story knifed through the residual fog of sleep. "What you two doing out at the Cut this time of night? Entertaining young men?"

"Oh uncle," Jean snorted. "We couldn't sleep, so we took a bike ride. That's when we saw it. Looked like some men on deck, but we couldn't be sure."

He scratched his head, glanced up as Lorraine sidled down the steps in her pink satin robe with the marabou collar, hair long and loose around her shoulders. Without a speck of makeup, she looked every bit of forty one. Not like her to let people see her bare-faced. He turned back to Jean. "What makes you think it was a German, not one of ours?"

Anna said, "It had this thing on the periscope our boats don't. A snorkel. See, it gets air to the engines so they can run even submerged. My husband told me about them. He's engineering officer on a sub out of Portsmouth."

Trying to arrange the girls' blurted facts into order, he continued to scratch at his thin hair until Lorraine ordered him to stop lest he lose what little was left. "Well, I'll be damned. A U-boat then. And you say she sank right out there?"

"Or submerged."

He snorted. "No more'n ninety feet of water in that channel. Not likely a sub'd go under if she didn't have to. Well now. You girls sure about all this?"

They both nodded. "So we've got to get word to the sheriff. And the Navy," Jean said. "We tried waking Connie Diggs to open the switchboard, but she never came to the door. Maybe if you go."

He stood still a moment while his mind churned through their information. Then, as a plan formed, he said, "Hell and damnation, if this ain't something! Lorraine, go make a pot of coffee while I get into my pants. Ain't none of us going to sleep after this."

By the time he'd dressed, the smell of perking coffee filled the small house. He belted the cup Lorraine handed him while he repeated the story to the girls, making sure he had details right to relay to the authorities. By now the enormity of the event had swollen his mind with possibilities, all dire. His plan was simple: First—call the sheriff in Rockhampton. Then get Connie to ring every house on the island warning that saboteurs might very well be ashore, bent on God knew what despicable acts. Almost every farmer had a rifle or two; those that didn't, could arm themselves with pitchforks, pickaxes and sledge hammers, even kitchen knives. Anything to defend their homes, their women and children. And the free soil of Maine. Then, after this Paul Revere duty, he'd fire up his boat and take her out on the Sound for a look-see. Maybe get Chester Philbrick to come along for an extra pair of eyes. Likely when they heard what'd happened, every islander with a boat'd want to join the search.

Returning the empty, still-steaming cup to the kitchen sink, he left by the back door, crossed the yard to the stable, coaxed the Model-A pickup into sputtering life, then left it to warm up while he went back to the house for his .45. The women were at the kitchen table drinking coffee now, but the brandy bottle stood open in the center. He grabbed it and tilted it to his mouth, allowing himself a generous swig as he went by.

"What're you gonna do with that gun, Cleve?" Lorraine demanded.

"Hell, woman. What do you think? Now you girls lock the doors and stay put, and whatever you do, don't go back to the hotel. No telling what them Huns is up to."

"Don't you take any chances either, uncle," Jean warned. "Leave it to the law."

He grunted, had another swig and headed into the darkness. Frost heavy as a light snowfall crunched underfoot; his moon shadow was sharp against the white crystals. By God, he thought; this was how the English would feel, preparing to defend their island against the depredations of the filthy Hun. He'd been in the First War, had believed that'd taken care of them for all time. Sure, he thought now; like getting rid of all the rats in his barn once had taken care of the rat problem forever.

By the time he'd driven through the village, he was quivering with excitement. He parked in Connie's drive and blew the ay-ooo-gah horn for a couple minutes until he saw light chinks behind the front room curtains. Only when she aimed the flashlight's beam at him, however, did he climb out of the truck.

"Cleve Cropper," she called, "you better not be drunk again." All these years and she still didn't trust him. Some things women never forgot.

He followed the light toward the steps. "Hell, no. But when you hear what I got to tell you, you might wish I was."

When Cleve hadn't returned by two, the coffeepot was empty, most of the brandy gone, and the ashtray overflowing with cigarette butts. Lorraine and Jean had smoked almost a whole pack while the three of them had gone over the incredible event. Over and over, mining it for even miniscule additional details of possible significance. Finally, sated with the subject and eyes stinging with smoke, Anna asked if she could rest somewhere. Lorraine directed her to a guest room at the top of the stairs. A bright place with flamingo pink walls, twin beds covered in crazy quilts, lime green carpeting, saffron yellow woodwork. On one wall hung a Sacred Heart of Jesus print, on another, a gaudy plaster plaque of Madonna and Child. And on the night stand between the beds, a small photograph in a filigreed silver frame. Expensive. The sort used to hold the photo of someone significant. Someone beloved.

Anna picked it up for a better look; the priest's face was shadowed, but with a wide, dimpled grin that reminded her of Dan's. Even on the back there was nothing to identify him. So she replaced it, kicked off her boots and stretched out on the bed. Thanks to alcohol and caffeine, her body was drowsy, but now emotions she'd been too occupied to notice before had begun to surface through the residue of unlikely facts. Earlier than evening, she'd been electrified by the act of war she and Jean had witnessed. And the circumstances that had combined to bring them to the intersection of time and place where it had happened. That unlikely sequence of events was still flashing in her brain, like the sporadic lightning of a recent storm.

The evening had been uneventful except for a minor incident during the first aid class in the town hall auditorium. That session, she'd been lecturing on bleeding, starting with forms they could control, as from the nose or after a tooth extraction. Next she'd touched on the internal sort, from a ruptured aortic aneurysm or the fracture of a major bone, as well as heavy external bleeding where a tourniquet could be used. Finally she described the frank hemorrhage of esophageal varices, a complication of cirrhosis of the liver. "For this, you need to get medical help as fast as possible so the patient doesn't exsanguinate."

Hands had shot up all over the room at the medical term, so she'd explained, "In other words, bleed to death. See, left unattended, the patient vomits so much blood, he's at risk for shock. And death." Her only illustration was a grainy black and white photo in the manual. Even without full color, however, Lou Ellen Bemish, who ran the House of Beauty near the church, had quietly toppled from her chair.

Anna had rushed over, stretched her out on the floor, covered her with Frank Hardester's black and red flannel jacket, elevated her feet, and waved an ampoule of Aromatic Spirits under her nose.

After Lou Ellen came to, Anna had dismissed the class and sent her home with Frank. Then she and Jean had cleaned up the auditorium and gone back to the hotel. Too exhilarated to sleep, they'd drunk Chianti on the hotel's front porch, watched the moon rise over the ocean, and talked of men they'd known who'd dared wartime seas. And been lost. Though the cold bit into her fingers and toes, Anna felt the mellow, poignant discussion had woven a small bond between them, tenuous as a spider's filament. Sixteen days since she'd arrived, she no longer wondered how long she could tolerate Jean, but whether these slender connections would ever link them in true friendship.

Later, still too keyed up to sleep, they'd taken the old bikes from the shed and ridden out the road along the island's spine to the cut between Hope and Little Hope Islands. Geologists claimed that unknown millions of years before, all three in the chain had been one contiguous land mass. Until prehistoric seas chewed through the rocks almost as neatly as dynamite blasted highway cuts in mountains. Early in the war, this narrow channel had been mined when the military recognized that coastal Maine, where so many England-bound conveys formed up, was a magnet for German U-boats.

At the end of the road, she and Jean had squatted on a makeshift bench just beyond a large barricade with DANGER! painted in crude red letters. A plane had gone over, so low its roar had set nearby farm dogs into a frenzy of howling. Anna'd shivered, said she felt eerie. Jean pooh-poohed the comment, of course, blamed it on the moonlight. When the racket had faded, Anna had become aware of a faint hum in the distance; it increased in volume so gradually she concluded it was a slow-moving blimp on anti-sub patrol. Except this engine noise seemed to emanate not from the sky but the sea.

Craning, she'd peered at the moon-glittered water. Until she'd made out a dark silhouette, a shape so familiar she gasped with shock. Surely a mirage, that long, low hull, the conning tower, periscope mast, deck gun—and something else: the small breathing device on its own mast.

"My God," she'd whispered, not daring to speak aloud. "It's a sub. A German sub!"

Jean had squinted where she was pointing. "How the hell do you know it's German?"

"It has a snorkel. To get air to the engines, even when they're submerged. Our boats don't have them." Barely breathing, she'd stared down as the boat approached the narrow channel between sheer rock walls. Moving fast, it quickly slid though the gap and out into the Sound. As it passed below them, a whiff of diesel exhaust had risen to envelope them. For Anna, a sudden, poignant link with Dan's boat. Then her rational mind had clicked in. She'd jumped to her feet and set the bike upright. "Come on, Jean. We've got to report this to somebody. But who?"

Jean had been slower to react, had continued to stare as the U-boat crept toward the mainland. "Oh, I guess the sheriff. Or the Navy. Cleve'll know."

Anna had already mounted the bike when she heard the muted explosion. It was soon followed by a sudden flash, a second concussion and a distant rumble, like underwater thunder. Though the vessel had continued to move forward, she could no longer hear its engines, and it appeared to be slowing and submerging.

Escalating disbelief had held her motionless, her gaze fixed on the boat. Even as she'd stared, it had gradually slid from sight. In the moonlight, she'd made out water swirling around the conning tower as it went under, submerging both periscope and snorkel. Without realizing what she was doing, she'd crossed herself.

Now, as she replayed the scene in memory, it seemed a dream, or a movie. Not quite real, not quite believable as more than a trick of the eyes and the moonlight.

Of course, her mind assured her it was real. The only seeming unreality was that she and Jean had been in just the right place at just the right time to witness it. So highly improbable that she immediately discerned the hand of the Lord in the event. But why? To reinforce her old fears for *Wolf Fish*? To make her eyewitness to a disaster she'd imagined for as long as she'd known Dan? And now that the galvanizing immediacy of it was fading, to speculate on possible outcomes?

Ironic; she'd left home basically to escape the constant reminders of Dan that lurked everywhere in Portsmouth. Still, a hundred and some miles up the coast, far from any large naval presence, she'd had a real-life demonstration of the vulnerability of all submersibles, a virtual enactment of her worst fears. The boat she'd watched come to grief had not been his, but she'd seen it, and heard it, smelled the familiar engine exhaust and felt the multiple concussions that might have ripped it apart. Now she easily pictured crewmen huddled in water-tight compartments within the hull. Expecting to escape? Or resigned to death?

Their fate would depend on whether this boat had been fatally wounded, or just crippled and still capable of sustaining the lives of those aboard. At least until the American Navy arrived. Had the mines—there had been two major explosions—hit forward, perhaps in the torpedo room, which could be sealed off? Or had the second bumped along her hull, to explode further aft? Or deeper, damaging the keel and causing the batteries to blow up? And what of the men topside, those conning her from the bridge; had she really heard their faint shouts of alarm? And had there been men clustered around rafts on the afterdeck? Or were all these suppositions no more than the outpouring of her imagination?

And where, in all this, was the engineer? Whatever damage the boat had sustained, he'd have been below when the mines hit, would now be working frantically to control damage even as he recognized the futility of his efforts. Was he a married man? Back in Germany, was his wife pregnant? Who would notify her of his loss? And would she able to endure that truth without risking her baby?

Finally, exhausted by speculation, it came to her to pray. She had no idea what to ask for; an intercession on behalf of the enemy seemed traitorous. Maybe a generic, all-encompassing prayer might be best, maybe just *O hear us when we cry to thee, for those in peril on the sea.* Loving Dan had taken her into deep waters where there were no simple answers even to questions like, Who should she pray for? Because a wartime disaster that befell an enemy sub might menace any boat, under any flag, on any sea.

She wished her own patriotism were simpler and more exclusive. Like Cleve's. But the same global waters that might already shelter the remains of *Wolf Fish* might now cover this U-boat. And there would be no joy in heaven at the loss of either.

Unable to reason further, she knelt beside the bed and whispered the only words that made sense: "O Lord, thy will be done. And whatever that may be, grant me the courage to accept it."

Chapter Seven

The morning after the U-boat incident, Jean observed everything the Navy did with a profound interest she carefully cloaked with indifference so that Anna wouldn't notice. And begin to speculate. And perhaps guess at the possibility in her mind.

First, a PBY from Brunswick circled low over the sound before it landed beyond the breakwater and taxied into the harbor. There, it launched an inflatable raft in which an officer and three sailors paddled ashore. Later, *Molly B* pulled up at the pier with a dozen more sailors and two officers. Cleve reported their mission was to search every nook and cranny on all three islands; they'd even hired him to ferry them over to Little and No Hope once they'd scoured the main island for survivors.

Later, a lieutenant commander with a scarred pink face and a Naval Academy ring questioned her and Anna in the Lunch Box, asking the same questions over and over, as if trying to catch them in a lie. Later he commandeered the Town Hall Auditorium as quarters for his men. And the next day, a small gray ship appeared off the north end of the island and began making slow circles in the sound. From the hotel porch, Anna scanned it with binoculars and pronounced it a mine-sweeper. Jean was peeved, surmising

Anna was showing off, as if having been married to a Navy man had forever endowed her with special powers of discernment.

Wednesday morning the mine-sweeper was gone, but a larger Navy ship steamed into the sound and anchored close to the area where the sub had gone down. Anna identified this as the *Falcon*, a submarine rescue vessel based in New London. Shortly behind it came a sturdy sea-going tug. "Maybe they're going to try raising the wreck," she added, handing over the binoculars. "At least send divers down for the crypto equipment."

"Oh, for crying out loud, Anna," Jean couldn't resist saying, "didn't you and your husband ever talk about anything but the Navy?"

"Sure. But I remember that better than anything. "She paused, gazing at a thin brown haze wafting from *Falcon's* stack. "Besides, I grew up in a Navy town. A submariner's town. And I worked in the base hospital. I picked up a lot before I ever met Dan."

Jean said "Hmmph," and crossed her arms over her chest. Earlier that week, she'd heard from Cleve that the Navy had rounded up two Germans in a rubber boat on the beach near the East Point light house. They'd also found the corpse of a third sailor drifting in raft a few miles down the coast. "They ain't saying," he'd continued, "but Fletch says they think another Kraut got clean away. Probably heading for a fifth column hideout in Portland."

"That mean they've stopped searching here?" she'd asked nonchalantly.

"Ay-yuh." He studied her a moment, causing her heart to race. No, he couldn't be suspicious. He hadn't even been on the island when she'd known Wil. Anyway, the sliver of possibility was so miniscule as to be non-existent. Just another apparition from the closet in her mind where she stored childhood dreams. Moldering, rusting, and mostly forgotten. Like old toys, once cherished. Like Wil Himmelreich.

Two days later, a launch left *Falcon* and put into the town pier. Two sailors waited outside while a lieutenant came into the clinic, asked for her and identified himself as the ship's Executive Officer. She hoped he'd come to tell her what was going on; after all, if she and Anna hadn't seen the U-boat, the Navy'd never have known it was there. But no, what he wanted was permission to bury the nine dead Germans in the Cropper family cemetery on the hotel property.

Anna interrupted. "Nine. What about the rest of the crew? Did any of them survive?"

The man's face constricted, as if with sorrow. "Those are just the ones that would have washed ashore if we hadn't picked them up. There are still more in the wreck, but in sealed compartments. We'll leave them there, and the boat will become a War Graves Site."

Anna debated only a split second before she said, "Sir, my husband's the engineer on one of our subs in the Pacific. So I know a lot about the dangers of submarines. Maybe I shouldn't ask, but Miss Cropper and I saw this one go down. Can you tell me anything about what happened?"

The officer's face was weary and work-worn, his sigh morose. He lit a cigarette before he answered, waving the match into a clamshell ashtray on the desk. "Well, let's just say the first mine did the worst damage. And the second one sealed her fate."

"I heard multiple explosions after the two big ones. So I wondered if the keel was damaged and the batteries blew up."

His nod was barely discernible. "The second hit was shallow, just below the water line. The control room. That's where we found most of the bodies."

"Oh…" Anna breathed out. "The engineer was probably

in there."

"Possibly. At least one was an officer. Anyway, please keep this confidential."

"Of course. I'd tell my husband if I could, but his boat's been missing since June."

The man's eyes narrowed and he inhaled the next puff deeply. "Sorry to hear that. Which one is it?"

"*Wolf Fish.* She was built in Portsmouth, then spent a month in New London qualifying for fleet readiness. So you might've seen her there. Right after we got into the war."

"More than likely. Been there half my life. Anyway, don't give up hope. You could still get good news."

By now Jean had lit a cigarette too but had said nothing. Until she cut in, "How come you're not burying these bodies in the church cemetery? Why do you need mine?"

"Oh mainly because we've been advised islanders wouldn't approve. Lots of bad feeling against Germans around here."

She nodded, scrutinized him with narrowed eyes. "Where'd you hear that?"

"Uh, Cleve Cropper. Your uncle, I believe. He's the one told us to ask you."

She shrugged, sighed. "Doesn't matter to me. Plenty of room up there. Do what you want."

Looking relieved, he withdrew some papers from a brief case and asked her to sign. "To make it official, of course."

"Sure." Without reading, she scribbled her name on three pages, and shoved the documents across the counter again.

"Thanks, Miss Cropper. We'll try to do it the next couple of days then. You won't have to do a thing except show the burial detail where to dig. We'll take care of the rest. Including a funeral service and grave markers." He snapped the briefcase closed. "Your uncle said your fiancé died when his ship was torpedoed in the North Atlantic. I was afraid you wouldn't want anything to do with Germans, even dead ones."

She shook her head. "You can't hate people just for doing their jobs."

When the officers left, Anna said, "Don't know how everybody else will see it, but I'm glad you're letting them use the cemetery. It's one of those turn-the-other-cheek acts Christians are supposed to do, but usually don't."

Jean sniffed and began stuffing charts in an overfilled file drawer. "That's not why I'm doing it. See, I don't consider myself a Christian. Or anything else. But I knew a German family once, and they were good people. Kind people. It's the sort of thing they'd do." She slammed the drawer closed, glanced at the clock. "Damn. Thought you'd never stop talking to that man. Better get a move on if we're going to see any patients before dark."

For the next three days, *Falcon* and the tug lay at anchor in the Sound, work boats coming and going to buoys that Anna said marked the wreck. The funerals had been Sunday afternoon, a day of dull sunlight and light southerly breeze; the ship's commanding officer read a funeral service from The Book of Common Prayer, thanked Jean, then left with the four Negro sailors who had dug the graves and lowered the wooden coffins into them.

On Tuesday, cloud layers folded across the sky and the wind took on a sharpness that gradually intensified into a gale. That afternoon, plumes of dark smoke belched from both ships' stacks; Anna identified activity on deck as the securing of anchors, booms and small boats prior to getting underway. Then both vessels came about to a southerly heading, screws chewing white swaths on the black water. Even before darkness closed in, the only sign the Navy had ever been there two thin gray smudges on the horizon.

"Suddenly it's all over," Anna sighed from a rocker on the back porch, where they'd been watching. "Let's go in and get some wine. Cold out here."

"Go on. Be there in a minute," Jean said. Instead, she walked around to the front and stared across the dune toward the fresh graves inside the iron picket fence. The small cemetery also held those of her grandparents, who'd built the hotel, and her father, who'd died in 1937. But her mother was buried in a Newfoundland churchyard Jean had never seen. The summer before the war, she'd gone back supposedly to visit relatives. But for reasons no one ever learned, she'd jumped off the ferry as it was coming into St. John's, died without leaving a note or any other clue to her motivation. Cleve always said she was tetched. But Jean knew better: her mother had killed herself because she couldn't escape her own complicity in her husband's death. Even now when she thought about her mother, her heart hardened into an inert lump that felt incapable of sustaining life. Consequently, she thought of her rarely and only as long as she had to before she slammed the book on those acid memories once more.

Chapter Eight

Saturday afternoon, Jim came in from hospital rounds as the grandmother clock in the hall was striking five and just as the phone began to ring. He picked up the kitchen extension with apprehension that he'd have to go out again, drag his leg back into the car and hope the pain didn't affect his bedside manner. Instead, he heard Anna's voice, but with a tight, guarded quality he immediately intuited had to do with keeping the operator in the dark about some matter that wasn't her business. From long experience, he knew a doctor's calls were, for bored PBX operators, a rich source of vicarious drama.

Anna began by asking if he was free to talk. "Yes, of course. Why? What is it?"

"Uh…Well, I saw a new case this afternoon. And I don't think I can handle it myself. So I was wondering, could you come over some time tomorrow? Hate to bother you, but…"

"What's the problem?"

"Probably pneumonia. Fever 103, with a tight cough, shortness of breath, congestion. Maybe dehydration too. Anyway, I've put him on strict bed rest and fluids, and aspirin, but I'm thinking maybe an oxygen tent…?"

Noticing she'd said "him", he asked, "Who's the patient? Anyone I know?"

"Mm, no, I don't think so. Somebody…uh, somebody visiting."

"I see." Aware she was skirting some private matter, he said, "Best I see for myself then. I'll call Fletch; see when he can bring me over. Let you know what time in the morning so somebody can meet me at the pier."

"I'll meet you. Cleve can bring you back in case Fletch doesn't want to miss preaching."

He laughed. "That'll be the day."

After he hung up, he fixed a half-inch of bourbon with tap water, and a peanut butter sandwich. He was hungry, but too weary to get himself over to the boarding house or back to town for a proper meal, meat and potatoes and real coffee in the hotel coffee shop. Once in a while, lately more and more often, a widow named Betty Grimes had been inviting him to dinner at her house after church. To reciprocate, once he'd taken her to the Coach and Four for an expensive meal. But the past week she'd waited for him outside church, then sat with him during the service. He was uneasy, lest sharing a pew signify couple status to the congregation. Well, maybe that was her intent. If so, he realized he was going to have to step away in some painless but obvious fashion. Like going to 8 AM Morning Prayer instead of 10:30 Holy Communion. Or not showing up at all.

Meanwhile, he sat at the scarred table in the hideous old kitchen that both his mother and his wife had refused to work in, and told himself this was a hell of a way to live. A hell of a way for a man to spend what was left of his life. Maybe he should get a cat. Something to talk to. Something to touch. Something that loved him, if only because he fed it regularly. But he was gone so much; no pet would thrive in such isolation either. Maybe two cats, then. But not Betty Grimes.

He poured more bourbon and limped up the hall to his office where the week's mail was a formidable tower on his desk. Earlier, he'd planned to go through it that evening. Instead, he had a sudden urge to get drunk. Only twice in his life had he let himself fall off that cliff, but now he wanted to experience again the numbness, the sloshing, euphoric disengagement from his conscience. Of course, he wouldn't, because somebody might need him. Among the warnings his grandfather had issued when he first went into practice was: if a doctor ever got the reputation as a drunk, however hard his life was now, it'd get worse.

Of course his life was dull. But not intolerable. Especially tonight, when he could cosset the expectation of seeing Anna in the morning. He threw the bourbon down the sink and poured a glass of milk instead.

Huddled into a Navy peacoat, she was waiting on the pier when Fletch brought the trawler alongside. Sunday runs were not on his schedule, so Jim was the only passenger. "Sure you don't need me to wait, doc? Wife'll understand if I don't show up for preaching."

Jim stepped down the gangway and waved him on; the engine roared as the boat reversed into the harbor. Walking toward him, Anna gave him a smile that warmed his heart and seeped into the rest of his body. Even better than bourbon. They headed toward the station wagon and she thanked him for coming. He waited till they were inside before he asked, "Now. Who's this patient you couldn't talk about last night?"

Shaking her head, she shifted into reverse and backed onto the street. Her sigh sounded exasperated. "You won't believe it. A sailor from the U-boat. He's been hiding out since it went down, mostly on Little Hope. Then yesterday Jean saw a white flag in the trees over there, so she and Cleve took the long boat over. And sure enough, there he was, much the worse for wear. Now he's in her bed in the hotel. Temp was down this morning, and he's diaphoretic, but his lungs are still congested."

He inhaled slowly, assimilating her array of unlikely facts. "After two weeks exposed to the weather? No wonder. Surprised he's even alive. We'll probably need the O-2 from the clinic, but Cleve can go down for it later."

She nodded and drove across the deserted square toward the road that ascended to the island's high ridge. "But if you think that's incredible, would you believe Jean used to know him?" She gave him a quick look. "His family stayed at the hotel a couple of summers before the war. Then they went back to Germany and he went to seminary. Till he was conscripted into the navy."

He frowned, took off his glasses and polished them with his pocket handkerchief. "Really? And he was on the U-boat that went down?"

"When we saw it, I thought there were men on the afterdeck. I mean, behind the conning tower. With rafts. Evidently they planned to join an espionage ring in Portland. He said he was picked for the mission because he knows the area. But he claims he was going to turn himself in instead."

"Incredible. Have you notified the Navy yet?"

She shook her head vigorously. "Jean won't hear of it. His name's Wilhelm Himmelreich, by the way."

"Himmelreich?" He allowed himself a small grin. "If I remember my high school German, that means 'kingdom of heaven.' Ironic, given the circumstances."

"Did Jean ever mention him?"

"No. But she may have told my sister about him. Why, was there a romance?"

"According to her, they were pretty serious. She thinks that's why he's here--to see her. She wants to hide him till the war's over."

He sighed with horrified disbelief. "That's crazy, Anna.

Just crazy. I don't care what the fellow's story is, harboring an enemy fugitive's an act of treason. And she damned well ought to realize it."

"Maybe she would if romance wasn't involved. Apparently he was the love of her life. Not the guy that brought all the wine."

He slumped against the seat, staring out the windshield without taking note of the familiar landscape. He was hesitant to voice the foreboding that had begun chewing on his gut, but wanted Anna to be aware of it. "Don't know how you feel, but from where I sit, this situation has all the makings of a tragedy."

She sent him a shocked glance. "Why…why do you say that?"

"Damned if I know. Just a feeling. Dread, I guess."

"Dread! Of what?"

He hunched his shoulders. "The potential for trouble."

"Oh yes. Yes, I agree. But….but what can we do about it"

"Nothing. Except treat the fellow's pneumonia and try to talk sense into Jean. Then call the Navy. Knowing her, she'll probably see it as betrayal. But it doesn't matter. They've got to be told." He sighed heavily. "You with me on this?"

She seemed to hesitate before she said, "Of course. It's the only thing we can do."

Still sensing her reluctance, he wondered if he seemed cold-hearted. It bothered him that she might perceive him that way, but not enough to change his mind. Some matters were beyond the sway of personal opinion.

Meeting the patient solidified his resolve. Beyond the scruffy beard and unkempt, tangled hair, Wil Himmelreich in no way resembled the clean blond stereotype of the Master Race. He was emaciated, eyes sunken and dark-rimmed, but a pale, soft blue. Not what Jim had expected; easier to see the man as a seminarian than a saboteur. And despite fever and labored respiration, he willingly answering questions about his general state of health and his two weeks in a fallen-down summer cottage on Little Hope.

Ready to examine him more thoroughly, Jim asked the women to leave the room. "For privacy," he explained, though what he really wanted was to give the man a chance to speak in confidence.

He wasn't prepared for the next surprise either—the fugitive's tearful confession, told in unaccented English—that he'd killed his assigned partner in espionage. "He was a Nazi. We were together only because I know the area. I don't believe in murder, but I had to kill him and send the body off in the raft so I could find Jean again. And ask for asylum."

Stunned, Jim willed composure into his voice. "Did you shoot him?"

"No, no. I wanted it to appear he'd died when the boat hit the mines, so I took a rock to his skull. While he slept, so he felt nothing."

Aghast at the calculated brutality, Jim shook his head; the seminarian image faded. "Well, I'm not going to judge you for that. Still, we can't go on hiding you here. You know that, don't you?"

Wil frowned. "But I have information that will aid your authorities to round up saboteurs in Portland. So if I turn myself in, they'll be lenient, won't they?"

Jim shrugged and bent with the stethoscope to listen to the bony chest. "I don't know what the policy is on that. I only know there are laws against harboring enemy fugitives."

Wil closed his eyes and turned his face away as Jim listened to his heart sounds—racing, like someone with severe anemia, or in extreme fear. Well, that figured; maybe he knew too much about the risks fugitives faced. Perhaps during training, would-be saboteurs were warned of grave consequences for anyone who betrayed the Fatherland on this mission. As well as for those who were stupid enough to be captured.

Finished, Jim washed his hands in the bathroom and came downstairs. Jean, Anna and Cleve were in the parlor, all three tense, jumpy and pacing. First he asked Cleve to fetch the oxygen bottle from the clinic. Then at the dining table, he wrote out medical orders as the women hovered nearby. While he was explaining them, Jean sighed loudly, shifting her weight from one foot to the other, twisting a hanky in her fingers. Finally, she broke in. "Listen, Jim. Anna can tell me all this later. Right now I need to get some juice for Wil."

"Just a minute, Jean," he called. She paused in her dash toward the kitchen. "You know I have to report this, don't you?"

She stared for such a long moment, his gut clenched with apprehension. Her eventual nod was reluctant. "Yeah. But not yet. Not while he's so sick. At least wait till he's stronger. Till he's back on his feet. Maybe a week."

"But if they came for him now, he'd get antibiotics. And heal faster."

She snorted. "Sure. And then what what'd they do to him?"

"That depends. If they believed he planned to turn informant, he might get amnesty. If not, well, I imagine he'll go to a Prisoner of War camp."

A bitter expression twisted her face. "That's a lot of ifs, Jim. And if they consider him a saboteur, he'll get the firing squad. And he knows it. So you've got to give him more time."

"Time? Sure, I could do that. But what about Mrs. Leech? You can hardly keep him a secret from her. After that, everyone on the island will find out. Hell, even Fletch asked why I was coming over on Sunday. Once this gets around, no telling what people will do. You know the strong feelings against the Germans. Would you rather take a chance with a lynch mob?"

Her eyes flashed with the rage he knew well, its onset always sudden as a summer squall. "You just can't give him a chance, can you?"

He scribbled his official signature on the sheet. "Sorry. My hands are tied. I'll hold off till Wednesday to make sure he's on the mend. But that's all I can promise."

She shook her head and stomped off like a kid with a tantrum. He sighed, pushed up his glasses and rubbed his eyes with a weariness that generally waited till later in the day.

"Don't mind her," Anna said. "She'll get over it, once she realizes it's the only way."

He eased back his shirt cuff to check his watch. Just past ten. "Maybe Cleve can talk some sense into her. Or Lorraine can. Somebody needs to."

Anna picked up the orders and scanned them. "Oh, there's an infected wound on the heel? Didn't notice that yesterday."

"When faced with fulminating bi-lateral pneumonia, I wouldn't have either."

She smiled. "Kind of you to say so. And thanks. Thanks for coming today, Hope it didn't interfere with your church time."

"I can miss once in a while. As you said, Episcopalians aren't Puritans."

"Oh, you're one too?"

"From the cradle."

Her smile widened, touched her eyes. "Well, if you aren't in any hurry, how about some breakfast? I fried some nice lean bacon earlier. And squeezed some oranges. Or did you already eat?"

He pulled himself up on the cane; a twinge in his bad leg

reminded him he'd have to take the stairs again to get the oxygen started. "I can always go for bacon and eggs."

"Good. Then come out to the kitchen while I cook."

Abruptly uneasy about letting her wait on him like a domestic servant, he sat at the oilcloth-covered table and sipped juice while she made toast and fried eggs. And asked the sort of innocuous personal questions with which ordinary people come to know the superficialities of each other's lives, a relief from the enigma of Wil's immediate future. Yet even as he answered, he sensed the dullness of his, the utter lack of color in his existence. The most remarkable thing about him, he thought, was that he'd been crippled with polio. Not quite as severely as Roosevelt, just enough that if he wanted to, he could claim some kinship. But there it began and ended, and even that required a stretch of the imagination.

Her face was flushed when Anna set down a gold-rimmed plate with two strips of bacon, two over-easy eggs and two pieces of toast hot from the mica-and-wire toaster. Then she sat across the table with her own plate, which held only one of each. He eyed it. "Appetite still poor?"

"Oh no. It's much better lately. At least when I drink wine. Too early for that, of course."

He nodded. "Any news of your husband?"

She paused, a piece of toast halfway to her mouth. She shook her head and resumed eating.

"Sorry. Maybe I shouldn't have mentioned it. But I thought of him when…when I heard about the U-boat."

"That's funny. See, when I first got here, I prayed for a sign. I mean something to let me know if he's all right or not. Then this happened."

"I see. So is it a sign?"

She cleared her throat, sipped coffee. "Not sure. At first I thought it meant he was gone. Especially when they found the bodies. But now…now there's a survivor. So maybe it is a sign. That Dan's all right. Of course, that's what I want it to be." A dim smile, humorless and fleeting.

"I see." He chewed bacon a moment. "Uh… how long have you and he been married?"

"Almost two years. Since the day before Pearl Harbor. His boat left Portsmouth a couple days later. We had some weekends in New London, but the only time we really lived together was last year when his boat was in San Francisco. In a shipyard, for four months. So I went out and rented us a garage apartment. They left in March, and I went back to my parents." She swallowed visibly and pushed slivers of egg around on the plate with her fork. "Dan wanted me to come home to have the baby. Guess it's good I did, the way things worked out." She blinked a couple times in quick succession before she jumped up. "Would you like to see his picture? Dan's, I mean?"

"That'd be nice." He wondered why she'd asked. Oh, that was easy, wasn't it? Because he was sympathetic and kindly and concerned, like an older brother or uncle. Or an employer who went out of his way to treat her decently so she wouldn't quit before her contract ended.

When she left the kitchen, he resumed cleaning his plate, remembering the flush of her cheek as she'd stood at the coal range. And the vague lines of her body under a loose sweater and slacks. Yet even as he'd noticed, he'd rebuked himself for failing to regard her through the same lens he used with the widow at church--one without overtones, without emotional attachment. Much easier to maintain that view of Betty Grimes, though his logical side suggested she'd be a perfect wife: good-natured, complaisant, undemanding, loyal. A woman about his age, whose late husband had been a Portland surgeon; who'd moved to Rockhampton to be near her daughter. A good person, who served on the hospital auxiliary and the board of the Penobscot Maritime Museum and the Altar Guild at All

Saints. He didn't know if she'd be considered attractive; she dressed well and her hair was always curled, and often she smelled like brass polish, but her looks on him were always fond.

Then he wondered, if he married her, would that render him incapable of noticing this much-younger woman who wasn't even a bona-fide widow? No, he decided; he'd rather yearn for one he couldn't have than end up yoked to one whose need for him was so apparent. With such a potential for smothering.

Anna returned with a tinted 8 x 10 studio shot in a photographer's folder; the lips were too red, the eyes an unnatural electric blue, the cheeks rosy enough to hint of a fever. He wore a naval officer's dress blues with a dolphin-and-propeller insignia above a double row of service ribbons. "Fine looking man," Jim said heartily as he pictured them together-- dancing, walking a beach, sailing. Being whole and young. Being lovers. "I surely do hope your prayers are answered."

She closed the folder, set it on the sideboard and returned to the congealed remains of her breakfast. "Thanks, Jim. But I have to wonder. Ever since I've known him, he's told me about things that can go wrong on a sub. Little things, but they happen so fast the crew has no time to reverse them. And they go to the bottom. Like *Squalus*, a few years ago, if you remember."

He nodded. "As I recall, about half the crew survived. They even brought her back up, didn't they?"

"She's still in service too. But a happy ending's the exception, rather than the rule. Anyway…" She swallowed coffee, stared at her plate with eyes that seemed to be watching an internal newsreel of all those disasters. "Anyway, before they came to San Francisco, they'd had a close call with a Jap destroyer. They almost didn't make it back. Dan was never the same after that."

Jim pushed his cup around on the saucer until she got up to refill it. “I guess that would change a man.”

She returned to her chair, wiped her mouth on a blue checked napkin. “The thing he worried about most was going dead in the water. Then drifting down to crush depth. He used to say, ‘If that ever happens, I hope carbon dioxide gets us before we implode.’”

He stared, marveling at her ability to speak the words evenly and calmly. Did she have any notion that death in a sub below crush depth wouldn’t likely be the relatively easy one of asphyxia, that the same pressures which collapsed a steel hull would also crush the body-- lungs, eyes, bones and vital organs? But mercifully, only until inrushing seawater put an end to that misery. He swallowed the last cold coffee in his cup. “That your worst fear?”

She regarded him with her level gray gaze. “One of them.”

“What’s the other? Capture?”

She nodded, face pale, voice flat. “Like the guys on the Bataan Death March. And that could’ve happened to them too. See, the Japs don’t always report it when they take prisoners at sea.”

When he realized she was revealing some of her soul scars, he wanted to reach across the table and clasp her hand. Instead, he settled for patting it and quickly withdrawing his own. “Wish I knew what to tell you, Anna,” he said, regretting his own inability to offer palliation for her pain. Not the kind that a scrip for codeine or morphine could assuage.

“You know, I think what you told me the first day…that’s still good advice. You said I shouldn’t lose hope. I’ve always remembered that.”

He shrugged, touched that she did. “Just words.”

“No, not just words. When you say something, you believe it.”

Even as the moment pulled him toward her, he heard Cleve banging up the porch steps. The front door opened and fresh-smelling wind blew down the hall into the kitchen. "Doc? Got the oxygen. Now what'll I do with it?"

"Haul it upstairs, please." Grimacing slightly, he got to his feet and prepared to launch himself again up the long steps to the hotel's second floor. By his watch, he'd been talking to Anna for over a half hour. Not nearly long enough. Oh well, he thought; if they'd had more time, he'd probably only have said something he'd regret afterward. Might even have confided Wil's confession, then expected her to keep it under her hat. No, all things considered, it was best the visit had ended when it had. Maybe if he was lucky, she'd share more of her painful story another time. And give him a chance to discover whether the qualities he admired in her were more than superficialities.

But it wouldn't happen today, if ever.

Chapter Nine

By Wednesday, Wil was well enough to sit in a chair, walk around and wolf down every bit of food they set before him. His cough still rocked the hotel, but now it was loose and productive. After Jean shaved him and cut his hair, Anna was surprised at the gentle face under the tangled beard. Hardly the demoniacal hard-jawed, steely-eyed Nazi in American propaganda posters.

When she spotted *Molly B* approaching the island that morning, she drove down to the pier at top speed. Jim's face was grim when he got into the car. "Well, this is the day. Even if he's still spiking a temp, I've got to turn him in. Think Jean's ready?"

"No telling. We haven't talked about it. Actually, I don't see her much. Stays busy with Wil, wants to do everything herself, even take his vitals. And she hasn't come to the clinic all week." She blinked in a burst of sunlight between cedars along the road. "In fact, sometimes I half-expect them to be gone some morning when I get up."

"Gone! You mean, run off? In what, Cleve's little boat?"

"Uh-huh. See, she's in love, not thinking straight. Nothing she did would surprise me."

"But running off…that'd be crazy."

"I know. But sometimes love is. I mean, sometimes it

makes you do stupid things."

He smiled ruefully. "You don't have to tell me."

"What?" She turned quickly, brows raised. "Oh no. Not you. You're much too sensible."

"Well, I hope I am now. But I haven't always been. Sorry to disillusion you."

She inhaled, felt the heat of a blush. "Will you tell me about it some time?" When he didn't answer, she added, "Of course, you don't have to. But I'd be interested."

"Maybe. If you ever make breakfast for me again."

"Be happy to." But then she wondered, would she ever? Unable to imagine why he'd need her to, she didn't comment further. Still, she was curious about details of his life, like the woman Jean had told her he'd married. And other minutiae, such as his relationship with his parents and the impact of his sister's death. So much she wanted to know, but sensing he kept a protective fence around personal matters, would never ask. Had even been surprised to hear herself blurt out the question. Why was it important anyway? Weren't they just employer and employee, doctor and nurse?

At the hotel she came upstairs when he went to examine Wil. As he did so, Jean hovered in the background, her sullen expression a rebuke, especially when Jim pronounced Wil out of danger. "Well, young man," he added, "I guess you know what that means."

"Yes sir." The voice was gravelly, as if long unused. "You have to turn me in."

"I've waited too long now," Jim said. "Considering how these islanders feel about what your U-boats are doing to our convoys, I'm doing you a favor. If they ever found out you're here, they might turn into a lynch mob."

Wil shrugged, shoulder bones prominent under Jean's brother's plaid flannel robe. "I'll be a dead man anyway if the Navy doesn't believe me."

"Not necessarily. Not if you tell them everything you know about fifth column activity in the area."

Jean said, "Jim Millett, you don't know what the hell you're talking about. Listen, when the Navy was looking for survivors, I asked an officer what'd happen if they found any. And he told me, plain as day. Wil knows too. In fact, they were issued cyanide pills to take if they were captured. So they wouldn't be tortured and shot."

Jim stood silent a moment, staring at Jean, then at Wil. "Where's yours?"

"Overboard. I kept it while I was hiding out, but got rid of it when Jean and Cleve rescued me."

He took a deep breath, gaze flickering to Anna's with the tacit question Do you believe this?

She shrugged, wishing she knew a way to make his decision easier.

"Sorry. Don't really have a choice," Jim said. Then to Anna, "Now. Let's get down to the clinic and see some patients. I'll call the sheriff from my office."

"You're a bastard, Jim," Jean spat. "I'll never forgive you for this."

"It's all right, doctor," Wil said. "Only following orders. Like I had to."

In the car again, Jim sat stony-faced, black bag clutched in his lap. At the clinic, he charged back to his office and closed the door harder than usual. Out front, the light on the counter phone glowed for a few minutes, indicating he was using the one on his desk. Trying to maintain a business-as-usual face, Anna began logging in patients. She was sure everyone was aware of Jean's fugitive, and was relieved no one mentioned it. She hadn't previously worried about a lynch mob, but now Jim's supposition seemed frighteningly plausible.

When the light on the phone went out, she knocked on his door, waited for him to tell her to come in. "Ready to see patients yet, doctor?"

His face was gray and haggard, that of a man who hasn't slept well in days. He nodded. "Keep your eye out for a plane. Sheriff's office patched me through to Brunswick. They're sending one this afternoon. Sorry, but you'll have to drive the Navy men to the hotel."

She couldn't speak, could barely breathe for a moment. "It's all right. I'm not intimidated by Navy men." She managed a deep breath and switched her mind to ordinary matters. "Now. Who do you want to see first—Lavinia Forbes with a stomach ache? Or Lou Ellen Bemish with an infected hangnail?"

"I don't care, Anna." His voice was as flat as his expression, and he shook his head for a long while. "Does it matter?"

"No. Of course not. Well, their charts are on the examining room doors, so take your pick. And tell me when you want lunch." She waited but his only response was a vague nod. So she went back to the desk and continued to log in patients until just before noon, when the familiar silhouette of a PBY materialized in the southern sky.

In the waiting room, word of the plane spread quickly. When she left to pick up the Navy men at the pier, the front windows were filled with curious patients apparently hoping to see the drama unfold. She wondered if even Jim was watching from his office, perhaps blaming himself for what Jean deemed his betrayal. He hadn't equivocated about turning him in, but now he'd be paying a steep emotional price for ignoring the wishes of a long-time friend.

Stupid, bitter woman, she thought as she waited for the Navy men to climb up from the raft. Jim was no more responsible for Wil's predicament than anyone else on the island. It was all circumstances, and Fate, and the inevitability of grief. As if no matter what you did, it was always hovering just beyond the horizon, waiting to roll over you like a cold fog.

The Navy had sent the scarred-face Lieutenant Commander and two sailors in pea coats and helmets, with sidearms. She tensed as they approached the car. The officer opened the door, touched the brim of his cap. "Morning, Mrs. Donovan. I assume you're here to deliver us to the hotel."

Her throat was tight, her "Yes, sir," reluctant

He motioned to the sailors, who clambered into the back seat. As he eased into the front, spicy, too-strong aftershave fumes filled the car. "I also assume you know why. At least you're aware Miss Cropper's been harboring a fugitive from the U-boat."

"It'd be hard not to be aware." She backed around and aimed at the hill, shifting gears roughly in frustration she wouldn't otherwise express. "But are you aware he was near death when she found him?"

"Regardless, we should've been notified right then. So we could've questioned him earlier. Now we've lost four days we might've used to round up the espionage ring he was joining. And he might have escaped."

Indignation seethed. "Listen, Commander, four days ago he was too delirious to talk, let alone escape. I'm the wife of a Navy officer myself. Don't you think I'd have called you immediately if I thought Wil Himmelreich was any threat to us?"

His fist slammed the dashboard so hard the windshield vibrated. "Damn it, that was a judgment you had no right to make! Neither did Dr. Millett. You both knew we were looking for those sailors, but you chose to delay calling. In wartime, that could be considered an act of treason."

The last word set her hands trembling on the wheel. Hoping he hadn't noticed, she willed calm surety into her voice. "Sir, the doctor and I are medical professionals, not military experts. Our decisions were based on the man's physical condition. If we'd wanted to keep his presence a secret, we wouldn't have called at all." She wondered where the strong speech had come from, flowing like a script she'd long since memorized. Like something Dan would have said if necessary, even to men who outranked him and held his future in their hands.

Commander Stark snorted like an impatient horse. "Listen, Mrs. Donovan. If your husband was captured by the Japs, do you think they'd have given him the same consideration?"

"Ah, but isn't that the difference between us and the enemy? We're humane enough to let him recover before we turned him in."

His face flushed crimson. He sputtered a little before he finally said, "Well, we're here now, that's the main thing."

At the hotel, he told her to wait, then swaggered up the steps ahead of the sailors. She thought about going in, but decided she didn't want to watch the surrender. Or witness Jean's impotent rage when they took Wil away. Yet as it worked out, she had to anyway, because they brought him out handcuffed between the two sailors, and all three squeezed into the back seat. Behind them, Jean and Cleve followed in his pickup.

Uneasy about her involuntary part in this drama, she drove in silence. No one else spoke either. At the pier, the commander directed her to park as close as possible to the piling where the raft was tied. But when the sailors opened the back door to escort him out, she turned and said, "I'm sorry about this, Wil. I hope it works out for you."

"Not your fault, nurse. You took good care of me. Maybe even saved my life." And then they were gone, the officer bringing up the rear as they herded Wil toward the raft. Beside her, the pickup squealed to a stop and Jean raced toward them. Anna closed her eyes to avoid seeing their last embrace, or the expressions of the guards. In silence, she breathed the Jesus, Jesus prayer, the one with no specific intent. Except today she asked for reassurance of the Lord's presence in their lives.

When she looked up again, Cleve was still at the wheel of his vehicle, staring straight ahead as the men climbed into the raft. They began paddling toward the plane while Jean stood on the edge of the pier, wind flapping her coat. Anna couldn't see her face, but knew it would be hard and bitter.

Damn war, she thought, wondering what Dan would comment about this event. Would he see the pathos in it? Or would his judgment be colored by the enmity he was expected to feel for all Axis submariners, his sworn foes? And what of Jim, one of the lucky ones who never had and never would face combat? Except maybe facing death yourself was easier than sending another man to his. Her heart ached for all of them, even Wil.

Finally, bucking the wind, the raft reached the plane; hands in the doorway pulled the men aboard, then wrestled the inflatable inside. The hatch slammed, the propellers spun, emitting clouds of gray exhaust. Slowly, like some massive prehistoric bird, the plane swung about and lumbered toward the breakwater. Once it was outside, the engines revved up and it began to move down the Sound. Clumsily, it bounced across the waves, then began to rise, wings wobbling in the wind that lifted it higher. Anna watched it climb steadily, until it was only a speck against the pallid winter sky.

Mouth tight, eyes downcast, Jean walked rigidly back to Cleve's old pickup without so much as a glance toward Anna. Just as well, she thought; what would she say anyway? A feeble I'm sorry? When the other woman withdrew into the dark cave of her own thoughts, nothing could bring her out. This retreat would surely be the deepest of all.

Chilled, Anna drove across the square and watched the

pickup climb the hill before she parked. Inside the clinic, those in the waiting room kept their eyes downcast as she walked back to Jim's office. He wasn't there, so she logged in the rest of the patients, then went down to the Lunch Box for two ham sandwiches. She didn't know whether he'd want to eat with her or preferred his own company, but she'd take one to him anyway. And later, drive him around on the usual house calls. And tell him, if he asked, about the scene on the pier, that small fragment of drama that marked the end of the U-boat incident. For everyone but Jean, of course. And, because she lived with Jean, for her as well. And certainly for Jim, because he was their friend, and unwillingly complicit in the fact that it had ended, perhaps tragically.

Just as he'd predicted.

Chapter Ten

By the time Anna arrived that wintry Sunday afternoon, Lorraine had added everything she'd been able to find to the Cajun stew she called her Louisiana Gumbo. The small house was full of spicy, garlicky steam, windows misted like sheer curtains over the early December snow that had been sifting down since early morning. Cleve answered Anna's knock, helped her out of her coat, called, "Anna's here," then went back to reading his newspaper by the front room coal stove.

Anna came to the kitchen doorway, cheeks and nose red from the cold. "Sure smells good, Lorraine. What're you making anyway?"

Lorraine wiped her hands on her faded print apron. "Something I learned from my mama. Only I can't get half the things she used. Like Shrimp. Okra. Creole sausage. But I make do."

"I can hardly wait to taste it. Hate to tell you, though--Jean's not coming."

Lorraine scowled. "What's her excuse this time?"

"The usual. Just doesn't feel like seeing anyone."

"Well, I'll be damned. Six weeks now, she ought to be getting over it. Didn't take her near this long to get over Kenny dying."

"That would've been different. She couldn't blame anybody, except the Nazis. This time, though, we're all her enemy." Her voice dropped. "Especially Jim."

"Poor guy." She lit a cigarette, pulled out a chair at the table, beckoned Anna to sit. "Care for a glass of wine?"

"Thanks. Maybe it'd warm me. Between the cold and the damp…" She rubbed her hands, then blew her nose.

Lorraine poured some of the sherry she kept for cooking into two small glasses once filled with Olde English Pimiento Cheese, then sat across the table with the ashtray. "She come back to work yet?"

"No. And we need her there. Jim says we're going to have to find someone else if she's not back soon. Don't know who, though."

"I declare, if that ain't something." She took a drag, let it out slowly, eyes narrowing in the smoke. "You know, her mother got like that toward the end. Oh not at first. I mean when I came in '38, she was just, well, moody. Thought it was because her husband'd only been dead a year. But these moods, they just kept getting worse. Like storm clouds in her mind, I guess. So, summer of '40, when she said she was going home—Newfoundland, I mean—going back to visit some cousins, I thought, well, that'll be good for her. That'll help." She took another long drag. "Then, by God if she didn't jump off the back of ferry coming into St. John's. Nobody ever did know why. Some said she didn't want to go on living without Malcolm. But Cleve, he said no, that wasn't it; they was never that close to start with. Not like some husbands and wives. Besides, she had Jean and Alex for company, except the boy, he was at MIT, so she didn't see him much. Jean, though, she was living right there where she is now. Already helping out in the clinic, like she is now. Or was till the Navy took Wil away."

Anna sipped a bit of wine, set the glass down again. "She never told me that story. Just said her mother died in

Newfoundland."

Lorraine nodded. "Now Eve could be right warm, in her way. Always was with me, even when nobody else was. But she was hard-headed. Made up her mind to something and that was it. Jean's the same way. Made up her mind she was gonna hide Wil till the war ended, until Jim put his foot down. Too bad. 'Cause she's gonna need him pretty soon, if I'm any judge of these things."

Anna's eyes widened. "What things?"

Lorraine ground the cigarette into the ashtray. "Don't know if you've noticed how bad she looks lately. Cleve says it's grief, but I say it's more'n that. I say she got herself in trouble with that boy. What'd you think, being a nurse and all? Think she's in the family way?"

Anna's expression didn't change, but her breathing slowed. "Why do you say that?"

"She slept with him, didn't she? Even when he was sick as a dog."

"Well, he was in her bed, and she was taking care of him. I don't know where she slept, but there's a big chair in there she could've curled up in."

"Huh. Well, let me tell you, I had a baby once, so I know the signs. Last time I saw her, she asked me to put out my cigarette 'cause it smelled bad. Now that, that's a real sign. That, and coffee and bacon don't taste right."

Anna gazed toward the slow drift of snowflakes at the window above the sink. "That's right. I noticed that myself in the beginning."

"You lost that one, didn't you?"

Compressing her lips, she nodded and glanced down at her hands.

"So did I. In a manner of speaking. Lost my child, I mean. Oh, not the way you did, but see, I was only seventeen, and I couldn't marry his daddy. So I gave him away. To the Little Sisters of Charity. In Baltimore. Twenty-five years ago come Christmas." She shook her head, trying to return to the present. "Still seems like yesterday."

As she spoke, she sensed Anna's gaze intensifying, curiosity deepening. Then she asked, "Is that your son in the picture in the guest room?"

The question rocked her like an earthquake, until she remembered Anna had rested there the night the U-boat had gone down. "Whatever makes you think that?"

"Oh, I just wondered if he was a priest."

Lorraine shook her head, took a long drink of the sherry, stared at her rose-tipped fingernails. "No. That was his daddy. The baby—I never seen him again. I don't know where in the world he is. Or what he's doing. Sorry to say." She drank again, felt the warmth spreading, melting the ice of that memory. "One of them things you never get over."

"I guess it would be. Well, at least he's alive."

"Not necessarily. He could've died and I never knew." She shrugged, pushed back from the table and got to her feet, carrying the empty glass to the sink. "Now then, time to get Cleve in from the barn for dinner. Afterwards, think I'll take a dish up to Jean, along with a little piece of my mind. High time she got over this childish tantrum. If she's in the family way, she'd better grow up before it's too late."

After they ate, she waved off Anna's offer of help with the dishes and packed a Pyrex bowl with a good helping of the gumbo. Cleve went back to the barn again, so Anna drove her up to the hotel. The snow continued sifting down aimlessly, softening the island's rocky profile, whitening dark evergreens, coating the gravel road. When they got out at the hotel, a fog horn bleated somewhere offshore. Lorraine shivered; the sound touched off a loneliness she could never have described, particularly in the mood that had descended after she'd told Anna about her son. Normally his existence was like so many other aspects of her life—another unchangeable in which she felt neither pride nor regret, just a peculiar empty spot in her memories that never filled in, never ended, even though the child could well have died without her knowledge. At least Anna's loss was finite.

When she'd come to the island as Cleve's mail-order bride, she'd told him all about the baby, because husbands and wives shouldn't keep important secrets from one another. Now she never mentioned her son, because she was content with their life and didn't want Cleve to suspect otherwise. Once in a while, however, usually as she regarded the family at Christmas dinner, she considered trying to find the child. But the lingering shame of his conception and birth would flare again, convincing her she had no right even to look.

As they climbed the hotel porch steps, she wondered if Jean would be feeling the same sort of shame, possibly even worse because she'd slept with an enemy sailor. No, she wouldn't see it that way; according to her mother, Jean had loved Will Himmelreich from the time he and his parents vacationed on the island the summer of 1931. Love at first sight, with all the attendant drama and passion such feelings ignited in kids of seventeen. They'd had two more such summers, with letters in the interim pledging eternal love. But in early 1934, the family had returned to Germany, where Wil entered a Jesuit seminary. All that summer, Jean had pined and refused to see friends. And then Louise Millett had died, and given her grief a new focus. Lorraine thought it had hardened her heart, so the engagement to Ken Renaldi and that subsequent grief had no foundation of love. Nor had his death undone her more than briefly.

At the hotel, Lorraine set the covered dish in the refrigerator while Anna put a kettle on the stove, then asked, "Why don't you go up and talk to her while I make a cup of beef bouillon. And some toast. If she's nauseated again, maybe that'll stay down."

"So she's had the morning sickness, has she?"

She nodded, removing the gingham cover from the toaster on the sideboard.

"Ever ask if her monthly was late?"

"No. If she is pregnant, eventually she'll tell me. Didn't want to send her into another tantrum. Anyway, I'll bring a tray in a few minutes. Hope she doesn't throw it in my face."

The upstairs hallway was dark, all the second floor guest rooms closed off except the two at the end. Lorraine knocked softly on Jean's door. Getting no response, she thumped again, harder. "Jeanie, if you're sleeping, wake up. I want to talk to you."

A muted, "Go away, Auntie," from inside.

Lorraine turned the knob, pushed inside. Snow whiteness gave the room an underwater light. Jean was in the disheveled bed, a tattered patchwork quilt pulled up around her ears.

"Let me alone," Jean said. "I feel too bad to talk."

Lorraine came further in, sniffing the sweetish, sick-room air. On the far side of the bed, she lowered herself into a tattered overstuffed chair and studied the girl. Her auburn hair was uncombed, her eyes dark-circled, cheeks sunken.

"My God, Jeannie," she said. "You look like hell. Best you let Jim have a look at you next time he's here."

"Jim! Don't even say his name to me. After what he did to Wil."

"Oh, don't be so hard-headed. What else could he do? But listen, I'm not here to talk about that. I want to know if you're in the family way, and that's why you're too sick to go to work these days."

Jean's face darkened. "Anna been telling you things that're none of her business?"

"Don't need Anna to figure out what's wrong with you. See, I had a baby once—your mama likely told you, didn't she? So I know how it starts. Long about six weeks, that's when it gets bad. Now I'd like to know, what're you gonna do about it—lie here till you die? Quit life like your mama did?"

The girl turned away, huddling deeper under the quilt. "None of your business what I do."

"No, maybe not. But it's Cleve's business and I'm married to him. And believe you me, I don't want that man hurt again like he was when Malcolm passed. And what about Wil? How'd he feel if he knew you quit? He'd hate it, Jeannie. Hate to think you could've had his baby but you rather've died. He didn't want to die, but that's probably what happened, isn't it? I mean, he had no choice. You do. And even if he's gone, why, one day after the war, maybe his family'd be glad to know you're raising his child. Might give them comfort. For that matter, might comfort you too."

Jean didn't move except to close her eyes. Footsteps approached in the hall, then Anna pushed open the door and entered with a tray. "Jean, I've made some beef tea and toast. If you eat it slowly, you'll feel better. Maybe even good enough to get out of bed and wash up. And come downstairs for a while. What do you think?"

Jean glanced up, anger distorting her face. "Oh, look. It's Little Goody-Two-Shoes herself. You and Auntie here you have all the answers, don't you?"

"Of course not. Only a suggestion that might make you feel better for a few hours."

"Huh. And what about tomorrow? And the day after that? What then?"

Anna's gaze brushed Lorraine's. "Start with a few hours. And take tomorrow when it comes. That's what I've had to do the last few months. This isn't the end of the world, you know. Anyway, I'll just leave the tray and you can do what you want. Just remember, though, nothing's going to seem better till you do something to help yourself." She set the tray on a cedar chest at the foot of the bed, then shaking her head, left the room.

Lorraine sat quietly, realizing she and Anna had said enough. Maybe more than enough. Now it was up to Jean to fight off the same darkness that had swallowed her mother. If she could. Finally, she thought of one more small argument to pull her back. "You know Cleve and I'll help you with that baby, don't you, Jeannie? And we'll love it like our own, just wait and see. At least like our own grandbaby."

When Jean didn't answer, she got up, switched on the dresser lamp and pulled the blackout curtains closed. As she glanced at the bed, she realized Jean had begun to cry, silently, one hand over her mouth. Lorraine had never seen her cry before, not when Cleve told her about her mother's death, or at Louise Millett's funeral, or when she'd got word of Ken Renaldi's death. Or even when the Navy took Wil away. She was startled, then strangely relieved that the pain had begun to break through the crust of Jean's resistance.

She eased onto the side of the bed, using her own hanky to wipe her cheeks. "Oh honey," she crooned. "I know. I know. It's awful." Her own eyes filled as she stroked the unwashed hair away from the girl's face. "But it'll be better. I promise."

Jean shook her head and continued to weep soundlessly. Tears crawled down her cheeks, leaving shiny little tracks like snails left. For a moment Lorraine could only wonder what to do, then remembered when she'd been in a similar predicament, her mother had rocked her in her arms. So she bent and lifted Jean's shoulders and wrapped her arms around the girl's shuddering body. She didn't stop crying, but Lorraine knew the reservoir of pain was too deep to empty any time soon.

After a long while, when the weeping subsided, she whispered, "There. Doesn't that feel better?"

Jean pulled back, blew her nose, shook her head. “I hate being a crybaby.”

“Don’t worry. Nobody’s business but yours. Now. You just drink some of this beef tea, then you’ll perk up. And the world’ll look a little better.”

Yeah, she thought; for a few hours. But that was how things worked, wasn’t it? You got a few hours of feeling better, and then you went down to the grave again. Off and on like this until gradually, you came out of it, at least enough to go on living between the hours when you thought you couldn’t.

Sooner or later, it was an art almost every woman had to learn.

Chapter Eleven

Wednesday morning, Anna was on the pier when the trawler crunched through the overnight crust of harbor ice and tied up at the town wharf. In a dark topcoat and the usual fedora, Jim came down the gangway and headed toward the station wagon. The sight of him warmed her like a hearth fire. Well, of course; even before they'd met, their telephone conversations had inspired hope for her personal restoration. Now the relief was almost as sweet, because he was here again after two weeks of nasty storms that had kept even the intrepid Captain Hood in port. Not that they'd been out of touch; she'd phoned almost every night with medical questions, but kept the calls brief and impersonal, steering wide around any gossip the island operator might have relished. Especially about Jean's delicate condition.

As he neared, she resisted the urge to get out and open the passenger door, or to let the smile take over her face. God forbid she should behave like a teenager with a crush: these feelings were more adult, more professional. She wouldn't even say she'd missed him, because it wasn't part of her job to miss him. Or worry about him. Or allow herself to think of him intimately. She merely worked for the man.

His cheeks were red with cold, and he was bundled in

earmuffs and a scraggly plaid scarf. Was she imagining it, or did he seem more lined, more tired than he had two weeks ago? She wasn't sure, but she remembered reading somewhere that for the rest of their lives, polio victims were plagued with worse health than the rest of humanity.

"Hi, Jim," she said as he tossed his medical bag into the back seat. "Good to see you again."

He grinned. "You too. You have no idea how much I miss this place when I can't get here. Even though you're handling everything as well as I could."

She put the car in reverse and backed around. "Don't know about that." Aware her heart rate had sped up, she took a deep breath. "Now. Would you like some good news?"

"What's that?"

"Jean's back at work again. Only afternoons, though, after the morning sickness passes. And she stays in the back office. Doesn't want to see anyone. Thinks people are gossiping about her. And from what I've picked up, they are indeed. Haven't told her that, of course."

His eyes narrowed as the tires crunched through small patches of frozen snow from the most recent storm. "How'd you convince her to come back?"

"I didn't. It was Lorraine. Sunday before last."

"Hmmm. That mean she's going through with the pregnancy?"

Anna gave him a quick look. "What else can she do?"

He shrugged. "Well, I could arrange a therapeutic AB. Easy enough to claim the fugitive raped her. Or, if she won't hear of it, she could go to the Florence Crittenden home in Augusta and have the child adopted."

Parking at the town hall, Anna switched off the engine, set the brake. "I have no idea what she wants. She refuses to discuss it. Probably not real to her yet. That's how it was with me at first. I mean, I knew what was happening, of course. But it was all so remote, it took a while before I believed it with more than my mind."

He sighed, seemed about to say more. Instead, he opened his door and swung the cane out.

She grabbed for his medical bag before he could. "Here. Let me bring this, bag, Jim; it's too icy to try to carry it yourself."

He grinned. "Well, okay. Just this once."

Jean didn't appear till they were eating lunch; Cleve brought her when he came to the clinic to coal up the mammoth old furnace in the cellar. "She's here now," Anna murmured to Jim, "if you want to talk to her."

He nodded and got to his feet. "Wish me luck, Anna."

She wanted to say she'd pray for him but hated to sound sanctimonious, the way people expected a parson's daughter to sound. When it served her purposes, she could put on a self-righteous act, but this was hardly the time, not when she was nervous about the outcome of his talk with Jean. Even focused on pulling charts for house calls, she was aware of the muffled rise and fall of voices down the hall. How would Jean react if he suggested abortion? She had no idea, though she herself was shocked, not so much that he'd mentioned it -- she'd known other doctors who managed such favors for special patients -- but that Jim might be one of them. This flew in the face of her image of him; since she'd learned he was Episcopalian, he'd become a younger version of her father--above reproach, spotless and pure of heart. Hardly a man who'd violate the law, even for an old friend.

She'd dug out all the charts and stocked their medical bags before Jim emerged from the rear office. She could barely contain her questions till they were in the car. "Well, did she actually talk to you?"

"Let's say she tolerated my talking. She mostly listened. Or seemed to. Except for a couple of pretty strong No's when I suggested AB or adoption."

"Thought she would." She sighed and steered them onto the lower road, which led from the village along the shore toward the northern end of the island. The sun was low behind them, shadows long and purple across snow-covered fields, the air still and frosty.

"Then I talked to her about prenatal care. Told her if she wanted to have a healthy baby, it was important to get started early. She wasn't quite so negative, but she didn't exactly jump at the idea of seeing Ben Simon anytime soon."

"That doesn't surprise me."

"At least she didn't suggest I handle her case. She's been a family friend so long, I'd be uncomfortable with that. Fortunately she didn't ask."

Of course not, Anna thought, remembering Jean's aversion to the notion of Jim's touch on her private areas. "Then I'll talk to her. About seeing Dr. Simon, I mean. Maybe since I've been pregnant myself, I can get through to her."

For the rest of the afternoon, they talked about only the patients they were visiting. Until they were heading to the pier, racing to get there before the sun disappeared.

"Tell me something, Anna," Jim said as they rounded a curve and the harbor came into view, ripples shimmering in the last golden light. "When you were pregnant, did you see a doc early on?"

"Oh yes." She gripped the wheel more tightly. "I went to a Navy dispensary in San Francisco as soon as I'd missed the second period. Ironic. Because in my case, early care didn't guarantee a happy ending." She swallowed the sudden constriction in her throat. "For that matter, I was working in the OB clinic at the hospital when the hemorrhage started. They took me to the OR stat, but still it came to grief. So maybe…maybe I'm not the one to preach to her."

He was quiet as the road wound down the slope to the village. "Did you have any premonitions beforehand?"

She shook her head.

"Anyone ever give you an idea what might've caused it? The abruption, I mean. Like some trauma you discounted at the time?"

"No, nothing. Except anxiety about Dan being missing. Dr. Fielding had a theory that two months of worry might have caused an imbalance in the pregnancy hormones. Does that make any sense?"

"Hmm. Interesting theory. OB's not my specialty, but I could ask Ben Simon what he thinks. If you'd like me to."

"Oh, I suppose." She cleared her throat. "At least it wasn't due to some anatomical abnormality, so it's not likely to recur."

"Well, that's reassuring."

She didn't answer, and he asked nothing more until she pulled up on the pier. As if on signal, Fletch cranked the trawler's cold engine. The last red sliver of sun disappeared behind the far shore. Dusk thickened around the island; in the west a single brilliant planet glowed. Star light, star bright, she thought, wishing she still trusted nursery rhyme magic to effect happy endings. But the simplicity of childhood beliefs had faded with every passing day of her adult life. Now she'd come to believe that happy endings weren't endings at all, but fleeting milestones along a road increasingly littered with the bones of defunct illusions.

Jim left the car quickly without any special words to summarize their day together. As she watched him limp up the gangway, a bereft feeling closed her in as it inevitably did when she'd talked about the baby This pale, still evening, in the aftermath of the rapport she'd felt while telling him, it seemed worse than ever. An old scar whose edges were still raw and sensitive.

She watched the boat put out of the harbor and churn into the Sound, until all she could see was the pale red mast light fading in the twilight. Then, suddenly chilled, she went back to the clinic. Jean had left, so she filed the charts and neatened the examining rooms and straightened Jim's desk, then locked the doors and drove up the hill toward the hotel. And what was probably going to be a pointless discussion with Jean about Jim's supposed perfidy. So pointless, she decided she wouldn't even get into it that night. Or any other, if she could help it.

Chapter Twelve

Shivering in the bitter wind off the water, Alex Cropper huddled on the afterdeck of the trawler and studied the island as they approached. Not exactly looking for changes—the place hadn't changed a whit in all his twenty-seven years—but absorbing the familiar topography: rock-fenced pastures, dark pines and up-thrust boulders, now ice-encrusted, along the shore. At the crest of the steepest hill, the hotel loomed against the silver December sky. Like the dreams he'd had the year he'd been gone, like the fading pictures he'd carried to war so he could study those grainy black and white images of Jean and Cleve and Lorraine, and his long-dead parents, and a girl from high school who'd sworn to love him forever, but who'd stopped writing six months ago. And now, a new photo, of the English nurse from the hospital where he'd just spent two months recuperating from a brush with death.

Oh, the irony that of all the men he'd come to England with, only he had survived twenty-five missions, then, celebrating his upcoming furlough, had come close to buying the farm on a borrowed motorbike in a narrow country lane. His left arm was still in a sling, the shoulder still frozen, his future as a pilot in doubt. Not just ironic, but so ignominious that he'd invented a more glorious story for the folks back home. In his revised version, the ship had been shot up returning from that last mission; two motors were out, half the crew was dead and the pilot had passed out from blood loss, which left him to wrestle the crippled Fortress into a wheels-up landing on a ploughed field outside the base. "Rough as hell, and I was tossed around a bit," he intended to say in a modest tone, "but my injuries are nothing compared to the others'."

The story went well with the uniform and the service ribbons and wings on his chest. And who'd ever know it hadn't happened just that way? After all, the plane had been hit, and one engine was out, and the tail gunner was dead, and a tire had blown on landing, so he was stretching the truth only slightly. Besides, when your time was up, it didn't matter whether you were taking flak in a B-17 over Frankfort or charging down a Kent lane on a rickety motorbike. He'd already tried the more heroic fiction on Fletcher Hood, adding details for verisimilitude. Like a flock of sheep they'd barely missed on landing. There actually had been sheep, but they'd been crossing the lane when he came rocketing along too fast to stop.

Fletch had shaken his head. "I declare, Alex Cropper, you always have been one lucky son-of-a-bitch."

He'd given a Ronald Reagan chuckle. "Guys in the squadron called me Lucky even before this happened. When I had to bail out of my first ship over the Channel." That at least was partly true; the captain had ordered everyone to jump, but Alex had decided to ride the plane as far as he could, which was to a wheels-up controlled crash in a field near Dover. And the men who'd had bailed out had been picked up right away; so this story could have happened very much as he'd recounted it. Anyway, plenty of other guys he knew embroidered their adventures when necessary.

The trawler's engine slowed as they swung past the breakwater into the ice-filmed harbor, close enough now he could make out Uncle Cleve and Auntie Lorrie and Jean beside the pickup. Couple other townspeople were there too, but no one he could identify as the new nurse from the clinic. When Jean had written about her, he'd been intrigued that she was basically a widow. Well, maybe she didn't see it that way, but from what he knew, subs went down as often as planes, with even fewer survivors. So for all intents and purposes, she could date him if she wanted. Sure, there were girls in Rockhampton who were dying to go out with him, but he'd become partial to nurses. They were earthier, less scared to be physical with a man. At least the one back in England had always been quick to restore a bloke's will to live. By now, he'd learned to fake losing his real well.

Dragging his duffel bag, he was the first one down the gangway, was instantly locked in one of Cleve's bear hugs, then embraced by Lorraine. Then Jeannie, smaller than he remembered, thinner of face, eyes dark-circled under shaggy brows, and wearing no lipstick or any other feminine adornment. He pulled back, stifling the urge to chide her for having helped the German sailor. No sense marring his hero's welcome yet.

He waited till that evening at supper at Lorraine and Cleve's, after he'd met Anna Donovan, heard Cleve's version of the rescue of Wil Himmelreich, and had three stiff bourbons.

"Jeannie, what the hell were you thinking of, taking him into the hotel like that?" he demanded over apple pie. "Suppose he'd taken you hostage or something?"

"Oh don't be silly, Alex," his sister snapped. "It wasn't just any German sailor. It was Wil. You knew him before the war. You even taught him to sail."

"Never cared much for him, though." He held out his glass for a refill, but Lorraine only poured water into it.

"That's nonsense," Jean came back. "You followed him

around like he was some sort of god. You were a damned pest, the way you tagged along everywhere we went."

"Well, back then he wasn't the enemy. Hadn't seen how good those Nazi bastards are at knocking down our planes. Didn't know how they'd treat the fellows that got down alive either. And wasn't it a U-boat sank your boyfriend's ship? Maybe even Wil's boat? How could you help him after that?"

She snorted. "He was only a cook. He wasn't responsible for what his boat did."

He regarded her with disbelief, then left the table to get the bourbon bottle himself. "I don't believe it, Jeannie. You're still sweet on him. Even under the circumstances."

Jean lowered her gaze to her clenched fingers. "He was my first love. Of course I still have feelings. Not that it matters now. If he hasn't already been executed, he soon will be."

Aware Anna was watching him, he said, "At least Doc Millett had the good sense to turn him in. Or you could've been locked up too. Maybe next in line for the firing squad."

"That's enough about Wil," Lorraine put in. "He's gone and it's over, and no harm's done."

Alex forced a grin, which he turned on Anna, sitting beside him but not close enough for his taste. "What do you think about it, nurse?"

Her casual shrug conveyed only indifference. Or a reluctance to comment. "We had to help him, of course. But I agree. It's over. And as Lorraine said, no harm was done. Except to Wil. And he was only following orders."

Cleve snorted. "So he said. But I say he knew what he was doing. Likely even volunteered 'cause he knew this place so well. And hell, his family lived in Portland; maybe they were part of a fifth column group. And that crap about asking for asylum, all hogwash. Sure, it's over and no harm came to any of us, but it could've. That's the thing, Alex. It sure as hell could've."

Jean shoved her chair back, gathered an armful of soiled plates and stomped over to the sink. As if on signal, Anna rose and began clearing the table too. Lorraine told them they needn't; she'd get Alex to help with the cleanup. "Bet you know all about KP from the army," she said with a wink.

"Are you kidding, Auntie? Pilots don't do KP."

"Then it's high time you learned, so some girl'll think you're wonderful when the war's over. Never mind diamonds; surest way to a woman's heart's through the dishpan."

He guffawed, then got to his feet and began stacking pie plates with his good hand. "Oh, okay. I'll help you. But only if you give me another inch of bourbon."

"Well, we'll be going then," Jean said primly.

"Let me help you girls with your coats." He followed them into the parlor, where their outer garments were heaped on the rocker next to the coal stove. First he held Anna's, then Jean's, hoping he was making points for good manners. As he walked them to the door, a new notion sprang into his mind. "Hey, girls, how'd you like me to take you Christmas shopping one of these days? How's that sound?"

"I've finished mine, thanks," Jean said in her tight-lipped way. "Found everything in the Sears catalog."

"What about you, Anna?" he asked hopefully.

She pulled on a toboggan and knotted a matching scarf at her neck. "What do you mean, take us?"

"Well, I could borrow Uncle's boat, and get a buddy to pick us up at East Point with his car. After you did your shopping, we could have dinner somewhere too. Even take in a movie. If you want to, I mean."

Her frown was barely discernible. Still, it worried him that she didn't jump at his offer.

"I don't mean a date or anything like that," he explained in his Van Johnson voice. "I know you're a married woman."

The frown congealed. "Let me think about it. Anyway, I couldn't go till Saturday afternoon. Clinic hours in the morning."

He shrugged, which hurt his shoulder and caused him to wince. "That'd be fine."

"Are you in any shape to pilot the boat, though? Looks like you're still in pain."

"Oh that. Just a little twinge now and then, when I'm tired. Be fine by Saturday, wait and see."

"I'll think about it," she said again, her manner still maddeningly aloof.

He stood at the door while they drove off, until Cleve hollered at him to stop letting cold air in. Back in the dining room, he loaded up some plates, but when he came into the kitchen, he made a show of discomfort for Lorraine's benefit. If she noticed, she failed to comment, so on the next trip, he purposely dropped a handful of cutlery. "Lazy man's load," he said as she came running to pick them up. "Guess the old arm's not as strong as I thought."

"Oh, go fix yourself another drink. I'll finish up. Just keep me company."

From the table, he couldn't see her face as she stood up to her elbows in dishwater, but the set of her shoulders warned him she had something strong to say. It took a good ten minutes, however, until she got around to it. Until she turned to fix him with her dark-eyed gaze. "Now you listen to me, Alex Cropper. Don't you go bothering Jean any more about that German boy. For one thing, he's probably dead by now. And another thing…."

He waited as she lit a cigarette, then brought it over to the table. "Ain't you going to offer me one, Auntie?"

She held out the pack of Luckies, waited for him to light

one, then poured herself a bourbon from the bottle on the table. "Now, as I was saying, there's more going on with her than you know. See, when he was so sick, she took care of him night and day. Wouldn't even let Anna help. So now, well.... now, sad to say, she's in the family way."

He almost choked on the smoke he'd just inhaled. "What the hell? Knocked up? Really?"

"And she won't hear of...you know...getting rid of it. Even giving it out for adoption."

"No kidding. Jeez, that's the stupidest thing I ever heard. You tried talking sense into her?"

Lorraine nodded, sipped bourbon. "I have. Jim has, and probably Anna too. But you know Jean. Hard-headed as y'all's mother was. So she ain't just grieving that boy, she's worried about how she's going to take care of a baby with no daddy. And what people are going to say. That's why I don't want you giving her any more guff about Wil."

He stared at her in disbelief. "But it's guff she needs, so she doesn't ruin her life with a Nazi bastard. I can't believe she's actually going to have it."

Lorraine's face clouded. "That's where we disagree. I say she should do what she wants, and Cleve and I'll help her every way we can. Didn't expect you to understand; you're a man. For y'all it's easy. Just get into a girl's pants and have your fun, and let the devil take the hindmost. But it ain't so easy for the girl, 'specially when she's in love."

"That's hogwash, Auntie. I know girls who don't think twice about abortions. That doesn't mean they're bad. Or never want kids. It's just the circumstances. So don't tell me not to talk to her about Wil. I'm going to tell it like I see it. And if she doesn't like it, tough shit."

"Oh Alex," Lorraine sighed. "Hold your tongue. Else you'll put up a wall between you and her. And suppose you don't come back next time? Sure, you've been lucky. But luck can run out. I'd hate for her last memory of you to be like this, like you turned your back on her in her time of need. Like you couldn't forgive her doing what thousands of girls do every day."

He stared through the miasma of tobacco smoke enclosing the table. "Thousands of girls don't give aid and company to enemy sailors, Auntie. I don't care how good his folks were, he helped kill plenty of American boys. And he would've sabotaged the war effort if he hadn't been caught. Any girl sleeps with a man like that'd sleep with the devil."

Before he realized what she was doing, Lorraine reached over and flung the contents of her glass into his face. Fortunately, only a small splash. "Now you listen to me, Alex Cropper. No more of that talk while you're staying in my house. You hear?"

He wiped his face on his shirt sleeve and gave her a wry grin. "Not if you're going to waste good bourbon like that."

"Well, good. Then we understand each other."

"Be hard not to, Auntie." Which, he concluded, meant she thought he'd agreed not to confront Jeannie about her pregnancy. Well, if Lorraine wanted to think he'd backed down, let her think it. Only thing a drink in the face had really done was convince him to say what needed saying. Lorraine was sweet, but too romantic for her own good. Cleve'd understand; Cleve had been in the First War, knew all about the Huns. Including the fact that the world didn't need another, even if Jeannie was its mother.

The morning after Christmas, Anna drove down to the pier where Cleve, Lorraine and Alex were huddled in the pickup watching *Molly B* crunch into the harbor. Waving, Lorraine climbed down and walked over to the station wagon. She was bundled in Cleve's Christmas present—a long coat of rabbit fur dyed to imitate mink. From a distance, it looked like the real thing. As she approached, Anna ran down the window so she could lean in and ask, "What's the matter? Jeannie sick again this morning?"

"No, she's fine. Just upset about Alex's attitude toward her condition. You know, she always takes it personally when someone doesn't agree with her. In fact, she's still barely speaking to Jim for turning Wil in. Now this, with her own brother."

Lorraine glanced back at the pickup; Cleve was lugging Alex's duffel bag from the rear compartment. "I begged him not to say anything. But I declare, he's hard-headed as she is. Still, her baby'll be his flesh and blood too. So, if anything happens to him…"

Anna nodded, left the car, wrapped her scarf more tightly against the frigid wind, and regarded Alex Cropper. In uniform, with his cap at a jaunty angle, he looked like a recruiting poster, especially if you overlooked the sling immobilizing one arm. More ifs followed—if she didn't know him so well, if she hadn't let him take her Christmas shopping, she might still find him a dreamboat. Oh, not dark and sexy like Dan, but in a blond, wholesome All-American-Boy way. Unfortunately, that he was handsome and funny was superficial, the least of what he really was. She'd discovered his other side Saturday night when he'd drunk himself into oblivion, and passed out on Cleve's boat at the East Point pier. Not wanting to share the crowded cabin with him, she'd almost called Jim from the pay phone on the pier to ask if she could stay at his house. But that she'd gone to dinner and a movie, and later to a night club with Alex and his high school friends might have given Jim the idea that she was fast. Loose. Easy. A fun-loving not-quite-widow.

So she'd walked up the hill to the boardinghouse and banged on the door till Mrs. Goulding finally let her in. The next morning, she'd She left early, before Jim might appear for a kippers-and-eggs breakfast. Then she'd roused Alex, still breathing alcohol fumes, to take them back to the island. And for the rest of the week of his furlough, had avoided him as much as possible with them both living at the hotel. That he'd judged Jean so harshly was the last straw. She'd almost decided not to see him off this morning too.

Then she'd thought of Dan. When he'd sailed on his last voyage, she'd already left the Bay Area for home. But other dependents would have been there to wave as *Wolf Fish* backed away from the pier, pushed into the bay and headed west; other wives would have sniffled into their hankies as the black boat disappeared in fog lingering over San Francisco Bay. Only Dan would've had no one to wave farewell before he went below, no one to observe the moment when his link with home and country was severed. Perhaps for the last time.

So Alex Cropper, a man she barely knew and held in no high regard, must be hugged and wished well, and waved off on his outbound journey to rejoin the war. Even though her heart wasn't in the gesture, she regarded it as one of those Christian duties a priest's daughter was morally obligated to do.

She and Lorraine joined the men as the trawler tied up, as the gangway was run down. Then, smiling his brilliant toothpaste-ad smile, Alex wrapped his good arm around her, hugged her against his body. "Jeannie still pissed off at me, Annie?"

She nodded. "She'll get over it. Just not today."

"You know she's ruining her life, don't you?"

Anna was compelled to speak truth as she saw it . "Well, it is her life. And if it turns out badly, we still have to support her. Meanwhile, you take care of yourself. And be sure and write when you find out where you're going."

He gave her a rueful grin. “First I gotta convince the medics I can fly again. That’ll take some doing. But hell, they need pilots, and I’m a damned good one. Plus now I’ve got this new beef with der Fuehrer. So just wait and see. I’ll be back in the cockpit in no time at all.”

“If that’s what you want.”

“You bet I do. So wish me luck.”

“Oh, I do. I do,” she said as sincerely as she could.

“And listen…” He lowered his voice and leaned closer. “Keep an eye on Jeannie for me, will you? See if you can talk sense into her about this…you know, this bastard she’s having.”

Swallowing disgust, she said, “Even If I thought I should, it wouldn’t do any good. See, she has a different way of looking at the situation than we do.”

His face hardened. “Jesus. When this gets out, folks are really going to give her a lot of shit.” He shook his head sorrowfully. “If she wants to go through with it, though, least she can do is go somewhere nobody knows her.”

Anna glanced away, at Cleve and Lorraine standing aside, at Fletch ambling down the gangway toward them. “Better get a move on there, Alex,” he called, “if you’re gonna catch the noon bus out of town.” Stooping, he grasped the ties of the duffel bag and hoisted it toward the boat.

“Well, folks, guess this is it.” Alex’s grin was wide, but she saw moisture in his eyes, a faint tremble to his chin. They all hugged. Then he astonished her with a full lip kiss before he pulled away and raced toward the gangway.

Huddling for warmth with the others, she watched the boat leave the pier. Alex stood on deck, waving with his good arm till they’d cleared the breakwater. He didn’t go into the pilothouse until they’d plowed into the wind-roughened sound.

“Well, there he goes,” Lorraine sighed with a shake of

her head. “I love him like a son, but he’s a self-righteous fool, the way he treats Jeannie.” Her gaze followed the receding craft. “Hope he gets a chance to make up for it.”

Cleve took a chaw of Red Man and headed toward the pickup. “Don’t worry about him, Lorrie. That one’s a cat with nine lives. Be back safe and sound before you know it.”

She shook her head, her expression funereal. “No. No, he won’t. I have a premonition.”

“Oh, you and your premonitions! Come on, get in the truck. Unless you want to walk home.”

Anna told him to leave; she’d drive her home. Cleve sputtered away in a cloud of yellowish exhaust and Lorraine climbed into the station wagon. Some of the past week’s snow had melted in the sun, but most remained, piled high and crusted over in the long shadows across the pier. Wind made Anna’s eyes water and chilled her thighs like a lover’s cold hands, so she started the engine and turned up the heater. Spray from the harbor had begun freezing on the windshield, but she could still see the trawler heading into a froth of scudding whitecaps. Shivering with more than cold, she crossed herself and mentally said the Jesus, Jesus prayer.

“Say, Anna. You ain’t Catholic, are you?” Lorraine asked.

“Uh, no. But Episcopalians use some of the same rituals. Including making the sign of the cross on occasion.”

“Well. I left the Church a long while ago, but it can’t hurt.” She crossed herself too, wrapped the fur coat closer and frowned out across the churning water. “If anything can keep him safe, it’s Our Lord.”

“That’s what my father always says.”

“That’s right. He’s a priest, ain’t he? Think he’d pray for Alex too?”

“I’m sure he’d be glad to.”

“And Jean too. Lord knows, she needs our prayers just as much. Maybe a whole lot more.” She reached into her coat pocket for a crumpled handkerchief, wiped her eyes, blew her nose loudly.

"I told him about her predicament on the phone yesterday, and he said he'd pray for them both."

"Yeah, I heard you talking." She sniffled back more tears, lit a cigarette. "If it wasn't winter, it wouldn't worry me so bad. But winters here…they always make me wish I could go South with the birds. Florida or somewhere warm. Like Louisiana. Except …"

Anna waited, wanting to prompt her, yet reluctant to pry.

"Except if I did, I might never come back. I mean, if I went home."

Remembering the photo of the priest who'd fathered Lorraine's child, she wondered if she'd been ostracized in her home town. Shunned, gossiped about, forever held up as an example of a fallen woman. But something in her balked at asking such a personal question simply for her own curiosity. Besides, she could easily imagine how her having compromised a priest would sit with his parishioners. Never mind that he was probably ten years older and cloaked in vows of celibacy; she'd have been blamed for tempting him. As for Jean, God knew what she'd have to endure for giving sexual aid and comfort to an enemy. Maybe Alex and Jim were right, then; maybe she should terminate the pregnancy before she caught the wrath of puritanical locals.

Still time for an uncomplicated first-trimester abortion. Or, if she was determined to keep it, at least leave the island and raise the child elsewhere till the war ended. And islanders had more to think about than a brief romantic encounter between two lonely, frightened souls who happened to be on different sides of a war.

Lorraine's voice cut into her speculation. "But what about you, honey? I know you was homesick yesterday. Did calling your folks help?"

She smiled, her parents' voices still clear in her memory

despite a long wait for the call to go through, and a staticky connection. She'd joined the family for dinner at Lorraine and Cleve's, then used their phone when they'd insisted. Constrained by conscience not to talk too long, she'd been embarrassed when her mother ran on and on. As if she didn't report every speck of news at least twice a week in letters.

"Oh yes," she said now. "The call was wonderful. And the church service was lovely." As it had been, in late afternoon by candlelight, with carols accompanied by a wheezing, groaning pump organ and a fine Congregational sermon. But no communion, not even with Wonder Bread and Welch's Grape juice.

"When I came here," she went on, "I didn't plan to go home for a year. I mean, if I can call where my parents live home. See, it's the rectory of my father's church. I grew up there, but when he retires they'll have to move." She shrugged, sighed, pressed her lips together. "Guess no place'll seem like home till my husband gets back."

Lorraine reached across the seat and patted Anna's gloved hand. "I pray for him too, you know. Him and Wil and Alex. And my own boy, of course. Never miss a night asking the Lord to keep him safe. Wherever he is in the world. This one or the next."

Anna bit her lip and put the car into reverse. Realizing Christmas would be a difficult anniversary for Lorraine, she wanted to say something of comfort and consolation to her, but empty to come up with any such words, even for herself. Even before Dan's boat had gone missing, she'd discovered that merely standing and waiting for news demanded more patience, faith and optimism that she could summon. Prayer didn't help, though she'd never admit that to her father. He wouldn't blame her, but within herself, she often doubted her faith was as strong as it should be for someone raised with his personification of the Christian virtues. Or did they develop only with time?

And if so, how long did it take?

Chapter Thirteen

As she dressed that February morning, Anna found herself humming *I'll See You Again*, without meaning to. She didn't know all the words, except it was a love song, which was embarrassing because a love song was hardly appropriate to express her anticipation of seeing Jim again. In the three weeks since he'd last been here, the weather had been so consistently fierce that Cleve had made the run only a couple times and then only to bring basics like food, coal, kerosene and the mail. This morning, however, the signs were auspicious – sun shining, albeit feebly, only a wisp of wind blowing, most of the roads cleared of snow. And just the night before, Jim had assured her nothing would keep him from the clinic that day.

But as she'd finished dressing—too cold for a cotton uniform; now it was sweaters, slacks, woolen sox and boots—Mrs. Leech called up the steps. "Doc on the phone for you, nurse. And he don't sound good."

She groaned and clattered downstairs in a sudden cloud of dread. Sure enough, his voice was thick and now and then he had to break off to cough. The hard, tight sound told her he was sick before he got the words out.

Remembering the hell-or-high-water promise, she whined, "But last night you were fine."

"I know. But around midnight, I woke up with a fever. And this cough. Likely bronchitis." He cleared his throat lengthily. "Thought I'd be better this morning, but I feel so rotten I've asked Fletch to run me up to the hospital."

"Oh no," she gasped. "You must really be ill."

"Well, I can't take care of myself in the best of times, so thought I'd let the nursing staff keep me from getting worse."

She forced cheer into her voice. "That's sensible, Jim." Then the panic crept in. "But who…I mean…is there anyone I can call if I need medical advice?"

"Fred Anderson. A GP in town. Covered for me other years I was under the weather. Jean has his number. A crotchety old coot, but a good doc."

"Well, then. We'll be fine. Now. Don't worry about anything. Just concentrate on getting better."

"Whatever you say, nurse."

As she came back upstairs, her spirits deflated like a pin-pricked balloon. Jean met her at the top. "What ails Jim?"

"He thinks bronchitis. He sounds awful. And has this deep cough. He's turning himself in to the hospital, so it must be serious."

"Oh, he'll be fine. He comes down with something every winter and has to take a couple weeks off. Except…well, he's never gone into the hospital before. Hmm. Makes you wonder."

Suddenly unable to speak, Anna rushed into the bathroom, and brushed her teeth for five minutes while fear blossomed in her like a virulent weed. In four months here, she'd learned to live with mild professional fear. But this was different; this wasn't for some patient whose condition she had to manage. This was what she might have felt had she learned her father was sick: a combination of impotence and anxiety that arose from a surfeit of medical knowledge she had no way to put to use. Besides, winter bleakness was getting into her bones, as Lorraine had warned. Not that winter here was vastly worse than it was in Portsmouth—there was just more of it: snow, gales, sunless days, black and white landscapes, and a frigid dampness that penetrated even layers of woolens. Worst of all was the isolation, almost like being on a ship locked in ice at the South Pole. With the mainland only a dim gray smudge on the western horizon, and sea and sky like dirty rumpled blankets, the rock-studded mound of Hope Island could've been in the middle of nowhere. A place of dark evergreens, dark buildings, dark water in the cove freezing white every night until *Molly B's* steel hull crunched through it. Mini-icebergs scudded the sound, surf turned into ice sculptures along the shoreline, frozen spray crusted the trawler's deck house on almost every crossing.

During January, Fletch had been able to make the run only a couple times a week. When the harbor froze over, an old interisland ferry back-and-forthed over it. Every morning afterward, Cleve's little boat broke the overnight layer. She wasn't built for rough water, but her red hull splashed cheerful color against a monochrome background where the only other bright spots were the hotel's mansard roof, a few barns and the sleigh Jean's father had made for her one Christmas. Hitched to Cleve's black mare, it took her to remote patients whenever the car bogged down in snow, chains useless against chest-high drifts. Or ice coated the roads. Or the station wagon wouldn't start.

She hadn't minded. She was, after all, able to talk to Jim every evening, usually with some question about a patient she might've answered herself, but preferred to rely on his opinion. Most, she realized, were just excuses to hear his voice. She took heart from the fact he never hurried her, or rushed his responses. Once in a while she even let herself believe he was just as happy to share their conversations. She cut short such speculation, however, when her imagination slid off the straight and narrow into the impenetrable and forbidden forest of his personal life.

Her last house call that afternoon was to a ramshackle cottage on the Upper Road. Henry Ewell was an elderly bachelor, a ward of the state she checked on every week to make sure he was caring for himself. As she parked now, however, she noticed the snow on the footpath was untrodden. And no smoke rose from the stovepipe on the roof.

Apprehension pecked at her like a hungry bird. Silly, she decided; he'd probably gone to his sister's in the village for the rest of the winter. But as she walked toward the cottage, she heard his hounds baying inside. Her knock drove them into a noisy frenzy. When she pushed the door open, the two low-slung dogs almost bowled her over in their haste to get out.

She stepped inside with increasing dread. The wood box was full, but the pot-bellied stove wasn't even slightly warm. The grapey stench of dog urine filled the air; droppings littered the floor. "Henry?" she called, eyes adjusting to the dimness. "Time to wake up now."

Then she saw the quilt-wrapped bundle on the daybed. Unmoving, inert.

"Henry?" she said again, with no response.

Even as she crossed the rough plank floor, even before she touched him, she knew he'd be cold and stiff. Still, she felt for the carotid pulse, watched for signs of breath. Nothing.

Crossing herself, she whispered, "Dear God", and backed away, uncertain of her next move. Who was she supposed to notify? And what would happen to the body? Jean would know, but she'd stopped going on house calls once the snows started. She hadn't yet seen the Rockhampton OB man, but her mothering instinct somehow warned her to avoid slippery surfaces. And falls.

After her ragged thoughts leveled out, Anna returned to the station wagon, drove too fast to the clinic and burst in the back door. At the desk, Jean glanced up with a frown. "My God, Anna. You look like you've seen a ghost."

"Not a ghost. But a dead man. One of our patients." Her voice came out low and solemn, like the tone her father used with the grieving. "Old Henry Ewell. And I don't know what to do. I mean, who do I call?"

Jean reached for an index card box and riffled through the contents. "Coroner over to Rockhampton. Probably tell you to send the body with Fletch this afternoon. Oh, and you'll have to tell his sister, of course. Can't do that on the phone, though. Have to go see her." She paused, brow furrowed in thought. "First I better tell Fletch not to leave, then ring the coroner. Meanwhile, go up to the hotel and get Cleve. He'll know what to do next."

Jean jiggled the book to get the operator and asked her to track down Fletch, who was usually at the Lunch Box this time of day. Anna was heading for the hotel when she saw Cleve's truck at his barn. Pulling in beside it, she blew the horn till he came out.

After she blurted out the news, he stroked the beard he'd grown for the winter. "Dead, eh? Ay-yuh. That's how it goes sometimes. Well, let me find Chet, then we'll come get him. And don't you fret none, nurse. Not your fault, don't you know?"

Reassured, Anna drove back to the cottage; the runaway hounds were back now and scratching at the door. She let them in, found a bag of meal under the sink and filled a chipped china bowl beside the stove. They tore into it so ferociously she wondered if she hadn't found them when she had, would they have gone after their master's body?

Shuddering, she refilled the bowl a couple times until they'd had enough, then let them out again. Now, alone with the corpse, she pulled a chair up to the daybed, and tried to devise some special ceremony to fill the minutes till Cleve arrived. Something to honor Henry's spirit, if it still lingered near his cast-off body. To give it peace and send it on its way.

But all she could think of were the stories he'd told during her visits, long-winded tales that always used more time than she could spare. Interesting nonetheless, a record of his eighty-eight years on Hope Island: accounts of horrific Atlantic hurricanes with wind-driven tides that flooded the village. Winters so severe the Sound had frozen solid enough to skate across. Blizzards that had blown ships onto the rocks below the hotel, and dramatic rescues he and other islanders had risked their lives to effect. Fires at sea they could see but not reach in time to do more than retrieve corpses. And another blaze that had wiped out a colony of elegant summer cottages on the island's north shore. "Every bit as fine as them down to Newport," he'd added. "Don't know why they never rebuilt them."

Once she'd asked if he'd ever married. He'd wagged his gray head a long while. "Nope. Came close, though. Pretty little thing, she was. Folks were summer people, up from Worcester. Real palace of a house. I kept their boats shipshape, so I saw her every year. Watched her grow from girl to woman. Had feelings for her, and she for me." He'd fallen silent, watery eyes staring into the past. "Afore we could marry, though, she took sick. The consumption, they said. Doctor back to Worcester, he sent her to one of them places in the mountains. Didn't do her no good, though. She weren't but twenty-two." He'd swallowed visibly, sniffled, wiped his nose on his sleeve. "That was back in 'eighty, and all them years since, I never found me another like her."

The poignancy of that lost romance, and of his death,

alone except for his dogs, brought tears to her eyes. When she wondered how else to honor him, she knew immediately what her father would do. Leaning over his body, she made the sign of the cross on Henry's forehead with her thumb. She hadn't memorized any of the proper prayers, so she murmured only, "May the Lord receive you into his kingdom and grant you eternal rest." Then she picked up his hand, so cold and gnarled it felt like a bunch of twigs. More obviously lifeless than the claw of the old man on the train.

As she held it, she pictured her father's thin hands, bones and blood vessels prominent through the age-spotted skin. And prayed silently for old men in their homes, and young men "in peril on the sea". And for herself as well, for strength to endure the solitude of life here. Once Jim had warned that not everyone could handle it; she'd been sure she could. Until today, when solitude seemed more a presence than an absence. A cold and heavy presence that dared her to continue working on this desolate, lonely outpost if Jim Millett didn't come back.

When Cleve's pickup finally sputtered to a stop outside the shack, relief warmed and softened her. Huddled in their mackinaws, he and Chet ordered her to get out of the way and leave everything to them. Without arguing, she drove back to the clinic. Jean met her with the news that the county coroner wanted the body brought to the hospital. Fletch was waiting to cast off till Cleve delivered it to the pier.

"Now," Jean went on, "only thing left is, go tell Henry's sister. Best do it now so she can see him before Fletch leaves. Know where she lives?"

As Anna drove toward the house on the lower road, she rehearsed ways to give the news. What would Jim say? No matter; there were no good, better, best ways to deliver this sort of information. In the end, though, she had only to tell Mrs. Warren she had bad news. Before she could say more, the old lady said, "It's Henry, ain't it?" Anna had nodded and begun to explain, when the other interrupted. "You know, nurse. I ain't surprised, not the least bit. See, I seen it coming. Watched him go downhill all last year. You know. Stopped caring about anything, even them hounds of his. I told him, 'Henry, you know what's good for you, you just move in here with me, least for the winter.' But he wouldn't hear of it." She wagged her spit-curled gray head and hunched her bony shoulders under a moth-eaten sweater. "Nothing nobody can do with a hard-head like that. Still, hate that he had to die all alone in the cold like that."

"Well, at least he didn't suffer," Anna said, though she couldn't have sworn that was the case. But it was something that seemed to comfort next-of-kin. "Now. Can I do anything for you? Or drive you down to the pier to see him before they take him to the hospital?"

She said she'd appreciate a ride. By then, Henry's body, still shrouded in quilts, had been placed on the mate's bunk aboard *Molly B.* Anna paid her respects, then went back to the car and waited to drive the old woman home again. Twilight still banded the west in pink, but cold and darkness had taken on a life of their own, becoming a physical presence as they did every evening. By that time, she was more than ready to go home—she called the hotel home now—but stopped off at the clinic first to let Dr. Anderson know what had happened.

She used the phone in Jim's office. Afterward, she swiveled in his chair and studied the miscellany on the desk: A calendar from a drug manufacturer. A blotter covered with jottings, phone numbers and scribbled names. A Merck Manual and PDR, both well-thumbed. A stack of medical journals weighted by a porous white rock from a World War I battleground. Some pencils, a fountain pen, a dog-eared address book. And a Bible with gilt-edged pages. On the flyleaf a small, neat hand had inscribed, "To dear Jim, with thanks for your help. Margaret. Christmas 1940." She riffled through it, found no other mementoes.

Still curious, she slid open the few unlocked drawers. And wondered what was in the others. The only personal item was a folded handkerchief, linen, monogrammed with the initials JEM. On impulse, she stuffed it in her coat pocket. Then, unnerved by a strong sense of his absence, she secured the clinic and locked up before she got in the car again, heading for the hotel. And the warmth of the kitchen, the smell of a chicken pot pie in the oven. And a glass of Jean's fiancé's rather awful Chianti. And Jean herself, more cheerful than she'd been in months, wanting to hear the grisly details of Henry Ewell's demise.

Nothing seemed to cheer her quite as much as a medical story with an unhappy ending.

Chapter Fourteen

It was long past midnight when the phone bell cut into Anna's rest. Not yet true sleep; an hour before, a cold front had slammed through, leaving brutal winds that pounded the hotel and screeched at the windows. A night of such foreboding, she'd drifted off several times, only to be brought awake again by the thump of a loose shutter or the creaking of the building's old timbers. Then wide-eyed, she'd stared at the window while her mind took her to places she didn't want to go—to Henry Ewell's shack, *Wolf Fish*'s sardine can wardroom, and her own hospital room after the C-section. Just before the doctor had come in with the bad news.

She'd begun to think she might not sleep again at all, when she heard the phone. Racing downstairs, she lifted the receiver with dread.

The caller was a Mrs. Dennett from the village, no one she'd met before. The patient was her husband. "He's got the worst belly ache, and he's feverish, and he can't keep anything down. Hate to bother you on a night like this, but I'd feel better if you'd come look at him."

Anna's mind swiftly turned clinical. "Be happy to. Meanwhile, if you have an icebag, or even a hot water bottle, pack it with snow and keep it on his belly till I get there. Now. Where do you live?"

When she came back upstairs, Jean met her in the hall in a decrepit chenille robe. Her eyes were wide with what looked like fright. As if the phone had brought bad news about Wil. "Who was that?"

Anna went into her room and threw on the usual layers of clothing. "A woman in the village. Sounds like her husband has appendicitis."

"What can you do if he does?"

"Try to keep it from getting worse till we can get him to the hospital."

"Then I'll go with you. I probably know even more about appendicitis than you do."

When they were in the car, Anna asked, "Where'd you learn all that?"

"From personal experience. See, my father died of it. Back before we had a doctor or nurse on the island. And by the time one came over, the appendix had burst. Oh, they took him to the hospital and operated, but peritonitis had set in, so nothing they could do."

"Oh, I'm sorry."

"The worst of it was, it was all my mother's fault. She thought he was constipated and gave him castor oil. Then put a hot water bottle on his belly. Jim said those are the worst things for appendicitis. She said she was trying to make him feel better." The words came out clipped and bitter. "I say she didn't give a damn if he lived or died."

Stunned at the vehemence, it took Anna a moment to say, "Were you close to your father?"

"Yeah. And she hated it. I mean, talk about a jealous bitch. Of her own daughter!"

Anna's failure of words persisted well beyond their arrival at the Dennett apartment above the village ship chandlery and hardware store. While she hoped to penetrate Jean's story enough to understand more, the other girl's logic often defied comprehension. Perhaps a wall she'd built around herself as a shield against painful reality. And behind which she existed in a world of her own design. Like the delusion that she and Wil might have escaped to the mainland and lived a life of happy deception in perpetuity. If Jim hadn't turned him in.

The patient was the forty-something summer lobsterman who also owned the store. The wife had packed snow into a hot water bottle, but seemed too distraught to understand why. Despite the cold pack, his pain was intense, so Anna gave him a shot of morphine. Meanwhile, Jean wrote a sheet of instructions for his care until they could arrange to get him to the Rockhampton hospital. "The shot should keep him quiet till morning," Anna added. "But keep using the ice, and don't give him anything to eat or drink except small sips of water. If he needs to pee, use a jar, but don't let him move around more than absolutely necessary. Now. Do you understand everything?"

The woman nodded, her expression bewildered.

"And call me if there's any change. Otherwise, I'll be back first thing in the morning."

Satisfied they'd done all they could, she and Jean headed back to the hotel. "Thanks for coming along. It helped having you explain to the wife. Too bad your mother didn't know what you do."

"Huh. Wouldn't have made an iota of difference. See, she had to care for him her way, even though it killed him. But she paid the price afterward. The guilt drove her mad. That's why she did what she did."

Anna was about to ask what that had been, but remembered Lorraine's story that she"d apparently killed herself. Averse to discussing it further, she told Jean she'd check with the Rockhampton doctor to make sure she'd done all she could for Mr. Dennett.

"Who, Doc Anderson? That old pill! Probably take your

head off for calling so late."

"Can't be helped. This seems like one of those nights when nobody sleeps."

"Like the night we saw the U-boat."

There was so much more they might have said, Anna mused, but anxious to call the other doctor, told Jean good night as she plodded up the stairs. She was only three months pregnant but had already begun walking heavily, with a slight waddle. Observing, Anna wondered if she'd done that too. When old sorrow stung her, she slammed the lid on the thought and picked up the phone on the dining table.

On the other end, it rang five times before a woman answered, then almost reluctantly, put him on. As Anna explained the situation, his comments were barely more than grunts. Until she asked, "Is there anything else I need to do right now?"

"Not unless you know how to excise a hot appendix."

What, a joke at this time of night? "Sorry. All I know to do is send him over on the boat in the morning. I'll call when I know what time, so you can arrange for an ambulance at the pier."

His sigh seemed exaggerated. "Well, I certainly can't get there. Between Jim Millett's patients and my own, I hardly have time to eat. Or sleep."

"I understand. And…uh, how is he?" She hoped he didn't hear her concern; far too intense for a nurse who was supposed to be objective.

"Frankly, not rallying the way I expected. Anyway, we'll talk more in the morning."

When she'd hung up, she went back to bed, but slept only in fitful bursts as the doctor's words about Jim echoed through her mind. Not rallying the way I expected. No, she thought; he had to rally, had to recover. Any other alternative was unthinkable.

***

Jean was working on the accounts book in the back office when Anna came in from seeing Mr. Dennett off on the trawler. “He was stable this morning, thanks mainly to the icepacks. And your help last night.”

Pleased that the nurse acknowledged her assistance, she’d murmured, “Least I could do for an old friend,” though she barely knew the man. He’d been here long enough, had bought the hardware store in the late thirties and moved his wife and kids up from some town on Cape Cod. But they were quiet folks who kept to themselves, so she’d talked to them only the rare times she was in the store. Until that night, when the notion had seized her that maybe Mrs. Dennett was as ignorant—or malicious—as her own mother.

Even now, expecting the man would survive, she felt the sting of old resentment. That her father, her own good and kindly Papa, had not. And mainly because her mother, her mean-spirited and whiny mother, had done all the wrong things. And not casually or in good faith, but with tight-lipped determination to have her way. Cleve had always called her hard-headed. Jean could only see her as evil.

“Sure wish I could’ve gone along with the patient.” Anna’s tone was mournful now. “To the hospital, I mean. But Fletch couldn’t wait long enough to bring me back. Storm’s closing in.”

“The hospital? Why? To see Jim? Now that’s downright silly, Anna. No need of you worrying about him. He’s in good hands.”

“I’ll only stop worrying when I see him for myself. That’s why I wanted to go along.”

Well, Jean thought smugly; if that didn’t prove her case. For months she’d wondered if the two weren’t secretly sweet on each other. Not that either had said anything. Probably wouldn't even admit it to themselves as long as Anna's husband was only missing. But she'd noticed the way they looked at each other, with soft-eyed gazes and a certain tilt to their bodies, like two lines curving toward each other. Surprising of Jim: his principles were like the rocks that ringed the island—stronger than any human consideration. She'd always recognized his professional inflexibility. But never as fully as she did since she'd become the victim of it. In this case, his insistence on turning Wil in. Doing the lawful, the moral thing, no matter who suffered.

Whenever she remembered, anger snared her like a trap for an animal. Because if Jim had looked the other way, Wil'd still be here, and she wouldn't be alone. By now, they'd have escaped from the island, maybe in Cleve's boat. Wil had assured her they'd have managed, gone down to Portland where he knew his way around. And had contacts who could provide forged documents—a draft card indicating 4-F status, a Social Security card, even a driver's license. And he was handy enough to do any kind of work without the tell-tale tinge of accent that might have given him away.

He'd planned every detail so thoroughly it was easy to believe it possible for them to appear just another anonymous hard-working young couple. The baby wasn't part of it, but Wil wouldn't have minded. Now, he probably didn't even know she was in the family way: she wrote letters every night and sent them to an address the Navy had provided, but with never an answer.

So Jim's fine principles had torpedoed the life they might have had, that halcyon happily-ever-after she'd come to trust the few days of intimacy during his convalescence. When the Navy had taken him away, another hole had opened in her heart, one even larger than the one caused by her father's death. Once she'd thought Ken Renaldi might fill it, but when he died and she felt only peculiar, numb relief, she concluded he'd been merely a poor substitute for Wil.

Therefore, even if Jim admitted his feelings for Anna, she'd never tell, not the nurse or anyone else, especially bleeding-heart Lorraine, who'd try to match-make. No; the best vengeance she could wreak on Jim Millett was making sure he lived without love too. Like she'd probably have to the rest of her days.

Except that even if Wil never came back, she'd have her baby, a child who'd love her forever, as no man ever would. A son, she hoped. A boy who'd grow up to be a dead ringer for his father, a young man who'd make her proud, take care of her and never leave. Never forsake, never betray, never abandon. Maybe that was the best any woman could hope for—not starry-eyed romance with some worthless dreamboat, but mothering a son in whom she could imbue virtues like her own father's.

Her mother, damn her, certainly hadn't done that with Alex. Despite the uniform and the heroic tales, he was still the same sonofabitch he'd been since the day he was born and blinded Eve Cropper to the needs of both her husband and two-year-old Jean. She'd made so much of him, in fact, by the time he was four he was getting away with transgressions for which Jean would've been switched till her legs were raw. He lied, he cheated, he stole from their mother's purse and shoplifted from the Variety Store; when he was fourteen he took their father's De Soto joyriding and overturned it on the high road. When she'd heard that news, her greatest hope was that he'd been killed. But no, the lucky bastard had escaped before it rolled down the side of the hill, crashing against the rocks and into the sea, never to be retrieved. And what'd happened to him? A few bruises, a bloody nose, a lecture from their father and his promise never to do it again.

Well, of course he wouldn't. Because soon afterward, he discovered girls and sex, which beat joyriding hands down. As Nature would have it, one of his little cuties turned up pregnant. To save his skin from the girl's shotgun-toting father, he'd promised to marry her. Yet only days before the ceremony, she'd miscarried, and let him off the hook. Jean hated his good luck, that, and the way he jumped from one escapade to another with some empty promise and no requirement he pay the piper. Even in the war, at least so far, he'd been luckier than most men. Maybe, as her mother claimed, he'd been born under a lucky star.

As her mind scanned memories of her brother, Jean's anger rose until she was rigid with it. Then she felt her baby moving inside her, tiny, hesitant thrusts she'd once assumed were gas. Now they reminded her of the promise she'd felt earlier. When she let Imagination take her deeper into this promise, anticipation began to soften her tense muscles. Before long, her lips curved upward in one of her increasingly rare smiles.

Chapter Fifteen

The next morning, Anna had a call from the daughter of a woman with congestive heart failure: she'd just found her mother dead. Anna left a message for the coroner, alerted Fletch he'd have another body to take to the mainland, and went to sit with the family. Stoics to the core, they'd known it was inevitable.

"Between Mom and Henry Ewell, that's two this week." The daughter shook her permed and bleached hair, the color and texture of excelsior. "You know, death always comes in threes. Hope the next ain't Doc Jim, sick as he is."

Anna started, barely concealed the acetic horror surging in her.

"It's that danged hospital, don't you know? Nobody ever gets better there."

She swallowed hard and forced a smile of false confidence like the one she used to convince patients they had nothing to worry about. "Sure they do. Why, just yesterday, Mr. Dennett had his appendix out, and he's doing fine."

Her long face was morose. "But he's not Doc. Mark my words, he'll be next."

"Oh no," she said, still with that pasted-on smile. "No, he'll be fine."

Yet for the rest of the day, this homespun prophecy

buzzed around like an angry hornet in her head. Later in the clinic, she jumped when Dr. Anderson phoned. "Is it Jim? Is he worse?"

"Well, no. But he's no better either. That's usually the way with double pneumonia. At least till the crisis."

She squeezed her eyes closed, clutched the receiver tighter. "Is he in an oxygen tent?"

"And having respiratory therapy and intravenous hydration. One of those new wonder drugs might help, but no go. Too bad. You'd think they could find some for a physician so many people rely on."

She sighed. "I wish I could come see him, but I can't leave the island."

"Oh, but he can't have visitors anyway. Except that priest from his church. By the way, I'll be sending your appendectomy patient home the first of the week."

"Well, that's good," she said without conviction. "And please tell Jim I'm praying for him."

She drove to the hotel later in a cloud of gloom that didn't dissipate even after two glasses of wine and a pep talk from Jean about not letting worry get her down. "After all, you have a responsibility to your patients, no matter how you feel personally."

Anna winced at the lecture, but nodded. "I know. It's just that…well, if anything happened to Jim, I couldn't go on working here. I mean, without a doctor."

"Oh for God's sake. Stop borrowing trouble. Even by yourself, you can do a hell of a lot more than you think. When you have to, I mean."

Mrs. Leech usually did supper dishes the next morning, but craving some simple, rote activity, Anna washed, dried and set them in the cupboards, all the while maintaining a litany of silent prayer. When she was ready for bed, she tucked Jim's handkerchief into the pajama pocket, knelt at the side and opened the Book of Common Prayer to

"Visitation of the sick". Twelve pages of psalms, antiphons, collects and prayers. Skipping through them, she came to "Unction of the Sick". In a loud whisper, she read, "I anoint thee with oil in the Name of the Father, and of the Son, and of the Holy Ghost, beseeching the mercy of our Lord Jesus Christ, that all thy pain and sickness of body being put to flight, the blessing of health may be restored unto thee. Amen." Then she pictured what her father often did for someone ill—laying hands on his head and anointing him with oil of chrism.

This done, he would've taken off his stole and closed the book. She closed the book, set it on the night stand, turned off the light and opened the blackout curtains. The night beyond was unrelieved by stars or moon, and she heard snow, or maybe sleet, ticking against the window. She could see nothing, but she stood staring into it a long while before, chilled, she climbed under the covers and drew them up around her ears.

Now the weariness of the day caught up with her. But even after she shut her eyes, her thoughts stayed on Jim. So persistent she gave up trying to shift to another matter, her parents, or Dan, or Jean, all of whom needed prayer too; right now, Jim's need was the greatest. Maybe her strange compulsion to pray was adding to his strength, speeding his healing. Hastening his eventual return to the island, and to her life. Whatever the cause, she chose to believe this with all the faith she could muster.

On a Tuesday night two weeks later, a quiet, intense snowfall blanketed the island with eight powdery inches. In the morning, Cleve drove her to the clinic in the sleigh, then parked on the pier to await *Molly B.* The sun was brilliant on the fresh white layer, but the cold was numbing. She'd wanted to meet the boat too, but patients had been coming in since she'd unlocked the doors. None had a major complaint; most apparently just wanted to lay eyes on Jim again. Just as she did, but more so.

By the time the trawler tied up, the waiting room was packed. Cleve urged his horse to the foot of the gangway. From the front window, she watched Jim leave the boat, climb into the red sleigh and ride over to the clinic. When they reined up out front, she trailed a crowd of patients to the lobby and watched him step down on his cane. The first thing she noticed was the beard he'd grown—darker than his hair, but salted with gray. And wild. Unkempt. The rest of him was so well ordered, it totally transformed his look. Then she noticed that the scarf she'd knitted him for Christmas was wrapped around his neck. Its alternating colored and white stripes added to the wild look. She was pleased; she hadn't expected he'd wear anything that gaudy.

After stamping snow from their boots, he and Cleve finally came into the lobby. In the rush of those welcoming him back with restrained Down East hugs, Anna hung back until everyone had had a turn and he'd made his way into the clinic. Finally she helped him out of his overcoat and scarf and hung them on the coat tree behind the counter. Backing away from the others, he motioned her to follow to his office. He went in and she closed the door, breathless for no reason except his presence. At last. Yet all she said was, "Good to have you back, Jim," in a quiet, professional tone. "Seems like forever since you were here."

He grinned, stroked the straggly tan and silver snarl on his chin. "How do you like the disguise?"

She laughed. "Well, it's more civilized than Fletch's, but it covers so much of your face I can't tell if you look healthy or not." Not exactly true; his cheekbones were prominent, skin sallow and pale, eyes dark-circled. Still, this close, she smelled fresh air and Bay Rum. And faintly, the masculine scent of his hair and skin.

"Don't worry. I'll shave it off the first warm day we get. Before it starts itching."

"You'll look more like yourself then." She waited, hoping he'd get around to offering an embrace of his own.

But he only glanced down at the desk. "Looks like you've kept things running just fine."

"Jean's been pitching in too. I couldn't have done it without her."

He raised his gaze, seemed about to say more. But when he did, it was only, "Well, guess we'd better get on with business."

"Of course." Despite mild disappointment, she smiled her competent nurse's smile. "I'll get the housebound patients' charts."

Except that someone had brought a celebratory chocolate cake which everyone nibbled on throughout the day, the hours passed in quiet, ordinary routines. With twice as many patients as usual, it was after one before they could leave on house calls. As they headed for the sleigh, Anna asked Jim if he needed to rest first.

He gave her a curious look. "No, I'm fine. Getting back to work's the best medicine I've had in weeks."

"Well, that's good news. This has been the busiest month ever."

His face sobered. "I know. Saw the case histories. Sorry you've had so much extra work. I promise I'll take better care of myself from now on." His gaze clung to her a moment, fortunately not quite long enough to start her face flaming.

Later, after *Molly B* had taken him away, she climbed down from the sleigh and stood in the fading day as the boat was swallowed by the indigo twilight. The familiar routine reminded her again that her life and Jim's were separate, linked only by their service to this island, not the ephemera of feelings, those vague emotions that came and went, as fleeting as clouds at sunset.

Deep in contemplation, she ambled back to the clinic. The snow was crumbled and powdery, numbing her toes in spite of woolen socks and boots. Strange, she told herself; Jim had recovered, returned to work for a day, then gone back to his mainland duties. He hadn't even hugged her, though he had almost everyone else. Winter still covered the world, and spring was a promise so remote she could take no heart from it.

Suddenly she was overcome with a yearning to see her parents again. Except for briefly at Christmas, she hadn't missed them till now. Their predictable routines, their simple admonitions, even her mother's affection that was so often cloaked in disapproval of some silly little something or other. She couldn't imagine taking a week off for a trip home, but maybe if she pleaded and begged, they'd come to visit here. So they could see the island where she lived and worked, and meet the friends she mentioned in letters.

Most of all, she wanted them to know Jim, even if in their infinite wisdom one or the other of them decided she was inappropriately fond of him.

Chapter Sixteen

On Tuesday, the sixth of June, Cleve lugged a big Emerson table radio to the clinic and set it on the counter so everyone could hear news of the Normandy invasion. Of landings on French beaches code-named Omaha and Jupiter and Sword. Of the massive fleet that had ferried thousands of Allied troops across the English Channel. And the mighty air umbrella protecting them from what was reported as feeble German resistance. Easy to conjure up a powerful machine rolling over the Nazis on their own continent. Optimism filled the air like the sweet fragrance of rambler roses cascading from fences all over the island.

But the next day, when reports of casualties began filtering in, Cleve took the radio home again. Jim was in the clinic, so Jean ventured from the back office to work the front desk while he and Anna saw patients. They were inspecting the bloom of a German measles rash on a toddler, when Jean knocked on the examining room door. Her voice was tense. "Anna, your father's on the phone."

Jim glanced up. "Take it in my office."

Her heart thudded with alarm as she picked up the receiver. "Dad? What is it?"

"Sorry to call at work, sweetheart." His voice was the

deep one he used for solemn occasions. "But we just got a telegram . . . from the Navy."

She sank into the chair facing the desk. "What . . . what does it say?"

"Don't know. Didn't want to open it without asking."

"It's okay. Read it, please." Hope lit her like a lightning bolt; maybe the boat was safe with all hands. Or maybe they were in a Jap prison camp. Wherever they were, it had taken the Navy a year to find out.

Her father cleared his throat. "Okay." More throat clearing. "Regret to inform you…'"

"Oh no." She had an urge to stop him, rewind the moment, return to the prior one of blissful ignorance.

"Sorry, sweetheart. Shall I read the rest?"

"Yes," she said, meaning No, no, no! Let her pretend the news was good for a few seconds longer, to prolong the past year of such pretense. But the practical voice in her head told her there was really no choice but to know. Now or later? "Now. Get it over with."

"Okay." He enunciated slowly and precisely, the way he read scripture at funerals. "Regret to inform you your husband Daniel R. Donovan LTJG USN missing in action since 15 June 1943 now reported killed in line of duty. USS *Wolf Fish*, presumed lost with all hands Pacific Theater of Operations on or about that date. Letter follows."

The breath went out of her. "Oh. Oh my." As if she were surprised. As if she hadn't had all those signs. But she hadn't known. Not the way she did as these clipped, official words—"Lost with all hands"-- slammed the door to her future.

Then her mother came on. Anna didn't want to talk to her, but knew she had to or her parents would worry about her composure. So she listened to homilies about faith, then her sentimental description of a layette the ladies' guild was sending Jean. "Nice new things, they are. Just like we give mothers in the charity ward."

After she hung up, she sat with one hand still on the phone, absorbing her parents' disparate conversations. Jim came in and asked if anything was wrong. Anna shook her head, swallowed the new truth, and got to her feet. Time to resume clinic duties. Put on the mask of cheerful courage again. Swallow one more bitter dose of grief. This was the worst, but at least it would be the last.

The rest of the morning, she felt Jean and Jim's concerned glances, but waited till lunch before she told them. Both murmured appropriate condolences, asked if they could help.

"No, I'm fine." She gave them a bright smile. "Remember, Jean, when you told me what happened to your fiancé, you said, 'The truth was hell, but at least I couldn't argue with it.' That's how I feel now." She couldn't imagine what else they expected her to say. Or do. So she did what she always did Wednesday afternoons when Jim was on the island.

But during house calls, a numbing fog crept into her mind, blurring her focus on patients' complaints and Jim's responses. On the way to the pier, however, he finally grabbed her attention when he said he'd set up an appointment for Jean with the Rockhampton OB man. "High time," he added, "being she's in her seventh month now."

Anna nodded. "At least everything's normal so far. I mean, her vital signs are good." Groping for words, she had to speak more slowly than usual.

Jim didn't seem to notice. "He'll see her Friday afternoon at four, so you can close the clinic early and ride over with Fletch. I'll pick you up in East Point."

"Both of us?"

He nodded; she noticed a flush to his cheeks. "Sure. You come along too. I mean, if you want to. Afterward, we'll have supper somewhere, then you girls can stay the night in my sister's old room at the house. What do you think?"

She stared for a moment as the brain fog thickened. "Oh. Well, I guess so."

His gaze turned serious. "Be good for you to get off the island for a while. You know, a change of scene. Might take your mind off today's news."

She could only nod.

"Can't tell you how sorry I am, Anna."

"Oh, thanks. But…well, it wasn't really a surprise."

"Still…" He reached across the seat and patted her hand. "Must've been a shock."

She wanted to say something bright and philosophical and reassuring, but Fletch already had the trawler's engine running. So she merely nodded and thanked him for his compassion. Then he was gone, limping across the pier and onto the boat. By the time she'd backed the car around and driven back to close the clinic for the day, the mental fog was pea soup. Fortunately, she knew the routines well enough to handle them by rote.

She and Jean had the usual wine with supper—Mrs. Leech's "special" chicken croquettes, new potatoes and fresh peas from local farms. In one of her more intense silent moods, Jean hurried through the meal as if trying to avoid discussion of Dan's death. Then, mumbling something about writing letters, she hurried upstairs while Anna washed the few dishes.

Finished with the chore but more restless than she'd been all day, she stepped out onto the back porch and contemplated the placid evening tinting the dunes, the beach below the cliffs and a line of small breakers in opalescent tones. Peaceful and serene, as if the world beyond the horizon wasn't bathed in blood.

Absorbing the familiar panorama, she stood motionless a long while. Until an urge to be close to the water sent her down the steps to the gravel path past the Cropper family cemetery, to another set of stairs to the beach. At the bottom, a demi-lune crescent of sand stretched between rocky bluffs rising like walls on either side. Beyond the tidal detritus as the base of one, the venerable longboat was pulled up where Jean and Cleve had left it after they'd rescued Wil from Little Hope.

Grasping the splintery rail, Anna stepped cautiously down the steep, rickety steps. The sea breeze was damp and cool in the warm evening, faintly salty on her lips. Drawn by the curling splash of breakers, she walked to the edge of the hissing ebb and flow, then hunkered onto a large flat rock just above the reach of the waves. And focused again on her father's call that morning. And the ultimate news about Dan.

As she stared over the sea, she felt the peculiar calm of knowing with certainty that he was gone, that she no longer had to wonder, or try to imagine what had happened. This was not so much a clearly defined knowledge with details of where, when, or even how the end had come, rather a dark emptiness where she'd previously sensed his presence. Like having watched an engaging movie to a climactic scene, only to have the film break and the screen go blank before the denouement. For a year, she'd waited for this story to resume. Until today, when she'd learned there was no more film, no more story. The end had come without so much as a sign, a dream or any other small coincidence she might have interpreted as a final message from Dan.

Perhaps, however, there had been one she'd missed at the very moment of his death. On or before 15 May 1943. Around the second anniversary of their meeting, what might she have failed to notice? A passing flutter of her heart? An inexplicable whiff of his aftershave on the breeze? A fragment of *All the Things You Are* on the radio of a passing car? Or a sudden violent scream only she could hear? Something to mark the moment when, ten-thousand miles away, her husband had drawn his last breath. For surely she should have known.

God, his last breath. Had it been peaceful, during the deadly sleep of anoxia after the masks were depleted and carbon dioxide had risen to deadly levels? Suffocating, had he retreated to his narrow bunk with the photo of her taped to the bulkhead? Had he ripped it from the black electrical tape and clutched it to him as he whispered his final supplication—a rote Our Father or Hail Mary? Or maybe her personal prayer of last resort, the simple Jesus, Jesus she'd once told him about? Yes, he'd liked that one best.

Or had that last breath been forced from him during the sort of cataclysm he'd avoided the year before? Perhaps in total darkness after the batteries were exhausted and all hope of reprieve gone, the boat had gone dead in the water. Settling ever deeper into the crushing depths, her steel frame and skin would have groaned as pressure warped them toward the breaking point. Could the crew still hear the enemy—the ping of sonar, the thrum of destroyer engines approaching and receding, the crash of depth charges? Or was the end of *Wolf Fish* and the seventy souls within her mercifully silent, except for the warning crunch of impending implosion? And the last prayers of the doomed?

Immersed in speculation, she watched an unfolding drama only her heart could see. Thirteen months before, by the Navy's reckoning, a day that would forever remain her Easter Saturday. Unlike that experienced by Christ's followers in their ignorance of the coming resurrection, however, her bleakness was lit by the church's promise of eventual reunion. But eventually wasn't soon enough, by God. She wanted his earthly presence—his living, breathing, eating, drinking, cursing, lusting, in-the-flesh earthly presence right now. Just as she'd ached for the baby when a chaplain had assured her she'd see him again; heaven wasn't soon enough for her wounded soul's reunion with husband and child.

Pierced by keen fresh sorrow, she sat unmoving, hands on her knees, palms up as if to receive the grace that could lift her above it. But nothing came, only the sense of staring into a black hole through which Dan had passed into infinity. The ultimate end of all her previous fears, her fading hopes, or the prayers for his safety in which she'd wrapped him.

Behind her, the sunlight faded; dusky blue shadows lengthened across the beach. Aware that she needed to return to the hotel while it was still daylight, she was about to get to her feet when a quivering gleam on the horizon caught her attention. Still unmoving, she watched it flare up into a just-past-full moon. Rising almost imperceptibly through the translucent cloud layer, it ballooned into a brilliant golden presence that shimmered on this placid sea just as, five hours before, it would have brightened the bloody surf of the previous day's Normandy beaches. And hours before that, the far reaches of the Pacific.

Since the first telegram the year before, she'd often imagined that somewhere in the world, maybe a Jap prison camp, Dan would be watching the same satellite's ascent and thinking of her. Tonight, however, she knew with certainty that it hadn't connected them for over a year. How much time, she wondered now, had she wasted on such hopeful speculation? Trying to assure herself of a happy ending that wasn't meant to be?

No answers even whispered to her heart. At last, putting the light behind her, she rose from the cold rock and turned toward the hotel's dark silhouette against the still-glowing western sky. Following her pale shadow, she picked her way across the rock-strewn beach, up the switchback steps and along the path across the dunes. As she approached the small cemetery, a vertical shaft of light, brighter than the moon and more silver than gold, caught her gaze between the graves of the German submariners. Curious, she stepped closer. And gasped to see a naval officer, in dress blues with the dolphin insignia of the Submarine Force above the service ribbons on his chest and the gold stripe-and-a-half of a jaygee on his sleeves.

Barely breathing, she recognized her husband, unquestionably and undoubtedly her husband. Her heart went into a wild, unreasonable dance that rocked her whole body. "Dan? Is that you?" she called. "Is it really you?"

He held out his hands and smiled the eye-crinkling dimpled grin that had first attracted her. Smiling too, she hurried toward him, a matter of just a few yards. But even as she came nearer, the light began to dim. And while she watched, he faded into the moonlit night. By the time she reached the iron picket fence, nothing was left but a swirl of mist between the bronze markers of the Germans' graves.

She groaned, "Oh, Dan. Don't go. Please? Come back, come back."

Nothing. Desperate to find him again, she pushed the gate open and picked her way across the uneven ground to the spot where he'd stood. Only the mist was visible now, but a faint trace of diesel fuel and cigarette smoke hung within it, as to confirm he'd actually been there, a fleeting but flesh-and-blood presence. Impossible, except for this ephemeral proof.

"Dan?" Her voice rose to a wail. "Oh Dan, where are you?"

Hardly daring to breathe, she paused, one hand on the cold granite of Jean's father's stone. The scent faded, the mist dissipated. Finally as returning reality squelched this stubborn new hope, she forced herself to leave the spot and walk the rest of the way to the porch steps. At the top, she turned quickly and surveyed the cemetery, dunes and beach below. The only movement was the incoming sweep of the moon-gilt waves. Dan was gone as surely as if he'd never been there.

Suddenly drained and limp, she sank into the nearest rocker. Covering her face with her hands, she let tears burst from the past year's reservoir. Whereas walls of false hope had previously contained them, now there was nothing to keep them in check. And no reason not to let them flow. No one would hear her sobs; no one would counsel faith, hope and optimism. Jean might well tell her to buck up—or grow up—but her room was on the other side of the hotel and at the far end. Yet even if there had been witnesses to her grief, there was no longer any way to reason with it.

She had no idea how long she wept, but when the tears had run their course, her pocket hanky was damp, the moon had turned white and climbed halfway up the sky. Finally, she struggled to her feet, and, feeling she'd left something valuable behind, went into the dark kitchen's smell of fried croquettes and old coffee grounds. By the time she'd plodded up the stairs to the second floor, the wonder of what she'd seen had been diluted by the tears. In her room, she pulled the curtain aside, stared into the night and waited for another sign of Dan's presence. But none came. In the bright darkness, the surf continued its ceaseless ebb and flow. And Dan did not appear again.

Exhausted now, Anna kicked off her shoes and lay on the bed watching the moon ascend. And prayed for strength to write Dan's parents about the new telegram. She might never tell anyone else, but they also needed to know about the apparition in the graveyard. Marie Donovan would probably correct her: no, it was not an apparition, a trick of the moonlight, or her own wishful thinking, rather a sure and certain glimpse of the transfigured Dan, bathed in the light of heaven. She was already convinced that the baby had been instantly received by the angels. "So now he's one of the lambs of God," she'd written after Anna had sent news of that loss. But for a devout Catholic, this sign that Dan was also with the Lord would afford the ultimate solace.

For Anna, however, it was just the last of all the signs she'd had that his presence in her life was destined to be only temporary. Only long enough to let her experience the breadth and depth and heights of first love, with all its passion and promise. And potential for heartbreak.

And now she had. Now she knew full well the scope of love found, and love lost. All she had yet to learn was how to live the rest of her life without it.

Chapter Seventeen

Friday afternoon, Jim dropped Anna and Jean off across the parking lot from Penobscot Memorial Hospital. Dr. Simon's office was on the second floor of a utilitarian brick building that also housed a dentist, an optometrist and a podiatrist. In the waiting room, Anna felt conspicuous for being the only woman with a flat belly. When Jean ignored her attempts to make conversation, she lost herself in a *Woman's Home Companion* story about a war widow and a wounded pilot. So rich with moonlight-and-roses that it gave her the half-sick feeling of having eaten a whole box of chocolates in one sitting. Maybe you had to fall for moonlight-and-roses once; after that, if you were smart, you recognized them as one of life's great romantic mirages. Like happily-ever-after.

When they'd arrived, the waiting room had been full. Within an hour only one other patient was still there, a honey blonde about Anna's age. With dimples, hazy blue eyes, and a suntan set off by the white collar of a navy blue smock, she might have been pretty except for a chin as pointed as a Hallowe'en witch's. Anna noticed these details with only the edges of concentration, until she realized the woman was staring at Jean.

"Excuse me, miss," she said. "Didn't your family used to

run that hotel over on the Island?"

Jean nodded, picked up a *Popular Mechanics* and began flipping through it.

"Lost your boyfriend a while back, didn't you?"

Jean nodded again, frowning now at the magazine. Apprehension began to chew at Anna's gut. Was Blondie just sociable, or on a fishing expedition?

Then she added, "Well, looks like you've found yourself a new one now."

By this time Anna was reading the same paragraph over and over, but trying to appear uninterested in the dialogue. Jean's lips were so compressed they could've been a pink scar.

"Heard somewhere," the woman persisted, "he's another sailor. That right?"

Intuiting Jean's trapped feeling, Anna wanted to intervene, but knew a careless blurt might well aggravate the situation beyond repair. She tightened her jaws.

"But this sailor, he's not one of ours, is he? Story is, he's not even on our side."

Anna sat rigidly, swallowing scathing retorts. Until she remembered words of Jesus and cut in. "Excuse me, madam." She forced false kindliness into her voice. "May I ask what that is to you?"

Before the blonde could answer, a bubbly young nurse summoned Jean inside. Inhaling deeply, Anna returned to her magazine but couldn't find her place in the story as anger stewed and seethed.

"Well, of course, it's none of my business," the other woman went on. "But if Jean Cropper's a friend of yours, you ought to know what people are saying."

Anna glared. "I never listen to idle gossip."

"More than idle gossip, miss. Everybody knows what she did. So listen, just tell her she'd better not have her…her little Nazi bastard here in this hospital. Or she might be sorry."

It took all Anna's resolve not to slap the self-righteousness from that smug face. Instead, she lowered her gaze and pretended to read further. She was still rigid with indignation when Jim came in fifteen minutes later.

Heading for the chair beside her, he called, "Oh hi, Nancy," to the blonde. "How're you doing?"

"Good, thanks, Dr. Millett. Only six more weeks till the baby comes. Jack and I can't wait."

"Give him my best." He sank wearily into the seat and turned to Anna. "Jean still in with Simon? Thought he'd be finished by now. Oh well, probably being extra thorough."

She jerked her head toward Nancy, now squinting at an old *Reader's Digest* as if she were actually interested. "Jim, do you know this lady here?"

"Uh-huh. Her parents are my patients. You two met?"

"Not officially. But she was telling Jean some malicious gossip. Says she shouldn't have her baby in the hospital here."

He frowned at the blonde. "What's that about, Nancy?"

"Oh, Dr. Millett, really. I was just trying to be friendly. People have such strong feelings about what happened over there last fall, I thought she should know. For her own good."

He flinched. Lines deepened around eyes and mouth as his face tightened, but he said nothing. Still, when the nurse called Nancy into an examining room, she fluttered her fingers as she went by. His gaze followed her across the room. "I was afraid of this. Should've known talk'd get around. Damn. Could be trouble."

"You'd have been proud of Jean though. She didn't say a word to that…that witch. Thank God she didn't hear her call the baby a little Nazi bastard."

He closed his eyes, slowly shook his head. "God, how cruel. Wish I'd been here. I'd have set Nancy straight. Not that it would've done any good."

"Oh, I don't know. When a respected member of the community speaks out, people listen. That's what my father always says."

When he didn't reply, she sensed his disgust and frustration were as acetic as hers. She wanted to hear more from him, but right away he grabbed a *Life* from the table and began flipping pages so fast he couldn't possibly be reading. His face was hard, but he said nothing more until Jean emerged from the inner office.

Her expression was grim-- it almost always was these days -- as she handed him an envelope. "Here. Dr. Simon's report on my condition."

They headed for the door, his arm around her shoulder. "Good. Well now, let's get supper, shall we?"

Feeling somehow excluded, Anna followed them down to the car and sat quietly in the back seat while Jim piloted the Buick through Rockhampton's placid side streets. As they neared the bay, she caught sight of a weathered frame building perched on skinny pilings just beyond a boat yard. Jim nodded toward it. "Clam Bake okay with you, Jean?"

"Good as anywhere."

As they walked from the parking lot, a warm breeze wafted the odor of iodine from puddled black muck. The tide was out and a fleet of derelict boats lay on their sides like beached whales. In the distance, Penobscot Bay shimmered between rock-rimmed shores. "Best lobster anywhere," Jim told Anna, "If you don't mind the casual setting."

"I'm sure it'll be fine." If anything would, she thought, after the encounter in the waiting room. Following the other two up the ramp to the entrance, she suddenly regretted having come today, and having witnessed the ugly scene. As well as being part of Jean's drama, and the complications she seemed to make for herself. Like her grudge against Jim even as he worked to ensure a happy outcome to this ill-begotten pregnancy.

Most of all, still reeling from the confirmation of Dan's death, she longed to be alone with her journal, not caught up in this convoluted relationship; But she'd had no choice. In this and in so many other aspects of life, she had no choice but to soldier on.

Inside, Jean excused herself to go to the ladies' room while Jim led Anna to a window table with a view of the boatyard. Red oilcloth covered the long tables; the air was heavy with hot grease fumes and noisy with the clatter of plates. It was early, only a few other diners in evidence. No menus here, just a stainless-steel counter serving lobsters, steamed clams, fried cod, french fries, coleslaw and corn on the cob. Roving waitresses supplied beverages and paper cups of marigold-yellow melted margarine.

He'd expected Anna to sit beside him, but she took a seat across the table. Silhouetted by low-slanting sunlight, her face was in shadow, expression difficult to discern. Nonetheless, he sensed she'd found the contretemps in Simon's waiting room unnerving. He'd been momentarily unbalanced as well, more than he'd let her see. Because it had given new life to his niggling premonition that Jean's situation would end badly.

Hoping to raise Anna's spirits, he pulled the OB man's report from his pocket. "Give me a minute to look this over, then we can talk. All right?"

"Of course."

He scanned Simon's slanted scrawl, noticed nothing that signaled problems, and glanced up again. "Seems okay, but I'll take a closer look later and make sure."

"Everything's normal then?"

"Apparently. Too soon to tell if she'll need a section, though."

"But what about the things that woman said? Is she likely to cause trouble? Should Jean deliver somewhere else?"

He took a deep breath and leaned the chair back on two legs, the way teachers always warned you not to. "Might be a good idea. In fact, she could stay with my cousin in Camden till term, and deliver up there But she'll probably just say, 'Nobody's going to tell me where I can have my baby.' You know how she is."

A quick nod confirmed she did indeed know, perhaps even better than he did after living with her for eight months. "But surely no one would try to hurt her in this hospital."

He shrugged. "Never call tell what folks'll do when they feel betrayed. Besides, Jean's not well-liked around here. Even in high school, she was too outspoken. Too quick to put people in their place. And now this…."

He felt Anna's speculative gaze, as if she was considering how to reply. Then she said, "You don't have much faith in human nature, do you? I mean, in people's basic goodness."

"Well, do you?"

"More than you, I think."

"Maybe because you grew up with a priest for a father. And haven't been in medicine long enough to be disabused of the notion."

Her shoulders moved under a red and blue striped sundress. "Long enough. Between nursing school and working, seven years. So I know plenty about human foibles. Still, I can't believe that woman's typical of folks around here."

"Maybe she isn't. But if there's even one person like her working in that hospital, well, that'd be enough to cause trouble. Not to mention mental anguish."

Anna took a deep breath, let it out in a sorrowful sigh and shook her head. But didn't comment. As if her mind was not wholly on this particular matter.

Of course not: only two days before, she'd finally learned of her husband's death. What was he thinking now, dumping his pessimism on her? His first instinct was to reach across the table and clasp her hand. But not only might she misunderstand, he'd never been one to express compassion or any other emotion in physical gestures. So he said, "Sorry, Anna. Hardly the time to get into that. After the news you got the other day."

"It's okay. Actually, it didn't really surprise me. Because…well, from the time I met him, Dan told me so much about the things that can go wrong on a sub, I never stopped worrying. And having premonitions. It was worse after they had a close call on one of their first patrols. And then, when they left San Francisco, I couldn't watch them sail. See, somebody once told me, as long as you're there when they sail, they'll come back safe."

He had no idea how to respond, except to murmur, "That must've been difficult."

She nodded, averted her gaze, clenched and unclenched her hands on the table top. "Funny, though, when the baby was stillborn, I took that as a sign Dan was okay." A tremulous smile seemed to suggest she'd soon realized her own folly. "For a while, I was comforted by the idea that the Lord wouldn't possibly let both of them die. And that gave me hope. But before long, I realized I was just grasping at straws." She shrugged and blinked quickly as the smile melted.

By now, the urge to comfort her physically had become almost irresistible. To dissipate it, he pressed his eyes closed and inhaled deeply. "Sorry. Didn't mean to pry."

"You didn't. But I guess maybe now it's time to stop

thinking about my losses. Move on to something more positive. Close the old book, and start a new one."

Start a new one? What was she trying to tell him? He had to know. "You're not talking about finding another job, are you?"

"Oh goodness, no. I still have four months on my contract."

Relief softened him. "Glad to hear that. Because you're doing a fine job here. Takes a load off my mind, the way you handle things. Like Henry Ewell's death and that appendicitis case. You knew just what to do."

"Jean helped a lot too."

"Sure. But I want you to know how I feel. Likely haven't told you before."

"Didn't expect you to. But thanks."

"Anyway, I'm damned grateful for everything you do. Couldn't be happier."

Now there was a bold-faced lie, he thought, forcing himself not to imagine the many ways she might make him happier. Just for openers, if she only reached across the table and clasped his hand, the warmth of her fingers could easily ignite a chain of even warmer responses. A luxury he could not allow himself to savor. Their mutual respect was too valuable to risk by yielding to adolescent fantasies. They were for men who lacked the foresight to predict the negative consequences of indulging them.

Before he could say more, Jean straggled back to the table. Her eyes were dark-circled, the fatigue on her face obvious. At seven months, women were supposed to glow. She merely looked burdened. If not by the child she was carrying, by the circumstances of its conception and gestation. Nearing the table, however, she turned on a smile and eased into the chair beside him.

"You two talking about me?" The smile lingered, not touching her eyes.

Jim settled his chair back onto all four legs. "Actually, Anna and I were just discussing that nasty woman in the waiting room. Don't think there's anything to her threats, but maybe you should stay with my cousin in Camden for the rest of your pregnancy, then deliver in the hospital up there. She's your age. She and Louise were close, so you might've met her a few years back. Kittie Meltzer?"

Jean's expression congealed into its usual hard planes. "Maybe. Don't remember. But why should I go up to Camden? My home's here." She wrinkled her nose. "And I hate hospitals, but at least I know this one. And Dr. Simon knows my case."

"Oh, just thought you might not want to run into Nancy Tweed again," he said.

"That bitch. In high school, she always looked down on us islanders. No siree, I'm not going to let the likes of that one run me out of town."

His gaze flickered to Anna's: See, told you so. "But she's probably not the only person who thinks what you did was…well, treasonous, to say the least."

"Too damned bad. Listen, Jim, I'll have my baby here. And anyone who doesn't like it can go straight to hell. Now. I'm starving. Let's get our food and eat."

That night, she and Jean shared a second-floor room at Jim's house that had been his sister's before her death ten years before. Her presence still lingered in the faded pink and pink and green floral chintz draping twin beds and a big bay window, in books and trinkets on the shelves, in her picture in cap and gown on the dressing table. But in the tiled bathroom across the hall, a frayed plaid robe on a door hook, and a shaving mug and brush atop the toilet tank were obviously Jim's. For Anna, noticing the everyday accoutrements of the ordinary man she worked with suddenly felt too intimate, too personal. Almost an invasion of his privacy. Even worse when she closed the door, the robe brushed her cheek with the smell of his body. She blushed, though he and Jean were still talking downstairs.

Later, when she and Jean were in their beds, she waited till the other girl had finished her nightly letter to Will before she asked, "Did Jim ever live here with his wife?"

"Oh, for a year or so. Why?"

"Just curious. And then she left him, right?"

"Uh-huh. Nobody was surprised. Only that she'd married him in the first place. Or come up here with him. Things might've been okay if they'd stayed in Boston where all her friends were. And she had plenty of parties to dress up for." Her voice turned sour. "Of course, Jim was never much for parties. All he wanted was to take over his grandfather's practice. So he moved her into this old house and told her to decorate it any way she wanted." Her sniff was derisive. "Only did one room. Her boudoir, of course."

Forcing herself to ignore the boudoir remark, she asked, "When did she leave?"

"Sometime the summer of 'forty-one. Don't remember exactly."

"Had she been his nurse?

Jean's laugh exploded mirthlessly. "Hell, no! Too classy for that. High society. Back Bay snooty. Don't know what she ever saw in him. Could be she just pitied him. Because he'd probably never been laid before she came along."

Anna rolled her eyes. "Gosh, Jean, sometimes you talk like a sailor. Where'd you learn that? From the guy you were engaged to?"

"Don't be silly. Everybody says those things. Anyway, according to Fletch, Jim was head-over-heels for her. Hard to imagine, isn't it, as straight-laced as he is."

Anna sighed, letting her imagination wander only to the

innocent fringes of his infatuation. “She was probably his first love. Like Wil was for you, and Dan was for me. Maybe we never really get over that first love.”

Jean’s tone turned strangely wistful. “Maybe if you can spend the rest of your life with each other. You know. Marry. Have kids. Buy a house. Get old together.”

“That’s right. Get used to each other.” Another sigh. “I never did with Dan. I loved being married to him. Except for the submarine part. But we only really lived together for four months, not nearly long enough to have all there is. What we did have was wonderful, maybe more so because we knew it was going to end.” The next sigh was heavy with old regret. “I can’t imagine ever feeling that way about anyone else.”

“Well, at least you had four months. When Wil was here summers with his family, we were together constantly. But we were young. And innocent. Besides, he was planning to become a priest. So we were sort of…you know…pure.” She was quiet a moment, her voice tearful when she spoke again. “When he was here last fall, though, things were different. Because we both knew it might be all the time we’d ever have. So, he was sick, but that was…well, it was our honeymoon. If you know what I mean.”

The vulnerability in the admission stirred Anna’s pity. “Of course I know what you mean. After all, you’re pregnant.”

“Then Jim had to turn him in and ruin everything.” Jean’s voice had turned hard again. “See, we could’ve gotten away. We might have had to hide till the war was over. But even so, we’d have been together. Except Jim had to do the right thing. Narrow-minded bastard. Serves him right he doesn’t have his first love either.”

Damn, always the same song from Jean—Jim was the enemy; her brother was the enemy. Her mother had been the enemy. Never circumstances, the war, or human nature.

Enmity seemed to flow through her veins, poisoning optimism and hope and good cheer. Warping her perception of others, and strangling her sense of humor.

Was that what repeated loss did to you? Anna had no such armor, only this flat, cold place in her soul—the eternal absence of Dan. Jim would understand, if they ever shared it, of course. Meanwhile, he was her employer, signed her paychecks, directed her professional actions. She couldn't let herself perceive him in any other way, with pity or an urge to pry into his soul, even as a means of distracting herself from the latest wallop of grief.

When Jean finally began to snore, Anna hugged the pillow against her body and turned toward the windows, where the waning moon floated up behind a fringe of evergreens. The sashes were opens, curtains drifting on a warm, harbor-scented breeze. Outside, the chatter of night insects was like a whirring lawnmower. Closer, she heard Jim's cane on the stairs, then its thump approaching the bathroom. The door closed, water ran, the toilet flushed, his steps retreated, another door latch clicked. Despite her resolve not to, she let herself picture him in bed, possibly scanning Dr. Simon's findings on Jean's condition. Beneath this surface concentration, what thoughts swam through his mind? Or was ensuring Jean's safe delivery his only concern?

That was it, she decided; he'd ponder only those problems he might solve. Wouldn't waste time on emotions, not grief for his lost sister, nor the wife he was no longer married to, nor any other absentees, including his parents. Above all he'd never dwell on recollections of lost love.

How long had it taken him to recover? Or had he, even in the years since he'd lost it? In the beginning, had the weight of sorrow pressed so heavily he thought he might never rise? Or was she the only one who felt it could easily take her down, all the way to crush depth, where the wreckage of other first loves washed endlessly back and forth in the restless seas of eternity?

No, she told herself with a sudden sense of resolution. Other souls lived with loss; she would too. Dan Donovan himself would expect no less from her.

Chapter Eighteen

Early on the last Saturday in July, Anna struggled out of sleep when Jean began banging on her door. Her voice was harsh and urgent. "Anna, wake up. I need you."

Just after six by her alarm clock, sky golden beyond the window, the room already warm with early sunlight. Flinging off the sheet, she yanked open the door. Jean's hair was wet and uncombed, eyes wide in her pale face.

"What's the matter?" Anna asked, instantly alert. "Has your labor started?"

"I guess it's labor. Anyway, what'll I do?"

Adrenaline chased the last sleep cobwebs. "How close are the contractions?"

"Half an hour, I guess. But they're not contractions, they're pains. At first, it was just a bad backache, so I took a hot bath, but it didn't help."

"When did they start?"

"Not sure. See, my water broke right after I went to bed, but when nothing else happened, I went to sleep. Till the pain woke me a while ago."

Alarms began to ping in her head. "Your water broke last night? And you didn't tell me?"

"I would have if I'd been having pains. But I didn't want

to wake you."

"When did you take the bath?"

"An hour ago. I felt so dirty by then."

Anna drew a deep breath to calm rising panic. And overcome an urge to scold Jean for failing to mention the ruptured membranes. "Didn't Dr. Simon tell you to come to the hospital as soon as your water broke?"

"Yes. But it was dark then. Cleve wouldn't have taken the boat out till morning anyway. So no harm done."

If you're lucky, Anna thought. "Well, time enough now. I'll let Cleve know, then see what Jim has to say. Now, come on in and lie on my bed while I phone. And if you get more pains, deep, slow breaths will make them easier."

Still in pajamas, she ran downstairs and asked the operator to ring Cleve's house. He was in the barn, but Lorraine promised to have him at the pier in half an hour. "Oh my God, Anna. Is there time to get her there before the baby comes?"

"I'm sure. The pains are still a half hour apart. So it may be ten or twelve hours. First babies aren't usually in a hurry, you know."

Lorraine's sigh was deep. "Oh, don't I ever! In my case, it took twenty-two hours. Hope she don't have to go through nothing like that. Say, you're coming with us, aren't you?"

"Sorry, I have clinic this morning. Nothing I can do at the hospital anyway."

When she called Jim, his voice was sleepy, but he assured her she hadn't woken him, and agreed there was no hurry. "Still, Dr. Simon will want to see her soon as possible."

"There's something else he should know. Jean had a bath before she woke me this morning. I'm sure he must've told her not to the last six weeks. But I guess she wasn't thinking. Or didn't realize there's a risk of infection."

"How long after the rupture was that?' he asked in his

serious, medical voice.

"Not sure. Maybe six hours. Anyway, a while after the contractions began."

He groaned. "Don't like the sound of that. Well, I'll pass it on to Simon. Anyway, see you when you get here."

"No need for me to come. Besides, I have clinic this morning. Meantime, you'll let me know how things are progressing, won't you?"

"Of course. I just thought . . ."

"What?"

"Nothing. We'll talk later."

Sensing that for some reason he was counting on her to be there, she added, "Actually, there's no reason I can't come after I close the clinic. So I'll see you later."

By the time she'd helped Jean down to the station wagon, an hour had passed; the contractions were now twenty minutes apart, stronger and more intense. When they boarded Cleve's boat, Anna helped her into the narrow bunk behind the pilot house and asked Lorraine to watch over her on the way to East Point.

"Sure," she drawled. "Not that there's anything helps labor pains. Lord, knows, even all these years later, I can still feel mine!"

Edging out of the little cabin, Anna told Jean she was all set. "Jim's going to meet you on the pier and take you to the hospital, so you'll be in good hands all the way."

"Jim be damned," Jean's pinched face streamed sweat in the cabin's mildewed closeness. "Weren't for his meddling, I'd be with Wil now. He'd take care of me."

Anna wanted to remind her the Lord was taking care of her now, but there were times in a woman's life when she didn't want any man around. Maybe Mary then. However, given Jean's staunch disbelief in any higher power, male or female, such platitudes might only rile her up. It didn't take much even when she was in one of her rare cheerful moods.

As she watched Cleve's little red boat come about in the harbor and chug out beyond the breakwater, Anna imagined Lorraine trying to distract Jean with tales of her own delivery all those years before, that long agony unrelieved by any promise at the end. Only pain and separation, the ultimate punishment for her transgression, while elsewhere in the Baltimore that day, good Christian men rejoiced at the Savior's birth.

Ironic, she thought, that she herself might never know labor pains. She hadn't yet felt any when a sudden hemorrhage had indicated trouble and necessitated an emergency Caesarian. Because the uterus was considered weakened by such surgery, the rule was, all subsequent pregnancies would be delivered by section too, optimally before labor started. So Fate could well have cheated her of the natural process Jean was enduring.

Praying silently that all would be well with this mother and child, she stared at the boat as long as she could see it, then drove over to the clinic for a long morning with other islanders' less compelling medical dramas.

Chapter Nineteen

When she hadn't heard from Jim by the time she closed the clinic, Anna caught a ride with Fletcher on the afternoon run to East Point. From there he drove her to Rockhampton in his rattletrap pickup, and left her at the front entrance of the Penobscot Memorial Hospital. Despite imposing fluted columns and marble steps of the front entrance, the dark brick building looked like an illustration from a Dickens novel of an almshouse, some final stop for the hopeless. As if to enhance the image, across the parking lot the power plant stack poured black smoke into the pastel summer afternoon. Like nothing so much as clouds of doom, she observed.

Inside, the dismal ambience was reinforced by the dried-up little clerk at the information desk; she refused to tell her if Jean had delivered or not, seemed reluctant even to direct her to the third-floor maternity ward. Across the hall, the elevator was a groaning steel cage run by a wheezing geezer in a wrinkled gray uniform. And the waiting room was a windowless area furnished with wooden chairs, heaped-high ashtrays and a table littered with old magazines. On the flaking tan walls, the only decorations were signs promoting Red Cross blood donations and Quiet!

Looking as if they'd rather be anywhere else, Cleve and

Lorraine were alone in the room. They greeted her listlessly, as if all the energy had been sucked from them by the gloomy setting. Like the setting for tragic stage play , Anna thought, trying not to yield to the presentiment.

Lorraine lit a fresh cigarette, waved out the match and told her the baby hadn't been born yet. "And if you ask me, Jim seems worried. Says everything's fine, but he looks like he don't really believe it."

The news lit a new strain of anxiety in Anna. She quickly cloaked it with platitudes and her cheery nurse persona. "Well, I'm sure it won't be long now. Meanwhile, have you had any lunch?"

Cleve shook his head. "Don't want to miss nothing."

"We won't. See, even after she delivers, we won't be able to see her for a while."

Husband and wife exchanged gloomy glances, shrugged, then got to their feet.

The cafeteria was a dismal cave in the basement; chlorine fumes from the nearby laundry almost overpowered the bitterness of stale coffee and cigarettes. Huddled around a wobbly pedestal table, the three of them picked at egg sandwiches and Coca Colas, while a large young man in an Army uniform fed so many coins into the juke box that it blasted out *Chattanooga Choo-Choo* the whole time they were there. They could still hear it as they waited for the elevator under dripping, steam-hissing pipes.

Jim appeared just after they returned to the waiting room. "Well, not much longer now." His smile was feeble. "They've just taken her to Delivery. Let you know soon as there's any news." He left before anyone could ask questions.

Anna made her expression cheerful, said, "Well, that's progress," took a seat and reached for a dog-eared *McCall's.* It took her a moment to realize she'd seen it before—in a new London Hospital after Betty Marks had had a miscarriage. The same snowy day in January, 1942, that Dan's boat had sailed for the Pacific. God, two and a half years now. And here she was in another equally-dismal hospital with another friend in pain. She hadn't known the Exec's wife as well as she did Jean, but the connection hit her as ominous.

Come on now, she cajoled herself; you're just looking for trouble.

It was another long hour before Jim returned, now in blood-spattered scrubs. This smile was wider, but didn't light his eyes. "Good news!" His voice was unnaturally high. "She had a hard time, but she just delivered a baby boy. Eight pounds, seven ounces. Healthy and normal as can be."

The shock Anna felt told her she hadn't expected good tidings. Almost a year since her own pregnancy had ended in tragedy, obviously not long enough to restore her faith in happy endings.

"His head's somewhat out of shape," Jim went on, "and there's forceps marks on his face, but he's fine, considering what he's been through."

Cleve asked, "Jeannie doing okay, doc?"

Anna hoped she was the only one who noticed the subtle change in Jim's face, as if his cheery demeanor was a thin layer, easily cracked. No, the others wouldn't; they weren't as attuned to shifts in his mood, professional and otherwise.

Jim rubbed his jaw. "Well, she's lost a lot of blood, so she's getting a transfusion."

Lorraine gasped. "A transfusion! Do they need us to donate?"

"No. Had it in their blood bank Now, anybody want to see the baby? Just remember what I said about his head. Few weeks, though, you won't even notice it."

At the nursery window, Anna joined the others in cooing and exclaiming over the plump, red-faced infant. While they were still admiring him, she beckoned Jim down the hall where Cleve and Lorraine wouldn't hear her ask, "Why did Jean lose so much blood?"

His voice was serious in contrast to the thin wail of newborns behind the glass. "Uterus didn't contract after delivery. Simon gave her a shot of ergotrate, but the placenta still didn't come out intact. So he went in manually for the pieces." He sighed, took off his glasses, rubbed his eyes. "Said if she'd come in sooner, he'd have done a section. Oh well, what's done's done."

"You mean, all's well that ends well?"

His eyes narrowed. "It hasn't ended yet, Anna."

She stifled a gasp. "That sounds ominous."

He nodded. "See, heard some talk in the scrub room earlier. About the Nazi bastard we were delivering. Wouldn't be surprised to see a swastika on his crib. Or worse."

This time she did gasp. Then she walked back to the window and regarded the blanket-swathed infant in the bassinet. Pure innocence, despite the circumstances of his conception. Whereas her own baby—she shook her head to dispel the next thought. Remembering that tragic day still closed her down, turned her to stone, slowed the breath in her lungs. Froze the moment, as if to enable her to re-enter, and relive, and somehow change the outcome. Yet it never did.

Jim replaced his glasses, straightened his slumping shoulders. "Now, why don't we go down to Recovery and find out how she's doing?"

She'd seen plenty of women immediately post-partum, but Jean's appearance was a shock. She seemed small and flat, like a doll that's lost its stuffing. Pale and used up, perhaps by her longing for Wil as well as the protracted labor. A bottle of blood dripped into her arm from an IV stand by the bed. She was semi-conscious; her eyes glazed when she tried to focus on them.

Anna smiled, took hold of Jean's hand. Cold and limp. "Good work, Jean. It was a long, hard labor, but now you have a beautiful little boy."

Her voice was weak. "I know. Saw him right after he was born. Then they gave me a shot, I guess to knock me out. Why? Is he all right?"

"Perfect," Jim said in his hearty voice. "You'll see him when they take you to your room."

A smile flitted across her face, like a butterfly trying to land on unfamiliar territory. "Only thing I wish now is that Wil could've seen him." Tears welled. "It's not fair, Jim. And all because of you."

He sighed, patted her hand. "Sorry, Jean. Wish I could've done otherwise. Now. How about I send Cleve and Lorraine in to see you?"

After the others had gone in, he said, "Hate to leave, but I have some house calls that can't wait. Tell you what, though. After I get back, maybe we could all have supper somewhere. My treat."

But fatigue was so deeply etched on his face and his shoulders so slumped, she knew better than to count on seeing him again that day for anything short of a major catastrophe. On impulse she patted his arm. "That'd be nice. But all of us are so tired, maybe another time would be better."

He regarded her seriously for a moment, then nodded. "Guess you're right. Tomorrow then. I mean, if you're planning to come over again."

She hesitated. "Mmm, not sure. Some chores I should do. Besides, if nothing goes wrong, Dr. Simon will probably send her home early next week. I might just wait and see her then."

Jim studied her so long, she sensed he was weighing his reply. Yet when it came it was only, "Of course. Well, I'll keep you posted." But as he turned and walked away, his limp more pronounced than she'd ever seen it, she realized he was disappointed in her. And she had no idea why.

For the next twenty-four hours, she was aware of a curious knot of anxiety in her chest that she could attribute to nothing tangible, nothing real, nothing but her own heightened though nameless fears. Yet Jim's Sunday evening phone report was anything but ominous: Jean and the baby were in a private room, three private-duty nurses he'd hired were caring for her round the clock. Moreover, she wasn't bleeding abnormally, had begun breast-feeding and was even able to walk to the bathroom. "If she keeps on like this, she'll be home Tuesday or Wednesday."

"Oh, that's good news. Well, then, I'll see her in a few days. Meantime, give her my best wishes."

"Oh? Hoped you'd changed your mind and come over with Cleve and Lorraine today. So we could have lunch. Guess it's been just you and me though. The others claimed they weren't dressed for a restaurant."

She was surprised at the let-down in his voice, and in her own mind. As if they'd lost a chance to spend time together in a non-medical, even social situation. Not solely as doctor and nurse, but something else. What, though? What defined their relationship besides the professional connection? What commonalities might unite them beyond medicine? The fact that they were both quiet, hard-working people who'd lost their first loves? She couldn't imagine he'd ever want to share that experience. But perhaps his concern that she might leave the job had convinced her to give her more personal attention. Yes, that had to be it.

Nonetheless, she felt curiously cheated. And as she bent over the ironing board in the hotel kitchen, her attempts to talk herself out of the mood only dug her in deeper.

Chapter Twenty

The ominous change began Monday. When Jim called that morning, his tone was so somber Anna intuited some new concern even before he said, "Don't say anything to anybody, but Jean began spiking a fever overnight. Not high, just over 100. Complaining of pelvic pain too. Saw her at rounds, but she's not my patient, so I'm waiting for Simon to examine her."

Somehow this news didn't feel unexpected. "Could it be from her milk coming in? Or a reaction to the transfusion?"

"No way to tell. Have to wait and see. Thought you'd want to know though."

"Thanks. Sounds like something to pray about. I've been doing that anyway, but this sounds…well, so urgent I might ask my father to pray too."

"Couldn't hurt. Anyway, I'll call when I know more."

After lunch, she watched from the waiting room window as Cleve's boat set out for the mainland. Four hours later, she was closing up when it put into the harbor again. A few minutes later, Lorraine bustled into the waiting room. Her face was dark, expression troubled. Before Anna could even ask, she said, "Something's wrong, Anna. With Jeannie, I mean. Jim said anything about it?"

"Oh, just that she had a slight fever. But that was earlier.

What's happening now?"

"Don't know. But you can tell he's worried. So's her doctor, that Jewish fellow, Simon something or other."

"They are?" She swallowed the fear lump that had suddenly ballooned in her throat. "What do they think it is?"

"Some sort of infection. They're trying to get one of them wonder drugs for it, but they're all going to the troops. None for civilians yet."

"Oh my." She drew a deep breath, made her tone cheerful. "How did she seem when you saw her?"

"Sick, Anna. Just plain sick. Too sick to nurse the little fellow, even. So they've taken him to the nursery and started him on formula. That don't sound good, does it?"

"Oh, they just don't want him to get germs from her milk. He's all right, isn't he?"

A small smile lifted the corners of her mouth; remnants of deep red lipstick still smeared the edges. "Oh my yes. His little head's still caterwumpus, but otherwise he's perfect. Not much hair yet, just some blond fuzz, and when he smiles—you know them little smiles they always claim's just gas?—I swear he has dimples! Jean thinks he looks like Wil."

Anna stuffed the last chart into the file drawer and forced it shut. "Well, I guess the only thing we can do is pray. I'll call my father and ask him to say one too."

"You mean, he'd pray for a girl with a bastard baby from an enemy sailor?" She shook her head. "If what she done ain't sin, I don't know what is."

"We're all sinners, Lorraine." She felt prim and preachy as the words came out. "And Dad says sin's all the same to the Lord, none better or worse than any other. So of course he'll pray for her. He prays for everyone, even our enemies, though my mother says he shouldn't help them that way."

"Well, maybe his prayers'll carry some weight. As for me, all these years I've been begging the Lord to keep my boy safe, I've worn out my welcome. But what else can we do, Anna?" Her dark eyes glistened with tears. "Poor Jeannie. She done wrong, but she don't deserve to be sick, not with a new baby to take care of. Even if he is a bastard."

Anna scowled her disapproval. "Well, technically that's what he is. But we shouldn't call him that. You wouldn't want anyone calling your son a bastard, would you?"

Lorraine's dark eyes widened and her mouth gaped, but she only shook her head and walked quickly toward the exit.

That evening, Jim's call confirmed Lorraine's suspicions: Jean's infection was spreading fast enough to be termed "fulminating". A culture had identified it as staphylococcal. In the old days, it would've been called Childbed or Puerperal Fever. He was baffled about how she'd contracted it. "Not really surprised, though," he added. "Anyone who wishes her harm had plenty of chances to contaminate her after delivery."

Horrified at the possibility, she said, "I think they use sulfonamide for that infection. But Lorraine said all the wonder drugs are going to the troops."

"Unfortunately that's the case right now." He was silent a moment. "Unless I can get some from the base at Brunswick. What was the name of that officer who took Wil away? Maybe he could help."

"I think it was Stark. Commander Stark. But why would he help? After all, Jean wanted to hide Wil till the war ended."

"Yeah, it's a long shot. But what do we have to lose?"

"I'll add it to my prayers, then."

Tuesday morning he called her at the clinic before any patients arrived. "The Lord must be listening to you, Anna." He sounded almost cheerful. "Commander Stark's driving up this afternoon with two ampoules of sulfonamide. All he could get." He chuckled. "Apparently he didn't go through official channels, just appropriated it."

Comshaw, she thought, Dan's term for such unofficial acquisition. Apparently it was more widespread than she'd ever realized, a form of petty larceny most commanding officers chose to ignore. "Oh my goodness. I thought he hated Jean."

"On the contrary. Says he admires her spunk. Off the record, of course." He cleared his throat. "By the way, I asked if he knew anything about Wil."

When he said no more, she coached, "And?"

Another sigh, heavy with reluctance. "Sorry to say, he was shot… trying to escape from some camp in West Virginia. Couple of weeks ago."

"Oh no." She paused, picturing him going hand-to-hand over barbed wire, men with dogs and rifles pursuing, cornering him in a tangle of woods. And showing no mercy. "Are you going to tell Jean?"

"Don't know. What do you think?"

What did she think? She tried to imagine her own reaction to such news, but could only go back as far as the phone call confirming Dan's death. And the cold numbness that had immobilized her for hours afterward. "Telling her now might make her lose the will to live. She's been afraid he'd be executed, but finding out officially…well, if I were you, I'd wait a while."

"Then I'll take your advice and hold off till she's on the mend. By the way, is there any urgent reason for me to come to the island tomorrow? Anyone really sick?"

"No one who can't wait till next week."

"Then I'll stay here and make sure she gets the antibiotic. But let me know if you need me and I'll come over afterward."

"We'll be fine," she told him, faking more confidence

than she felt.

That evening his news was less dire but hardly uplifting. "Well, she's no better. But no worse either. Only gave her the second shot this afternoon, so maybe tomorrow she'll rally. Meanwhile, keep on praying."

She told him she was praying more fervently than ever, but didn't add that her petitions were plagued by the same sense of futility that had clouded those she'd raised for Dan the whole year between the missing and killed-in-action telegrams. As if her soul had recognized the quality of doom about them, the premonition that what she asked of the Lord was already an impossibility. In Jean's case, recovery might still be a viable option. If indeed the Lord's will was for her healing. She had a vague hunch that it wasn't. When she'd first met the other girl, she'd struck her as fey, marked for tragedy, maybe even destined for early death. As if she held onto life only because she had to. Now, given a choice, maybe she'd loosened her grasp and was letting it float away like an untethered balloon.

Well, Anna decided, if she was bound to leave the world, maybe she needed to hear about Wil after all. "You know, Jim," she said into the receiver. "I've changed my mind. I think you should tell her about Wil. If it were me, I'd want to know. Especially if I thought I was dying."

"She may already suspect she is. See, she told me today if anything happened to her, she wants Lorraine and Cleve to raise the baby."

The confirmation of her theory was startling. "Then you really should tell her."

"Can't promise, Anna. I'll wait and see if the second shot helps. If not. . . . " His voice was flat with fatigue and the retelling of a story he must have recounted a hundred times before: We're doing all we can, but now we just have to wait and see. Over and over to family members clustered outside hospital rooms, despair conflicting with hope in their eyes. How did he manage to deal with these recurring tragedies, then go home to an empty house, an empty bed, and the prospect of only more emptiness in his own life? What reservoirs of strength he drew on she couldn't imagine.

Unless, of course, his Christian faith was more robust than her own.

In Thursday morning's call, Jim no longer made even a pretense of optimism. If the sulfonamide had made any inroads on the infection, they weren't enough to reverse the tide of the infection. "In fact, Lorraine and Cleve are staying at the hospital tonight. Just in case," he added.

"You mean… she might not live till morning?"

"Can't say for certain."

Anna groaned. "But I want to see her again."

"Then I'll have Fletch come over early and fetch you. You said there's no urgent cases on the island, so don't worry about the clinic. Now, try to get a good night's sleep. And keep praying."

"Oh yes. Sure. You too."

But again, her prayers felt too puny, too weak to intercede. And sleep was elusive, full of distorted images, fitful dozes and sudden awakenings to the horror of Jean's imminent death. It was better not to know beforehand, she thought, but to deal with death only as a swift and sudden event rather than a train you heard coming for miles before it hit you. As it had when she'd lost the baby, with no prior symptoms to signal that his lifeline, the placenta, had begun to detach. Her mother, of course, would lecture, "Where there's life there's hope." What would her father say? Thy will be done, Lord? She'd intended to call earlier, but by now it was too late to ask her father to pray for Jean. Or offer the comfort of his faith to her. Besides, any words, however he intended them, would be too empty to cling to. In these long dark hours before sunrise, there was only the grinding reality of a looming tragedy she was helpless to avert.

Chapter Twenty-One

She was already dressed when the call came just before seven. Mrs. Leech left the stove to stand by the phone as Anna listened. “No change this morning.” Jim’s words were even more clipped than usual. “Fletch’s on his way to pick you up. I’ll meet you on this end.”

When she’d hung up, she relayed the news to Mrs. Leech. “Ah, poor Miss Jean.” Her corrugated face was suddenly awash in tears. “To think the next time I see her, she’ll be in her coffin. Well, I ain’t surprised. From the time her daddy died, nothing made her happy. Not even that nice fellow she was engaged to. Now…well, almost like life don’t mean nothing anymore. ‘Specially since the Navy took that German boy away. No, I ain’t surprised, not a little bit.”

Anna gave her a hug. Then, feeling like a hypocrite, reminded her to pray for a miracle, and went to get her purse.

It was just eight-thirty when *Molly B*, her engine smoking from running wide open, nudged the pier at East Point. The mate cinched the stern line to a piling and ran the gangway over. Anna was well off and heading toward Jim’s car before he'd secured the bow line.

She was barely seated when he shifted into low and eased the Buick up the hill. "How much longer to you think she has?" she asked, dreading the answer.

His shoulders moved under a wilted white shirt. On this warm summer morning, he was hatless, a seersucker jacket folded over the seat back. "Her vitals were so bad last night, I was surprised she was still with us this morning. All the organs are shutting down, so there's not much time left."

"Didn't the sulfonamide help at all?"

"At first, I thought it did, but then the infection came back, twice as bad. Almost as if too little was worse than none at all. Oh Anna. I don't know what more we could've done. Neither does Simon, and OB's his specialty."

Pointless to keep talking about it, she thought, to keep pushing the same facts back and forth in hopes that one of them would suddenly yield a new truth. So she said nothing more, nor did he, until he'd parked in the hospital lot. And then it was only, "Keep your fingers crossed we made it in time."

Though he'd urged hurry, on the steps to the main entrance he was slower than usual, his face reflecting the pain of such exertion. Inside, he directed her down a corridor floored in scuffed black and white linoleum. Two nurses nodded as they passed the station. Just beyond, a bent crone wheeled a laundry cart and a stooped man pushed a string mop in glistening arcs. From every doorway, odors of urine and feces mingled with whiffs of stale coffee, ether and pine oil disinfectant.

Jean's room was at the end next to an emergency exit. "If you want, you can wait here while I see how she is." He gestured toward a worn wooden bench against a wall with green paint flaking like colorful dandruff. "Or… you can come in with me."

She followed him inside.

The foul odor of purulence didn't shock her, but the change in Jean did: her skin was yellow-tinged, hair matted, and her fever-glazed eyes stared without recognition. Breathing shallowly in the stink, Anna approached the bed, forced a smile and touched Jean's hand. On the other side, Lorraine and Cleve huddled in chairs, holding hands. They acknowledged her presence with only a minimal nod. Jim picked up the chart and beckoned her to read it with him. Looking over his shoulder, she did so by rote, dutifully absorbing the various notations, the neat script of several nurses contrasting with Dr. Simon's almost illegible scrawl. All told of rising fever, deteriorating vitals and the advancing spread of what had begun in the uterus and was now a systemic infection affecting heart, lungs and kidneys. "Pt moribund," was Simon's dry conclusion noted an hour before.

Without comment, she went back to Jean's side and touched her forehead: dry and feverish. "Jean, it's Anna," she said in her most composed medical voice. "Can you hear me?" She didn't expect an answer, at least not with a voice. Still, her eyelids flickered and she turned her gaze on Cleve and Lorraine, silhouetted against the window. Lorraine smiled and murmured something low and hopeful. Cleve only glanced at Anna and shook his head.

Just then a pudgy nurse in a tight uniform bustled in. "Excuse me, folks. Got to bathe the patient, if you don't mind stepping outside for a few minutes. Won't be long."

Anna led them into the hallway; Jim volunteered to take them to the cafeteria. "All they have this time of day's coffee and doughnuts, but it'll hold you a while. " Anna said she'd wait with Jean. "Well, if you need us," he added, "you know where we'll be."

Aware that "bathing the patient" was a euphemism for changing the soiled sanitary napkin and emptying the jar of caramel-hued urine beside the bed, Anna waited a few minutes before she re-entered the room. The nurse had just given Jean a shot in her thigh. “Morphine,” she explained, washing her hands at the sink. “Dr. Simon’s orders. Said he doesn’t know if she’s in pain, but it’ll give her some ease anyway.”

And possibly speed her on her way, she thought, but said, “Dr. Millett’s in the cafeteria. If you want to take a break, I’ll stay with her till he gets back. I’m an RN too.”

The older woman nodded, said she’d be at the station, picked up a magazine and left.

Alone now, Anna tried to ignore competing smells in the close air of the small room, purulence and Lysol in shifting layers. Antiseptic and decaying bodily fluids; and she knew which would eventually dominate. What was the use of all these efforts--Jim’s and Dr. Simon’s and the nursing staff--except to make Jean comfortable at the end? Was that the best their combined years of experience could do for this young woman who, a week earlier, had been in robust good health? The sense of some deaths was unfathomable, as she’d always known, but not with the keen despair that filled her now.

Fifteen minutes later, Jim came back alone. Cleve and Lorraine had gone outside to smoke, he said, glancing over the latest chart notes.

As if it might matter, she suddenly remembered, “Did you ever tell her about Wil?”

His nod was brusque, almost dismissive. Without further explanation, he said, “Listen, Anna. I’ve got two other critical patients to check. If you notice any significant changes, ask someone at the station to page me. And Simon too.”

She closed her eyes briefly, murmured, “Yes sir,” and felt his gaze on her a moment longer before he retreated to other duties. Watching him leave, she realized that for all his professional demeanor, he was even more affected by Jean’s hopeless condition than she was. His shoulders were stooped, and though it was still morning, his hobbled gait was that of a crippled man at the end of a long day. She was tempted to run after him and embrace him, if for no other reason than to remind him their pain was shared. Or could be.

After he'd left, Lorraine and Cleve returned, but looking hopeful now, as if a miracle might still be in the offing. Anna hated to shoot down their hopes, but neither did she want to encourage them, so she explained Jean had fallen asleep after the morphine shot. But her basic condition hadn't changed.

Murmuring to each other, they hovered around the bed for a while before they resumed their previous seats in front of the window. They looked so old, forlorn and exhausted that Anna realized nothing she might say could restore their faith—or her own—in a happy ending to this drama. Though she'd been there less than an hour, she'd begun to ache with the tension of reining in her emotions, of making small talk, of trying to behave like the professional she was. So, claiming she needed some air, she excused herself and left the room.

For a while she walked the first floor corridor from one end to the other, then sat on the bench outside Jean's room and observed late morning routines--nurses bustling from room to room, orderlies pushing gurneys, an elderly doctor making rounds. Obviously, this wasn't the OB floor. Medical, probably. No responsible institution would put a septic patient in with other new mothers. She could barely imagine the revenge of the nasty blonde they'd met in Simon's waiting room if they had.

She was mentally comparing Jean's care here with that given maternity patients at Portsmouth, when she saw Jim get off a distant elevator. Relieved, she walked to meet him, even tried to smile as she approached.

"Any changes?" he asked.

"Sorry." Maybe the smile had misled him. "But I've been out here a while, so maybe…"

He nodded, gaze unfocused. "Jean might not approve, but I've asked Father Danner to stop by soon. He's rector of my church."

"Oh, that's good." Last rites, of course, unction, forgiveness, anointing. The pending sacrament filled her imagination with the final scene of a novel she'd read in high school. What was it? *A Farewell to Arms*, of course, though there'd been no priest for Catherine Barkley as she lay dying after childbirth.

She followed Jim into the room; Jean was still asleep, her breathing more shallow and irregular. He read her chart, checked her pulse, touched her forehead, shook his head, then sighed. "She'll be okay for a while, so I'm going down for some lunch. Anyone want to come with me?"

Shocked, Anna said, "How can you think of eating at a time like this?"

His eyes widened and he shrugged. "Sorry, Anna. Nothing else I can do right now."

Cleve and Lorraine exchanged apathetic glances. "Right doc," he said. Nothing we can do here. Might as well come with you."

"Go on then." Anna's tone was clipped and self-righteous. "I'll stay with the patient."

As if she hadn't spoken, the couple trailed Jim from the room, moving sluggishly, almost reluctantly out the door. Shuddering at the memory of the dingy cafeteria, Anna settled herself in the chair between the bed and the window. It was open just enough to admit the clean smell of outside air. Below, a trash can-lined alley separated the hospital and the rear of the Mansion House hotel where a scrawny young man in a white apron slouched with a cigarette on a loading dock. When he noticed her and smiled up, she turned her gaze quickly back to Jean. Still sleeping, breathing slow, shallow, labored. Anna took hold of her hand--limp and cool. And her forehead too was no longer dry and hot. As if the fever had left her.

Once she'd have considered the diminished temperature a hopeful sign; now she recognized it as a grave indication that Jean's body was no longer fighting the infection. "Oh no," she whispered, squeezing her hand. "You can't give up now, Jean."

Almost as if she'd been waiting to hear her name, the other woman opened her eyes, blinked a few times, looked around, then back at Anna. Her smile was barely noticeable, her voice ragged with disuse. "Is that you, Anna? Wondered when you were coming."

Stunned at the reaction, it took her a moment to say, "Sorry. I've been busy. But Jim told me to take today off just to visit you."

Jean's gaze drifted, then swung back to her. "Today? What day is it?"

"Friday. The fourth of August." The fourth of August, the date her own baby had been born the year before. The image of a small cake with a single candle flared in her consciousness a moment. When it flickered out, it left a darkness in which a distant voice was chanting the *Agnus Dei*.

"I had the baby Saturday, didn't I?"

Deep-breathing herself back to the moment, Anna nodded. "You've been sick ever since."

"Sick? I don't feel sick now. I feel wonderful. But where is he anyway?"

"In the nursery. See, you've been too sick to nurse, so they're feeding him till you can take him home."

"Well, I want to see him now. Right now. Go get him, will you?"

She nodded, jumped to her feet. "Be right back."

Panicked, she raced down the hall to the station and spoke with all the authority she could muster to the private duty nurse, who was reading her *Look* magazine at a rear desk. "Nurse, Miss Cropper's rallied, so go down to the cafeteria and tell Dr. Millett, then fetch the baby from the nursery. She wants to see him." She swallowed the emotions that rose with the next statement. "She probably doesn't have much time, so be quick about it."

Back in the room, Jean was leaning up on one elbow. Her eyes were unnaturally bright, her color high. "Where's Auntie Lorrie and Uncle Cleve? They've been here so much, but now…"

"In the cafeteria. They'll be right back"

Jean sagged against the pillow. "Good. I have to tell them something. See. I want them to raise the baby if anything ever happens to me." Her eyes clouded. "Because Wil's not coming back. They shot him when he tried to escape from the prison camp."

"I know. Jim told me. And I'm so sorry." Turning away, she ran cool water onto a clean wash cloth from a pile beside the basin. "Now. Shall I wipe your face? Warm in here."

As if she hadn't spoken, Jean said, "Well, at least I have my baby. My little boy. That's more than you have from your husband."

Despite tears behind her eyes, she had to smile at Jean's reversion to her usual blunt manner. Almost like the day they'd met. Maybe that was a good sign; maybe this wasn't just a final rally. Maybe she'd passed the crisis. Maybe all things were possible after all.

"You're right," she said brightly. "Compared to you,. I have nothing. You're really lucky. By the way, what've you named him?"

"Johann Malcolm. After Wil's father and my own. But where is he, Anna? You said you'd get him."

"The nurse is bringing him. Didn't want to leave you alone."

Jean stared at her a moment, blankly, as if the tide of consciousness had already begun to recede. Her voice was fainter as well. "You're a good friend, Anna. At first I couldn't stand you, but you got nicer."

The nervous laugh that burst from her was still echoing in the room when Jim came in, Cleve and Lorraine trailing. Their smiles widened when they saw Jean was awake, but Jim only limped to the bed, picked up her wrist and felt for a pulse. When his eyes met Anna's, she read the worst. All he said was, "I'd better call Simon.

"Why? What can he do?"

"He's the attending physician. He should be here." He left the room again as the nurse came in with the baby. Snuggly wrapped in a blue flannel blanket, he was looking around and whimpering, his pink rosebud mouth twitching.

Anna took him from the nurse and laid him on Jean's chest. As her arms enclosed him, her face was transformed, as if lit from within. "Oh look, Anna. He's hungry. Come here and help me nurse him."

The nurse quickly stepped up with a four-ounce bottle of formula. "Here, Miss Cropper. Give him this instead. He's been taking them since you turned so sick. "

Jean stared a moment, blinked a couple times, eyes suddenly unfocused. "Oh. Maybe in a minute. All of a sudden I'm just so tired." She lay back against the pillow, her hold on the baby loosening. In one swift move, Anna lifted him before he could slide to the floor.

"Then have a little nap, Jeannie," Lorraine coaxed. "We'll still be here when you wake."

Jean turned her face away from the window, toward Anna and the baby. Her eyes drifted closed and she smiled, as if cosseting some secret vision, perhaps of Wil waiting on a far shore. Her body relaxed. Her breathing grew more shallow, with longer intervals between inhalations.

Appalled to realize the final rally had so quickly run its course, Anna clutched the baby closer and inhaled the sweet scent of his hair. When he kept squirming and squealing, she offered him the rubber nipple. Initially he nuzzled it with disgust, then began sucking, small fists tucked under his chin.

Lorraine moved closer to the bed, made the sign of the cross and took Jean's hands in her own. Shaking his head, Cleve sank into chair by the door, turned his cap in his hands and stared at his niece with pleading eyes. Anna went on feeding the baby.

When Jim returned, Dr. Simon was with him; his bald head gleamed in the overhead light as he bent and spoke Jean's name. She didn't respond, so he listened to her chest with the stethoscope around his neck while Jim and the other nurse stood at the foot of the bed, eyes downcast. The only sounds in the room were the baby's contented gurgles as he swallowed formula.

Dr. Simon straightened up, shook his head at Jim, then excused himself.

"What's going on?" Lorraine asked, panic in her tone. "Ain't she just asleep again?"

Cleve rose from his chair, encircled her with one arm. "Come on now, Lorrie. Nothing more they can do for her, that's all."

Anna said nothing, rocking the baby as instinctively as if she'd had a dozen kids of her own, as if this soothing rhythm had been programmed into her by years of repetition. His warmth against her chest was comforting, but his innocent ignorance of his impending orphaned status tore at her heart.

There was no clock in the room, but Anna felt she could hear time ticking away as Jean's breathing slowed further. Involuntarily, she held her own breath between the other girl's diminishing inhalations. The last one escaped as a long sigh. Anna waited for the one that never followed, then raised her gaze to Jim's and signaled him with her eyes.

He walked silently to the bedside, observed Jean briefly and picked up her wrist to check the pulse. With a minimal shake of his head, he gently replaced her hand atop the sheet, but laid his fingertips on the carotid pulse in her neck. Finally, he frowned at his watch. "Nurse, please chart that the patient expired at one-twenty-three PM."

Lorraine's gasp broke the heavy silence. "Expired! You sure, Jim? Sure she ain't just sleeping?"

"Sorry, Lorraine."

"No. No. She's just asleep. She was tired, Jim. But she's better. Why, her fever's even broke."

Someone knocked and pushed the door open. A small, fragile-looking man in black clericals glanced in, wispy white hair haloing his head. "Oh, hello, Jim. Is this the patient you asked me to see?"

Without speaking, Jim led the priest back to the hall. Lorraine began to sob quietly. Cleve held her more closely as they stared down at the lifeless young woman on the bed. In Anna's arms, Jean's son sucked earnestly at dregs in the bottle. Jim and the priest returned, the latter with a black stole draped over his shoulders; Jim introduced him as Father Danner. He'd hoped to pray for Jean's recovery, he said, but now he could only commend her soul to the Lord.

Anna steeled herself for the familiar words. And wondered, had anyone prayed over her son after he was delivered, stillborn? She clutched Jean's baby tighter as he sucked the last milk from the bottle. Then as Father Danner began speaking, she hoisted him to her shoulder and patted his back to get him to burp. He did so loudly, just as the priest spoke the final words: "Receive her into the arms of thy mercy, into the blessed rest of everlasting peace, and into the glorious company of all thy saints. Amen."

Anna felt the pressure of tears waiting to explode. Compressing her lips, she prayed to maintain composure until a more appropriate time and place. From her earliest years as a priest's daughter, she'd been indoctrinated with the necessity of seemliness. Of comportment. Decorum. This had been reinforced in her years as a nurse, and later as a Navy officer's wife. Emotional outbursts were the province of those who hadn't been raised with her advantages. Surely this training wouldn't fail her now.

Father Danner folded the stole and went from Lorraine to Cleve to Jim, wringing their hands and expressing sympathy. The nurse handed Jean's chart to Jim, then held out her arms for the baby. "Here, miss, let me change him so he'll be ready to go home."

Anna handed him over and moved closer to the bedside. By now Jean's face was more relaxed and peaceful than she'd ever seen it. Lorraine kissed her cheek, tears dripping onto the tangled auburn curls. Cleve stood there longer and said nothing, but his eyes were full. Finally, he glanced over at Jim. "Well, nothing to do now but take that little boy home. You think of anything else, doc?"

"No. I'll take care of everything. You know… the arrangements. If you want."

Cleve's nod was brusque. "Glad if you would. Be right outside, Anna. We'll go soon's the nurse brings the baby back. And doc, don't you worry about driving us to East Point. We'll just take the taxi."

"Nonsense," Jim said quickly. "Least I can do. Anyway, we ought to stop off at the Rexall first and get some formula."

Slowly, slumping with resignation, Lorraine gave Jean's body a last tender look and shuffled from the room. Anna followed, Cleve behind her, only Jim still at the bedside. Saying goodbye, she reckoned, as he'd had to do to his sister years before. And who knew how many other patients who had also been personal friends?

They met the nurse with the baby in the corridor. Holding out her arms, Lorraine received him, carefully as women unaccustomed to handling newborns do, him in his neatly-tucked blue blanket and his fresh smell of baby powder.

When Jim joined them, his face was ashen and grim. "Now, Lorraine. Need anything beside formula before I drive you back to the boat?"

"Oh maybe bottles. And some diapers," she said vaguely.

"Jean has a layette at the hotel," Anna volunteered.

"Oh God," Lorraine sighed. "God, what are we going to do without her?"

"Can't talk that way, honey," said Cleve. "Got a little boy to take care of now."

No one spoke as they came down the wide steps from the main entrance. Brash yellow light winked off cars, filled the lot with stifling heat. Anna was surprised the sun was still so high, as if they'd been in the hospital far longer than four hours. And even after they rolled down the windows, Jim's black Buick was an oven as he drove toward the drug store on the square. Parking down the block under a huge maple, he asked Anna to come in with him. At first she thought he wanted to talk privately, then realized he needed her to carry the bags with nursing bottles, canned formula, diapers, baby lotion. Too much for man with a cane to manage.

Afterward, walking back to the car, she felt her steps slowing as a sudden, painful reluctance to return to the island dragged at her. She halted at a patch of dappled shade where tree roots had buckled the pavement.

Jim turned with a puzzled expression. "You okay, Anna?"

She shook her head. "Sorry, Jim. I feel sick….I mean, just thinking about going back to the island. At least right now."

Sunlight shadowed deep grooves alongside his mouth.

"Well, okay. You don't have to."

"But...but what about the baby?"

He gave her his gentle, professionally reassuring smile. "Between Lorraine and all the other good women on the island, he'll be fine."

"Maybe tomorrow, then."

He nodded. "Sure. You can stay here tonight. In my sister's room. Or the boardinghouse. Whichever you want. You'll feel better in the morning."

Would she? Was he voicing medical fact or wishful thinking? "If you don't mind."

"Of course not." He patted her arm, leaned on his cane and walked on again.

In the car, the sleeping baby was making mewling noises, like a kitten. Riding beside Lorraine again, Anna tried to calm herself with deep breaths, but the nightmare sense persisted even as Jim pulled into the street, drove around the square and headed south again. They'd just passed a big funeral home when she made herself tell the other woman, "I hope you don't mind, but I'm...I'm going to stay over here tonight." Lorraine shot her a bewildered look. "Sorry. I can't go back right now. I just can't." She cleared her throat. "Can you and Cleve take care of the baby?"

Lorraine blinked as if she'd spoken in tongues. "Sure, Annie. Can't we, Cleve? Can't we take care of Johann tonight?"

"Best you start calling him Johnnie, dear. That Kraut name'll just remind people where he came from. Don't want them hating him already."

"No. It's Johann. That's what Jean wanted, that's what he'll be. And woe betide anybody gives him any grief about it."

In the rear view mirror, Jim's gaze met Anna's.

Ten silent, heavy miles later, they pulled up at the East Point pier. That colorful calendar scene again, glassy harbor reflecting stacked lobster pots, dories trembling on tidal ripples. Across the sound, the islands of the Hope chain shimmered in the afternoon haze. Without speaking, they trooped down the pier to Cleve's red boat. Odors of bait, diesel oil and low tide hung in the still air. Cleve stepped aboard, reached for the baby. Lorraine handed him down, jumped in and took the Rexall bags from Anna. The engine coughed and caught. Anna unwound lines from the pilings and tossed them aboard. At the next pier, the freshly-painted green hull of the *Molly B* towered over them. The smaller craft drifted away; Cleve advanced the throttle and came about, bow slicing a path through the shimmering water toward the harbor mouth.

No one waved, though Anna and Jim stood on the pier until they'd turned north around the last rocky point. Within moments, the diminishing sound of her engine and the fanning wake were the only sensory reminders the little boat had ever been there.

Jim's fingertips brushed Anna's arm. "Well now. Want to go back to the house while I telephone patients?"

She nodded mutely and followed him up the rough-paved slope to the car. Inside she sat staring silently ahead as he started the engine.

"You can rest, if you like. Or have a cup of tea." He backed around and accelerated up the hill. "Later, if you want to come along on house calls, maybe we can talk about…oh, what happened."

Squinting into low sunlight, he seemed the pale shadow of an old man. Like the ghost of his future self. Her heart softened for the grief that must be racking him. Compared to hers, his would feel like a crucifixion.

They came into his house through the kitchen door at the rear, into a big dismal room filled with old appliances and other neglected reminders of previous women in his life. Passing the gas range, he pointed out a tarnished copper pot.

"Tea's in the cupboard, along with some cups. I mean, if you'll make it while I make a few calls."

"Will you have a cup too?" she asked dully.

He paused, face softening. "That was one of my grandmother's panaceas. She was English. Whatever happened, she made tea." He straightened, sobered. "I'll be in the office, if you need me."

"Mind if I use the bathroom?"

" Know where it is?"

"Yes. I've been here before, you know."

"Sorry. Not quite myself today," he explained. As if he needed to.

In the tiny lavatory behind the examining room, she combed her hair, splashed cold water on her puffy face, smeared on fresh lipstick. But nothing changed the blank stare of grief. When she left the office, Jim was on the phone, speaking quietly and earnestly. If he noticed her, he gave no sign. In the kitchen, she set the kettle on to boil, found tea and an ironstone pot in the cupboard near the cups, sugar in another, milk in the old refrigerator, spoons neatly lined up in an oilcloth-lined drawer.

While the tea steeped, she stared out the window above the sink at the four-square brick house next door, beyond the Buick in the drive. This curious numbness was familiar, like a layer of ice on a pool of pain. She'd felt it the year before after days of private tears shed into the pillow of her hospital bed. But when she'd gone home to her parents, she'd soon realized weeping into a pillow behind the closed door of her room wasn't private enough. So she'd swallowed each new freshet of tears with a knot in her throat, and made plans for a new life on Hope Island, where she'd expected to be beyond the reach of such sorrow. Yet two months before, it had stabbed her to the marrow when the telegram confirmed Dan's death. Now, here it was again.

When the tea was ready, she carried a cup and saucer to

Jim's office. He was still on the phone, so she sipped hers in the waiting room and stared into space, aware only of multiple clocks ticking off the minutes of this black day. In the background, his steady business-as-usual voice droned on. Never mind what was chewing at his soul, always the reassuring professional for others. Where did he find such strength? Where her father did? Or were they both of necessity skilled in concealing their own pain?

Despite the occasional chime of some unseen clock, she had no idea how much later he came to the doorway. He cleared his throat until she glanced up. "Uh…listen, I'm going to make a few house calls now if you want to come along. Then, I… uh, have to go back to town." He swallowed visibly. "Just talked to the undertaker. They… well, they need a dress."

She was slow to comprehend. "Oh."

He nodded. "It's okay if you'd rather not go."

She got to her feet, smoothed out creases in her skirt. "No. I want to, Jim."

"Good. I'd welcome the company. Afterward, we could have supper. Feel up to it?"

"Yes," she lied.

The first two house calls were in the village, the last up a rocky lane to a hardscrabble farm on a cliff overlooking a tidal inlet. She waited in the car, swatting mosquitoes and inhaling the pervasive odor of cow dung. Chickens scratched and stuttered in the yard. A couple of cur dogs sniffed, then peed on the tires. She noted these details abstractly, as through a mist. As irrelevancies, as a stage setting for the final act of Jean's life.

Jim returned, tossed his black bag into the rear. His limp was more pronounced than ever, his shoulders slumped, face weary. "Thanks for being so patient. Now. Let's try Benjamin's for the dress. Ever been there?"

"Christmas last year. Alex Cropper brought me over so I

could buy presents."

He gave her a quick look across the seat, then made a tight turn in the yard and headed toward the county road. "Jean go along too?"

"No. She wasn't feeling well. It was just me. Till he met up with some high school chums." She shuddered in spite of the heat, was tempted to tell the rest of the story. But now it seemed only another vague irrelevancy, like the world around them. A story that in no way affected or impinged on the larger story that occupied their minds. Like the bloated corpse of some dead animal at their feet.

Benjamin's was a three-story department store across the town square from the Rexall. Friday night, open late for shoppers with fat shipyard paychecks. So crowded they had to nudge themselves onto the escalator. Ladies' Better Frocks was on the second floor. A smooth-haired young blonde in a black dress glided over and greeted Jim by name. When he told her they were looking for something really nice, she eyed the rumpled blue sundress Anna had worn all day. "And would it be for madam?"

"No. A friend of ours. What color do you think, Anna?"

Her mind raced around the color wheel for one that would complement Jean's pale complexion. "Oh, green, I guess."

"And what size does she wear?"

Baffled, all she could think of was, "Smaller than me."

"Eight? Ten?"

"Oh, what does it matter?" She was horrified at the wail of her own voice. "She's only going to be buried in it."

The girl's alarmed gaze swung to Jim. "Well, I'll see what we have in green. Why don't you have a seat?"

The pink velvet settee looked like furniture for some indulged and pampered woman's boudoir. Anna covered her face with her hands, wondered aloud how she could have blurted that out. Jim rubbed her shoulder. "It's all right,

Anna."

She made herself inhale a series of deep, slow breaths, so by the time the clerk came back, she could focus on the dresses over her arm. The first was mint green, heavily ruffled.

"Not her style," Anna said. The next was bright Kelly, a tailored shirtwaist with silver buttons. Like a uniform for the women's branch of the Irish army. She shook her head. The third was mossy, soft jersey, with a draped neckline. "That one I think."

Jim nodded. They followed the girl to the register; he paid with a fifty-dollar bill. Outside, they stowed the string-tied box in his car trunk, then crossed the square to the canopied entrance of the Mansion House. The black and white marble-floored lobby was lined with armchairs, potted palms, and stand ashtrays piled with soggy butts. In contrast, Ye Olde Coffee Shoppe and Grille smelled of steam and hot grease, just like the Lunch Box on the island but without the thumping, flashing Wurlitzer.

"Best food in town," Jim murmured. The smiling hostess led them to a window table with a view of the square and the white-spired Congregational church. Late light spilled through the trees and glinted on cars. The bus from Brunswick rumbled by. A few minutes later, two officers in Navy air greens strode past carrying ditty bags. Her gaze followed them until they were out of sight, but an abrupt knife-thrust of sorrow for Dan lingered.

Jim ordered the Friday night special -- baked cod, macaroni and cheese, boiled beets. Anna did too, mainly because it was easier not to have to choose. Then they sat staring past each other at the life of the town, proceeding as usual. Well, why wouldn't it? she wondered. It was only an insubstantial piece of her world that had ended. A death not nearly as significant as those of Dan and her baby, yet oddly enough, part of her trilogy of personal loss, unconnected to the other two, except in her soul.

Aware Jim was studying her, she felt fidgety, as if he had something of great import to say but wasn't sure he should. She was tempted to pick at her nail polish, but subverted the childish urge by folding and unfolding her napkin. Well, he'd said that earlier, hadn't he—"Maybe we can talk about what happened"? As if any words would help. Maybe what he actually wanted was to analyze the events leading to Jean's death and figure out what he could have done differently. Why? So he might harvest a modicum of medical insight from the tragedy? Or calm a nagging conscience?

"Penny for your thoughts, Jim," she said after a long silence.

He shook his head. "Odd, how few I have. At least that makes sense. I just keep wondering why things happened as they did. And when…when did they reach the point of no return?"

She laughed nervously, hoped he'd hear the irony in her tone. "Oh, probably when they found Wil on Little Hope. I think right then things became irreversible."

His eyes narrowed. "In other words, it was beyond control from the first."

She nodded. "Didn't we both have premonitions?"

His face turned more sober than usual. As if he'd just acknowledged a hard truth, perhaps one he'd always suspected but never allowed himself to verbalize before. "That's right, Anna. We did. And for no sensible reason."

She shivered despite the steamy heat in the restaurant, wished she'd thought to bring the bolero that went with the sundress. Instead she hugged her arms to her chest as the waitress approached with their platters. The scent was so revitalizing, her mouth began to water. She picked up her fork and stabbed a tomato slice awash in orange Russian dressing.

Jim watched her, then plucked a pale Parker House roll from the basket. “Can’t believe how hungry I am all of a sudden. An hour ago, didn’t care if I never ate again.”

“But you would have, wouldn’t you?” she asked between bites. “To keep your strength up. In case you had to go out again tonight.”

He shrugged and slathered the roll with brilliant yellow margarine. “Never hurts to be prepared for that possibility.”

“Oh Jim,” she sighed, with no idea what she meant. Maybe just You’re so damned good. So damned careful. But it didn’t matter, nor did he question her.

Without speaking, they ate fast, then ordered glistening slabs of lemon meringue pie. Savoring hers, she felt strength resurging through her weary body. Good it was, she thought, given their next stop.

The funeral parlor they’d passed earlier—“Moreton and Sons, serving Rockhampton since 1928”—was a low brick building on the southern outskirts of town. Inside the flower-scented hush, a viewing was in progress, people milling about quietly, murmuring condolences to family members in chairs rowed near the casket. Greeting Jim, of course, with an affection verging on reverence. In the background, an organ was whining out *The Old Rugged Cross.* After a few minutes, a dark-suited man approached with the standard unctuous smile. He nodded at the department store box as Jim extended it. “Anything in here besides the dress, Jim?”

“No. What else do you need?”

“Oh, maybe a necklace. Some personal jewelry.”

Remembering the pearls she was wearing, Anna reached behind her neck to unfasten them. “Here,” she said before she could talk herself out of the impulse. “Use these.”

Jim frowned. “But…you’ll want them back, won’t you?”

She shook her head. “No. Jean should have them.”

One hand on her elbow, he steered her outside. “Didn’t

you tell me they were a confirmation gift from your parents?"

"I still want her to have them."

The sigh was baffled "But you were wearing them when we met.."

"It's okay, Jim. I know what I'm doing."

He stared a moment and squeezed her shoulder before they resumed walking down the flagstone path to the parking lot.

On the road south, neither spoke till they'd crossed the inlet bridge. Then, sighing again, Jim said, "I know it's pointless, but I keep thinking about that sulfonamide we gave her. If that officer found two doses, couldn't he have found more?"

The question startled her. "How much would it have taken?"

"Oh, maybe enough for ten days. Only know what I've read about its use in service hospitals. In Jean's case, I thought if there was a chance…well, it was worth trying." He braked for two young deer grazing beside the road; they scrambled into a thicket as the car approached. "Guess it was what we said before: too little was worse than none. Or maybe too little too late. Maybe she should have had it right after delivery."

She hesitated, connecting to her early days with Dan, not sure she should mention it now. She did anyway. "When I met my husband, he'd just had surgery for a fractured femur, from a motorcycle wreck. Two days later, he began spiking a temp and had to go back to surgery. Apparently the initial sulfonamide hadn't been enough to prevent infection. So maybe it wouldn't have worked for Jean either. Of course he got plenty afterward, being in a Navy hospital."

"Of course," Jim echoed with unusual irony. "In her case, though, there's the fact that I told her Wil was dead. Maybe that took away her last shred of hope."

As he talked, she wanted to touch his hand, stroke it, connect with him physically from the depths of their continuing aliveness despite Jean's death. She stifled the impulse, as usual. "I think it would have made me want to live. For the baby's sake. Then again, maybe she did too. We'll never know."

"Jesus." He said the name so softly it was more prayer than profanity "If only I was sure…"

"Sure of what?"

"Oh, that I did right by her. Especially after she delivered. That had to be when she was infected. But who would've done that?" He shook his head with a weariness beyond any she'd seen in him before.

"But she was Simon's patient, not yours. What does he think?"

"Only that the transfused blood could've been contaminated. As for the notion that someone meant her harm, he admits it's possible, but won't look into it. Says it's too far-fetched."

"So it's another mystery we may never solve. Even though someone who'd harmed one patient might cause problems for others too."

"Yeah, I told him that. He said if it does happen again—any more suspicious deaths. I mean—then we can investigate. But that's cold comfort tonight. Besides—" His slow shrug suggested that he believed this was one of the situations that were beyond medical management from the moment they began to unfold. Unstoppable as the wind. Or human existence through eons of wars, famines, plagues and cataclysms.

Or the delicious appeal of first love, even when it seemed predestined to end tragically.

Chapter Twenty-Two

Back at his house, they entered though the kitchen again. Jim started up the hall, then glanced back at her, almost as if he'd forgotten she was behind him. "Want to phone your parents or anybody before I start my evening calls?"

"No, thanks. But are you sure it's okay for me to stay here tonight? Or should I go to Mrs. Goulding's?"

The hesitation was almost imperceptible, but she noticed. "No, no; here's perfectly fine. Now then. Can I get you a sedative? Or a medicinal brandy?"

"Nothing, thanks. I'd just like to go to bed."

"Okay. When I come up, I'll find you some pajamas. Sorry to make you wait. But I try not to use the stairs more than once a day."

"Take your time."

In the twilight of the dust-smelling room with the faded chintz curtains and spreads, she sat on the bed she'd used when she and Jean had been here before. Beyond the bay window the sky was the dulled purple that precedes darkness. From outside came distant music, canned and tinny, the occasional car whining up the hill. Warm and damp, the southwest wind brought whiffs of tidal mud and the sweet fragrance of new-cut grass. Lying back, she wondered if the sheets had been changed since they'd stayed overnight. Or would the pillow on the other bed still smell of Jean's hair? She was tempted to find out. But why? She asked herself. What was the point? Traces of everyone lingered after they were gone, residual wisps of remembrance that only affirmed a larger, unchangeable absence. Like Dan's Chesterfields, still in the glove box of his car back in Portsmouth.

Half an hour later, she was still staring at the windows when Jim knocked on the door frame, startling her from a reverie as irresistible as it was pointless. "Here, Anna. The pajamas I promised."

She sprang up to take them from his hands. "Oh thanks, Jim. But it's so warm, I probably won't even need them." She winced, aware too late that the comment might sound off-color.

"And a sleeping pill." He placed a small paper cup in her palm. "Wish I could do more."

"Don't worry. I've lost people before, you know."

"Yeah. But dealing with loss isn't like rehearsing a play. You don't get better by doing it over and over. With death, each one's harder."

She stood straighter, made her expression confident. "Look, Jim. I'm young and strong. I'll bounce back before you know it."

"Sure you will. But right now you must be hurting as much as I am."

She shrugged, clenching and unclenching her hands. "Well, anyway, thanks for letting me stay over. Hope it doesn't give you a bad name."

"What?" His eyes widened. "Don't be silly. I'm so colorless, nobody notices anything about me."

She wanted to seize the remark and pick it apart, exploring it until she'd extracted every subtle shade of meaning. But, aware she was a single woman alone in his house with a single man who was also her employer, she merely thanked him again and said goodnight. He shuffled away, crossed the hall to the bathroom and closed the door. Water ran; the toilet flushed. She waited a few minutes after he came out before she went in to put on the pajamas. A little large, but of a cool fabric, maybe plisse; they smelled as if they'd been dried in the fresh air, then ironed. Who would do that? His cleaning woman?

Finding no washcloth other than the one he'd used, she splashed water on her face, dried it on the only towel on the bar, then brushed her teeth with a finger full of his Colgate. Back in her room again, she closed the door and lay staring at flashes of heat lightning against distant clouds. Somewhere nearby a dog barked, and an unseen multi-engine plane crawled through the darkness. She whispered the usual prayers for her parents' and Margie's safekeeping, and for all the boys in the service, then for the souls of Dan and their baby. And now Jean's. And tried to picture those three together, smiling in supernal bliss. But the picture wouldn't develop. Despite the Church's promises, no one knew what the next life offered. Maybe it was all a myth anyway, to keep the grieving from giving up. A promise that offered less comfort than a pat on the hand to a heart slashed by one loss after another.

Lost in contemplation, she scarcely noticed the tide of pain receding as a numbing oblivion rose from the darkness and gently immersed her in nothingness.

Trying to ignore the electrifying truth that Anna was just up the hall, Jim paged through one medical journal after another from the haphazard pile on the nightstand. This routine usually calmed him for sleep while keeping him current with medical advances. Tonight, however, unable to focus on any topic for more than the first few sentences, he skimmed more than he read. Until an article on the use of antibiotics in Army field hospitals grabbed his attention. But it failed to answer his questions about Jean, so he set it aside.

When the downstairs hall clock chimed midnight, he switched off the light and opened the blackout curtains. The steamy southwesterly that tumbled in did nothing to diminish the tropical heat in the room, and a mosquito at the screen whined like a distant dive bomber. The sheets felt damp, pajamas absurdly restrictive; had he been alone in the house he'd have slept naked, at least stripped down to his shorts, but didn't want to shock Anna should their paths cross outside the bathroom. He even considered getting a fan from the storage room, but knew he'd crash around so much she'd surely waken, even if she'd taken the pill.

He began to relax only when he noticed sporadic lightning flashes, still distant enough to be soundless, and felt the first cooling drafts of an approaching storm.

He was asleep before the rain began, but awoke instantly when thunder crashed overhead and rumbled off into the distance. The sweet scent of rain blew in the windows; the eaves were dripping; more lightning flared; receding thunder grumbled. For a moment, his mind was a blank canvas. Until memory began to paint the previous day, freezing the moment of Jean's death in a bleak picture he sensed would forever haunt him. Despair clutched him awhile, then faded as he forced himself to detach from his emotions. It was an art he'd learned as a child with polio, then honed through the death of his sister, the departure of his parents and Ellen, and the loss of countless patients. And now—especially now, when his imagination led him to Anna and tempted him with futile and frustrating fantasies.

By the time the clock struck two, he needed to urinate, so he pulled himself upright on the crutch he kept by the bed and hobbled up the hall. Outside the bathroom, he paused when he heard muffled sobs from behind Anna's door. The ensuing spurt of sympathy tempted him to barge right in to comfort her. But first he used the toilet and washed his hands. Only then did he cross the hall, rap twice, and push open the door.

"Anna?" he whispered into the chiaroscuro dimness. "You all right?"

The sobbing faded and bedding rustled. "Oh Jim." Her voice was thick with weeping. "Sorry. Guess the storm woke me. Then I remembered what happened today. And I…well, it just hit me. I mean, that Jean's gone."

Without debating the propriety of his actions, he limped over to the bed. In the next lightning flash, he saw she was sitting up, sheet pulled high over her chest. Wordlessly, he eased down beside her and slid one arm around her. He half-expected a rebuff, but she only let him pull her to him. This close, the scent of her hair filled his nostrils. Not sweet with shampoo, but dank with the sweat of the previous hot day. Intoxicating nonetheless.

Dropping the crutch, he stroked her face with his free hand, felt her tears on his fingertips, the trembling of her shoulders under his arm, and within him, the even greater trembling of a familiar old force reanimated by this warm presence beside him.

For a few moments, he tried to focus only on the mutual, unspoken grief that connected them. Silent, more eloquent than any words. But no sooner had he acknowledged it than it morphed into a need for more, for a more tangible connection, for everything else there might be. He tensed to pull away, but before he could, she raised her head so her lips touched his cheek. Instinctively, he turned his face to hers, not in a full kiss, more a hesitant suggestion. Or a question generated in the intense moments they'd shared that day.

Barely breathing, he felt her mouth open with greater urgency. Longing burst with stunning fury as hunger seized him, first for her lips on his, then the feel of her body under his hands, and her hands on his own private places. In only a few heartbeats, he was sucked into a Niagara of desire so powerful he felt incapable of extricating himself even as it swept him toward the brink. Toward a point of no return his mind could barely imagine, at least with her.

He could, however, too easily imagine the aftermath of passion recklessly indulged—the awkwardness, the shame, the sense that a good relationship had been forever tainted. The concept imbued him with the strength to pull away, to say, “Better let you get to sleep now,” in a voice like gravel.

She gasped, as if she’d been slapped out of a dream. “Oh no. No, Jim. Please. I don’t want to be alone. Not tonight.”

The deep, resolute breath shuddered into him. “Can’t, Anna. I respect you too much.”

“But I don’t mean…you know…that. Just hold me.”

“Hold you?” He laughed quietly, wryly. “Look. I’m colorless, not a eunuch.”

“That’s okay. I don’t care. Whatever happens, it’s okay.”

Subsumed in the heat of her body, the taste of her mouth and the musky smell of her skin, he felt choked. In the four years since Ellen had left, he hadn’t seriously imagined Anna or any other woman as a lover. But that swiftly, wanting her was life-or-death urgent. Nothing romantic about it. He was nineteen again, with that sense he’d die if he didn’t penetrate her immediately. Except that in the intervening twenty years, he’d become habituated to an inner debate that had kept him—except with Ellen—from such regrettable impulses. In this case, the overweening logic was that he was a cripple who couldn’t have intercourse in the usual position, but only awkwardly and ungracefully. And possibly for Anna, repulsively. That was the worst of it—that she’d be repulsed and disgusted as

Ellen had eventually become. And never perceive him in the same idealistic light again.

He pulled away, reached for the crutch and hoisted himself from the bed. "Sorry, Anna. I can't do that. You know."

She sniffled. "Don't you…I mean, don't you want me?"

"Didn't say that."

"Then…why won't you stay?"

He inhaled to the depths of his being. "Sorry. I can't." He leaned a light kiss on her cheek. "Look, we'll talk tomorrow. Now we both need sleep. Want another pill?"

"Still have the one you gave me earlier."

"Take it. It'll help. And in the morning, everything'll look better. Trust me. It will."

She didn't answer; he stumbled to the door. "Goodnight, Anna." He waited a split second, but she said nothing more, so he hobbled back to his room, his safe, empty bed.

There he lay in a torment of recurring desire until hours later when birds began to chitter and the sky paled. Then, loathing himself for his weakness, he strapped on the abhorrent brace and put on the clothes he would wear for another day as a respected man of medicine. The term had an ironic ring. That was what he was to the town and the area, yet in his heart he was just another lust-dominated male who would gladly have spent the past night screwing his eyeballs out with a woman to whom he was neither legally nor spiritually entitled. In that regard, he was morally superior to none of his patients, not even those who routinely took their carnal needs to streetwalkers, from whom they often contracted the clap, which they brought home to their wives, then to him for a cure.

None of his patients nor any of those proper Episcopalians at All Saints' might suspect him of such common desires, but now Anna knew. Knew he'd been tempted; knew he'd looked on her with lust-blinded eyes.

And hadn't the Lord Jesus Christ himself declared that that was the same spiritually as actual adultery? Or, since neither of them was still married, fornication, which he supposed was only slightly less reprehensible.

Previously only Ellen had known of the fever he'd so long suppressed. Ellen, whose regard no longer mattered. But now Anna knew. That was the worst of it, the last thing he wanted her to know -- that in his heart, he was just another common sinner. A very ordinary man indeed.

Chapter Twenty-Three

When she woke the next morning, Anna only dimly remembered taking the pill, but not exactly when. The memory was imbedded in fog so persistent she was sure of nothing but sunlight at the window, brassy and hot. And the hands of the clock on the night stand at nine AM. Stupefied, she fought her way back to Louise's room. And the previous day. To Jean's final moments. And another memory she prayed was only a bad dream.

More pieces fell into place. Until she was sure--Jean had died. And something else had happened. She followed the trail: to Jim's house calls, the dress, supper, the undertaker's. Then back here, to sleep in his pajamas. For a few hours, at least, until a storm had hammered her awake. And reality ignited sorrow so agonizing she'd cried aloud.

But surely what happened next had to be a dream—Jim had come in, sat beside her on the bed. Together in the lightning-pierced night, they shared their mutual loss. Silently, they'd held onto each other in the steamy darkness. Now she had no idea who'd initiated it, her only surety the longing it had kindled, sudden as wild fire through dry brush. They'd drawn even closer, craving more, craving all the rest a man and woman could share. At least she had, though she was sure he'd been caught up in passion too, had felt the quickening of his heartbeat and respiration, the tightening of his arms around her, the ardor of his kiss.

And then he'd pulled away, just like that, had backed off. As if repulsed. Or shocked. Or disgusted by her invitation to hold her. Of course, he knew what she really meant. Lie with me, Jim; make love to me. Have intercourse with me. She hadn't had to say the words. He'd been married; he knew the scent of desire.

And wanted none of it. For God's sake, of course not. She was his professional employee, his nurse. Yet she'd behaved like the wanton that the letch on the Brunswick bus had thought her. Oh God, how could she ever look Jim in the eyes again?

Eventually a full bladder sent her to the bathroom. From downstairs came the murmur of his voice, likely in the office. Probably on the phone again. He was scrupulous about maintaining contact with his patients. A man of principle and probity. Not a man to yield to the blandishments of just any woman. A man on whom, she was sure, the shadow of scandal had never come close.

Stung with remorse, she made herself as presentable as possible in the previous day's dress, then tiptoed down the front steps and waited at the office door until he glanced up. In unison, both said, "Good morning."

He averted his gaze, mumbled, "Coffee and cereal in the kitchen, if you're hungry."

Though he wasn't looking at her, she turned on a wan smile, said, "Thanks," and walked down the hall toward the smell of stale coffee. As he'd promised, a pot was on the range, a box of Wheaties, dishes on the drain board. She lit the gas under the pot, dumped flakes into the bowl, then took milk from the refrigerator, which was empty except for a bottle of Heinz ketchup and a jar of dill pickles. She doused the cereal with milk and sugar, poured coffee, then carried them to the white-painted table in the center of the scuffed black and green block-patterned linoleum. There, she sat primly staring out the back door at the sultry morning beyond.

She was still spooning up cereal when she heard his cane in the hall behind her. "Find everything you need?" His tone was formal, like the host's at some genteel, historic inn.

"Oh, yes. Thanks."

"Good. Sleep well?"

"Very well, thanks to your pill." Her gaze dropped to the soggy flakes, the gray coffee. She suspected she was blushing.

"Good." He cleared his throat. "Listen, I just talked to Moreton's. They'll have the casket at the pier by one. You going back then?"

She nodded, shoveled in more mushy cereal, gulped bitter coffee, swallowed with difficulty.

"Viewing's tonight, funeral tomorrow afternoon. I'll come then, but I can't tonight. Sorry. I've gotten too far behind this week."

"Business as usual, eh?"

His expression tightened. "No, not as usual, Anna. Why'd you say that?" Leaning on his cane, he seemed a forlorn, bewildered child, even to a lock of hair drooping over his forehead.

She was tempted to spring to her feet and embrace him, kiss his cheek, stroke the hair back into place. But obviously he didn't want easy affection. Or her clumsy attempts to comfort. "Well, you have to do what you have to do, I guess. Like soldiers in combat. You can't stop to nurse your wounds anymore than they can."

His smile seemed tight and forced. "Ah, maybe you do understand." Then the phone rang and relief softened his features. He hurried back toward the office, though there was a wall phone beside the refrigerator.

Forcing herself to finish eating, Anna washed the milky

dish and cup under hot water with a vegetable brush. Then, restless, she prowled the dismal, old-fashioned room, as if some clue to Jim's reality might be included on pantry shelves filled with jars of age-darkened preserves, and domestic items a woman would use—iron and board, toaster, waffle maker, Mixmaster under an oilcloth cover. A glass-fronted cabinet displayed mismatched china, bowls, glasses, vases, and platters. On the rear service porch a wringer washer stood beside soapstone tubs, with a line-up of laundry products like her mother's: Rinso, Oxydol, bluing, starch. Out back, iron clothes poles were set into the yard, but no line connected them. The grass was sparse, no flowers or shrubbery anywhere. If Jim's Buick hadn't been parked in front of the sagging garage, the place might have seemed abandoned. Empty. Maybe even haunted.

Like a metaphor for his life.

She used the back stairs when she went up again. After another ersatz tooth brushing, she folded the pajamas and took them to his room. Before she set them on the pillow, she leaned her face into it and inhaled the stale smell of his skin and hair. The longing it stirred verged on pain, even sharper than the night before. Breathing deeply and slowly, she was relieved to be distracted by a picture on the dresser. The woman looked older than she, dark hair in a well-behaved pageboy, full lips and wide, smiling eyes under well-shaped brows. Ah, the glamour-girl wife, she reckoned.

No wonder he hadn't wanted her, Anna; how could he ever forget a woman like the one in the photo?

Hearing patients arriving downstairs, she clutched her purse and hurried down to the front door as they went past her into the waiting room. In the tiled vestibule she stood with hand on the knob and wondered what to do with the two empty hours before the boat left. As if anything she might do could put her back together. Today she was

Humpty Dumpty, with no hope of restoration any time soon. The most she could hope for was killing time.

When an elderly woman with a cane turned in at the gate, Anna went out, nodded and walked past, then took the nearest cross street up to a weedy vacant lot on the hilltop. Below, the sound spread like a blue velvet cover; on the horizon, the islands were veiled in humidity. No wind dissipated the sultry heat, the sort to spawn thunderstorms and sudden squalls. But please God, she prayed, please not till after Jean's body had been delivered to the church. Let her final homecoming be tranquil.

In spite of gasoline shortages, wakes from two racing speedboats fanned out white on the cobalt water. The week before, Fletch had said there were more vacationers this year than since the war started. He thought it because, "People're feeling a lot better since D-Day." Paris had been liberated; Allied armies were pushing through France. Even Alex Cropper had returned to duty.

Oh God, Alex. Abruptly aware she'd have to write him about Jean, she stood for a long while absorbing the heat of sunlight on her skin. And her father too; she'd have to call him with the sad news, that his prayers—all their prayers—had failed. The prospects made her want to curl up in the dry grass like a wounded animal.

Instead, she yielded to gravity, letting it pull her down a succession of sloping streets to the harbor. On the pier, two middle-aged women in floppy sun hats and artists' smocks were dabbing at canvases on easels. *Molly B* was tied up beyond them, her hatch open, Fletcher and the mate tinkering with the engine. Anna wandered closer, sat atop an old barrel. The pungency of linseed oil and turpentine blended with the odors of tidal muck, diesel fuel and old fish. Rainbows of spilled oil swirled around pilings. Heat waves radiated from the pier planks.

Before long, one of the artists called, "Excuse me, miss,"

in a nasally New York accent. Odious, except when it had tinged Dan's voice. "Do you know if there's any place to stay over there?" She gestured at the hand-lettered sign nailed to a piling. *Hope Island Excursions. $2 one way, $3 round trip. See Captain Hood for schedule.*

Anna swallowed hard as Jean's memory intruded. "Well…the hotel's closed for the duration. But there's a boardinghouse in the village."

"And what about a restaurant, one with a nice harbor view?"

"Oh, the Lunch Box, I guess. But it's not very picturesque."

"Thanks. Maybe we'll ride over this afternoon."

When the noontime siren went off at the firehouse, Anna walked over to the snack counter for a bottle of Nehi and a lobster roll. The sandwich was more roll than lobster; it stuck in her throat until she swallowed warm soda. Aware of apprehension tightening her chest, she realized soon the hearse would arrive. Would Jim be there when the casket was unloaded? She hoped not; his presence had always been as calming as oil on water. But after their aborted tryst the night before, would he even want her as his nurse? Perhaps her out-of-control behavior had even poisoned their working relationship. After all, no self-respecting doctor wanted a sex-starved strumpet in his employ.

It was quarter to one when the Cadillac hearse, gleaming like polished onyx, purred down the hill. At the pier, two black-suited men rolled the casket onto a catafalque and pushed it to the trawler. The artists stopped painting and stared. Fletcher and the mate helped carry it aboard.

Anna headed toward the boat. "Doc coming along today, nurse?" Fletcher called.

"No, he's busy. He'll be there for the funeral though."

"Reckon half the town'll show up. Everybody knew Jean. Well, no sense crying about it today. Tomorrow'll be soon enough." He glanced at the artists. "You folks coming with us?"

They exchanged glances, shook their heads grimly and returned to their paintings.

On the boat, Anna hunkered into one of the folding canvas chairs Fletcher now supplied for tourists' comfort. He'd also rigged a canopy to shade the afterdeck. Today she was the only passenger to enjoy the amenities. The only living passenger, at least. At the stern, the casket was lashed to cleats and the sea was an undulating mirror, but he made the crossing at a reverent half-speed, agonizingly slow for someone accompanying a corpse.

When they came into the cove, Cleve and two other men were on the pier with the horse and wagon. For the first time since she'd arrived ten months before, Anna had to force herself to set foot on the Island. Still, she waited in the shade of a cedar while they unloaded the coffin, then she walked behind the wagon up the hill three blocks to the church. She didn't enter until they'd carried it inside and set in on an iron stand in front of the altar. Lorraine was already there with the baby in a frayed wicker perambulator Jean had had Cleve bring down from the hotel attic and paint white. The infant was sleeping on his stomach, hands under his chin, tiny mouth making sucking motions.

Fighting off waves of old regret, Anna admired him a moment. "My, he's such a beautiful baby. Was he good last night?"

"Oh yeah," the other woman said. "Best baby ever. Makes it even worse Jeannie's not here to take care of him."

Anna swiped fingertips across her cheeks. "But she'll watch over him his whole life. His guardian angel."

"Don't talk foolish, Anna. He needs a mother, not a guardian angel."

"Sure. But now he has both." As she spoke, she imagined Jean's reaction to her sweetness-and-light homily. She could barely stomach it herself.

Inside the church, flowers were banked on the altar, window ledges, even the floor. Improbable arrangements—sunflowers in tall vases, roses in cut glass, Queen Anne's Lace and wild chicory in Mason jars, zinnias and marigolds in juice glasses. A wild profusion from the island's gardens and roadsides.

When the men opened the casket, Lorraine and Anna lit candles. And made themselves look at her in the moss-green dress, in the satin-lined coffin, a white lace cover drawn up to her folded hands. Her dark auburn hair was a mass of tight waves, face chalky with make-up, stiff lips redder than she'd ever painted them. Anna's pearls glowed against her lifeless skin.

"Cleve doesn't want to leave her alone tonight," Lorraine whispered. "Some people still can't forgive what she done. He's afraid they might cook up mischief. So we're going to take turns watching. Want to help?"

"Of course. But… mischief? What kind of mischief?"

"The worst. See, a few years back, some islander went off to prison for shooting a man who seduced his wife. When he died, they brought him back here to be buried, but his body went missing in the night. Later they found it in a sunk boat washed up on No Hope." She shook her head. "It'd kill Cleve if something like that happened to Jeannie."

Shivering, Anna gestured toward the flowers. "Surely nobody feels that way about her."

"Don't want to take no chances, Annie." The baby stirred, whimpered. She jumped to pick him up, cuddling him on her shoulder till he quieted. "Be a while till I get used to having him all to myself. Lots of nieces and nephews, but this is different. I can't take no chances with this little boy."

When Cleve offered to drive her to the hotel, Anna said she wanted to walk instead. Her body resisted the idea, but plodding up the long hill in the August heat had the feel of a pilgrimage, inducing discomfort so intense it soon distracted her thoughts from the viewing, and the orphaned infant. Even Jim's rejection.

Mrs. Leech was in the kitchen peeling a potful of hardboiled eggs to devil for the funeral lunch. Her granite face was damp, her unexpected hug fervent. "Oh, nurse, whatever are we going to do without Miss Jean?" She blew her nose on a pocket hanky. "Cut down in her prime, like somebody in the war. Ain't none of us safe, are we?"

"It's a terrible loss." Her voice was as funereal as the undertakers' who'd delivered the body.

Upstairs, her room had been cleaned. Across the hall, Jean's room looked as if no one had ever used it, all her things gone: hairbrush, mirror, perfume atomizer, even Alex's framed photo. Only in the bathroom was there a trace—the yellow toothbrush next to Anna's in the porcelain holder. Of all her possessions, the most humble.

After a long bath, she lay on the bed, inhaled pungent sea air, listened to the surf below, and tried to imagine living here now with Jean gone. No matter how she tried, she couldn't picture it. Well, maybe that was telling her something. No point keeping the hotel open for one person anyway. Instead, maybe Lorraine would let her move in with her and Cleve and the baby.

Or maybe...maybe it was time to leave the island altogether.

Like a farmer plowing a field for the first time, she turned the idea over to see what lay beneath. Initially, it felt so drastic and surgical, she set it aside and concentrated instead on what to wear to the viewing. Her one black dress was a severe, high-necked linen that Margie claimed made her look like a nun. Well, then. Since she'd given away the pearls, she'd complete the image with a silver cross on a chain. Maybe this chaste persona would help Jim forget the wanton who'd tried to seduce him.

Then again, maybe there was no eraser for such memories. She sensed this one was destined to grow into a wall between them. High and frigid as winter ice floes on the beach.

The possibility brought back the idea of leaving, but now with more surety. Maybe it was indeed time to put Hope Island behind, time to reassemble her life in a place empty of so many chilling recollections. Ironically, the year before she'd left Portsmouth for similar reasons. Now she had no idea where she might go, nor did she try to decide. Enough that she'd acknowledged the first step she had to take.

Chapter Twenty-Four

The first few days after the funeral, the idea took on form and substance. By Wednesday morning, it felt so much like a fait accompli, she knew it was right as soon as she awoke. She'd already asked Lorraine if she could board with them until Jim found another nurse. Her parents too had promised to welcome her for as long as she wanted to stay. The only thing left was to tell Jim her intentions. And pack.

Her big suitcase was still in the basement, but the smaller would hold enough to tide her over for a few days. Summer things didn't take up much room anyway. Gathering her toiletries, she froze at the sight of the yellow toothbrush. Tempted to take it, she decided it should stay where Jean's hand had put it. When would that have been? Probably the night before she went into labor, when her life had begun sliding down that long last hill.

Tears came on, not a flood like the one at Jim's house, just a salting for her cheeks. She splashed cold water on her face, carried the bag downstairs and went to the kitchen to tell Mrs. Leech she was leaving. "But I'll see you again," she promised without conviction. They exchanged a hug, mutually tearful, and the usual clichéd good wishes before Anna headed for the door.

Driving away, she watched the hotel recede in the rear view mirror. With all the upstairs shutters closed now, the place looked forbidding, like a mysterious manor house on an English moor. Or one of those abandoned frame buildings that were often consumed by sudden, unexplained fires on windy nights. She sighed and glanced back at the road, relieved that if this one did go up in flames, she wouldn't be there to watch it die.

At Lorraine's, she unpacked in the colorful room where she'd rested the night of the U-boat incident, then walked down the slope to the clinic. Waiting for Jim, she rehearsed the little speech she'd prepared. He probably wouldn't notice, of course; he'd barely spoken to her at the funeral, or afterward at the hotel for the reception. If she hadn't had the bedroom experience with him, she might have realized he'd been monopolized by the priest from his church, and some old friends of Jean's and his sister's from high school. And then one of those ocean fogs had rolled in, moving Fletch to round up his passengers so they could get back to the mainland before it turned to pea soup. As it was, she interpreted their distance as yet another sign from God she was meant to leave.

When Jim arrived at the clinic, he beckoned her into his office, waved toward a chair, "Have a seat, Anna. If you're not too busy."

"No, not yet. What's on your mind?" She tugged the uniform skirt over her knees and clasped her hands in her lap, prim and chaste as any devoted churchwoman.

He ran a finger around his shirt collar. "Well, mainly . . . how're you feeling today?"

"Fine, thanks."

"Really?"

She blinked with surprise. "Yes, really. And you?"

He lowered himself into the squeaky chair behind the desk. "Sad. Just so damned sad."

"But you're not letting it get you down, are you? I mean, you're here, doing your job."

The frown was barely noticeable. "Anyway, I was hoping we could talk after the funeral. But then there was the fog. And the phone—well, you know how the operators are."

She nodded, tensing for a lecture. "Then maybe this is a good time. Because I need to tell you something. Something important."

"Oh? What's that?"

She closed her eyes in a slow blink, then studied her clasped hands so she wouldn't have to see his expression. "Well, mainly… just that…well, I'm thinking of leaving the island. Cleve's closing the hotel, you know, so it seems like a good time."

His jaw dropped. "Leave? What do you mean? Go home a while?"

"Well, yes. But I can't say for how long. I know I contracted to stay a year, but the way I feel now…. well, I'm not sure I can."

He winced as if slammed by a blow to the solar plexus. "But why, Anna? Because you miss Jean? Because it's too painful at the hotel now?" He made a broad gesture with both hands. "Tell me."

She shrugged and inhaled deeply while she chose the precise words. Finally, in a small voice, "Not just the hotel. Everything here hurts now."

"I don't understand. About Jean, sure. But what else are you talking about?"

She shook her head, forced her gaze from his, finally whispered. "Mainly, what happened with you that night."

He stared with such a hard gaze she had to look away. "Oh? What about it?"

Dear God, didn't he know? "Well, to start with, I should've gone back with the others. Or stayed at the boarding house. Because I, uh…I lost control." She paused, expecting his baffled expression to change, but it didn't. "And now I'm too ashamed to even think of staying in the job. Working with you again, I mean."

He blinked and cleared his throat, tugging at his necktie as if it were too tight. "Well now. Don't quite know what to say about that. Except…is leaving the answer?"

She swallowed a hard knot in her throat, with no idea what he'd be feeling. Disgust? Or relief? "It's the only one I can think of right now."

"I see." The stare continued to knife into her. "Well, that's what you should do, then. Get away for a while. Go home. Spend time with your parents. Maybe things'll seem better after a while. If they don't, well, you wouldn't be the first nurse who left before her year was up. Actually, you've stayed longer than any of the others."

Relief began to loosen her chest muscles. "Then maybe…maybe you should look around for another nurse. In case I decide not to come back."

Finally, she saw twinges of pain on his face, tightening the lines around his eyes, tensing his mouth. "Oh, Anna. I'd hate it if you didn't."

She shrugged again and clenched her hands more tightly.

"But if that's what you want, I understand."

"It isn't what I want, Jim. I want Jean to be alive. I want to erase that awful night. I want things to be the way they were before. But none of it's possible, is it?"

He continued to regard her with sorrowful eyes, then took off the glasses and rubbed his eyes. "No, of course not. We can't turn time back." He blinked a couple times, then slid the glasses back on his nose. "Actually, the nurse who helped me last winter's between patients at the moment. She needs the work, so maybe she could fill in for a while."

She hadn't expected to agree so readily, but said, "Good. When can she start?"

"Why? When do you want to leave?"

"Soon. Soon as possible. Tomorrow, if I could."

His sigh sounded like I give up. "Well, whatever you have to do. But I must say I'm shocked. Of course, losing your child, and your husband, and now Jean, that's been hard. But the other…for the life of me, I can't see why you're upset. I knew you were hurting that night. People do all sorts of things when they're in pain. It doesn't change the way I regard you."

"That's good. Because your opinion really matters."

He stared a moment longer, expression perplexed. "Don't you know nothing will ever change that? You're a fine nurse. A fine person."

She wanted to shout "Is that all I am?" But knew he'd realize an emotion beyond grief had inspired her bedroom advances. She'd always been sickened by women who begged for love, in real life, fiction or films. And now, oh Lord, she was turning into one. "Thanks. And I'm sorry. About letting you down, I mean."

He rose, leaned heavily on the desk. "You're not letting me down. I'm going to consider this just a temporary hiatus."

"Sure. It's a temporary hiatus. Then we'll all live happily ever after, won't we?"

His smile had a wry twist to it. As if he knew all too well that happily-ever-after came only in small servings. Like candy to bribe kids. "Anna, I hope you find what you're looking for while you're gone. I want you to come back. But if you can't, I wish you well."

Of course he did. This gentle man dealt lovingly with everyone. Even a woman for whom he had only the purest fraternal feelings. Dear Jesus, why did that truth have such a sharp edge?

***

That evening, she was helping Lorraine with the supper dishes while Cleve strolled around the yard with Johann in his arms. “He’s showing him the garden and the horse and those mangy old hounds of his,” Lorraine said. “He’s crazy about the little guy, but scared he’s going to break.”

“Having the baby here probably takes his mind off Jean.”

“As much as anything can.”

She realized she’d been drying the same plate for minutes. “Speaking of Jean, today I told Jim I need to go home for a while. Asked him to look around for another nurse. In case I don’t come back.”

The glass in Lorraine’s hand dropped onto the drain board and bounced into the dishpan. “Oh Anna, why? Because she died?”

“That’s part of it.”

Her dark gaze bored into Anna’s pretenses. “And what’s the rest of it? Jim?”

She gasped. “For goodness’ sake, why would you think that?”

“Well, when you didn’t come back after Jeannie—after she passed-- I wondered if something was going on. You and him…oh, I’ve seen sparks for a long while. So what happened? Did he go too far, and now everything’s changed?”

She shook her head. “He didn’t. I was the one. I . . . I threw myself at him. He wouldn’t, though. You know. Guess he’s still in love with his ex-wife. And now he’s upset with me. Probably thinks I’m a strumpet. So you’re right—everything’s changed.”

Lorraine studied her as if she were speaking in code.

“So, with Jean gone, there’s nothing here for me now. Only the job.”

Lorraine’s gaze drifted across the yard to her husband, cuddling Johann in one arm while he pointed to a gull soaring over the barn. “Oh, Anna, I know that hurts. Cleve and I have each other, and that precious baby. But I can see where you must feel awful damned alone. I wish you wouldn't leave, but if your heart's broken, well, I understand."

Later, in her room she studied the small framed picture of the priest who'd broken Lorraine's heart. Now her new anguish linked them in a sisterhood of grief with women the world over. If there was consolation in knowing she wasn't alone with her go-nowhere affection, it did about as much good as an aspirin for the surgical incision of an appendectomy.

Saturday morning, Jim phoned: the other nurse could start on Monday. "So you're free to leave whenever you want."

"Okay, then. Tomorrow," she said firmly.

"Very well. If that's what you want." His tone was…what? Cold? Sad? Even in ten months, she hadn't glimpsed the inner workings of this man. For all she knew, he could've been a robot left over from the World's Fair. A man with such magnificent control of his emotions he might as well have none at all.

The next morning, Cleve took her to East Point in his little boat. Once he'd intended to name it for Lorraine, but had never gotten around to painting *Miss Lorrie* on the stern. Now he talked about calling it *Jeannie;* what did Anna think of that?

"I think she'd like it," she murmured, eyes suddenly wet.

On the other side, she'd arranged to meet Fletcher for a ride to the bus, but instead, Jim was waiting on the pier. Surprised, she lugged the bag toward his car. "Where's Fletch?"

"Thought I'd take you myself. Not just to the bus, to the

train at Brunswick."

He opened the rear door. She set the suitcase on the seat, got in the front. "Kind of you, but I'd rather you dropped me off at the bus."

"Can't just let you leave the way you arrived, can I?"

"It'll be fine, Jim. And you'll have time to go to church afterward."

He shook his head, stepped on the starter. "Stubborn to the end, eh?"

She watched a small boy being tugged down the hill by a husky black Labrador retriever. "I never knew you considered me stubborn."

He ignored the comment, put the Buick in reverse, looking over his shoulder as he backed around. He was in his navy blue suit, a freshly-laundered shirt, a red and white striped tie she hadn't seen before, and Panama hat. Before he shifted to low, he glanced at his watch. "Well then, if I can't talk you into a ride to Brunswick, at least you'll make the ten-thirty bus. What time's the train?"

"Noon." She was wearing the black linen again, washed and ironed, very ecclesiastical with the silver cross. She realized black made her skin look sallow, but today the color was perfect for her mood.

During the ten miles to town, they spoke only of impersonal matters--how much clinic responsibility Beth could handle, little Johann's robust health, and Commander Stark's surprise rendering of the Navy hymn at the funeral. By the time they pulled up in front of the Rexall, she realized they were parting with as few connections as they'd begun with the first day. For her, the tingling anticipation of adventure was gone. So was any hope that on the island of that name, her old losses would be healed. The main difference was that now, with sharp new ones to deal with, she didn't feel the old quite as acutely.

Five minutes late, the bus wheezed to a stop. Grabbing

her bag, she murmured, “Goodbye, Jim,” and hurried toward a cluster of dressed-for-church ladies. He trailed on his cane, returning their greetings. She wished he’d waited in the car; enduring these pointless few minutes gave her the same death-watch feeling as sitting with Jean while her life had ebbed.

The bus door folded open. She held out her hand, blinked rapidly so he wouldn’t notice her watering eyes. “Thanks for the ride, Jim. I’ll let you know my plans.”

“Please do.” His grip was firm. “Take care of yourself, Anna.”

She got in line, but before she could follow the ladies up the steps, he leaned in to kiss her cheek. With the damp touch of his lips on her skin, she climbed aboard, paid the fare, then headed for an empty double seat. Outside, he was standing on the sidewalk, looking stricken, and leaning on the cane more heavily than usual.

The engine roared, the bus lurched forward. Sorrow squeezed her chest, but she waved and smiled again. And wondered, suddenly, if she was crazy to leave. Maybe working with him only one day a week--even with no prospects of love and that old shadow between them—maybe that was preferable to life without him. Maybe the pain of his presence would be nothing compared to the pangs of his absence. Well, at least she hadn’t burned any bridges, so if this hiatus proved that supposition right, she could always return. With a sigh of resignation, she leaned back in the worn seat and closed her eyes to sunlight flashing through roadside trees.

At Brunswick, the southbound train was right on the minute. An express, with a Diesel locomotive and matching Boston and Maine coaches, except for two from the Pennsylvania Railroad at the end. A grizzled sergeant led a ragged group of young men in civvies toward them. Still boys, skinny and gangly. She wondered how many would survive the war they were about to join. Once, their patriotism would've made her want to burst into *The Star-Spangled Banner.* Now she knew patriotism was no protection from harm. Just as love could shield no one from grief.

The trip was so fast, with so few stops, she took it as a God-sign she was doing the right thing. At Dover, her parents were waiting on the platform; even her mother seemed happy to see her. They'd wanted to come to Maine for the visit Anna had proposed back in the spring, but it had been during Lent, and her father had always been too busy with church activities. So in the ten months since they'd last seen her, maybe they'd finally accepted that she was no longer their little girl, grieving the loss of husband and child, but a full-fledged woman capable of meeting life on her own.

At the rectory, as she walked from the car at the curb, she noticed the service flag in the front window wasn't the one she'd improvised for Dan's missing-in-action status: this star was gold. Her heart clutched. "When did you get this flag?"

"Soon as learned about Dan's death," said her mother. "Was that all right?"

She nodded, unable to speak.

Inside, the entry was redolent of roast pork. "I know it's your favorite. So we waited dinner till you got here. Oh my. I hope you didn't eat on the train."

She hadn't even thought about food, but said, "Of course not. Because I knew you'd probably killed the fatted hog."

In the dining room, the best linen cloth, Havilland china and sterling flatware offered further proof this was a celebratory meal. While her mother brought forth the sacrificed hog, her father held her chair at her usual seat at the table. "But sweetheart, you're anything but prodigal." His smile was luminous; his eyes shone with tears.

It felt like a long while since anyone had loved her this much. It made her weep, not out-of-control tears, just a slow ooze. Damn. The last thing she wanted was for these people to witness this small frailty. The previous year, she'd become good at masking the larger pain with stiff, non-stop smiles. Now, she made no attempt. No one seemed to notice anyway.

After dinner, she helped with the dishes, then paged through the *Boston Globe*. The war news seemed unreal and distant, but on the radio, the New York Philharmonic's rendering of Beethoven's Fifth stirred up a biting sense of nevermore. When she glanced up, her father was smoking his pipe and reading, her mother knitting socks for sailors on the Murmansk run. Such an ordinary domestic scene, yet abruptly, she felt time blowing past her like a steady wind, one that would eventually carry her parents away. Like Dan and the baby and Jean, leaving behind more scattered images of loved ones no longer flesh-and-blood real.

Regret tightened in her gut. Jim was alive, but she'd walked away from him as if he'd ceased to be. As if he no longer mattered to the scheme of her life.

In her father's presence, she longed to confide in him. His homilies were never trite, never judgmentally preachy like her mother's. But she couldn't trust herself yet to speak of Jim equably and with detachment. Too soon, she decided, particularly in view of her ability to predict her father's counsel that she be candid with the man. And her probable reluctance to follow it.

Chapter Twenty-Five

The next day, focused on washing, ironing, mending and cleaning her neglected civilian wardrobe, she mentally invented a new life for herself. Not exactly new, though; in nursing school, she'd also considered joining the Navy Nurse Corps. But only briefly. Because at that time, she'd been engaged to Bob Hallowell, their future carefully mapped out. Then she'd met Dan Donovan, fallen hard for him. And jumped at the chance to become a Navy wife instead.

On Tuesday, she let her mother cajole her into making bandages with other church women in the parish house. As her fingers folded gauze into compresses, she pictured the field hospitals or ships where they'd be used, thousands of miles from Portsmouth, New Hampshire and these hair-netted Episcopal ladies who sterilized their hands in Lysol and joked self-consciously about how their products resembled Kotex. Even as she laughed with them, she felt drawn to the heroic dramas being played out near the scattered battlefields of this virtually ubiquitous war, where she could actively minister to the fallen rather than making bandages in this untouched part of the globe with these naive, well-fed friends of her mother's. Even as she laughed with them, the plan became more solid, more dimensional.

The first step was to determine if Dan's car was still operable. Wednesday at breakfast, she asked her father if he'd been using it while she'd been gone.

His look was surprised. "Well, of course, sweetheart. You asked me to. Fact is, when you said you were coming home, I had my mechanic check her over. And gas her up. So she's ready to go anytime you are. Why? Where are you off to?"

"Oh, just over to the hospital to look up some old friends."

Now his expression turned hopeful. "Thinking of coming back to work here when the year in Maine's over?"

She shrugged, gave him a fond smile. "I might," she lied.

Inside the '36 Plymouth, she noticed right away that the tinge of motor oil hadn't faded. Dan had bought the car in terrible shape, then done everything possible to renew it. But the smell remained. It hadn't bothered him, if he'd even noticed. On the boat the constant reek of diesel had apparently dulled his olfactory sense to anything less pungent. The pack of Chesterfields was still in the glove compartment, the four cigarettes untouched. And the chain of the St. Christopher's medal was still looped over the rear view mirror. Ironic that these minute traces of him remained despite the most significant change of all.

On the way to the base administration building, she drove as close as possible to the submarine piers. Security was heavy, but she managed to get close enough to see a new boat at the fitting-out pier. Another was approaching on the river. And even without looking around, she saw Navy men—healthy, whole, and busily carrying on. Because it was summer, they were in khakis or whites, not the dress blues she associated with Dan. Still, they were here, and he was gone.

It took a while to locate the right office and gather the forms for her purpose. On the way, a Nurse Corps recruiting poster chased her last doubts. While the picture of an attractive brunette in dress whites beside a hospital ship filled her mind with an image of herself in that smart uniform, healing wounded fighting men, facing hardships in exotic locations and using her training in situations far more urgent than any she'd encountered at the hospital here, or on Hope Island.

But before she could take the next step toward this goal, she needed to round up birth certificate, school and medical records, diplomas, work history and official notification of Dan's death. As she headed for the exit, she realized someone had called her name. She turned to see Chaplain Fogel hurrying up the corridor toward her.

"Anna? Anna Donovan, is that you?" His smile was the broadest she'd ever seen on his pale, thin face. "Thought you were working in Maine."

She nodded. "Well, I have been, but I'm home for a few days. Before I join the Nurse Corps." In his presence, she felt traces if the pain this man had witnessed the year before. First, when he'd come to the clinic where she was working, to tell her about the missing-in-action telegram. Later, in the women's club he'd organized. And finally, after her baby had been stillborn. "See, in June I got word that my husband's been declared killed in action. That makes me officially a widow. So I can sign up."

His expression, usually so neutral, turned sorrowful. "Oh, I'm sorry to hear that. About your husband, I mean. I'll be sure and tell the ladies in the group. They remember you so fondly."

"Well, we had a special bond. Glad to know you're still meeting."

"Oh my, yes. More need now than ever. In fact, one new member's a submariner's wife like you. Her husband was on *Sculpin* when it was lost last year. She got a telegram like yours and thought he was dead, but last month, she found out he's a Jap prisoner."

She inhaled sharply. "I thought for a while maybe Dan had been captured too, but apparently not. Well, at least her husband's still alive."

"He was one of the lucky ones. Some of his shipmates were on a Jap carrier that was torpedoed on the way to Japan, so they didn't even make it to the camp." He regarded her solemnly for so long she wondered if he was keeping something from her. "Anyway, we still get together Sunday afternoons if you'd like to join us while you're in town. We even have a name now—the Survivors' Club."

"Appropriate." She glanced at her watch for an excuse to break off this somehow unsettling conversation. She'd been away from Portsmouth so long she'd forgotten the deep emotional connections between sub force personnel. Now here they were again, with the loss of another boat she knew by reputation, had even seen back in May, 1939, when *Sculpin* was aiding recovery efforts for *Squalus*, her sister sub. She cleared her throat. "Not sure how long I'll be home, but I'll come to a meeting if I can."

"Good. We'll all be happy to see you again. By the way, how do you like the little stone your parents got for your baby's grave?"

This latest news added to her sense of being lightning-struck. Her mouth gaped, but she managed to say, "Uh…I didn't know there was a grave. I mean, I never asked my father what happened…you know, afterward."

He seemed puzzled. "You mean after the funeral?"

More surprise. "Oh, there was a funeral? Didn't know that either. Didn't want to know at the time. I thought the less I knew, the faster I'd get over it."

His eyes narrowed. "Oh, I see. Well, yes, your parents and I had a little service in the cemetery behind St. Stephen's. You were still hospitalized at the time. We used the prayer book. Very simple. They got the stone about a month ago and I helped your father consecrate it. He could've done it himself, but since I was with you at the time of the…uh, the tragedy, I wanted to be part of it too."

She inhaled deeply to loosen the sudden constriction in her chest. "Well, I'll have to ask my father about that too. I just didn't know."

"Something else you may not know either."

She steeled herself for more information, dreading it for no sensible reason. "Oh? What's that?"

"After the baby was born, seeing that your husband was Catholic, I asked Chaplain Anselm to baptize him post-mortem. I was going to do it myself, but your father thought it should be the Roman priest, since he officiated at your wedding. Hope that was all right."

She was barely able to nod before the winds of sorrow touched off unexpected tears.

"Excuse me, Chaplain Vogel, I've got to run." Turning quickly, she hurried toward the exit, and the parking area. There, inside Dan's car, she surrendered to a new explosion of the grief she hadn't realized was still so close to the surface.

When she got home, her father was in his study. From papers scattered on his desk as if wind-blown, she concluded he was working on his next sermon. She waited till he glanced up before she asked, "Is this an okay time to talk, Dad?"

He pointed to the well-worn leather wing chair where parishioners sat to confess their own sins, or gripe about someone else's. "Happy to talk to you anytime, sweetheart. What's on your mind?"

Her hands had begun to shake and her heart was pounding, almost as if this kindly old soul were a menacing stranger who held the power of life and death over her. She coughed a couple of times. "Well, when I was on the base today, I saw Chaplain Fogel. That wasn't why I went, though. See, I'm thinking of joining the Navy Nurse Corps. So I picked up the forms I have to fill out."

He blinked several times, then removed the bifocals he cleaned only when he thought he was going blind. "Join the Navy? You mean when you've finished the year in Maine?"

"No. I mean now. Soon as I can." Her throat felt raspy. "Anyway, that's when I ran into Chaplain Fogel." She paused to give him a chance to volunteer the news she'd just learned, a whole year after the facts.

But he only nodded. "Did he tell you he's put in for a transfer? Wants overseas duty. Something a little closer to the action."

"No. But he did tell me he helped you and Mother with a funeral for my baby last year. How come you never mentioned it?"

Her father suddenly seemed far older than his sixty-six years. Worn out with unending ministerial duties, perhaps with having to represent the Lord even when he couldn't divine the Master plan for himself. "Sorry, dear. Didn't think you wanted to know."

"I didn't then. But now…well, now I need you to tell me about it."

He wiped the glasses, replaced them on his craggy nose. "Not much to tell. A simple funeral in the churchyard. Nobody but Rev. Fogel and your mother and I. We said…" He paused, swallowed visibly. "We said the prayer book service. You know the one. For the burial of a child."

"I see." A deep breath enabled her to go on. "I used to think it was easier not to think about it at all. But Lorraine said nothing's worse than not knowing where your child is. Even if it's in a cemetery."

He blew his nose. "She's right, of course. So…would you like to see the grave?"

She wasn't quite ready to answer. More pain—old pain she'd thought had evaporated by this time---rose like the onset of some sudden disease. "Right now?"

He blinked moisture from his eyes. "No time like the present, they say."

Side by side, they followed the uneven brick path behind the church. The front of the burying ground was filled with mossy headstones from the Revolution, the Civil War, World War One and the great influenza epidemic. Between rows of dark granite, occasional marble monuments rose like white exclamation points. The path ended at an old oak, its massive trunk encircled by a scarred wooden bench. Beyond it, they stepped between graves to a small marble square near the back wall. Her father pointed to the chiseled words: *Baby Boy Donovan, 4 August 1943*. "We only got the stone last month."

Compressing her lips, she covered her mouth with one hand and lowered her gaze to the stone. Was there room to add *Lamb of God*? Either the words, or the small icon.

"Wish we'd had a name for him," her father murmured. "But you'd never told us what you wanted."

"No. It was so early, I hadn't decided. And Dan....well, he was missing by then too."

He gave her a quick, tight hug. "Now then. Suppose I let you have some time alone."

After he left, she continued to stare at the marker. Losing Dan had been a slow process, tempered by surges of optimism during the year before the second telegram had banished it forever. With this infant, however, one day she'd been full of active, promising life. The next, hollowed out, scarred and empty. By the time she'd left the hospital nine days later, she'd stuffed the event down in her memory. Just as fighting men had to do when death carried off one buddy after another.

Oblivious to the bustle of the town, she stood bathed in steamy mid-day sunlight, until the courthouse clock struck noon. Then she walked back to the rectory and stood in the study doorway until her father looked up. His eyes were full of unspoken concern.

"Thanks, Dad. For taking care of…oh, all that last year. I didn't want to know before, but I'm glad I do now." She felt her voice breaking, so she coughed a couple times. "Well, time for lunch. So I guess I'll go tell Mother my Navy plans."

"You know she won't be happy, dear. Proud of you, but not happy."

From the kitchen came the rattle and clink of dishes. She paused, halfway into the hall. "But first, something else I want you to know."

"What's that?"

"It's about Jim. You know, Dr. Millett? I'm embarrassed to admit it, but I've…well, I've developed feelings for him, Dad. I admired him right from the start, but once I got word about Dan, well, then they sort of blossomed."

"Feelings?" He seemed taken aback. "What sort of feelings? Romantic? Like you had for Dan?"

She shook her head. "No. That only happens once in a lifetime. These aren't that intense. More like…uh…affection. He's such a good man, so gentle, so kind to everyone. I really enjoy working with him. But now I want more. I want to be more than his nurse."

"Then why are you leaving Maine?"

"Because it's hopeless. He's still in love with his ex-wife. Between that and Jean's death, it's too painful to stay. See, I kind of…well, I threw myself at him. And he rejected me. So…"

Her father stared, then came to envelope her in his tobacco and mothball-scented embrace again. "That must've hurt, dear. But keep in mind that the man's lame. The service doesn't want him. Maybe his wife didn't either. So he's trying to avoid being hurt again."

"That's absurd. He just has a bad leg. Otherwise, he's a

beautiful person."

"And so are you. If he can't see that, he isn't the man I think he is."

Finding the necessary documents for the Navy meant poring through a trunk in the attic, but by nightfall, she'd found everything except her Mass General transcript. So the next afternoon she rode the local down to Boston, left her bag at Margie's new apartment, walked over to the hospital and obtained the record before the other girl came home from work. Anna was surprised: in the year since she'd seen her, Margie seemed to have become louder, brassier, sillier. Was that what working with sick kids did to you? Still, she felt Margie's covert scrutiny, as if measuring her too against recollections of their last meeting shortly after she'd lost the baby. And probably concluding Anna had grown even duller than she'd been in high school.

That evening, they joined some of Margie's work friends at a downtown nightclub. The place was so jammed and noisy, the air so thick with cigarette smoke, Anna felt smothered, almost to the point of panic with the recollection that two years before, almost five hundred revelers had died in a sudden holocaust at another Boston nightclub.

As they pushed through the mob, Margie apparently noticed her looking around for exit signs. "Don't tell me you're worried about fire," she said blithely. "This place is much safer than the old Cocoanut Grove. Besides, you need a little fun." Her narrow-eyed gaze took in Anna's dress—the black linen, of course. "And some new clothes. Looks like you're still in mourning."

"I probably am. I've lost a lot the last couple of years."

"Come on, then." She tucked her arm through Anna's and propelled her toward a nearby table. "Time you start getting over it."

She tried to smile. And act interested in the people she met—a couple of pediatric residents, three nurses and an Army doctor. Margie ordered Singapore Slings, then leaned closer. "Listen, I can see feeling bad about Dan and the baby. As for Jean, well, you ask me, any girl who sleeps with a Nazi's asking for trouble."

Anna had an urge to slap her, but good sense kept her sweet.

The next day at Filene's, her friend talked her into buying what she called "a really glamorous black dress." Silky rayon, square neckline outlined in black sequins. Later in the beauty parlor, she tried to convince her to have her hair bleached, but Anna's daring extended only to getting one of the new feather-cuts you didn't have to curl. After lunch, they went to see *Thirty Seconds over Tokyo*. Except for some actual newsreel footage of Billy Mitchell's B-25s lurching off the tossing carrier, the movie seemed too Hollywood to be believable. Especially with Van Johnson playing a heroic amputee.

That night while Margie went out again, she stayed behind to read a new Daphne du Maurier novel she'd bought that afternoon. Margie woke her when she came in after two. "I know it's late, but I met the cutest ensign just out of Newport. We danced till the club closed, and then he brought me home. In his convertible." She rolled her eyes.

Saturday, instead of going home as she'd planned, she let Margie convince her a trip to Provincetown with Ensign Convertible and a jaygee friend was just the sort of fun she needed. As they passed around a flask of Canadian Club, she realized it wasn't. The greasy shore dinner didn't help either. She ate most of it, but when they parked by the bay afterward, had to run from the car and throw up on the sand. After that the Navy men were in such a hurry to get back, they got a speeding ticket outside Barnstable. Margie pouted all the way into the city.

But by next morning, she had a new plan. "Today we're going to church. That big Congregational on the square. Nice class of eligible bachelors there. I mean, Christians, not Catholics." A reference to Dan Donovan, of whom she'd never totally approved. As a dreamboat boyfriend, yes, but not as a husband.

"I'm not interested in bachelors," Anna said. "Christian or otherwise. Maybe another time."

Margie's glance was sharp. "You mean, you still aren't ready to start dating?"

"Well, yes. But the only man I'd like to date isn't ready for me."

"Who? That Air Corps pilot?"

"No. The doctor I worked with."

Margie smoothed her silvery-blonde pompadour and smiled at herself in the mirror by the door. "You mean, the crippled guy?"

"He's not really crippled. He had polio, and one of his legs was damaged, so he has to wear a brace. But he gets around fine."

"Isn't he a lot older too?"

"Thirty-nine. Not that much older."

She stared open-mouthed. "Don't kid yourself. Thirteen years is a lot older. So now you've fallen for an old lame guy you'd probably have to take care of later. God, Anna. Don't you know he might be impotent too?"

"Oh Margie! Why'd you say that?"

"Listen, I hear doctors talking. Things they discuss would make your hair curl."

"Well, he and I never….you know…did anything. Not even a kiss. I would have. But he's still pining for his ex-wife."

"Ex-wife? Well, doesn't that just prove it? Of course, he's impotent. Maybe even a fairy. Listen, Anna, you're damned lucky he doesn't want you. There's thousands of healthy, normal men out there just waiting for a girl like you. You don't have to settle for some decrepit old Four-F. Or does he remind you of Bob Hallowell?"

Anna felt like slapping her again. She was saved by recalling it was the Lord's Day, and she was a priest's daughter.

But during the service, she kept wondering if that impotence theory was more than hot air. She was mortified to mention her botched seduction, but needing to know, she confided it while they waited for lunch in the Copley Plaza coffee shop. Memories of her brief honeymoon pierced her, until she took a deep breath and returned to the current discussion. Finally, she asked, "If he couldn't, why would he say he wouldn't take advantage of me?"

Margie broke off a piece of roll and smeared it with real butter. "Oh, Anna. You're so naïve. He said that so you wouldn't know he couldn't. Maybe he wanted to. Meaning he still has the equipment, but it doesn't work. And you never wondered before?"

"I thought it was because he still loves his ex-wife."

"Now there's the gal to ask. You want to know everything, talk to her." She shook her head. "Or read *The Sun Also Rises.* See, the hero has the same problem. Only from a war wound." She tittered. "It doesn't say, but maybe it was shot off. Anyway he and this girl are in love, but they can't do it. So he goes fishing in Spain and she sleeps with other men. Now, your guy's lame too, so there's not a whole lot you and he can do, is there?" She paused as an odd grin spread over her face. "You said he wears a leg brace? Maybe he needs a little tiny one too."

Anna felt her mouth pursing in disapproval. "Oh, don't be so crude."

"Crude's better than prude, Anna. Which is what you're turning into. A real prude. Listen, if you lose your sense of humor, life'll get you down. You've got to keep laughing. Keep having fun."

Watching her friend bat her eyelashes at a Marine at the next table, Anna wondered if she and Margie had always had different views of life. Or was she just now noticing, even after ten years of friendship?

Though the thought of living in Boston no longer appealed, the next day she made rounds of hospital personnel departments just to assure Margie she had. Experienced nurses were so scarce, she could pick and choose from the best positions. Margie even offered to share her posh new apartment. Anna said she'd think about it, knew she never would.

Tuesday morning they hugged goodbye before Margie left for work. "You know, Anna, it'd be swell if you moved down here. Why, in the Navy, you won't have any freedom. Or fun. Only advantage I can see, you'll be around lots of eligible men."

On the train back to Portsmouth, she tried to read Hemingway, but if the novel was a window into the psyche of an impotent man, it was curtained in more opaque dialogue than she could penetrate. If she hadn't borrowed it, she'd have left it on the seat when she got off.

It was after one by the time she walked home from the station. The Packard was gone, her mother up to her elbows in tomatoes from neighbors' victory gardens. Anna ate one in a sandwich with mayonnaise while she answered questions about Boston. Finally, her mother remembered that someone had called from the Naval Hospital. "You need to take the papers in tomorrow morning. And have a physical. That is, if you're still set on joining. Or did being in the city again change your mind?"

She shook my head. "That life's too fast for me."

Her mother scowled, stirred a steaming pot. The sweet, vinegary smell of chili sauce reminded Anna of all the summers of her childhood. Nostalgia dampened her eyes.

"You know, Anna," her mother said, "your father and I just hate to think of you in some god-forsaken part of the world, with nothing but pain and suffering all around. So far from home, with no one who cares about you. Bad enough you've been in Maine so long. Honestly, this latest notion of yours is breaking our hearts."

Notion? Was that all she considered her pending Navy service? "Then think of me as helping to heal all that suffering," she snapped.

In the morning, she turned in the completed documents, then a doctor poked and prodded, and lab technicians tested blood and urine. Four hours later, she signed forms that made her commitment to the Navy official.

She was scheduled to be sworn in Friday afternoon. That morning, she helped her mother polish every piece of altar brass and silver they could find. Being the dutiful daughter for a while longer, making a memory her mother might cherish, perhaps even brag about to her church friends.

After lunch she drove over to Kittery Beach and watched a desultory surf collapse on the pebbled foreshore. A steamy afternoon, almost tropical, with a polished sea, fuzzy clouds hovering over the horizon. Probably the South Pacific would look and feel like this. Wednesday, one of the forms she'd completed was the "dream sheet" request for duty stations. The duty yeoman had read it with a smirk. "Hate to tell you, ma'am, but generally BuMed sends you the exact opposite of where you want to go. So, your first choice being a hospital ship in WestPac, you'll likely end up at a dependents' clinic in Iceland." He tapped the form. "Take my word, you'll be surprised where they send you."

Her parents came with her to the commissioning ceremony in the CO's office. They were so early they had to wait half an hour in an ante-room decorated with framed pictures of submarines built in the Navy Yard there.

Nervous, Anna paced around, looking for Dan's boat in the lineup of official photos, taken dockside with ship's company posed on deck. She found *Sculpin* and *Squalus* in the top row; there was even one of *Squalus* renamed *Sailfish* after being rebuilt following her brush with doom in 1939. Then she scanned past Dan's first boat, *Bluefish,* to the shot of *Wolf Fish* a few pictures away. And there they were, Dan and his shipmates—Ron Grady, Ben Marks, Tony Unger, even CPO Steve Stevenson, and four others' she'd met but didn't remember. Pale sunlight shadowed their sober official expressions at the boat's commissioning in November, 1941, the latest of the big fleet subs the yard was turning out for a war everyone knew was inevitable. Still, she'd thought they'd have all the time in the world—to be married, live together, share their lives, have a child. And love each other. Especially to love each other.

For a fleeting moment, she was alone with him again. And the other men who'd gone down with the boat. This time, she was on the verge of a new connection to the same overarching service, the same commitment to the same great Cause. Dropping the thread of her old life and picking up his. A chill shivered through her. Until the secretary announced that the CO was ready to swear them in.

In his office, Anna, another nurse and four WAVE candidates raised their right hands for the oath of allegiance, were welcomed into the service, and received orders to report to Officers' Candidate School at Newport, Rhode Island, by 2400 hours on 31 August. Suddenly, she had only six more days as a civilian. She took a deep breath and tried to decide whether to go back to Hope Island to pick up the rest of her things. Or leave them until she needed them again, presumably after the war. Before long, however, she realized her real motivation was to see Jim again. Part of her balked: hadn't one parting been traumatic enough? Did she need to return for another?

But riding home with her parents, she decided to risk it. Being with him might only increment her pain and haunt her forever with a tragic sense of might have been. On the other hand, maybe it would free her to commit herself more totally to her new life. One way or the other, it was a risk she had to take.

Chapter Twenty-Six

As the decking on the old iron bridge rattled beneath the Buick's tires, Jim caught sight of a gray spire rising from the brick clutter of downtown Portsmouth. A current of excitement, palpable as an electric shock, jolted him at the notion that he was within minutes of reaching St. Stephen's on this surprise visit to Anna. Her father's telephoned invitation a few days before had been cryptic: "Doctor, if there's any way you can get down here Sunday morning, I think you ought to come."

He'd asked why, of course, a routine question under the circumstances. And Rev. Moss had said, "Because Anna's leaving for the Navy next week. And I know she'd want to see you before she goes."

"The Navy!" Jim had gasped. "She didn't say anything about the Navy when she left here."

"You ask me, it was a spur-of-the-moment decision. She says it wasn't, but…." The priest had sighed. "Maybe you can talk her out of it. She won't listen to her mother and me, that's for sure. But you—she thinks so much of you, maybe you can change her mind. At least come down and tell her goodbye, if nothing else."

He'd hesitated, envisioning his day off. Morning hospital rounds, the 8:30 service at All Saints' to avoid

Betty Grimes, then maybe a drive up to Camden for lunch with his cousin. Later he'd catch up on mail and shuffle through the reading material piled beside his bed. And wonder with a small corner of his mind what Anna might be doing at that moment. And even more so, what she'd decided about coming back.

Well, now he knew the answer to that one at least.

"Don't see any reason I can't get there," he'd agreed. "What time's your service?"

"Eleven."

"With an early start, should be there in plenty of time. Now, where's the church?"

So here he was, heading for the steeple as diligently as the wise men had followed the star to Bethlehem. With no idea what to expect, his heart was racing and his palms were sweaty on the steering wheel. Two weeks since she'd left the island; two weeks with no word, two weeks of impotent regrets and indecision so niggling he'd begun to regard it as a character defect, one that had made him cautious to a degree bordering on cowardly.

But earlier that morning, as he followed Route One through Portland, he'd been struck with an idea so sudden, so brilliant, it felt providential: he'd offer Anna a new job—working with him in his practice. Lord knew, he needed a nurse in the office almost as much as he needed a new right leg. Now, the notion of hiring Anna generated an excitement he could barely contain. And damned little of it was professional.

When he turned onto Church Street, it was barely ten-thirty, only a few cars parked near the imposing stone church. Slowing, he passed a brick rectory with a gold star in a front window, and a parish house set in a wide lawn, then pulled up behind a yellow Studebaker roadster with Virginia plates. A spit-and-polish Marine captain got out and opened the door for a slender blonde in a black straw hat. He watched the handsome couple walk toward the main entrance before he cut the engine and set the brake. Then, increasingly anxious, he focused on the view of the rectory in the mirror. When other cars began pulling in behind him, they blocked his vision, so he got out and leaned against the front fender of the Buick. To his dismay, a film of road dust had accrued since Fletcher had washed it the day before to impress Anna. He'd even considered bringing flowers, but didn't want to appear as pathetically anxious as he felt. Like a damned adolescent with his first crush.

Sweating in the warm sunlight, he returned the nods of others arriving for the service and tried to compose himself. Nonetheless he couldn't shake the same unease he'd felt the first time he'd taken Ellen out to dinner. Six years before, she hadn't been the first woman he'd dated, just the first who'd made him feel like an adult male rather than a neutered cripple. Nice while it lasted, but the aftermath had plunged him back into that effete identity with such force he'd never expected to emerge again.

By quarter to eleven, as he was wilting in the heat, Anna and her mother left the rectory and started down the sidewalk toward him. His heart thudded, his mouth went dry at the sight of the younger woman, shapely and slender in a yellow dress, hair cut short and wispy, almost like a girl's. She'd never impressed him as a beauty, but today, with the glow of summer on her face, she was lovelier than he remembered. And no longer just a fine person, nor a nurse he merely admired, but a young woman any man—or even a cripple—might lust for.

Abruptly conscious of their age difference, however he was rocked by a new wave of futility. Pointless, he thought, this last-ditch stand. Stupid too to think he could win her affections with one large, last gesture. All too easily, he pictured her husband in the studio portrait she'd once shown him--handsome, virile, energetic and vital. The Navy was full of officers like him. Even if she didn't join the Nurse Corps, she'd soon find love with another, and her life would proceed almost as if it hadn't been interrupted by Dan's loss.

Now he felt an urge to flee before he made a fool of himself. But Mrs. Moss had caught sight of him and given a little wave. Anna was staring in his direction too, but apparently without recognition. Until he smiled, held up his hand and started toward her. Closing the gap, she regarded him with wide-eyed surprise. "Jim. What are you doing here?"

He shrugged with a self-conscious grin.. "Wanted to see you before you left for the Navy."

"But…but how'd you know I was going into the Navy?"

"Your father called."

When Mrs. Moss rushed over and pumped Jim's hand, Anna said, "Mother, did you know he was going to be here?"

"Of course. But we wanted to surprise you, dear."

She flushed. "Well, I'm surprised, all right." Still smiling, Mrs. Moss urged them toward the church door. "But you needn't have bothered. See, I'm coming up tomorrow. To get the last of my things. And say goodbye to everybody on the island."

"Oh, I didn't know. Your parents didn't mention it."

"I haven't told them yet. If only I had, I could've saved you the trip."

"I don't mind, Anna, Wanted to see you anyway."

They came into the nave, cool and stone-smelling after the heat outside. From the sanctuary came the protests of a pipe organ being subjected to an inexpert rendition of a Bach prelude. An usher led them up a long red-carpeted aisle to a pew near the front. Nodding and smiling at everyone within range, Mrs. Moss went in first; Anna followed, so he ended up sitting beside her. An uncomfortable closeness, but sweet beyond words with her warmth and fresh-bathed fragrance enveloping him. And her father addressing the Lord from the altar. Jim tried to note every word of the sermon so he could make enlightened comments at dinner afterward. "I do hope you like roast lamb with mint jelly, doctor," Mrs. Moss had said on the phone. And he'd lied and said it was his favorite food. Oh, the white lies he would tell to get closer to Anna, even if he fell flat on his face on the way.

But all that spoke to him was the text from Psalm 77, the one about God having lost his right hand and how the world must feel very much like that psalmist these days. At communion, he followed the others up to the rail but because of his bad leg, was the only one not kneeling. He was embarrassed for Anna that the congregation had to see her with a cripple, though, of course, he might be just a family friend, not necessarily a new beau. Unless they read the warmth in his gaze or could tell how he had to stifle the impulse to touch her hand on the hymnal they shared. At least she commented that he had a good voice. Not an overpowering compliment, but better than nothing.

After the recessional, her mother pushed out ahead of them, explaining she had to put the finishing touches on dinner, which would be on the table promptly at one. Outside, mid-day sunlight was blinding after the reverently shadowed church. Now his insecurities had morphed into a staunch do-or-die sense that made him say, "Okay, Anna. Your mother said dinner's at one. So we have half an hour to talk. Can we sit somewhere?"

"Talk?" she echoed tensely.

He nodded. "Or, if you'd rather not talk, then just listen. I have a lot to say."

She gestured toward the rear of the church. "There's a bench under a tree in the graveyard. Nice and shady this time of day."

Leaving the rest of the congregation straggling toward

their cars, they set out on the brick path that led behind the church. He was about to tell her about the new job when she said, "Remember I told you I had a stillborn infant?"

"Yes, of course."

"Well, his grave's back there. I only found out last week. It was…it was the first I knew about it."

"Really?" His steps slowed. "How come?"

She shrugged. "Nobody told me before. And I never asked. Didn't think it mattered. Then Lorraine said it was important to know. So I asked my dad. And he showed me."

He wanted to tell her that had been a healthy gesture. But didn't speak, because it seemed a judgment he had no right to make. So they walked on in a silence he could barely endure for all that cried out inside him to be said. And today. Now. Finally, now.

"Would you like to see it?"

"If it wouldn't bother you."

"No. I'm fine." The bravado in her voice told him she wasn't really.

Beyond the big tree, in a new part of the cemetery near a brick wall, she pointed out the small square of marble with the few chiseled words.

"Oh, August fourth," he said. "Why, that's the same date Jean died this year."

"I know. I thought of it while we were waiting. You know. For the end. I remembered it would've been his first birthday."

Jim reached for her hand. "Did you have a name for him?"

Her voice was hoarse and rough. "Well, it was so early, and the only name Dan ever mentioned was Francis, for his brother who disappeared years ago. But after the boat went missing, I decided to call him Dan. If it was a boy, of course. Daniel Robert Donovan, Jr. But as it was, nobody ever wanted to know what his name would have been."

"Daniel Robert Donovan, Jr. Good." He nodded "First sons should have their father's names."

She swallowed visibly. "Okay. Now let's sit, shall we?"

Turning away from the grave, they walked toward the towering oak. "Getting back to Jean," he said. "Been twenty-three days now, but I feel--especially at the clinic, I feel sort of….well, haunted. Must've been even worse for you, having lived with her. No wonder it's painful for you there."

Close but not touching, they sat side by side in the dappled shade; a breeze rustled the leaves overhead. The sound was autumnal despite the heat. He took off his hat, pushed a damp lock of hair back in place.

Anna said, "But it's not just because she died. I told you that when I left."

He stared at his black wing-tips, one a normal shoe, the other with the built-up sole. "Still, I was shocked when your dad told me you were joining the Navy. Seems kind of sudden."

"No, not really. I mean, I thought about it before, in nursing school. And even last year, before I took your job. But then I was still married. Officially, I mean. See, married women can't be in the Navy. But widows can."

He regarded her a moment, then said, "Kind of ironic. Because I was going to ask you to come back. And work with me in the practice."

She turned with a questioning stare. "You mean as your nurse?"

"Uh-huh. I've needed one for years now."

"Oh. When…when did you get that idea?"

His gaze swept the cemetery, the looming steeple, the brick parish house and rectory beyond the emerald sweep of lawn. "Actually, today on the way down. If I'd thought of it earlier, I'd have asked you sooner. Or maybe not. Because I thought you needed time to figure things out. Anyway, too late now, I guess."

She slumped, looked away from him. "That's a shame. Sounds like a good job. Except I'd still be uncomfortable working for you. You know. Because of that night."

Silence wedged itself between them, louder than the hum of traffic behind them, or the rattle of leaves overhead, even the approaching screech of a low-flying P-38. The twin-tailed, twin-engine Air Corps fighter came out of nowhere; they glanced up as it roared southward and disappeared in the direction of Massachusetts. "We need to talk about that Anna," Jim said when the noise had faded.

"I don't know what more there is to say." She seemed to be waiting for his response, when her father came out the sacristy door, vestments over his arm. As he set off toward the rectory, he reminded them her mother hated to be kept waiting when she had dinner ready. "Well, we'd better go then," she sighed. "Sunday dinner's the Holy Grail. Especially when we have a guest."

"Then let's oblige her." He set the hat back on his head, leaned on the cane and got to his feet.

Walking beside him into the hot glare, she asked, "Are you driving back today?"

"Can't take two days off. Why?"

"Well, I was coming up tomorrow anyway, so maybe I could ride back with you, We could talk on the way."

"Oh, fine idea. I'd like nothing better." He turned with a mirthless grin. "That's a damned lie. There's so many things I'd like better. But I'll settle for a few hours in the car with you."

Her eyes narrowed, as if she wanted to hear exactly what he'd like better. Until her mother charged out the back door. "Oh there you are. Finally. Dinner's all ready to go on the table. Now Anna, don't you dare bring the doctor in through the kitchen. He'll think we're heathens."

She did anyway, with such a defiant look he

suspected that opposing her maternal parent was an old habit, one she was going to indulge as long as possible. He was mildly shocked, but inexplicably pleased at her independent spirit. Even though he realized it might occasionally work against him.

The meal was worthy of a bishop's visit, but Anna's appetite had fled, so she only picked at the food and gulped ice water to wash it down. Jim was silhouetted against a sunny window, his expression unreadable, but he ate a lot, which thrilled her mother. No one mentioned Anna's impending departure for OCS or the ensuing naval service. As if they regarded these issues as too private to discuss in front of someone who qualified as company. The result was such a stilted conversation, she could barely wait to finish dessert and coffee so she and Jim could leave the table, and get the hell out of Portsmouth.

Still, even before she cleared the soiled dishes, Mrs. Moss insisted they troop out to the side porch for more banalities. "Because who knows where you'll be this time next week?"

"Oh Mother," she said sharply. "Just down the coast in Newport, Rhode Island. You know that." Perched beside Jim on the glider, she twisted her hanky and tapped her foot, impatient with the spate of inane questions: "How long was the trip down?" "Was there much traffic" "Did you have any problem finding gas?" And on and on. Below the green awning, afternoon heat shimmered and shone. Jim complimented the meal again; Mrs. Moss simpered, "Oh, it was nothing. Nothing at all."

Finally her father asked, "Couldn't you stay tonight, doctor? So much driving for one day. Over a hundred miles, isn't it?"

"A hundred and thirty actually. Thanks. But tomorrow's a work day. As for the driving, Anna's coming along to help." He cleared his throat. "I was hoping she'd come back to stay. As nurse in my office. Haven't had help for years. Maybe if I'd had the idea sooner.."

"Oh, I wish you had, Doctor," wailed Mrs. Moss, wringing her hands. "But once she makes up her mind, neither heaven nor earth can sway her."

This last comment brought Anna to her feet. "For the love of God, Mother. Would you please stop making this into a tragedy. Now, talk about it all you want, but I'm going up and pack."

"Can you wait a minute, Anna?" Jim said. "I have something for you. A little gift in appreciation for all the help you gave me on the island."

A gift? Lured by childish curiosity, she returned to the seat as he handed over a flat green velvet box. Inside, a single strand of cultured pearls gleamed against the satin lining. Almost identical to the string she'd given the undertaker for Jean. She said, "Oh my goodness. You shouldn't have," but let him fasten them behind her neck.

Her mother sniffed. "Maybe since they came from you, doctor, she'll take better care of them than the ones we gave her."

His smile was gentle and fond. "You know, Mrs. Moss, I'd admired Anna for a long while, but when she wanted Jean to have those pearls, she touched my heart."

Confused, she wondered if she'd heard right. Was this an archaic, poetic way to express admiration? Or a hint at a sentiment deeper than appreciation? She mumbled, "Thanks, Jim. But now I really do have to pack."

The suitcase was almost full when her mother came upstairs, looked in to her room, then settled on the edge of the bed. She fingered some loose socks, mated them into pairs. "This trip to Maine. When will you be back?"

"Tuesday or Wednesday. In plenty of time to pack for Newport. I'll let you know."

"And where will you stay up there? On the island?"

"Not sure. Maybe Jim'll let me use his sister's room again."

"Oh, Anna. That hardly seems proper in light of your…your feelings. Your father told me about them. And it worries me. Being fond of a man makes a woman so vulnerable."

"Vulnerable to what? Indecent proposals?"

She reddened. "So to speak. Listen, I saw how he looked at you all through dinner. With that look men get."

"Oh pooh. That was just your imagination. Jim has no personal feelings for me. I'm just his nurse. And a friend."

"Oh, how sad. Being Episcopalian, and a doctor, he'd make such a fine…oh, never mind."

Before Anna closed the bag, she tucked the new black dress inside. Silly; she'd hardly need it on this trip. She was debating returning it to the closet when she noticed her mother's face in a slant of sunlight; it shadowed deep creases and highlighted a lone whisker jutting from her chin. Suddenly she realized the older woman was probably compelled by this one last chance to cram her with the final wisdom a girl needed. Small things she hadn't had time to share when Anna had married Dan. Now, after twenty-six years, one last moment with the daughter who was jumping into a life that for all she knew, might as well be on the far side of the moon.

Bending quickly, Anna swooped in with a hug, so fast Mrs. Moss had no time to pull away. Trying to avoid a teary scene, she turned away and closed the bag with the dress still inside.

Chapter Twenty-Seven

It was after three before she and Jim left. Looking forlorn and pitiful, her parents trailed them to the car. When Anna volunteered to drive, they warned her to be careful in all the Sunday traffic. As if she'd never driven anywhere before, including the steep hills and curving streets of San Francisco. She pulled into the street, then glimpsed them in the rearview mirror walking back to the rectory. They were so old and stooped, her heart softened.

Headed north at last on Route One, she took a deep breath, and forced her mind to ordinary matters. Something untinged by emotional coloration, some issue with which she could safely reconnect with Jim. First, the nurse he'd found for the island clinic: how was she working out?

"Better than I hoped," he said. "In fact, she and her husband want to move to the island. Cleve's looking for a house they can rent."

"Oh, that's good." Next, she rambled on about OCS. "It's usually longer, but this is a crash course. It'll be a grind, but they say active duty's a lot worse. And that's what I want. I mean, to be used in a good cause. So busy I can't think of anything but work. Sort of like you are."

"I'd have kept you just as busy in my practice."

She circled the notion like a plane coming in to an

unknown airfield. Much as she might have wanted to, however, she couldn't land here.

"Of course, you might have found it boring. Which is a moot point now, isn't it?"

She braked for the traffic signal in Kittery. "Maybe after the war." Before the light changed, she glanced over. His face was bleak, shoulders slumped. Maybe he was feeling the same sort of rejection she had two weeks before. She had a sudden urge to wrap him even tighter in the prickly wool of remorse. "Okay. Now can we talk about the night Jean died?"

"Ah yes, that fateful night. What about it?"

She drove on in a slow-moving clump of cars. "Oh, I was wondering if you've found out any more about the circumstances of Jean's death. And who might have meant her harm."

Before he spoke, she remembered Dan's habit of lighting a cigarette at significant or uncomfortable junctures in conversations. She wondered if Jim had ever smoked, and if so, did he wish he could now?

"Actually," he said slowly, "since then, I've conducted an unofficial survey of hospital staff. Not just those who dealt with her personally, but orderlies and nurses on other services, even some of the janitors. And Art Simon too. I tried to be casual so no one would suspect I was looking for answers. Anyway, I've finally concluded that no one really intended her any harm. Or deliberately tried to infect her. But most of them—maybe half—thought she'd been a traitor when she gave aid and comfort to an enemy. And she'd gotten what she deserved."

"Funny. My best friend in Boston said something like that too. I think it was, 'Any girl who'd sleep with a Nazi deserves what she gets.'"

He nodded. "Jean's thumb-your-nose attitude toward everybody didn't help either. So I believe some staffers got sloppy, or at least careless about antiseptic procedures. Like that last day, even though the private duty nurse I hired was right there, the odor in her room was inexcusable. It had to be negligence."

"Was Dr. Simon's attitude that casual?"

"Hard to tell. He still doesn't think the matter should be pursued. But in practice—well, I was right there after Jean delivered and he went in manually for placental debris. And he did everything by the book. Besides, that's a bloody procedure, but it doesn't carry a high risk of infection. More likely later, when there's less uterine drainage to flush out bacteria. In the old days, that's when Puerperal Sepsis was spread. When docs with dirty hands examined post-partum patients. Simon would never have done anything like that."

"Isn't he Jewish?"

Jim's glance was swift and puzzled. "Yes. But if you're implying he was vindictive because Wil was German, he'd be the last person I'd ever suspect of that sort of prejudice. Fact is, he's one of the most ethical men I've ever known." He sighed. "So we're right back where we were the night she died: we'll probably never know what caused it."

She pondered this truth a moment, then, "And it wouldn't matter if we did, would it? I feel that way about what happened to Dan's boat too. Even if I knew every detail, there's nothing I can do about it. Except if you decided to bring charges against someone, you'd need to find out."

"Criminal negligence is one thing, but this kind of negligence would have been unintentional. Benign, you might say. Good help's so scarce nowadays, everybody's overworked. So it's easy to let proper procedures slide. Especially in Jean's case, when so many staffers believed she was getting her just desserts." Another protracted sigh. "Sometimes even I find myself wondering if her baby's not better off with Cleve and Lorraine than he'd been with her."

The admission was startling. "Why do you say that?"

"Why do you think, Anna? You lived with her, knew the grudge she held against her mother. Would she have been a better mother herself? Or would she have infected the boy with her grudge against me? Convinced him it was good old Uncle Jim's fault he doesn't have a father?"

"Those are interesting questions. But more with no answers."

"I know, I know," he sighed. "But still we speculate."

"Maybe because we're medical people. We're curious about why things happen, so we can believe every problem has a solution."

He nodded, his troubled gaze on traffic ahead. "Speaking of problems, here's another for you. Actually, not a problem so much as a fact. One I haven't told anyone else."

"Uh-oh. Sounds ominous."

"It is. So would you rather not know?"

She hesitated: did she really want more details about Jean's troubled romance? Oh, what the hell, she decided; she'd never found ignorance nearly as blissful as it was said to be. "No. Whatever it is, tell me."

"Well, to begin with, it's something Wil confided the first time I saw him. That Sunday I made a special trip to the island. When we had a chance to speak privately. Remember?"

Impatient to hear the rest, she said only, "Of course."

Jim inhaled deeply as if summoning strength to recount the latest news. "Okay. So maybe you also remember that after the U-boat went down, they found a dead sailor in a raft down the coast a ways? And they concluded he'd been killed in the one of the explosions?"

She nodded, holding her breath for the rest of the story.

"Well, according to Wil, that's not what happened. See, the man was the shipmate he was paired with for that mission. But Wil intended to defect, so he planned to shoot him once they were in the raft, then come back and find

Jean. But when the sub hit the mines, they made it to Little Hope and hunkered down there for the night. The other man fell asleep, so Wil bashed his skull in with a rock. Dumped him back in the raft, then pushed it into the channel when the tide was running in. He hoped a head injury would convince the authorities he'd died in the blast. As indeed it did."

As she coasted to a stop at the next light, Anna could only blink with horror. "You mean, he killed a shipmate, basically in cold blood?"

Jim nodded, mouth tight, face grim.

"My God. To do that to someone he served with…I mean, if the U-boat service is anything like our Sub Force, the crew are more like brothers than shipmates. They have to be to tolerate the close quarters on the boat. Yet he bashed his head in with a rock?"

"Yep. Said the fellow was a Nazi who'd have killed him just as easily if he found out Wil planned to defect."

The light changed and she drove on, past the hamburger stand where she'd once stopped with Dan. Another summer now, nearby beaches crowded with families who appeared carefree and happy, at least at a distance. "Oh my," she sighed. "Dan had to shoot some Japs once, he and another man on a mission to Philippine guerillas. That really was kill or be killed. If he had any remorse, I never saw it. But what Wil did…God, I wonder if he ever told Jean?"

"I doubt it. He wouldn't have wanted her to know that side of him. Might have told the Navy though, to prove he was serious about defecting."

A shard of memory interrupted her thought process. "You know, maybe he did tell her. Because when I was taking care of him, I tried asking about his boat, not to get military secrets, just curious what it had in common with Dan's. But all he ever said was, he was only a cook, and when they needed him, a torpedoman. I had the feeling he might've said more, except Jean was always there, even when I was taking his vitals. I thought she was just trying to keep him quiet to conserve his strength. But in the light of what you just said, maybe she was afraid he'd tell me about the murder. And didn't want me to know."

"Could be, I reckon."

"Anyway, he was in a prison camp. So maybe the Navy didn't believe any of his story, and they were going to execute him, and that's why he tried to escape."

He turned with the hint of a grin. "Hey, we're still doing it, aren't we? Still looking for answers we'll never find."

"I guess. But at least now I understand why you think Johann's better off without Jean. Or Wil either. Gosh, what a heritage that child has."

He nodded but didn't answer. In the ensuing silence, she realized this conversation had connected them again, restoring her sense that all was well, that their friendship was still intact. There was, however, still one more issue to dredge up, with or without resolution.

As if his mind was on the same track, he finally said, "Now, let's talk about something more personal. The issue that troubled you so much you left the island. I still don't understand what you meant, at least not completely."

She took a deep breath, focused on the highway unreeling before them. "Well, it was the way I behaved that night. When you heard me crying and came into my room."

"Go on."

"I know you thought I was trying to seduce you, but I didn't have that in mind. Truly. I only wanted to be held. It wasn't really…you know…sexual."

He chuckled. "Maybe not for you."

She paused, not sure she'd heard him right. "You mean…?"

He nodded. "It took my last ounce of resolve to walk away."

"Really? Oh my goodness! Then why did you?"

"You ought to be able to figure it out. See, you were married to a younger man, one in the prime of life. Probably a perfect physical specimen, not an old cripple like me. Why? What did you think?"

Her voice came out faint and shaky. "Well, mainly that you were still in love with your first wife. And still felt married." She cleared her throat before she went on. "So the next morning I sneaked into your bedroom and saw her picture. And figured she was so beautiful you were still pining for her."

"Pining? Where'd you get that idea?"

"Well, when you wouldn't…you know… I figured you didn't want to be unfaithful."

"Good God, we were divorced years ago! And I stopped feeling married long before it became official."

"So she wasn't the reason you didn't…you know…. didn't want me."

He smiled wryly. "Told you before, I did want you, Anna. So much it hurt. Hell, it was all I could do to walk away that night."

She forgot to breathe. "Then…then why? Why did you act so damned pure? Or were you afraid I'd get pregnant and disgrace your name?"

He laughed. Of all the ways he might have reacted, he laughed. "Hell, I could've lived with that. And not one soul in eastern Maine would've considered it a disgrace. Because I'd have married you in a heartbeat. But you're right. I was afraid of something. Something I couldn't do a damned thing about."

"What in the world was that?

His voice dropped. "Disappointing you."

Margie's suggestion lit up her mind like an aerial flare. "You mean, you think I might have compared you to Dan?"

"Maybe you wouldn't have intended to, but on some

level, you couldn't help it."

"Oh Jm. That's just plain silly." She wanted to come up with an argument more compelling than silliness, but realized he might be right: maybe his first wife had been one to make such comparisons. And thrown them in his face when the grand passion had cooled. She clamped down on the words like a stern school-ma'am. "Anyway, it's good we didn't. Because if I'd conceived, I'd always wonder if you married me for love. Or duty."

He didn't answer, but his eyes went soft. "Oh Anna. Have you no idea?"

God, how she wanted to believe! But believing would mean that by joining the Navy she'd lost a chance to be more than just his nurse. Staving off regret, she forced anger into her tone . "Then why didn't you say something sooner? Like before I left the island"

He slid closer, extending his arm over the back of the seat so his fingers could gentle her shoulder. "Mainly because I didn't think a woman like you would ever want me."

"Wouldn't want you? For God's sake, Jim, what did you think was going on that night? Of course, I wanted you. Oh, it started with needing comfort. But I won't pretend that's where it would've ended. I was sure you knew. And were shocked. Because I behaved in a totally unprofessional way. Anyway, the next day you seemed so cold. So disappointed with me. As if we could never work together again, so I just assumed...."

He shook his head slowly. "You had it all wrong, Anna."

She brushed away a cobweb of old possibilities and came back to this placid afternoon on the busy Post Road in southern Maine. There was no answer to his statement except yes, she had misinterpreted. And based her subsequent decisions on a false assumption from which there was now no retreat.

Spotting an Atlantic station ahead, she squinted at the gas gauge. "Look. Only a quarter tank left. Should I pull in?"

"Might as well. Always fill up when you can." He chuckled. "Like telling someone you love her. Do it before it's too late."

She swerved in alongside the pumps; told the attendant to fill the tank. Had Jim just said, Like telling someone you love her? Inhaling garlicky gasoline fumes, she was rocked by the thud of her heartbeats as the words replayed in her mind. So insistent she lost track of time, was surprised when the boy wiped the windshield. Jim counted out ration coupons and dollar bills, then asked, "Want me to take the wheel now?"

"No," she sighed, started the engine again. "Just talk to me. Tell me more things I don't know."

"Like what?"

"Well, first, why did you let me leave without saying one word about your feelings?"

He gazed out at a pebbly beach, a colorful mosaic of families, umbrellas, kids splashing at the lacy edge of the surf. "Told you before. Thought you needed time away. Didn't know…"

"What?"

"Didn't know you were going to burn your bridges."

"Well, I wouldn't have if I'd had any idea you felt like I do."

He sighed. "Guess we let each other believe the same lie. Maybe because we were still trying to make sense of Jean's death. And it was too soon to trust our feelings about anything else."

She drove numbly, hearing lines from Whittier in her head: *For of all sad words of tongue or pen/the saddest are: "It might have been!"* "Damn you, Jim Millett," she muttered, sensing his shock. "That makes me so mad. At both of us."

"Well, then. Look at it this way. It just wasn't our time."

"And maybe it'll never be. Maybe we lost the only chance we'll ever have."

He reached over and clasped her hand on the wheel. "No, we didn't. I love you, and I believe we'll get another. Even if it isn't till after the war."

"But who knows when that'll be?"

"Hell, I've been waiting so long, what's another year or two?"

Despite her own frustration, his optimism and stubborn belief made her smile. Almost like her father's mantra that all things worked together for good. "And then what?"

"Then what? Well, maybe you'll come to work with me in the practice. And decide if our feelings could lead to something more permanent."

Joy twitched in her, tentative and fragile as the first movements of a developing fetus. "What do you mean by 'something more permanent'?"

"Oh, maybe being engaged."

"After the war, you mean."

"Right."

"But that's a long time to wait. In the meantime, can we have tonight?"

He turned quickly. "Tonight?"

"And maybe tomorrow and Tuesday night too. I don't have to go home till Wednesday." When he didn't answer, she added, "Or are you still too noble to take advantage?"

He slid closer, moved his free hand to her thigh. "Right now, I don't feel noble at all."

Breathless, she said, "Well, that's okay. Your heart is pure. And you intend to make an honest woman of me someday."

"Anna, you're already the most honest woman I know."

She laughed, and pulled up her skirt so only the thin tissue of her hose was between his fingers and the flesh of her upper leg. She wondered if he'd be shocked if she suggested he unfasten her garter. But before she could, he got the idea himself. And she was the one who was shocked. And pleased beyond words.

North of Portland, the sky turned sullen, the air so cool they cranked up the windows. As they passed the high fencing around the Brunswick air station, drops spattered the windshield. By the time they stopped for the signal at the Bath Iron Works, the wipers were working hard and the car was cool and damp.

The light changed. Jim turned on the heater, then leaned a kiss on her cheek. The space between them no longer felt like a hearth without a fire, but had begun to glow with the warmth that presaged a new sort of relationship. A man and woman thing at last, after almost a year of propriety and professionalism. Would it endure for eternity, or just for the next few nights before she left for the war? She had no idea. But in the meantime, she and Jim would explore the desire that had begun to glow between them. After that, her commitment to the Navy would take over and toss her into the bloody whirling vortex of the war.

But only after she'd finally tasted love in Jim's bed. And made up for all the time she'd behaved like a damned nun with him.

Chapter Twenty-Eight

As she drove around the Rockhampton town square, wet paving shimmered and yellow leaves swirled in the headlights. Jim said he needed to pick up a prescription, so she parked at the Rexall, and took the Brownie to the counter while he went back to the rear pharmacy. By the time the clerk had loaded her film, Jim was waiting, a white paper bag in hand. "Hope you don't mind, but I have to make rounds too."

"Always on duty, aren't you?"

His quick, shocked look made her bite her tongue in remorse.

While he was in the hospital, she pulled a sweater from her suitcase and huddled into it. But the chill persisted, especially when she tried to picture the coming night. If only Margie hadn't planted that damned seed of doubt. Not that it mattered; she was determined to love him even if the most they could do was hold hands. Still, she was restless. For a while, she tried to distract herself by studying the camera she'd borrowed from her father, then an old *Penobscot Gazette* on the floor. The last distraction was the bag behind the seat. She peeked in, expecting brown bottles or white envelopes. Instead, there was a gray cardboard box stenciled with black letters: *Condoms, latex, 12 dozen.*

She gasped, read it again. Condoms indeed. Why in the name of all that was holy? Did he expect to need them with her? But twelve dozen? A hundred forty-four? Unless he had a side she'd never suspected.

Oh, dear Jesus. Did the kindly, overworked doctor persona disguise a satyr? Maybe that was his secret vice. Maybe he spent his carnal urges on prostitutes and loose women, then played the saint with her and the good people at his church.

Well, so much for Margie's theory. If he had a problem, impotence jolly well wasn't it.

She replaced the bag and squeezed her eyes closed against images so disgusting she was tempted to bolt from the car, run back to the Rexall and catch the next bus south. Never mind friends or clothes left behind on the island. Without a word, she'd simply disappear from Jim's life. And one day, from the safety of a distant Navy assignment, write and explain why: "Yes, I wanted to make love with you, but not if I was part of a crowd".

Before she could move, however, he slid in under the wheel; he smelled of fresh air and damp wool. "Damn. It's really turned cold. Now. Ready for a little supper?"

"I guess," she muttered.

"Don't mind Ye Olde Coffee Shoppe, do you?"

"It'll be fine." Cold and tension set her shivering, her teeth chattering.

He drove back to the square, talking now about his hospitalized patients. Her answers were so minimal, he gave her a quizzical look as he set the handbrake. "Sure this is okay?"

"Uh-huh."

"They have good clam chowder Sunday nights."

She opened the door and stepped out into the chilly rain. "I said it'll be fine, Jim." Inside the hotel, she waited till he'd caught up before she entered the restaurant. Only a few tables were occupied, so she ignored the hostess and headed for a quiet corner. As he limped over, Jim looked puzzled. She was gratified; if she was baffled, he jolly well ought to be too.

He took a seat and wiped drops from his glasses. For the first time since she'd known him, she had to force herself to look him full in the eyes. The waitress brought menus, but he waved them off and ordered the chowder and pimiento cheese sandwiches. "That's okay, isn't it?"

"Whatever you want." She folded her arms, crossed her legs, and directed a scowling, tight-lipped gaze toward some noisy teenagers nearby. Laughing, joking, as if they'd been to a church meeting and believed the Lord would always be their shield and buckler, shepherding through every danger, even those caused by their own stupid behavior. Abruptly, she resented their insouciance and their assumptions that they were indestructible. Like a bunch of damned submariners who raced motorcycles and couldn't wait to get into the war in their stinking steel coffins. Well, before long the little snots would learn nothing was as pretty as the church painted it.

"Anna," Jim said, outside her thoughts. "What's going on?"

"What?" She swung her gaze back to him. "What do you mean?"

"Well, just that you were so sweet earlier, and now you act…oh, angry. Or hurt." His eyes narrowed. "Oh my word. You didn't look in the Rexall bag, did you?"

She swung that hard look back to the kids. "You were gone a long while. I got bored."

"And now you want to know what the hell I'm doing with all those contraceptives, right?"

"Well, it's none of my business. But I do have to wonder if you've got a couple of hot tomatoes on the string somewhere."

"Hot tomatoes?" His eyes crinkled. "Mother of God, that's the most ridiculous thing I've ever heard! Don't you know me better than that?"

She shrugged. "Then why…?"

"Because I have some male patients who can't stay away from those…those tomatoes, and end up with VD. And plenty of married men who can't figure out why their wives are always pregnant. Condoms are rationed, but I can get them. So I show them how to use them…with a test tube."

Her face warmed. "Oh. Well…that makes sense."

"I keep some on the island too, in a locked drawer."

"Oh, I see."

"Or did you think I had some big plans?"

She flushed, lowered her gaze to the pink polish on her nails. "Not really. I didn't—I mean, I was just so shocked. I didn't really think about it."

He reached across the table to clasp her hand. "Sorry. Didn't mean to upset you. Should've told you right away."

She was finally able to return his smile. And realize how silly she'd been—jumping to the worst possible conclusion. Mistrusting him now seemed as ridiculous as impugning her father's spirituality.

It was almost eight when they pulled into his drive. He unlocked the kitchen door, preceded her inside, and switched on the overhead light. Shivering, she set her bag on a chair. "Better get you a brandy for that chill," he said. "Don't want you going into the Navy with pneumonia, do we?"

She followed him to a formal dining room redolent of mildew and dust, ancient oriental rugs and dry-rotted damask drapes. In the glow of a grimy crystal chandelier, he poured from a decanter on a Victorian sideboard, then handed her a snifter. She sipped; the burn in her throat made her wince.

"Now. Guess what I have to do next," he said.

"Call patients?"

"Right. You know me too well."

Back in the kitchen, he grabbed her bag and carried it up the hall, then unknotted his tie and draped it around the newel post at the foot of the stairs. "I'll try not to be too long."

"How long does that mean?"

"Oh, an hour or so." He grinned. "Why? Impatient?"

"No, of course not," she said primly. "What's another hour?"

"If you want to, you can wait upstairs."

"Where? In your bed?"

The grin touched his eyes, melted her fatigue. "I wouldn't mind."

"First, though, may I have a proper kiss?"

He leaned toward her, just brushing her lips with his. "There. Proper enough?"

She laughed. "Maybe I should've said an improper kiss."

He held out his arms. Setting the snifter on the lamp table, she walked into the cautious embrace of a stolid Down Easter, one obviously unaccustomed to romantic advances. His kiss was so hesitant, so abashed; it reminded her of Bob Hallowell's first amorous advance. At age fifteen, neither she nor he had any idea what they were doing; Bob never did quite figure it out. But she had. though Jim still seemed reserved. Until finally, his arms tightened around her. Down the hall, the grandmother clock chimed the quarter hour.

Breathless, she backed away, gestured toward his office. Light from the hallway spilled across the desk. "You make your calls in there, don't you?"

He nodded, watching curiously as she assessed the leather swivel chair to determine if it was sturdy enough to support the activity she had in mind. The prospect, naughty and daring, made her giddy. Aware it might shock him, however, she swallowed more brandy for courage, then groped through the dark examining room to the lavatory. There, she stepped out of her panties, but, feeling even more wicked, left the garter belt and stockings on. And wondered, peripherally, if this whorish behavior would disgust—or excite him. She knew only how Dan had reacted when she'd taken the initiative. She had to risk it now.

When she returned, he was sitting at the desk, cane propped against it. From the glass lamp globe, pale green light glowed on the condom bag. He'd pulled the phone over and picked up the receiver to jiggle the hook for the operator, but she took it from him and hung it up. "Can your calls wait a while?"

"Sure." His voice was rough.

She drained the brandy, then felt in the bag for a tinfoil-wrapped packet in the condoms box. "I hate these things," she whispered, "but I don't want to turn up pregnant at OCS."

"No, of course not." His hands trembled as he folded his glasses into his shirt pocket and pushed the chair back. "Might ruin your career."

Hoisting her skirt, she straddled him. The hard metal of his brace pressed against her thigh, but when he didn't wince, she assumed he wasn't in pain. So, clasping his face between her hands, she kissed him again, and again. Until she knew beyond any doubt: Margie'd been wrong. Thanks be to God, she hadn't known what the hell she was talking about.

For a few moments, the roaring in her ears blotted out all sound except the squealing protest of the chair's casters. Until he gasped. And clutched her so tightly her breath was stifled.

When the hall clock chimed the half hour, his hold finally loosened. "Good God, Anna," he breathed. "You certainly are inventive."

"You didn't mind, did you?"

His laugh took her by surprise. “Hell, no. What’d you think?”

“Well, I didn’t know. I thought…see, last week in Boston, my girlfriend told me sometimes men who’ve had polio are…uh, you know, impotent.”

He went on laughing, tilting his head like a happy kid. “Look, dear. I may have a bum leg. But everything else works fine.” His face sobered. “Supposed she’d been right, though. What would you have done?”

“Loved you anyway,” she glibly, though she had no idea.

“Even if we couldn’t have normal relations? Or children?”

“Of course. But I’m glad she was wrong.”

He kissed her again, this time with the placid tenderness of a satisfied lover. “Well, now that I’ve passed that test, will you think about marrying me?”

“I can’t right now. Can’t be married in the Navy.” She got to her feet, smoothed out the severely creased skirt of the linen dress she’d worn to church earlier.

“Then think about getting engaged. That’s permissible, isn’t it?”

She nodded. “Okay. I’ll think about it. Now you make your calls. I’ll wait in your bed.”

“Haven’t had enough for one night?”

“Not when we have so few nights left.”

His face darkened. “Oh God, don’t remind me.”

Upstairs, she went through her usual evening rituals, even put on a chaste plisse nightgown, then crawled hesitantly into his rumpled bed. The sheets smelled faintly of a man’s body she didn’t yet know intimately. Rain whispered at the windows, the curtains fluttered inward on a damp breeze. A year and a half after Dan had sailed for the last time, she felt womanly again, tingling with remembrance and promise. But even as she recalled the coupling with Jim, she was back to the first time with Dan, with any man. Nothing like this, except the physical similarity.

That night, they'd just returned from visiting his parents in Brooklyn and had told hers of their plans to marry. In her modest Kittery apartment, she'd made bacon and egg sandwiches, he'd given her the engagement ring that had been his mother's, then said he needed to get back to the boat. But before he left, she'd asked—come right out and made her intentions plain—for a little loving first. He hadn't had a condom with him, but when she assured him it was a safe time of the month, he'd been convinced. He'd always been so easily convinced.

That first time had seemed sacramental, almost like Eucharist, an outward symbol of their love, their commitment. And though he'd left almost immediately afterward, she'd felt forever anointed. Forever Dan's.

Yet on this night less than three years later, she'd made love with another man. Not spiritual this time, less symbolic of a new commitment to Jim than to the end of the previous one to Dan. The final chapter of their romance, marking not just his loss, but of her faith that her first love would last forever

Strangely now her thoughts were all of him; would he understand why she'd moved on? Or had he believed her a woman who would feel such passion only once? And forever after remain alone with memories, her only companions, her solace till the end of time?

Too late now, of course; what had just happened with Jim was irrevocable. Dan would've said, "It's not like it's a light bulb that you can unscrew." The deed was done, the tentative new commitment sealed by the same sacrament that had sealed the first. And all she could do was pray that even if he didn't understand, wherever he was in time and space, Dan's spirit would forgive her for moving on.

She was pondering the combination of circumstances that

had led her across the past year and a half-- from Dan's bed in San Francisco to Jim's in East Point, Maine-- when she heard his steps on the stairs, his cane in the hall, then approaching the bed. In the pale darkness, his hands were warm, and he was impatient to love her again, this time without haste, and thoroughly, with none of the previous awkwardness or pretense.

Yet as soon as the fireworks had subsided, even while they lay entwined with the scent of rain and lovemaking between them, she became aware of a heaviness drifting over her, like the harbinger of a squall spawned in summer's heat. Before she could take shelter in reason, it crashed down, leaving her with no more control of her emotions than she had of the weather.

As it raged, part of her wanted to assure Jim he hadn't caused this storm of tears. But she was unable to calm herself long enough to even mumble the words. Still, he held her to him, tightly as a mother might enfold a fretful infant, rocking, stroking her hair, kissing her face. His voice was blurred, but his consolation and compassion were unmistakable.

Eventually, the deep sobs subsided to a shallow residue of hiccups. He reached a handkerchief from the night stand and put it in her hand. She sat up, blew her nose and took slow, deep breaths until her throat loosened. "Sorry, Jim," she murmured, "I was so happy. And then…then I was hurting. And I don't know why."

His fingertips massaged her neck. "Things caught up with you."

Because she already had a good idea, she didn't ask what things? but retrieved her nightgown, and felt the way to the bathroom. In the harsh glare of the wash stand light, her reflection was bleary-eyed, with puffy cheeks, straggly hair, dripping red nose. And spasms convulsing her chest every few seconds. Hardly the image of their first night she wanted him to cosset in her absence.

She let the tap run cold, soaked a washcloth, pressed it to her eyes. Combed her hair, drank a glass of water and went back to his room. She didn't notice when the hiccupping stopped, but as soon as she was in the bed, he pulled her to him again. "Sorry," she told him once more. "Couldn't help myself."

"It's all right, Anna. Been a long day and you're worn out."

But as she felt the throb of his heart next to hers and the warmth of his hand on her hip, she realized everything wasn't all right: she was still connected to Dan, even after his death, and to the baby, and Jean, and other women who didn't live to raise their infants, and babies who didn't live to be born. And to the old fellow she'd found dead in his shack, and all the strong young men who went to sea in ships that didn't return.

All the lost souls of her lifetime.

Why tonight, when she'd finally reconnected to the joyous essence of life, was she so conscious of the immanence of death? As if she were suspended between the two realities, belonging to neither Dan nor Jim, but to the perils of the world beyond, that world of war she'd chosen to join before this week ended.

She wanted to tell him of this darkness in her, but couldn't speak of it. So she blew her nose again and concentrated on the reassurance of his arms about her, his warmth close beside her. Still sleepless when he began to snore, she reviewed the past twelve hours since she'd met him outside St. Stephen's. When the world had begun to shift, altering her view of the future again. Far too much to make sense of now when she was worn with the events of those hours.

And with the emotional detritus of them still whirling in her mind, even prayer felt beyond her. Except for the simple

Jesus, Jesus petition, unadorned by any others. And tonight, uttered with the certainty that nothing more was needed.

Chapter Twenty-Nine

The next morning, leaving Jim to the routines of his practice, she went back to Hope Island on *Molly B.* Déjà vu might have gripped her if she hadn't been in the company of the nurse who'd replaced her in the clinic. She'd taken to Grace Foye right away, probably because she was older, and serene of manner and face. Plumpish, with gray hair tucked into a bun, and soft brown eyes, motherly in a way Anna's own mother had never been.

On the other hand, Grace's husband, Matt was a rough-hewn giant who towered over everyone. When he spoke, which he did only rarely, haltingly and almost too softly to hear, his watery gray eyes stared into space. According to Jim, this was what shell shock looked like all these years since World War I had ended. And nothing could heal it.

While Matt stayed in the pilothouse, Anna sat with Grace under the afterdeck awning. And talked of plans, Grace's to move to the island, Anna's to go into the Navy. "And after Newport, then where?" she asked.

"I'm hoping a hospital ship. In the Western Pacific, where all the fighting is."

She clucked her tongue. "Oh my dear. I can scarce imagine the sad things you'll be seeing. Hope it doesn't change you. I mean, like the Great War changed my poor husband."

"I'll be fine. And when it's over, Jim and I plan to be married."

"Well, that's the kind of news I like to hear!" Her eyes shone with approval. " I've known Jim Millett since he was a sprout. Even before the polio. Years and years now. He's always been a man after God's own heart."

"And mine," Anna murmured so quietly the other women didn't hear.

The last time she'd entered this mirror-calm harbor, Cleve had been waiting for Jean's body. He was on the pier again now with the same wagon, the same black mare. Beside it, Lorraine rocked the baby buggy and Beth waved a greeting. As the boat splashed toward them, Anna's vision blurred with nostalgia. Before she could turn tearful, she snapped a picture to help her remember the poignant moment.

At the foot of the gangway, everyone hugged her before she grabbed Johann for a cuddle. Almost a month old now, he'd doubled his birth weight, Lorraine boasted. Anna wasn't surprised that holding him ignited a brief flare of loss for her own baby. To banish it, she blurted out her good news about Jim. "Of course, we'll have to wait till after the war. Married women can't join the Navy. And if they get married afterward, they can't stay in."

Lorraine's bright red smile faded. "Oh, that's too bad. He's waited so long for a woman like you." She shook her head. "Have to tell you, Anna, if I was you, I'd go for love."

Vaguely unsettled, she said, "I only wish it were that simple," and hoped Lorraine didn't challenge the statement. She needn't have worried; as they walked toward the clinic, the others caught her up on island happenings, such as they were. Nothing new, no big events, just the ordinary routines she'd come to know well in ten months here. But now, aware of her outsider status, she even caught glimmers of envy because she was leaving for adventures they could only imagine. As if when she put on that glamorous uniform, her life would become one long romantic movie featuring tropical seas, a noble purpose, and endless attention from handsome Navy men.

Later, Cleve drove her to the hotel and dragged her big train case up from the basement to her old room. Sunlight laid tiny gold stripes on the pine floor under the louvers of the closed shutters. As she filled her bag with moth-balled winter clothes, packets of letter, photographs and an old diary, he sat on the bare mattress watching.

"Right good news about you and Doc." His jaws worked on a plug of Red Man. "Sure hope you come back okay, though. Hate to see him disappointed after all this time."

"I'll be back," she said with more conviction than she felt. "The war's going to be over soon anyway."

"Oh, I pray so." He shook his head. "After what happened to Jean, hate to lose you too."

Murmuring her standard, "I'll be fine," she bent to hug him. The pungency of straw and horse manure, chewing tobacco and sour sweat enveloped her. "Now, tell me how you and Lorraine are making out with the baby."

A rare smile lit his crinkled face. "Only problem is, she can't keep taking him to work. Getting too lively. Pretty soon she'll have to decide whether to go on working, or just be a mother. Me, I say anybody can run a post office. But not everybody can mother a little boy."

Lips tight, she nodded, snapped the bag shut, then glanced into the bathroom. Jean's toothbrush was still there. She touched it with her fingertips, then joined Cleve at Jean's grave; the mounded dirt was still fresh. It was just behind her father's and her grandparents'. And across the cemetery from those of the U-boat sailors. Where Anna had seen Dan—or his ghost—the June night after she'd learned he'd been dead for a year.

She was still staring at the spot when Cleve reminded her that Fletch wanted to leave by one, so they hurried back to the station wagon and rode down to the Lunch Box.

As if it were any ordinary Monday, Lorraine, Grace and Beth were waiting for her, had even ordered her favorite ham sandwich on rye. She choked it down while new tunes on the juke box -- *You'd be so Nice to Come Home to*, and *I'll Walk Alone*—reminded her she no longer worked here, but was shipping out for parts unknown. As if it'd slipped her mind.

Besides Cleve and Lorraine, a surprising number of islanders were on the pier to see her off and say things like, "If you see any Japs, thumb your nose at them for me." She snapped pictures of all of them. Fletcher carried her suitcase aboard, started the engine and revved it as a few last tourists hustled toward the boat; she was the last to climb the gangway. As they came about in the harbor, she stood misty-eyed waving at those on shore long after they'd cleared the breakwater. The island receded, like the life she'd lived there. Leaning on the rail apart from the day people, she sniffled all the way back to East Point.

After he'd secured the boat, Fletch drove her to Jim's in the old Model A pickup in which he'd brought her here the day she'd arrived in Maine. The Buick wasn't in the drive, but the back door was open. He brought the bag inside, then grabbed her for an unexpected hug. "You be careful out there, nurse. You hear? Don't take no chances with them Japs. 'Cause everybody wants you back safe and sound. Specially Doc." Blinking, shoulders hunched, he hurried out.

With time on her hands and a newly proprietary interest, she wandered through Jim's house. He'd been raised in this boxy, high-ceilinged Victorian his grandparents had built in 1878, where his grandfather had practiced medicine before him. And where, she imagined, he'd want to continue to live after they were married. She could barely imagine it: the woodwork was too dark for her taste; there was too much bric-a-brac on display, too many threadbare Oriental rugs, gloomy paintings, faded drapes. At least by now, his ex-wife's picture was gone from his bureau, replaced by a studio shot of Anna her mother had given him the previous day. In nurse's whites, cape, and frilly pleated Mass General cap, she was smiling with the confidence that all things were possible to those who loved the Lord. And worked like the devil.

Five years before, had she really believed that simplistic homily? Probably. Since then, however, life had taught her about complexities she'd never have believed, back when she was engaged to uncomplicated, undemanding, uninteresting Bob Hallowell. Back before she'd met Dan Donovan, a man whose nature was so complex, she wondered now if she'd ever have understood him, even if they'd been married sixty years.

She was rooting through the kitchen cupboards when Jim pulled into the drive just after five. His greeting kiss was wet and warm. But when she suggested they make love on the examining table in his office, his look was so astounded she realized she'd shocked him even more than she had on his desk chair the night before. She could barely imagine his reaction if she told him how sexually adventurous Dan had been. Some things he was better off not knowing.

But then he laughed, and glanced at the slacks and shirt she'd worn all day. "Wouldn't mind, but I made reservations at the French restaurant in town. Folks tell me the food's only passable but it's plenty romantic. So why don't you get into that pretty dress you wore Sunday and we'll see how we like it." His voice dropped. "Figure I owe you one romantic evening before you leave."

The yellow linen was so hopelessly wrinkled, she decided instead on the new black rayon, with his pearls. As they made their entrance to the pink-painted mansion on the Rockhampton waterfront, everyone in the dining room turned to gawk at them. As if amazed to see the good doctor—colorless, sensible Jim Millett, whose first wife hadn't been worth spitting on—squiring a well-turned-out younger woman who was obviously smitten with him. Or so she hoped as she clung to his arm and smiled her fondest smile. A heavily-accented waiter led them through the candle-lit ambiance to a window table overlooking the bay. The menu was huge, but all in French, so she let Jim order for her. When he also asked for champagne, she said, "So you're fluent in French. What else don't I know about you?"

He reached for her hand across the small round table. "Anna, from the day we met, I felt you could read me like a book. At least, everything important."

"I had the same feeling about you." She paused. "Funny, though, neither of us knew what was really going on the night Jean died."

Candlelight flared on his glasses when he shook his head. "Thank God we do now."

The waiter brought the champagne, made a fuss over the pouring and tasting. Finally he was gone. When they'd toasted and sipped, Jim withdrew a small, square box from his jacket pocket. Even before she lifted the lid, she knew it held a ring. The platinum solitaire was so imposing, she gulped, remembering the old ring of his mother's Dan had given her for their engagement. And the tiny diamond that now lay amid the rubble on the Union Pacific right-of-way somewhere between Sacramento and Donner Pass.

"I wasn't sure it'd fit," Jim said, "but if it doesn't, I'll have it sized tomorrow."

As unobtrusively as possible, she slipped her wedding

ring into her purse, then put on the new one without any of the difficulty she had with Dan's ring. "Oh, it's beautiful," she sighed, twisting her hand to maximize the glitter. "And it fits perfectly."

"And if you're not allowed to wear it in uniform, I bought a silver chain so you can hide it around your neck. If you want to."

She nodded, extended her left hand to touch his. Unable to speak, she swallowed more champagne. This helped. "Maybe it's good I'm leaving so soon. Otherwise I'd be so happy, I'd burst."

"I know. Crazy, isn't it, how life can be wonderful and sad at the same time? I haven't felt anything for so long, and now….all this." He shook his head.

"When was the last time? With your first wife?" As she asked, she realized again that story had no bearing on this one. Still, curiosity was an old compulsion.

He toyed with the diamond, stroked her fingers, gazed out the window at the harbor. As if reconnoitering the past for the answer. When he looked at her again, his eyes were soft. "Listen, dear. You have to understand that was nothing like this. It was just, well….heat. No light, just heat."

"Oh." She inhaled sharply, wishing he hadn't confirmed what she'd suspected. How ridiculous, she thought; she'd known heat before too, irrational and consuming. Why shouldn't Jim? "And now…" she said, "now what is it?"

He grinned. "Both. Heat and light. The way I always thought it should be, but never expected."

She tried to imagine how Emily Dickinson would have responded to this sentiment, but all she could think of was, "Oh. That's nice. I …I really like that."

Driving home, he said he didn't have to call patients, in case she wanted to turn in early. She wasn't tired but realized these three nights might be the only honeymoon they'd ever have. Switching her thoughts from pathetic to practical, she said, “Something I’ve been meaning to ask, Jim. When are you going to let me see your bad leg? ”

His gaze swung from the road. “My leg? Why?”

“Well, last night you undressed in the bathroom. And this morning you chased me out before you got up. But sooner or later, you’re going to have to take off your brace in front of me. Are you worried I’ll be squeamish?”

“No, of course not.”

“Because I’ve seen what polio does to limbs before, you know.”

“Well, last night, I didn’t want to interrupt the mood. And this morning there wasn’t time. Though I don’t see why it matters.”

“Because it’s part of you. You can’t live with someone and keep something like that hidden.”

He inhaled deeply. “Oh, it’s possible.”

“But how?”

He was silent, as if wrestling with an old demon. Perhaps one generated in his childhood experience with polio, then nurtured by his wife in ways Anna didn’t want to imagine. It seemed a long while before he muttered, “Separate bedrooms. Meeting in the dark. And only when necessary.”

She wanted him to define necessary, but knew introducing that aspect of his past would only intrude on these swiftly-flying moments. Instead, she ran her hand over his thigh and felt the steel cage again. “Well, I’m not going to be that kind of wife. I’m interested in your whole body. Not just the sleeping giant.”

He chuckled. “The sleeping giant. A Navy term?”

“No, learned it in nursing school. Nurses can be quite irreverent about body parts, you know.”

“Med students are even worse.” He patted her hand. “Anyway, if that’s what you want, sure, I’ll get undressed with you. But it has to be mutual.”

***

Tuesday morning, while he saw office patients, she tried to organize his files. His last nurse had left three years before, so they were such a rat's nest she was relieved she wasn't coming to work for him. At lunchtime, she fixed tuna sandwiches, then rode along on house calls and to the hospital. While he was making rounds, she walked two blocks to the Loblaws Market for a half pound of ground round, two baking potatoes, some green beans and six large mushrooms. When she told him the supper menu, he said, "You don't have to cook for me. My mother never did and my wife wouldn't even try. Said the kitchen was too old-fashioned."

They hadn't discussed it, but she surmised his mother had been a party girl, with no tolerance for discomfort, as witnessed by the fact she and his father had peremptorily run away to Florida after his sister's death. They hadn't been back since, only rarely called, and Jim seemed averse to talking about them. Nonetheless, Anna assumed they spent their days on a boat or the beach, their evenings at parties or country club dances, pouring martinis down their throats and trying to be F. Scott Fitzgerald and Zelda. The very thought of parents neglecting their only son—particularly this special son—made her bristle.

"I hope I never meet either of them," she said. "Your mother or your first wife, I mean. Because I'd probably forget I'm a Christian. I'm not the best cook in the world, but by golly, I can still make the effort."

His face softened. "You're going to spoil me, Anna."

"High time somebody did. Only wish I had longer."

He didn't answer, but his jaw tightened.

Trying for festivity, she set the breakfast room table with a linen cloth, candles in silver holders, and his grandmother's good silver and china. But by the time they sat down, her thoughts were so filled with the dark truth that this was their last night, she barely tasted the food. And could think of nothing cheerful to divert him from noticing her mood.

Fortunately he had good news. "Had a letter the other day from a med school friend." He folded a slice of bread and wiped up mushroom gravy. "Wanted to know if I'd be interested in taking him into the practice when he gets out of the Navy. Lord, if he only knew how interested, he might be scared off."

"Well, good. Time you had some help here. And after we start having children…." Laying fingertips on his arm, she felt underlying muscles and bone through the shirtsleeve. And in spite of two nights of passion, craved his body again.

He stopped chewing. "Children? Uh…how many do you want?"

"Well, one right away. I mean, after we get married, of course. And a couple more after a decent interval. At least three."

His expression turned grave. "But Anna," he said in his quiet, serious voice; "You've already had one section. Three's the limit, you know. As for me, even one child's more than I ever hoped for. See, I never even expected to marry again."

"You didn't? Why not?"

"Well, for one thing, my parents' marriage didn't inspire me. And my own knocked all the hope out of me. Then I met you. " He grinned. "Still seems too good to be true. Except for tomorrow. Your leaving's all too believable."

Their fingers intertwined. Desire pulsed in her bloodstream, sorrow retreated. She inhaled a good deep breath and said, "Mind if I just stack the dishes for now? I need to pack so we can get an early start in the morning. What time, do you think?"

"I'll set the alarm for six, so I can take you to the bus

before I go to the island. As for the dishes, sure. They'll give me something to do tomorrow evening." He swallowed, pushed overcooked beans around with his fork, eyes downcast. "I have to tell you, dear. I hate to think of going back to my old life." He glanced up, face a study in sorrow. "Easier to live without love if you've never known it."

She gripped his hand, saw the moisture in his eyes, the tightened lips. She shoved back her chair. "Come on then. Let's go upstairs."

They loved each other for what seemed all night, though now and then she dozed off, only to wake with a start, remembering their time was running out. When the sky grayed with dawn and he leaned over to kiss her, she said, "Do you have any condoms left for your patients?"

His laugh was subdued, forced. "A few. Next year we can blow them up and use them for balloons at Johann's first birthday. I mean, if you're home by then."

Always the return to that reality. Forgetting lasted only a moment or two, for the space of a kiss, or the duration of intercourse. Then the world closed in again. And the future rushed at her like a dive bomber bent on the destruction of her remaining joy.

They ate breakfast—the usual bad coffee and stale Wheaties—at the scarred kitchen table. She sniffled continuously; Jim looked grim. Upstairs, she brushed her teeth, then left the brush in the holder. If she never came back, would it become a *memento mori* as Jean's had at the hotel?

When she came downstairs, he'd already loaded the big suitcase into the car. All she had to do was carry the overnight bag and try not to look back at the life she was leaving. True, she was marginally exhilarated by the coming Navy adventure, but another part of her was tortured by a recurring sense of *it might have been.*

Leaving East Point, neither spoke till they we were on the

bridge over the inlet and Jim reached for her hand. His tone was strangely formal. "Anna, dear, I want you to know, whatever happens while you're gone, I'll always cherish this time we've had together."

She shot him a stunned glance. In that distant, solemn voice, the words rang untrue, like a speech he'd written and memorized and rehearsed. Perhaps he had; perhaps using the right words was the only way he could even hint at his deepest fears. "But nothing's going to happen," she said.

His smile was ironic. "Oh, I didn't mean in the obvious way. More like, suppose you meet someone else. Younger. With two good legs. Someone who can take you dancing and sailing and mountain climbing. Somebody colorful and whole."

"Oh Jim, that's silly," I said automatically. "I'm going to marry you. I love you."

He twiddled the new ring on her left hand. "I know you do. And I believe you're sincere. At least right now. But who knows how the war's going to change you?"

Her eyes filled, causing the pastel morning to shimmer as if underwater, pink and pearly light glowing on vague shapes of houses, boats and trees. "If you think that, why did you give me the ring?"

"Because I want you, no matter what. Want to feel connected while you're gone. On the other hand, I don't want you to feel tied. It's only an engagement ring, not a legal obligation."

Her gaze followed shadows flitting across the road ahead. "You just can't believe in happy endings, can you?"

"Lord knows, I want to." He cleared his throat. "Well, at least we've had these three days. I feel so loved right now, I could let you go. If I had to."

Suddenly she was beyond tears, gripped by an aching tightness in chest and throat, with no idea how to assure him of her faithfulness. The past three days had been so intense, she was too used up to try. Then she remembered what Lorraine had said after Anna had told her about the Navy's ban on married women: "If it was me, I'd go for love." For her, a black-and-white choice. Love trumped duty every day of the week.

Had he thought that was Anna's guiding principle too? "Tell me something, Jim. The last few days, have you been expecting me to change my mind about the Navy?"

The sudden inhalation and widening of his eyes hinted at the answer, though all he said was, "Of course not. I know you're committed."

"But I could still get out of it. Shoot myself in the foot, or marry you. Either way I'd be excused without dishonor."

"Shoot yourself in the foot, or marry me? That's a hell of a comparison."

"A figure of speech. You know what I mean."

He nodded, face grim and tight. "'I could not love thee, dear, so much, loved I not honor more.' Is that it?"

"Well, I don't know if it's honor, or duty. I mean, a chance to do something important in the war. Something I've been trained for, something there's a real need for. God, Jim. Of all people, I thought you'd understand. Duty's your middle name."

He sighed; the car slowed. "Told you before, I do understand. And I certainly haven't tried to change your mind."

"Yes, but maybe you hoped I'd change it myself. For love. Because I'm a woman. That's what we do, isn't it? We fall in love, and nothing else matters. Like Jean, with Wil. We get caught up in romance, and making love with our beloved. And that's the end of everything. Oh, except motherhood. Maybe since I've already lost a baby, you thought I'd be that way too."

"No, no," he said quietly. "I swear, I never thought that."

"Well, maybe not with your mind. But some part of you

is disappointed. Some part of you thinks if I really loved you, I wouldn't leave. So now I'm just one more woman who doesn't love you enough to stay with you. Like your mother and your wife. Isn't that how it feels?"

His silence gave her the rest of the answer. By now they were passing through the seedy outskirts of Rockhampton, with only a few minutes left to resolve this contretemps. If resolution was even possible in such compressed circumstances. She felt like an hourglass emptying for the last time.

As he steered them toward the center of town, he said, "Sorry if I seem cynical, Anna. But you know my background."

"Yes. But I'm neither of those women. I'm going away, true. But I'm not leaving you in any way except physically. I'm taking you with me in my heart."

He shrugged and stared straight ahead. "Taking me with you in your heart? Don't know what that means. Guess I'll just have to wait and see."

Frustration mingled with despair like a physical ache in her chest as they approached the town square. As words failed her. As time ran out.

The bus was already at the Rexall when they came up behind it. A long line was boarding, mostly shipyard workers with lunch pails. Jim parked, then dragged the larger bag from the trunk. Tight-lipped, she followed while he summoned the driver to stow it in the baggage compartment. She was about to hand over money for the fare, but Jim paid before she had a chance.

More desperate than ever to make him understand, she clutched his hand. But all she could think to say was, "I'll write soon as I get to OCS."

He nodded; oblique sunlight highlighted every crease in his face, making him look old and haggard. "Now, promise me something?"

"Anything."

"Don't forget me. Even if you change your mind about marrying me, don't forget me."

Her throat constricted so painfully she could only whisper, "Of course not. I told you, you're in my heart to stay."

When everyone else had boarded and the driver gunned the engine, she leaned a quick kiss on Jim's mouth and hurried up the steps. Standing room only, clear to the rear. As the bus lurched forward, she caught a glimpse of him through the back window. Then, heading south, they turned a corner, and she lost sight of him.

Leaning on the cane, he watched the green bus turn left in front of the church, pause at the stop sign on the corner, then, in a cloud of exhaust, roar onto the southbound lane of Route One. When he could no longer hear the engine, he got back into the Buick again, aware that he needed to hustle if he was going to cover the ten miles back to East Point before eight. Fletch wouldn't leave without him, of course, nor did he want to keep him waiting. But for a few minutes, he felt incapable of even the simplest effort, like stepping on the starter and guiding the car around the square. Not merely a physical weariness, though that was part of it: with Anna beside him in the bed, he hadn't wanted to waste time sleeping when he could savor her warmth, her smell and her reality for the brief time remaining.

Though the fatigue was understandable, he was similarly weighed down by an anticlimactic sense of having received all the gifts he'd ever wanted at one time. On one spectacular birthday or one unbelievable Christmas morning. In this case, in the space of seventy-two hours. This fleeting and finite happily-ever-after had already ended, as he'd known it had to, and in no way had he been disappointed. And yet, this very morning, only a few minutes earlier, he'd pushed Anna away verbally, preemptively giving her permission to love someone else, someone she might meet in the Navy. Someone who might kindle the same passion he suspected Dan had.

Why had he done that? Because he didn't trust her promise to marry him? Because in some dim closet in his mind he recognized she still belonged to Dan? Or because he himself was incapable of enjoying happiness in ways other men took for granted?

Perhaps that was it: life, and Ellen in particular, had inoculated him with cynicism. And yet…and yet…he couldn't forget the first day Anna had come to Maine. At their initial meeting, it had taken him no time at all to recognize that her soul had been maimed by the loss of husband and infant. And now, Jean had died too. Not that the two women had been close in the manner of lifelong friends. But for the past ten months, they'd worked in the same clinic, eaten meals at the same table, shared a bathroom, and most recently, been united by the experience of pregnancy. Regardless of Jean's prickly ways, Anna had tolerated and supported her with a loving spirit few other young women might have managed. So however Jean regarded her, Anna saw her as a friend. And her passing would have left yet another hole in her soul.

Now she was off to war, that great new adventure she hoped to find on a hospital ship on the far side of the world. A big floating emergency ward where young men torn apart in combat arrived in endless streams; a place of wearying, grinding duty and injuries he could barely imagine. Recently, he'd read an article by an Army doc who'd been on a D-day beach; it described insults to human flesh no training had prepared him for. As well as the numbing Sisyphus syndrome—the emotional stagnation of repeating the same healing rituals over and over, with never an end in sight.

Yet, in light of her years of nursing, Anna believed herself ready for anything. And she probably was, professionally. But emotionally? He could only imagine this duty would add to and magnify all previous losses. And exacerbate her unconscious need for comfort, respite, palliation. And passion so compelling it could briefly anesthetize the low-grade soul pain she lived with. Even as he'd shared the explosive, obliterating pleasure of lying with her, he'd recognized it as excessive.

Not that he'd minded. Like a starving man at a banquet, he'd ingested riches that might never be offered again. And grasped at her promise to marry him, even as he'd realized it was one she might not keep. The greatest of all the gifts she'd just given him was also the most ephemeral, the most illusory; the one most likely to be blown to smithereens by the war's stresses. He'd never been a gambler, but he knew the odds that Anna would actually marry him were all stacked against him. Yet he'd jumped at the chance to put the ring on her finger.

Just as she must have when Dan had proposed. When she'd wed him despite the likelihood that their marriage was doomed by the gods of war. It was all a matter of hope, he reckoned; hope led lovers to gulp the bittersweet cup of risk; Hope fanned the flames of impossible attraction, promised forevermore, but delivered only fleeting moments. Then whispered that love only merely remembered was preferable to love left unexplored.

The blare of a passing car horn brought him back sharply to the Rockhampton town square. Good Lord; next he'd be trying to remember exactly what Emily Dickinson had said about "the thing with feathers." Emerging from the pointless reverie, he started the engine, put the car in gear and made the turns that took him back the way he'd come earlier, when Anna had been sitting beside him, when the sight and sound and smell of her had subsumed him in the imminence of parting. Now, he tried to convince himself that whatever happened, his gratitude for this interlude would suffice for perpetuity, whether she came home to him or not.

As he drove across the inlet into the glaring sunlight, he wondered how long it would take to cool his newly-awakened memories of carnal delights. But he'd put them aside before, after Ellen. Now he was three years older, three years more sensible, so maybe recovery would be quicker now. Maybe by the time Anna came back he'd be so wise and self-sufficient she wouldn't even tempt him. And if she'd found someone else, he wouldn't be crushed.

He almost laughed aloud; the fallacy was heroic, but it was still a fallacy.

By the time he reached the pier at East Point, his thoughts had begun shifting to the ordinary routines ahead, to the calming effect of familiar disciplines and the resumption of interrupted normality. Hefting his medical bag in one hand, cane in the other, he left the car and limped toward the boat, just as he'd done almost every Wednesday morning the past five years. As if nothing had changed in his life, or in his heart. So if Fletch and the mate had been speculating about Anna's effect on him, they'd see he wasn't brooding because she'd left. That he was the same old Doc Jim—perpetually placid, perpetually more concerned for his patients' needs than his own. And perpetually dull. Maybe, though, if he smiled more than usual, they might nudge each other and wink, assuming he and Anna had been lovers. He hoped so anyway, so they wouldn't worry about his state of mind, or give him the sort of pitying glances he'd endured after Ellen had left. With a little luck, the only sympathy he'd get now would be because his fiancé was away at war.

Everyone would understand how that felt.

***

Clutching the overhead strap, Anna pressed her eyes closed to memorize the last sight of Jim as the bus roared southward. Her head ached, her cheeks stung where his beard had abraded them, her thighs were smarting, and the first cramps of an approaching period bit into her belly. God, maybe she shouldn't have insisted they be so careful; maybe she should've let nature take its course. Surely getting kicked out of the Navy for an unexpected pregnancy wouldn't have torn her into little pieces the way this precipitous dissension did. Too late now, of course, to reverse the course of their history.

So why hadn't she taken the risk? God knew, when she let herself imagine motherhood, she craved another baby with every cell of her body. Or had Jim been right to question her commitment to him? Had she wanted only a romantic interlude, and nothing more?

Behind the lumbering bus the miles flowed out, widening the space between them and pushing her into a future clouded by this sudden personal storm. On her left hand, the diamond glinted with a promise she no longer trusted. No answers came. All she could do was hold on and grit her teeth.

Most of the passengers filed off at the Bath shipyard, so she sank into a window seat. And watched her life running backwards, like a movie rewinding, canceling time. Maybe when she reached Dover, the previous eleven months would have been erased, along with this final day.

The train was late, slowly jolting down the map of coastal Maine, starting and stopping, loading, unloading, reversing that first trip. Like looking at the past in a rearview mirror and reviewing old memories as they hurtled by. And making sense of none of them.

When she'd called her parents the previous day, she'd told them not to meet the train: she'd take the local bus to Portsmouth. But at Dover, her father was in the crowd on the platform, smoking his pipe and holding out his arms. He'd always assured her of the Lord's guidance, but as she rushed toward him, she was uncertain that she'd ever followed God's will. Only a few hours before, she'd been convinced loving Jim was right, but now his doubts reverberated through her consciousness. Like cannon fire in the distant war.

She couldn't tell her father that, though; his response would be too predictable: "This may not be the way you want things, dear, but the Lord has other plans. You just have to trust him."

Later, when they pulled up at the rectory, he gave the horn a couple of toots. By the time they'd pulled the bags from the trunk, her mother was halfway down the walk, still in her apron. Her smile was wider than any since the day of Anna's confirmation. And her embrace surpassed all others for warmth. But when she inspected the engagement ring, she gasped. "Oh my! A diamond that big is almost obscene. You can't wear it in the Navy. Someone might kill you for it."

"Don't worry, Mother. It'll be on a chain around my neck."

As they approached the house, she noticed a second service flag in the window by the door. When she'd left, only one with a gold star had hung there. The new star was blue.

"That's for you, dear," her father said. "Now that you're officially in the Navy." He scowled. "Need to move it, though. Hung it too close to Dan's."

True; the flags were so close the red borders overlapped. Sunlight shimmered on the gold star, touching it with a radiance she hadn't noticed before. She took a deep breath and blinked a couple times. "No, leave them like they are. Nice to know you're proud of me too."

Her mother hugged her again. "Of course. What parents wouldn't be? Now, come along and see what I've made for lunch. Creamed chipped beef on toast. Bet you won't get that in the Navy."

The one time Anna had served it to Dan, he'd called the dish by a scurrilous Navy slang term that would have sent her mother into a swoon. So she just said, "Oh, my favorite," and followed her into the welcoming old-books-and-stale-cooking smells of the rectory.

In the entry, she glanced over her shoulder at the flags in the window. Backlit by the noon light, they seemed to merge into one, the points of the stars just touching. Like fingertips across time and space for the split second before they became two again.

Warmed by the momentary illusion, she hurried toward the kitchen for her special homecoming lunch.

The End

ABOUT THE AUTHOR

Born in 1929, Joan Hartzel La Blanc discovered the joy of fiction writing during her childhood in Philadelphia. While she set this addiction aside to raise four children, it later enabled her to survive marriages to two career Navy men and one with Alzheimer's Disease. Now, in her "golden years", it continues to offer romance, travel, and the adventures of an international spy without the associated dangers. After a "real" career as a PR and non-fiction writer, she crafts circumspect prose for church publications between visits to the various parallel universes that still provide inspiration and creative fulfillment.

THE ANNA DONOVAN NOVELS

Here presented in an enriched and enlarged revision, MINISTRY OF ANGELS is the second work in a deeply researched, historically accurate four-novel series about young nurse Anna Donovan. [The first, INNOCENCE OF ANGELS, recounts her romance and short-lived marriage to submarine officer, Dan Donovan.] The third volume, ODYSSEY OF ANGELS, takes her deep into the hell of the Pacific War as an ensign nurse aboard USS *Compassion,* a Navy hospital ship. The final book, ORDINARY ANGELS, follows her return to marriage, civilian life, and a measure of peace. All are available from Northampton House Press in both hard copy and ebook editions.

Northampton House Press

Northampton House LLC publishes carefully selected fiction, as well as lifestyle nonfiction, memoir, and poetry. Our logo represents the muse Polyhymnia. Our mission is to discover great new writers and give them a chance to springboard into fame. Our watchword is quality, not quantity. See our list at www.northampton-house.com, or Like us on Facebook – "Northampton House Press" – to discover more innovative works from brilliant new writers.

www.ingramcontent.com/pod-product-compliance
Lightning Source LLC
Chambersburg PA
CBHW070808180626
46818CB00001B/164
* 9 7 8 1 9 3 7 9 9 7 4 5 8 *